# Black Knights, Dark Days

The True Story of Sadr

by

J. Matthe,

---

"A gripping, astonishing insider's account of the April 4, 2004, ambush of a First Cavalry Platoon in Sadr City that changed the course of the Iraq War. With great candor and skill, Matt Fisk interweaves the chaos and adrenaline of modern combat with the continuing battles with PTSD at home. An intense, vivid, deeply personal portrait of men at war that is up there with the very best books of the genre."

—Mikko Alanne, screenwriter and producer,
*The Long Road Home, The 33*

"Matt Fisk's *Black Knights, Dark Days* hits the reader square in the gut from the first line—"I've just killed a child, and I'm waiting for my conscience to tell me it's a bad thing"—and doesn't let up. It is a rare first-hand look at the 2004 Black Sunday ambush in Sadar City from a grunt with Shakespearian sensibilities. A beautifully told story of sacrifice and loss, devotion and redemption, this book should be required reading for veterans and civilians alike."

—Erin Celello, *Learning to Stay*

# Black Knights, Dark Days

The True Story of Sadr City's Black Sunday

by
J. Matthew Fisk

WARRIORS PUBLISHING GROUP
NORTH HILLS, CALIFORNIA

Black Knights, Dark Days: the True Story of Sadr City's Black Sunday

A Warriors Publishing Group book/published by arrangement with the author

PRINTING HISTORY
Warriors Publishing Group edition/December 2016

The article "Lancer Legacy Ranch provides a new life for veterans with PTSD"
is used by permission of Alex Meachum, KTAL News.

Martha Raddatz gave permission for use of her discussion of her book, *The Long Road Home.*

ISBN: 978-1-944353-12-4

The name "Warriors Publishing Group" and the logo
are trademarks belonging to Warriors Publishing Group

PRINTED IN THE UNITED STATES OF AMERICA

10 9 8 7 6 5 4 3 2 1

This book is dedicated to the men and women of Task Force Lancer, Operation Iraqi Freedom II, who stood by each other in the darkest of days; to the brave warriors from Alpha and Charlie companies who charged to our rescue in unarmored trucks, without hesitation or regard for their own safety; and to Eddie Chen, Ray Arsiaga, Ahmed Cason, Israel Garza, Stephen Hiller, Forest Jostes and Casey Shehan.

"Beloved and pleasant in their life, and in their death they were not parted. They were swifter than eagles. They were stronger than lions." 2 Samuel 1:23

# Acknowledgements

I would like to thank my wife Lisa for a life time of friendship and the daily encouragement necessary to complete this work.

I'm grateful to my parents for giving me the confidence that comes from being loved.

Erin Celello, author extraordinaire, was an excellent mentor and coach to a guy that wanted to tell a story.

To the men of Charlie Company, 2-5 CAV, who always had my six: thank you, brothers.

And most of all, I thank God who was with me in the alley, who kept my feet from slipping and delivered me from a host of ten thousand.

# Prologue

IT'S ALL THERE in black and white. I sit numbly reading the Newsweek article that explains why I have another human being's blood on my boots. They even managed to label the battle. *Black Sunday* the writer called it. I suppose I should have seen this coming. It's July 2004, a hot month in Iraq, and for weeks the reporters have been crawling all over each other to get out to Forward Operating Base War Eagle. We would see them sitting in our brand new Dining Facility (DFAC) dressed in the reporter uniform of khaki cargo pants, light-color t-shirt, and blue flak vest. If they were feeling particularly daring, they would swap the flak jacket for a tan cargo vest.

They were here to fish. Their questions were meant to hook a trophy Bush Bass, Cheney Trout or Walleyed Rumsfeld. Our commanders had prepared us for their arrival by issuing daily talking points. These points all focused on the same theme: we are here to win the hearts and minds of the good people of Sadr City. After what happened on the 4th of April, it was all any of us could do to say that without any sense of irony.

I wondered, as I sat newly returned from three days in hostile territory, if any of the intrepid correspondents actually cared what was really going on. They were so hell-bent on nailing the administration to the wall that the larger picture escaped them.

"Bush only invaded Iraq for the oil—gasp!—and is using these poor, dumb grunts as pawns in his evil, neo-colonialist bid to spread America's influence." Well, no shit. Every Soldier knows that we are the final extension of diplomacy, and we like it. Last I checked, not a single one of my brothers-in-arms had been drafted.

"Cheney started a corporation that is making untold millions in profit—double gasp!—from the blood of American Soldiers!" Who cares? Did they honestly think that we gave a crap about anything once we left the wire other than watching out for the man to our left and right?

"That creep Rumsfeld sent the military into harm's way without the proper equipment to keep them safe"—swoon! Don't underestimate an American Soldier's ability to thrive on adversity. Every time America defeats her enemies, the first thing that short-sighted politicians do is heed the media outcry to reduce the size and funding of the military. Then they all want to sound outraged when America once again has to stand against bullies—emboldened by our relaxed posture—without the latest and greatest gear.

No, none of this concerned the average soldier. The story that the reporters missed in their frenzy to play political gotcha was that we understood these things, either tacitly or unconsciously, and did our job anyway. Political corruption and greed, is that really news? What about courage in the face of overwhelming odds? What about loyalty and devotion that transcends race and skin color? What about mourning the tragic loss of young warriors who stepped from this mortal coil with honor?

As my eyes scanned the glossy magazine pages, I had an epiphany: Someone was going to write a book about *Black Sunday*. One of these louts, desperate to be the next Mark Bowden, would chronicle our deeds in order to score cheap political points. Even as this revelation made me furious, I accepted the fact with resignation. Of course they would; it was just the way things were done.

Someone had to get it right. Someone who had actually pulled a trigger should tell this tale. Why not me? I grabbed my small tape recorder and went looking for someone to interview. I would do my best to get it right. For Eddie.

# The Question

I'VE JUST KILLED a child, and I'm waiting for my conscience to tell me that it was a bad thing. Not just one child but three all at once, gone before my eyes could register that a cloud of red mist floats where three little heads used to be. Didn't I used to be a teacher? Yeah, I'm pretty sure that's true. I taught Spanish to at-risk teenagers. Sure, they were a handful as only pubescent males can be when made to do something they didn't want to do, but I can't recall that I ever blew their heads off for it.

Waiting. Not a peep from my soul, which probably means that I've killed that, too.

I had talked with Sergeant Bellamy and a few other bored soldiers about this moment less than a week before. We lounged on our cots, young lions who had never tasted the kill, discussing what it would be like in the abstract manner of the ignorant. Jokes—gutter humor mostly—floated in the air as though we were passing around a joint in some gratuitous Vietnam War movie scene. Everyone was nervous about crossing the border from Kuwait to Iraq, yet no one would admit it.

"Think you could do it, dude?" I'm as unsettled as the rest, the teacher recast in a post 9/11 mold as a warrior. It's an identity that I'm trying to reconcile, my mind full of questions, speculations, myths about what it would be like to take another human's life.

"What?" Sergeant Bellamy is younger than me and looks it.

"Waste a kid." I can't make my mouth say the word "kill." Using the word 'waste' makes it seem as innocuous as throwing away a piece of scrap paper.

"Don't know." He scowls as if the thought had been just birthed from his subconscious. "Hope I don't have to."

The subject came up as we passed the time away watching *Blackhawk Down*. We don't know war, not yet, so we grapple with the ineffable questions using the oracle of the day: war movies.

"I'd do it in a heartbeat if they draw down on me," declares one grunt with his nose in the latest copy of *Swank* magazine. I can't tell if it's bravado or calculated.

"I couldn't do it. No way," said another. He was a big guy with a newborn baby. The parallels struck too close to home.

Some guy from Boston was quick to chide him, "What? You sayin' that some raghead sonofabitch tries to put a bullet in your head, and you'd just let him?"

"Better that than having to live the rest of my life knowing I had killed a child."

More than a few untested warriors laughed and swore at him for being a pussy. I admired him for sticking with the conviction of his beliefs, even if I didn't share his certainty.

Still, I said nothing and mulled different scenarios over in my head. Killing a man didn't seem out of the question. We shot man-shaped targets all of the time, ostensibly to get us used to the idea of putting the shape of a man into our sights. I wore a sharp knife that I had prepared myself to plunge into someone's throat if need be. We had trained daily to use jujitsu both to detain and to kill. The mechanics of the deed were well known to all of us.

But what would it be like? Again, my only yardstick was the Hollywood tome of wisdom compiled by philosophers like Kubrick and Spielberg. War movies portrayed soldiers who killed as full of deep regret and post-homicidal angst. Even cops who took part in a clean shooting routinely checked out of life and into the nearest bottle of booze. Assuming these cliché archetypes bore any resemblance to re-ality, was it a price I was willing to pay to survive?

My answer came later that week during a routine patrol on my fourth day in Iraq. The proverbial Shiite hit the fan with hurricane force. Our platoon—four Humvees and 19 soldiers—was ambushed by a local militia, estimated at 10,000 strong. Within five minutes, two of our vehicles were disabled. The gunner on my vehicle was killed, shot through a gap in his body armor. His job fell to me, and I didn't want it. Any glamour that my mind attached to combat flew out the window with Sergeant Chen's soul.

I popped up through the turret, expecting to die that moment as a fusillade of bullets struck the armored plate of our vehicle. I looked behind us. No one followed. We were alone.

Left behind in the thickest part of the ambush, two of our vehicles could no longer move and the trail Humvee was trying to help them. Our mirrors had been shot out and no one could hear anything on the radio due to the deafening barrage of weapons—both ours and the enemy's. When he realized that our comrades were still locked in combat, the platoon leader ordered his driver to turn around and drive back into the ambush to get them. The driver wasn't happy about it. I wasn't happy about it. We did it anyway.

We were surrounded on both sides by three- and four-story buildings. Helplessness engulfed me as the enemy continued to pound our vehicle with unrelenting fire. Riddell drove so fast that I couldn't see a target.

Movement! A blur of motion caught my eye. I looked up to my right and glimpsed three small figures dressed in black. They huddled together on the roof of a four-story building. Children. Yellow-or-ange flame exploded from their midst. Muzzle flash.

Now I would answer the question posed five days and a lifetime ago.

This was wrong. Where had everything gone so wrong? I used to be a teacher. I love kids. Almost a year ago I was on a youth ranch in Arkansas. By day I taught Spanish in their on-site high school. At night, six of the children lived in my home. Sometimes I would play tag with kids. Sometimes we would play war. Bang, bang. I shot you. You're dead.

I put all three small figures within the iron, unforgiving circle of my front sight post. The gun roared. There was dust and there was blood.

I continued to scan for targets as we raced to save what was left of our platoon, engaging anything that moved. Bullets snapped and whined past my head and careened off of the vehicle's armor. I didn't care. It no longer mattered. In dealing death, I had died. Blood was the price of life. It always is. There is no question.

### SO note by Weekes, Jennifer

*The chief complaint is: Memory loss, possible TBI.*

*Patient reports difficulties with concentrating, memory loss, increasing irritability and possible TBI. Patient reports being in several IED explosions in 2004/2005 during his deployment. He recalls an incident in which a mortar round landed very close behind him. After the incident he reports feeling dizzy for 3 days, hearing loss, and difficulty walking. He reports that after the incident, he consulted with a medic and was given time to rest. Patient reports another incident in which a rock [hit] him in the back of his head. Patient reports that he now feels withdrawn, has difficulties with his sleep patterns (waking up 3-4 times per night), having nightmares once a week or sometimes monthly. Patient reports his plans to write a book. He expressed noticing worsening symptoms as he tries to recall incidents from the past. He stressed "I will write this book if it kills me."*

**Assessment: 1. ADJUSTMENT DISORDER**

# ACT I: INNOCENCE

# IRAQ—2004

THE IRAQI MAN is tied to a chair with his legs stretched out in front of him and fastened to an iron bar. A soldier removes the unfortunate captive's shoes as he pleads for mercy. The soldier begins to strike the bottom of the man's feet with a bamboo baton. Fascinated, I never blink as the man whimpers in pain. I take a shallow sip from a soda can covered in Arabic writing. The scene cuts to an older Iraqi woman in a *hijab*, perhaps meant to be the prisoner's mother. She is weeping as she speaks to a pair of sympathetic men and gestures with B-film quality to a picture of the captive hanging in her living room.

With only a few shopping days to Christmas of 2004 I found myself, as I often did at two in the morning, watching Iraqi soap operas with mouth agape and mind 1,000 miles away. I could be watching one of a handful of British channels or even the Armed Forces Network, but I usually gravitated toward the Arabic networks after spending half an hour flipping aimlessly from one station to another. They are horrible, no matter which language you speak, and like watching a Special Olympics version of the running of the bulls. I lie to myself and say that I'm trying to sharpen my language skills. The truth is that I can't sleep. Most of us can't without pills or illicit alcohol. Sometimes I find Rollings or Puppet or Briones in the barracks TV room with the same expression on their face that I wear for such an occasion. We will sit together silently watching shows that put *Telenovelas* to shame with the magnitude of their schmaltz.

But on that particular night in December, I sat alone contemplating the future. Sergeant First Class Swope had gathered us NCOs a few hours earlier for the evening huddle to pass command information. "You can put out to your soldiers that anybody who wants to become an officer," he said, "can shoot for the slots they're offering for an ROTC Green-to-Gold scholarship. You can sit there and attend college while still on active duty and get your butter bar." I dutifully copied down the details in my green notebook without much thought.

Later I thought plenty about it, even as my mind wrestled with the concept of a McDonald's—*McArabaya*—commercial where the male Arab employees wore glowing white robes and desert head gear. When I first joined the Army in 1997, my recruiter noted my high ASVAB scores and college credits asking why I didn't want to be an officer. I told him that it wasn't for me. I wanted to be a Special Forces weapons expert. After I finished my first tour and volunteered to come back in after 9/11, the recruiter asked me again why I wasn't applying for Officer Candidate School. Not my style, I said. I just wanted some payback. And it really didn't seem to fit my personality. I came from humble means out of rural Arkansas and would never be the kind of guy comfortable around a West Point crowd. Plus, I didn't think I could do it, that it was beyond my ability.

But it's now December 2004, and I'm different. That other guy, the eternal optimist and slayer of dragons, died in a godforsaken alley on the 4th of April. He was the one who wanted to experience battle, to see if he had what it takes. The guy who took his place is one scary son-of-a-motherless-goat. He's the guy who, in the span of six months, has been on almost 200 missions outside of the wire. He has been shot at, shot, blown up, blown down and struck point-blank in the chest with a frozen chicken, among other indignities. He's the guy who laughs too hard at body parts littering the street after a gun fight. I don't recognize him when I catch his crazy eye in the mirror.

Only three months before, during a particularly grim and extended defensive action, he was knocked unconscious by a mortar round that landed a few feet behind him. It was not just a lucky round but had been directed there by a small child who had been sent in to scout their location. He hadn't killed the child, though he wished after the fact that he had. The blast evaporated a small puppy that he had been feeding only minutes before. They picked him up and sent him back to base to recover for a few days. When he rejoined his team, he left behind the last remnants of humanity and mercy that he had been guarding like childhood keepsakes.

Within minutes of assuming his post in the middle of hostile territory he was screaming at children who gathered below begging for *schokolata*. He began to shoot at the ground near them and was contemplating a center of mass shot when the company XO put a gentle hand on his shoulder. First Lieutenant Clay Spicer took five minutes to remind the young sergeant about who he was as an American and a human being. Five minutes and a calm tone of voice kept that young man from going to prison—or worse.

Though I have come to rely on that guy when the fit hit the shan, he also worries me. He's a guy I need to survive, a beast that enjoys his job perhaps a little too much. The X-O was right when he reminded me that other guy wasn't me. However, if I stay in this job, I will always need that other guy in certain situations and in desperate times. He will accompany me on every deployment with the rest of my gear. I had no illusions back then that the insurgency would end as soon as our year-long tour was complete. We would be back, again and again, most likely facing off against the children whose parents we had dispatched on previous deployments. And every time, that other guy—that beast—would be rattling the bars of his cage, demanding to be let out to hunt.

So I sit up late watching Iraqi soap operas and contemplating my options. Lieutenant Fisk? Captain Fisk? General Fisk? I laugh out loud at that. Why not? I could sell it to my wife as a bump in paygrade, more family income. I sell it to myself as a way to honor Sergeant

Chen and First Lieutenant Aguero. I suppose it is a way to escape what I am becoming. While contemplating this career change I had peppered Lieutenant Aguero with endless questions about what officer life was like, having only a glimpse into their world that I suspected was less glamorous than the war movies made it out to be. I am correct-a-mundo. Aguero himself is dreading his next promotion which will take him farther away from the rank and file. All the really high-speed door kicking, lead slinging, snatch-and-grabbing hooah-hooah type stuff was done at the junior NCO level or below. Ascending higher in rank, he explained, took you farther away from the troops and farther away from combat, the two things which I enjoyed most about this profession. While our officers are unusually involved in combat, that was generally the exception to the rule which declared that if a Lieutenant or above is pulling the trigger, something has gone dreadfully wrong.

This bit of knowledge is actually a two-edged sword for me. On one hand, I will have to bid a bitter farewell to the life I love. On the other, I can escape this ravenous war dog that I am becoming before it is too late to go back. At least, I so dearly hope that it isn't too late.

Amid the babble of Arabic actors emoting on TV, I close my eyes and run a different movie in my mind. It opens with a platoon of soldiers preparing for their first combat mission in Iraq.

----

"Fisk! Get over here!" I ran to the front of the convoy where the leader of each vehicle had gathered around a map laid across the hood of the Lieutenant's High-Mobility Multi-Purpose Vehicle, pronounced the world over as Humvee. Sergeant Lovett had his Kevlar helmet off and didn't look at all pleased. *What now?* I wondered. It was April Fool's of 2004, so I was wary of a prank. Two days ago, Sergeant York had filled Sergeant Bourquin's mouth with cheese-in-a-can as he slept

while we waited to leave Kuwait and drive into Iraq. College fraterni-
ties drew their inspiration from Infantry guys, so I wasn't taking any
chances.

"Specialist Fisk, you are going to be the L-T's recorder."

Had to be a joke. I stood there blinking for a second, waiting for
the punch line. "You mean he wants me to be his flute-like wind in-
strument?"

"No, smart-ass, you're going to be the L-T's battle-buddy. Wher-
ever he goes, you stick with him and write down whatever he tells you
to. Can you handle that, Grandpa?" I had just turned 31 in Kuwait,
making me his senior by five years. I was older than most of the guys
in the platoon. The senior citizen jokes just came with the territory.

"Yes, Ser-gent!" I peppered his title with a little extra basic training lilt at the end, grinning all the while.

"All right, then. Grab your gear and move to the lieutenant's vehicle. Step it out, Gramps—we roll in five mikes."

I double-timed to the third vehicle, grabbed my helmet and water
bottle, and slugged Deaver in the shoulder. "Catch ya later, ol' bean.
Big daddy's movin' to the head of the class."

"What do you mean?"

"Sergeant Lovett ordered me to babysit the L-T. Let me know how
that tan's coming." The two vehicles in the middle had no top and
very little in the way of armor, so the crew got baked by the sun. The
gunner stood in the vehicle's bed behind a makeshift Mad Max-type
gun turret. The vehicle in the front and rear were M-1114 fully armored Humvees with tops that could withstand a fair amount of punishment. I felt a momentary twinge of guilt for leaving my buddies
out in the open while I rode in a veritable armored Cadillac.

Lieutenant Aguero was still talking to the Track Commanders, so
I took a moment to check my gear in one of the vehicle's side view

mirrors. I was just over six feet tall, so I had to stoop a little. My canteens were full. The MOLLE vest, which was the platform for all of my equipment, held 180 rounds of M16 ammo, my compass, an improved Israeli field dressing, a small pair of binoculars, and another pouch containing Night Vision goggles. In addition, I had attached a small fighting knife made by my Uncle Jerry, widely considered the world's best blade smith. Two Kevlar plates covered my torso front and back, adding to the weight I carried. It was welcome weight, something an infantryman learns to respect and then ignore when he has worn it for a while. The poor-quality mirror couldn't tell me honestly if I had shaved well, so I rubbed a hand over my face to make sure that I had knocked all the hair off of it. I had missed a little spot under my unimpressive chin. I pondered using Uncle Jerry's razor-sharp knife to get what my initial effort missed, but that would likely result in a severed jugular, so I decided to leave it alone. My glasses, framing the blue eyes my grandfather gave me, sat askew as usual on my crooked nose as I straightened them for the bazillionth time and mopped beads of sweat from my bald head as the Iraqi sun beat down upon it.

"Fee-isk."

I slowly raised my eyes to find the owner of that oddly accented deep voice. "Yes, Sergeant Chen?"

"You still don't look any prettier." The muscular Asian behind the .50 caliber machine gun smiled slyly as he stared down at me. I always remember him smiling, but I can't remember if he ever laughed. The effect was a little unsettling. It was as if he understood a perpetual running joke that no one else got.

First Lieutenant Shane Aguero was irate. He mumbled some profanity to no one in particular and continued to outline the intended route to his assembled vehicle commanders. When he felt confident that his instructions were understood, he dismissed the gathering to prepare for departure. It was time for our first patrol as a platoon in the real deal. We had trained for this moment together for over a year. I scrambled to my seat behind the driver and plopped my Kevlar on my shiny dome. I was pumped.

Lieutenant Aguero, a slightly built, wire-tough man, slid easily into the shotgun seat beside the driver and began to organize the radio handsets, maps, and documents that clutter an Infantry Platoon Leader's life. Soldiering was all that he ever wanted to do. He had already served 10 years in the Cavalry Scouts, achieving the rank of Staff Sergeant before crossing over to the dark side to become an officer. He was experienced, highly intelligent, and loved his job. He also had very little patience or tact with bureaucratic types. He took a deep breath and affected his most detached and courteous radio voice, failing only slightly to convey respect and admiration for senior officers in the Combat Operations Center. "Lancer Mike, this is Comanche Red 1 requesting permission to exit the FOB, over."

Moments passed. I rubbed my right thumb against my weapon's safety. Then we heard a faint, static-riddled response. Garble, garble. The teacher from the Charlie Brown cartoons giving final instructions to our band of warriors. "Roger, Lancer Mike. Leaving the FOB…time now…with four Humvees, twenty-four U.S. Personnel, and one translator, over."

"That's a good copy. Comanche Red 1, out." Aguero slung the mike against the dashboard as if it felt great to get it out of his hand and waved Riddell forward. He continued to vent his frustrations as the National Guard artillerymen manning the gate opened up to let us pass. As the vehicles left FOB War Eagle he gave the order to lock and load. The familiar and extremely motivating—at least to me— sound of live bullets entering rifle chambers filled the cab. Above me I heard Sergeant Chen haul back on the charging handle of the M-2 .50 caliber machine gun. CHA-CHUNK! Just knowing that this weapon was hovering over me like a heavy metal guardian angel was a comfort. The Ma Deuce, as she is affectionately known, is a weapon so deadly and effective that our grandfathers and great-grandfathers had used it in wars long before our time. A few years before, I had attended a small-arms repair school and was astounded to see that they were still using the M-2 repair manual from the late 1940s. None of us had ever used it in combat before, but the general consensus was that it would tear a mo-fo up. Now we were heading out the gate into wild territory as green as we were and ready to put ourselves to the test. We were warriors, heirs of a long tradition of valor and honor, ready to take our place among the long line of soldiers who had fought before us.

The Iraqi countryside slowly rolled by as we made our way down a road that paralleled the low wall surrounding the FOB. A deep, stagnant canal lay to the right side of the road, and it reeked of human waste. Ahead, the dirt path fed into the only paved road connecting Forward Operating Base War Eagle—our quaint new home—to Sadr City. According to the lieutenant's map, it was called Route Silver.

"Where are we going, Sir?" I asked.

"Didn't your squad leader give you the mission, Specialist?" Aguero stared out of his bullet-proof window distractedly.

"Yes, Sir. He did. I just wondered what our first stop was. And, while we're at it, what exactly do you want me to do as your recorder?"

His eyes never quit scanning his surroundings as he answered. "Look, it's real simple. Write down whatever I tell you to. It's that easy. Our Area of Operation is on the far west central side of the city, and we're going to different institutions in our sector today to introduce ourselves."

"Winning hearts and minds, Sir?"

"Whatever. You speak a little Arabic, right?"

"I'm learning, Sir. I can ask if you like Arabic food and where to find the toilet."

"That's why I asked for you. We're going to be interacting extensively with the locals, so just pay attention." He turned to the translator sitting behind him—an elderly man named Monsoor—and began to ask questions regarding Muslim culture. I suddenly felt foolish as I realized that the Lieutenant was trying to avoid revealing our destinations in front of a man he clearly didn't trust.

*Gotta think about things like that,* I warned myself. Even though he and I both seemed cut from a philosopher's cloth, we had vastly different outlooks. I'm more like Ghandi with a gun; he's more like a chain-smoking Marcus Aurelius with a migraine and Tourette syndrome.

Specialist Riddell, the driver, gunned the engine as we approached Route Silver, turned right, and began to weave hesitantly through the bustling traffic. Our convoy into Baghdad in the early phases of the war had barely prepared us for the mad swarm of humanity that is Sadr City. I looked it up in a world atlas before I left the states and was puzzled to find in its place the name Saddam City. I asked Sergeant Fowler about that the night that we arrived at FOB War Eagle. He had been here for two weeks with the advance party and had learned a great deal of useful information. He told me, accurately or not, that the city was originally built by Saddam Hussein to house a troublesome Shi'a Muslim population as cheap labor for his factories. Saddam, a Sunni Muslim, would visit a cigarette factory on the city's edge to shoot random Shi'a pedestrians with a hunting rifle just for sport.

A religious man in that city from a respected family formed a nucleus of resistance to Saddam's regime. The dictator viewed him as a serious threat, so in 1999 he had the cleric assassinated. The elderly man, Mohammed Mohammed Sadeq al Sadr, became a martyr to the citizens who brazenly began to call their town Sadr City in his honor.

Two and a half million people lived here in an area seven kilometers, or two miles, square. Poverty and unemployment were high. Although the electricity was free to everyone, a big part of the city was without power for all but two hours most days, a technological nightmare when people began to connect their homes to the city power grid using any number of inventive and potentially lethal shortcuts. Each residential concrete telephone pole had a medusa of multi-colored wires spliced into the main line that ran through the alleys like an intricate web woven by a drunken spider.

As we turned off Route Silver on to Route Aeros, the Lieutenant yelled out over the roar of the engine. "They call this intersection Home Depot. It's basically an open-air building supply market." I peeked around Riddell's head and saw a wide open space crammed with ancient dump trucks, donkey-drawn carts sporting Michelin tires, and huge piles of gravel and sand. Bearded men in turbans wore long robes called *dishdashas* by the locals and man-dresses by American soldiers. The sellers haggled with all comers for materials that were used to build homes and walls and other domestic projects. Traffic was severely congested. Lieutenant Aguero gave terse orders to Riddell not to stop and to plow through the traffic jams or crowds if necessary. "Trust me," he said. "They'll move."

Riddell liberally employed his horn, emboldened by the orders, and squeezed the Humvee through almost impossibly small gaps in traffic. A fully armored M-1114 has no rear window, so I could only pray that the rest of the vehicles were keeping pace.

As we raced southwest down the western edge of the city, my eyes darted everywhere, searching for any sign of improvised bombs that we had trained so hard to spot. Used tires dotted the gutters like large licorice lifesaver candies. Empty plastic shopping bags wrapped themselves around concrete telephone poles and waved to us in the slight breeze. Cars on cinder blocks rusted quietly in the blazing sun, their dented hoods raised in salute as we passed. Rotten fruit littered the streets along with the carcasses of dead animals. *You've gotta be kidding me,* I thought. *How am I supposed to find IEDs hidden in this mess?*

The space in between Route Aeros and Route Bravo, which ran parallel, was just wide enough for a good soccer field or two. Through the right window, I could see children playing what the Iraqis called "futball" in the different fields with teams scattered according to age and size. Dirty children were everywhere playing in the dust, mud, and filth of these fields which had no grass to cushion a fall. Fine gray dust puffed up in clouds when someone attempted a slide tackle. Most of the younger children ran recklessly through the harsh, rocky ground without shoes. The older children—lean teenagers with shiny hair and beardless chins—sported new, colorful uniforms and carried out their practice with grim determination and violent purpose.

As our convoy rolled noisily down the road, the kids stopped playing and raced toward our vehicles in waves as word that Americans were coming spread like a prairie fire. Most cheered as we past, giving us the thumbs-up sign. I had been briefed earlier that this was, in their culture, an obscene gesture. However, this was always accompanied with a hearty, "Good Mister!" so I assumed that they were merely adapting to American customs. To my surprise, I heard them sing a song as we passed that was partly in English and used a few Arabic words that I knew. I asked Monsoor if he knew what they were singing.

He looked at me and smiled. "They sing good things," he said in heavily accented English, "They sing 'Good, Good Mister! Give to us the food. Give to us the water.'"

I pondered that as I fidgeted with my loaded weapon. Were they actually happy to have us here? Did they see us as liberators or oppressors? What did they want from me? Lieutenant Colonel Gary Volesky, our Battalion Commander, had repeatedly told us that our mission was to perform humanitarian aid and restore civil services to the city. Those of us who had been spoiling for a fight since airplanes crashed into the Twin Towers began to brace ourselves for a year of boredom and subpar chow.

Several hundred meters later, the dirt road became paved and the mud houses with colorful door-blankets became nicer houses with window panes, high walls, and metal doors. And trees—palm trees, date trees, and some sort of deciduous tree that I had never seen— sprang high over the multicolored walls that divided neighbors. I continued to watch the roads, alleys, and second-story windows for anyone full of naughty intent.

At length we reached Route Gold, a very busy east-west thoroughfare, and turned right. On the corner was a man in a bloody *dishdasha* who held a knife. As I watched he flayed the skin from a small animal which dangled from a rusty metal scaffold. It must have been a sheep. Two clusters of the forlorn, doomed animals huddled nearby awaiting their turn on the chopping block. One group was marked on the rump with pink paint, the other with green. A sort of brand, I supposed. A small child held a large metal tray upon which the butcher deposited one cut of meat after another. I saw no freezer into which the meat would go, nor anywhere to wash blood-stained hands, nor shelter of any type where they would find respite from the sun.

The Lieutenant suddenly burst into a vehement stream of invective which filled the cab of our vehicle with a bluish haze even as we slowed to a stop. I suddenly realized that words beginning with the letter F held great attraction for my platoon leader. Our current situation, however, seemed to have less to do with synonyms for 'fornication' or the judgment of God against fatherless children and more to do with being stuck in a traffic jam. As a game, I endeavored to record the number of times Aguero dropped the F-bomb.

Despite the Lieutenant's colorful encouragement, we remained securely stuck in a traffic swarm that gave no hint of dissolving. Aguero listened intently to his radio for a second and responded with a brusque "Roger." He turned to me and said, "We're dismounting to untangle this mess. Sergeant Chen! Bring the vehicle forward behind us. Let's go."

I threw the door open and untangled my long legs and weapon as fast as I could. The Lieutenant was moving quickly and I had to trot to catch him. We passed vehicles of every description and condition as another group of soldiers brought up the rear. French and German automobiles were common. White-robed Sheiks in brand-new Mercedes idled beside filthy merchants in beat-up Bongo trucks. Some familiar American models were also popular, most of which were GMC Suburbans. Some still had Texas license plates on them, evidence that they had come from other-than-legal markets. At times, among the unregulated, ozone-killing exhaust, I smelled something like a banana-flavored magic marker. I learned later that this was homemade ethanol, a clever way to circumvent the corrupt gas stations.

As we passed car after car, I attempted to use my fledgling Arabic. *Salaam a lechum* (peace be unto you) and *Minfa'adluk, ruuh,* (please go). People I spoke to immediately responded in kind or smiled beneficently.

The Lieutenant glanced over his shoulder and frowned. "Where's the interpreter?"

I shrugged. "Guess he didn't feel like comin', Sir."

"That's just great," Aguero growled reaching into his arsenal and dropping several more F-bombs.

We reached the spot designated as Checkpoint 1, which coincidently was the source of the traffic jam. Two-lane roads, holding three lanes of traffic, fed into a traffic circle at the corner of Routes Gold and Bravo. Germany has arguably the best implementation of traffic circles, aided by patient, orderly drivers, but German planners would keel over dead from culture shock if they saw what was happening at Checkpoint 1 that day in Sadr City. Iraq has no working traffic signals that I could ever discern. Couple that with sociopathic drivers who lean toward anarchy and you arrive at an epiphany in understanding Sadr City traffic. Uniformed Iraqi police officers and well-meaning civilians added to the chaos by attempting to give conflicting directions regarding who should go and who should stop in unsnarling the mess.

Our platoon sergeant, Sergeant First Class Swope came from behind us and took charge of the situation. He posted his soldiers at strategic locations and began to alternately wave people through or hold them in place. Staff Sergeant York, towering over everyone with his six-foot-five-inch frame, took post in the middle of the street and radiated motivation to overcome driver inertia.

In the Iraqi culture, you can ask someone to wait by extending your arm, holding your palm up and joining your fingers in a gesture reminiscent of Italians talking about food with their hands. When I used the gesture, I usually looked an Iraqi directly in the eyes and added the dialogue from an old TV commercial: "That's one spicy meat-a-ball." The response was usually positive.

There were a lot of those gestures and several others used within the five minutes we needed to clear a path through the snarl and maneuver our vehicles through to the other side of Checkpoint 1. Once clear, we left the task of clearing the residual to the Iraqi policeman who seemed genuinely puzzled at how we had just accomplished such a feat. We mounted our vehicles and continued to our first scheduled stop.

Crossing the two-and-a-half-mile sprawl of Sadr City took just minutes once we breached the traffic circle. Automobiles still crammed the streets, but they all seemed to be moving in the same direction at the same speed. Tall buildings lined the streets, and almost all of them seemed to house some sort of commercial enterprise in three to five stories of brick and concrete. Brightly painted signs bearing Arabic lettering were sometimes augmented with English words. I could read 'Faisal for Clothing' as we crossed Route Charlie and a little after, 'Abdul for Dentist.'

The Lieutenant rattled off street names for Riddell as the young Oregon native wove our vehicle around a mix of European import cars and donkey carts. "You see that wall with graffiti that says Down USA?" Aguero asked. "That's Route Echo. You see that sign on the left with the word Kurdish? That's right before Route Fox. Route Texas is just after that. When you can't go any farther, you've reached Route Golf and the far western edge of the city. You're gonna turn right there. Come on! Give it some gas. You can't be scared to drive aggressively in this city."

Our first stop was a hospital. A high wall, painted aquamarine, surrounded the facility. Our convoy parked nose-to-tail just outside the entrance where a guard force watched our arrival with interest. Swope began to bark orders in his unique, quietly intense way. In short order, he had chosen those who would accompany the Lieutenant inside and left Staff Sergeant Davis in charge of the perimeter security. Staff Sergeant York and I followed Lieutenant Aguero to the gate where the uncertain guards awaited our arrival.

Aguero gave the standard Arabic greeting and the guards responded in kind, tapping their chests with their right palm as a sign of sincerity. Through Monsoor, he told them of his desire to meet with the hospital administrator. Once they had summoned the chief of security, a well-fed man named Monther Fahker—no, I am not making that up—Aguero began to ask Mister Fahker a set of questions regarding the guards' status. Had they been paid? Did they all have weapons and uniforms? Were there any problems? All of these questions and answers were haltingly relayed by Monsoor and dutifully copied down into my little green notebook.

As Security Chief Fahker led us deeper and deeper into the hospital, I noticed that the only decoration on the walls was the same colorful poster placed at random intervals through the hallway. I paused for a second to examine it. The writing was Arabic, which I couldn't read, but the images were gruesome—civilians torn up in one form or another in bloody batches. Inset at the top of each poster was a picture of a man wearing the black robes and turban of a Shi'a cleric. His fat face was rimmed with a mature beard and dark circles underlined dark, fierce eyes. He was shown jabbing a finger in the air as if warning viewers to heed his words—or else. I paused long enough to grasp the message, and our visiting party got ahead of me, so I had to run to catch up with Staff Sergeant York. He knew all about the posters and the cleric depicted.

"That's Mookie," he told me, identifying the intense man as Sadr City's Big Man on Campus, Muqtada Al Sadr. I had heard a lot about this man, but this was the first photo of him that I could remember seeing. Suddenly it seemed important to know what the Arabic words meant. When our party passed another poster, I asked Monsoor to translate. He read the words and it looked like he was struggling to put them into English. I got the feeling he was trying to decide how literal he wanted to be in telling me what the message was. Finally, he just shrugged. "This is religious poster saying how bad is the violence. It is not bad, this saying. It is from the Prophet, peace unto him."

While I tried to correlate the bloody imagery with any kind of peace, Aguero concluded his interview with the hospital director and led us back to the vehicles. Our next objective was close enough to walk, so we set out on foot while the Humvees shadowed us at a slow pace. There were only two large structures on the street, the hospital compound behind us and another tall, brick edifice at the far corner to our front. A wall ran the entire length of the street, festooned with posters proclaiming the greatness of Muqtada Al Sadr. On the far side of the street was a block of apartment buildings from which noisy groups of children scampered to follow us, skipping and shouting. This romping made everyone nervous until we saw the toothy smiles and heard them shouting in fractured English. "Mista, Mista! Good, good Mista! I luff you, Mista!" Shifting my rifle to free a hand, I engaged in a long series of high-fives with the kids and tried some of my Arabic. That was met with wondering looks from some and applause from others. I felt a little like a rock star struggling through a mob of adoring fans.

A few hours later, the radio brought orders for us to visit an Iraqi fire station on the south side of the city. This was way out of our Area of Responsibility or AOR, but since we were the only patrol then outside the wire, we got the mission. The firemen at the station had reported a big pile of explosive devices that civilians had turned in, and they wanted someone with sufficient expertise in disposing of it to take possession. Our company commander, Captain Troy Denomy, wanted us to see what they had and give him our opinion of what should be done with it.

When we finally found the station, the Fire Chief greeted us warmly. His uniform was clean and pressed and his gray mustache was meticulously groomed. He led us to a fenced area beside the station and pointed to a pile of stuff that seemed to be mostly old 60mm mortar rounds plus some old Soviet rockets and a few land mines. I didn't know the details, but Aguero did. As he identified each item, I carefully recorded it in my book. We photographed it all and then returned to the vehicles where the Lieutenant got on the radio to make his report. Then the waiting game began.

While we milled around waiting for instructions from the Company Commander, Swope decided curious locals were approaching closer to our vehicles than he was willing to abide. He told the squad leaders to keep the civilians at a distance and outside our hasty perimeter. The lieutenant had nothing specific for me to do, so I moved around from soldier to soldier on the perimeter, trying to keep myself from being a static sniper target. Specialist Joseph Thompson was in position at the intersection nearest our position and I spent a little time with him. Thompson was on a second tour in Iraq and not very happy about it. I tried a little Jimi Hendrix on him to improve the mood. "Hey, Joe, where you goin' with that gun in yo' hand?"

He almost smiled through his usual dour expression. Thompson was chunky and what is usually considered overweight for an Army infantryman. Fortunately, he carried the weight with surprising speed and endurance. Thompson was the only man in the platoon with a mustache, and he wore mirrored sunglasses that made him look like a stereotypical State Trooper.

"How do you like being the L-T's little whipping boy?" he asked and let the smile come through as he waited for my response.

"Hey, I get to drink *chai* among the high muckety-mucks with my helmet off while you guys are out here sweatin' buckets. I'll take that deal any day." Joe was a friend and I'd always felt a sort of brotherly concern for him. He had been married for more than a year but had spent less than a week with his wife. He told me the forced separation caused some strain in their relationship. I decided not to mention his domestic situation and pointed at a cluster of kids staring at us from across the intersection.

"Just a bunch of kids saying give me this and give me that," Joe responded. "I hate these little pot lickers."

"They're just kids." I shrugged and surveyed said pot lickers. They didn't look very dangerous to me.

"Say that when they start chunkin' rocks at your head." Joe was the only one in the platoon who had been deployed for the initial invasion a year ago. He'd volunteered to be a driver when the call went out, but his unit hadn't seen any serious action. That didn't keep him from a jaded attitude about Iraqis and Iraq in general.

"You just gotta know how to talk to them, Joe." I turned toward a nearby youngster, maybe 16 and wearing a faded pink t-shirt. He was carefully studying us and just as carefully trying to appear that he wasn't. I tried my Arabic on him and asked him to approach. He looked startled and pointed at his chest. "Yes, yes, you. Come here." Apparently my Arabic communicated. He stood and walked quickly over to us seeming relaxed and unafraid.

"Peace to you."

"And to you, peace," He responded and laughed with delight at conversing with an American in his native language.

"My name is Mathias," I said, using the Arabic translation of Matthew. "What is your name?"

He laughed again and said, "My name is Mohammed. You speak Arabi?"

"Little," I replied, having reached almost the limit of my vocabulary.

Mohammed surprised me with some broken English. "Mista Mathias, you like Iraq?"

"Yes, excellent," I lied in Arabic.

"You have baby?"

"No."

"You have wife?"

My thoughts went instantly across the ocean to Texas. "Yes," I said and felt crushing loneliness settle in my chest.

"You show me picture?"

I pulled out my old black wallet and showed him the two pictures that I always carried. One was a picture of her with her brown hair up, her full lips almost in a pout. The other was one of us holding each other and smiling. She looked so small next to me, her arms around my shoulders. Her hair was curly and her face was radiant. Her oval-shaped glasses and tiny nose conspired to make her look like some cute little pet shop rabbit. As I looked at the pictures with Mohammed, I ached to hear her voice.

Mohammed made some clicking noises as he examined the photos. "Very good, Mathias. You make baby?"

Unsure how this conversation would develop, I turned the tables and began to ask him how to say different things in Arabic. While we talked, some younger kids had mustered the courage to approach and crowd around us. Suddenly it seemed that my desire to foster good will with the natives had drawn too much unwanted attention. From the corner of my eye I saw Swope approaching. He did not look pleased.

"Fisk!" He hissed at me. "Move everybody back. The last thing we need is for one of them to shoot a soldier in the back of the head."

"Yes, Sergeant!" I shook Mohammed's hand. In Arabic I said, "Goodbye. Please go away." Mohammed tapped his chest in respect and led the smaller children away with him. I went back to the lieutenant's Humvee and sat down to wait until higher gave us instructions.

It was around 1530 hours when Staff Sergeant Darcy Robinson called our attention to a van moving slowly along Route Pluto. Young men were hanging out the windows and waving large red, black, and green flags. They were chanting a slogan in Arabic so loudly that we could hear it clearly. It was rhythmic and repeated several times. It started out "Allah! Mohammed!" and after that came words that I couldn't pick out until the chant finished with an emphatic, "MOOK-tada, MOOK-tada, MOOK-tada!" It seemed to be some sort of peppy, cheerleader-like slogan, but the shouters were angry young men. We watched tensely, anticipating that the drive-by pep squad would become a drive-by firing squad. They passed us and continued down the street, chanting all the while, as if they were performing just for us. I was unimpressed and wanted my money back.

EOD arrived 20 minutes later and asked us to watch their back while they loaded up the suspect munitions. We agreed in a fit of brotherly compassion despite being hot, sweaty, and way overdue to shrug out of our combat gear. By 1630 hours, The Explosive Ordnance Disposal techs determined the munitions were stable enough to transport. We led them out of the neighborhood without incident and when our routes diverged, we turned onto the road leading back to the FOB. We had been patrolling outside the wire for eight hours, but nothing about the experience was like any nine-to-five job.

Our cooks had established a dining tent for our culinary satisfaction to serve the 2/5 CAV warriors until the Change of Responsibility with 2nd ACR scheduled a few days hence. It was, without a doubt, the most dismal fare ever spawned. Navy cooks, after they leave the service, are qualified to work as gourmet chefs at five-star restaurants. Army cooks, by contrast, are barely fit for fast-food duty.

Chow consisted of a variety of foods packaged in large tin cans that were heated by immersing them in boiling water. Cooks then open the cans and dump the contents into serving pans. The usual treats are beans and rice, peas, cubed potatoes, hamburger-like patties of some vaguely carbon-based life form, and chicken. Lots of chicken.

The Army has a sick fascination with the chicken. If you eat Army chow long enough you will begin to hallucinate, mistaking the eagle on the Army seal for what my daddy called yard bird.

When you find yourself in this sort of situation, you cope by using vast amounts of whatever sauce or seasoning you can find. For a hot minute my heart beat with delight when I saw the familiar and soothing shape of an A-1 steak sauce bottle. I almost tore off the cap in my eagerness to get at the brown gold inside. I was chagrined to discover, however, that the cooks were receiving only sauces produced right there in the good ol' Middle of East. The stuff was hideous. In the dark I had failed to perceive that the label was blue and advertising in Arabic letters what must have said "Good Good Mista Sauce." Back in the states I would religiously dump A-1 sauce on just about everything, up to and including scrambled eggs. I would think twice about dumping this stuff on the ground lest I receive punishment from the Environmental Protection Agency.

I wanted to buy some Gatorade to flush the taste of the imitation chicken meat—not to mention the damned sauce—from my mouth, but we were not allowed in the PX until after the fourth day of the month for some reason. A dark, angry cloud was beginning to form over my head. I stomped dejectedly toward the shower that I had promised myself earlier.

When I had finished washing myself in water deemed unsafe to brush our teeth in, I returned to our bivouac site. The FOB was actually an old chemical weapons plant and prison under Saddam's regime. The existing buildings were occupied by 2nd ACR and those few soldiers from our own unit who had come here a month earlier as part of the advance party.

The walls enclosed a rectangular area that might have been 800 meters by 400 meters. Guard towers were dispersed at even intervals along the low wall. To our south was Route Silver, a spread of Iraqi farm country, and then the city of Baghdad. To our west was a narrow dirt road, a canal full of feces and fish, a large open tract of farm land, and an impoverished collection of shacks known as Triangle Town. Clusters of brick houses huddled against our eastern wall. Another military compound adjoined our northern wall housing the Iraqi National Guard. A door in the wall connected our two camps.

Since the base was relatively new, they had not yet finished the barracks we were to occupy. We could see them, though. Large white-washed two-story buildings built of reinforced concrete were designed to house one company of soldiers each. They were all complete except for the plumbing and electrical work. Eventually—soon, we were told—there would be running water and air conditioners. For the present all we could do was pine for them.

Our company was sleeping in the oily dirt of the motor pool on the end of the camp closest to the Iraqi Army installation. Our gear would not arrive for several days, so those infamously uncomfortable Army cots were a rare, highly sought commodity. Those of us who could not find one slept in vehicles, on vehicles, on rucksacks or anything that would get us off of the ground and away from wandering scorpions and camel spiders. I stretched out on a row of duffel bags, keeping my M16A3 and M-14 sniper rifle within arm's reach.

There was no indication, lying there on those duffel bags at the end of my first mission in Iraq, that demons lurked and a year later I would be fighting an intense battle with them like so many other soldiers scarred by intense battlefield experiences.

----

At dawn on my second day in Iraq, I struggled up off the duffel bags, groaning and stretching an aching body. The sun was still a mere suggestion of light in the eastern sky. Most of my comrades were dozing in the pale morning light. A mist hung over the FOB, lending a mythic air to the routine activities of an Army unit coming to life. Soldiers generally try to exercise noise discipline by conducting business quietly, even in a relatively safe environment, but gas-powered generators purred here and there around the base. The smell of diesel exhaust, an ever-present odor in third-world countries, barely muted the stench of raw sewage and other odorous filth wafting over our compound's short walls.

A line was beginning to form at the latrines. Male warriors of all ages and ethnicities stood patiently in line, towels slung over shoulders, personal hygiene bags in hand, weapons safely slung. It struck me then that normal people don't wait to brush their teeth while clutching a rifle. The wait didn't seem worth the reward, so I strolled to our dining tent, grabbed a tiny apple, and filled my aluminum canteen cup with hot water. Back at the Lieutenant's vehicle, I lathered up to shave the face reflected in a side-view mirror.

Nearby, Sergeant Chen was sitting cross-legged on top of the M-1114 next to the huge .50 caliber machine gun wrapped tightly in a poncho liner. He looked like Buddha incarnate—an extremely muscular Buddha who could rip your arms off, but most likely wouldn't from the placid expression on his face. Always hard to tell what he was thinking. Maybe he was pondering his fiancée back home or planning for law school, which he claimed was his intention if he survived deployment. Or maybe he was just cold. The morning air in Iraq had to be chillier than it was on Saipan where he'd once served as a police officer. Among the few things I knew about Sergeant Yihjih "Eddie" Chen was that he liked country music and was very proud of his pickup truck. I was determined to get to know him a little better. Before I could strike up a conversation, Lieutenant Aguero approached looking both angry and thoughtful.

"How's it going, Sir?"

He spent a few profane moments complaining about "those assclowns" at battalion headquarters and then pointed at Chen. "Make sure your crew's equipment is ready to go within the hour. We have a mission to the DAC at 0800."

That sent me to work on my rifle as everyone began to gather and check their individual gear. My hands worked over the weapon easily from long practice as I watched the platoon get ready for a second day of activity outside the wire. The lieutenant didn't specify, but apparently something at the District Area Council (DAC) needed attention and whatever it was, our platoon was going to handle it. Specialist Deaver sat down to keep me company, and we both carried out the soothing ritual of weapon maintenance without much to say. When he finally spoke, I had to strain to hear.

"Look at that LMTV." He motioned vaguely toward a big four-wheeled Light Medium Tactical Vehicle that was the Army's replacement for the standard family of five-ton trucks. It had an unarmored three-man cab with a weapon mount in the roof and huge wheels that kept the chassis high off the ground. To make up for a lack of armor, our platoon had spent a good deal of labor lining the vehicle bed with sandbags to reduce IED blast effects. "Can you believe those morons sent us through IED Alley in the back of that mobile sandbox? How's a thing like that gonna stop a firecracker much less a freakin' high-yield explosive? Are these people nuts? Or are they intentionally trying to kill me? I swear to God, if they make us go on patrol in that deathtrap, I will create whole new definitions of workplace violence."

All I could do was nod in the appropriate places. He was right. The road from Kuwait to Baghdad which we had traversed mainly packed into LMTVs was known officially as our MSR or Main Supply Route, and soldiers who traveled that route called it IED Alley due to the number of road-side bombs encountered.

The DAC was a large two-story structure with an open rotunda balcony that peeked over high concrete walls. The gate was nothing more intimidating than a large pole manned by lethargic civilian guards, but the facility was surrounded by snarls of serpentine concertina wire or razor-wire. The street in front of the DAC was closed to civilian traffic, which made it a tad less likely that some loon in a car stuffed with high explosives could conduct the dreaded Vehicle-Borne Improvised Explosive Device or VB-IED attack. Across from the DAC was a block of two-story brick buildings containing shops that all seemed to be closed at this early hour.

We parked in front of the gate and dismounted to form a protective perimeter. While our Company Commander went inside to meet our Battalion Commander, there was nothing much for us to do but stand around and watch the clumps of kids that were beginning to gather. A gaggle of them were playing soccer on the pavement of what had been a parking lot before the Army conscripted the building. Most wore no shoes, but that didn't deter them from running full-tilt up and down the area littered with gravel and broken glass. Specialist Christopher Rusch approached carrying his automatic rifle at the low-ready position. I pointed at the kids playing in the near distance. "Do you see that? Playing barefoot in all that junk."

Rusch stared for a few moments, probably wondering what his infant daughter was doing back in Texas. He was half Dominican and he'd inherited handsome Latin features from his mother. He had an enormous head that barely fit inside the standard Kevlar helmet and a tough time communicating. He often seemed to be searching for the right words either in English or Spanish. "Tough kids," he finally said.

"Durned skippy, they are." I watched one of the older boys conferring with a younger one. There was some conversation that we couldn't hear, and then the older boy stared at us. He wanted the younger one to follow him in our direction, but the little kid was having none of it. Finally, the bigger kid picked up the little one and walked toward us. They didn't look threatening, so I turned my attention to my assigned security sector. I had a soft spot for kids, but we'd all heard the horror stories about kids bearing bombs or grenades. And there was always the sniper threat if you let yourself get distracted. There had been no recent sniper attacks in Sadr City, but there was always a first time and I didn't intend to be a target. I was scanning the buildings in the area so closely that I almost didn't notice that the two kids were rapidly approaching our perimeter.

"Stop!" I ran through the standard Arabic warnings. "We are American Forces. You are safe. Go away." Immediately I felt foolish about the shouting. It was a big fat duh and nothing if not obvious to a couple of Iraqi kids. The older boy seemed shocked to hear an American speaking Arabic and stopped in his tracks. He squinted at me for a few moments, apparently trying to decide on his next move. The kid he was carrying on his hip stared wide-eyed and sucked his thumb.

"Good Mistah, good Mistah—you my friend, Mistah." He raised the smaller child a little higher on his hip as if to show him off and smiled. "Baby, Mistah." I looked at Rusch who just shrugged.

I asked the boy his name. He replied, "Mustafa" while patting himself on the chest and grabbing his passenger's leg. He showed us a deep gash in the sole of the younger boy's foot and said something that sounded like Do-wah. I had no clue what that meant, but it was obvious that he wanted some sort of medical treatment for the boy's injury.

Motioning them to approach, I got a closer look at the younger boy's foot. It was a fairly bad gash, likely from one of the glass shards littering the parking lot playground. They were both dressed in dirty clothes that looked like they'd been picked up at some stateside yard sale in 1979. The cut on the little guy's foot would need more than a Band-Aid. I looked around for our medic and spotted him hanging out near the rear of one of our vehicles.

"Hey, Doc! Guzman, come here a minute!"

The medic started in our direction in no particular hurry. Guzman was a New York Puerto Rican with no accent and pale mocha complexion. His middle name was Aristoteles, the Spanish spelling of the great Greek philosopher. He was an intelligent guy and a solid aid man in our platoon.

"What do you want, Fisk?" he asked, and then spotted the gash on the kid's foot. He went directly to work. "That's a pretty good one," he said. "Somebody get me some water."

Rusch fetched a bottle from the nearest Humvee and we watched as Guzman washed the wound and the kid's filthy foot. The injured kid didn't make a peep while Doc cleaned and bandaged his wound.

When I asked him for his name, he meekly replied, "Hamed."

"Mathias," I replied tapping my chest as I had seen the Iraqis do.

The kid nodded enthusiastically and I reached into a pocket for some Tootsie Rolls saved from my last MRE meal. I handed him one and gave another to his rescuer, brother or friend. They were much more interested in the candy than the medical treatment. "Go on, now," I told them. "Go home."

"Thank you, Mathias. You good Mistah." Mustafa walked away still carrying Hamed who was now wearing a big smile and had a mouthful of chocolate. I had a warm feeling at that moment. Maybe we could do some good here after all.

----

### Neurobehavioral Assessment by Ortiz, Felix @ 15 JAN 2013

*CPT Fisk is a 39 year old, right hand dominant, divorced Caucasian; OD who was referred for neuropsychological screening secondary to concussion and difficulties in concentration, memory and hand writing (ideomotor apraxia like) related difficulties.*

*CPT Fisk has 13 years of military service. He has had three combat deployments. He was deployed to Iraq (2004-05), (2010-11). During his first deployment he faced many firefights; he was an infantryman at the time. In regards to mTBI related events, he was involved in a rocket blast that occurred approximately five feet from him. He was thrown across the room. Later his section leader woke them up. He received quarters for three days and experienced vertigo for three days. He described multiple events in which his vehicles were hit by IEDs and/or RPG.*

*CPT Fisk described his second deployment as uneventful*

*Overall, CPT Fisk total score on the RBANS was at the 90$^{th}$ percentile indicating superior performance in cognitive functioning at this time. Post-Traumatic Stress Disorder-hyperactive amygdale with hippocampal atrophy, resulting in heightened state of arousal.*

----

Hours passed before we got a new mission. It seemed simple and promised a little sightseeing to boot. We had to transport a Civil Affairs captain to another large U.S. base in Baghdad, located near a former tourist attraction called the Martyr's Monument. That frequently photographed destination was an onion-shaped building built by Saddam as a tribute to Iraqis who died in the war with Iran during the 1980s. It was comparable to the Vietnam Memorial in Washington, D.C., as the names of the dead were etched on walls inside the cavernous structure.

The American base was also located near an abandoned amusement park where the rusted steel structures gave the place the look of a dinosaur graveyard. It was a weird juxtaposition of dead structures and monuments to the dead as we pulled into yet another security perimeter and listened to Sergeant First Class Swope outline the plan.

"We're gonna sit here and use their PX," he said. "Ya'll better sit there and go to finance while you're here and get your checks cashed and whatever. Be back here no later than 1545. Move out."

Swope was a short, quiet man. He spoke without the stereotypical Senior NCO bluster and so quietly that we often had to strain to hear him. Likely a hangover from his Texas childhood, he peppered everything he said with the phrase *sit there,* no matter whether or not what he was ordering us to do could be accomplished by sitting there or anywhere else. Swope was usually calm, but if you pissed him off, you could expect lightning to strike in a hurry. He could go from serenity to explosive rage, and that produced lightning-quick responses from his subordinates. Swope's occasional tirades had the effect of a nuclear detonation. I was never able to figure out if that was calculated or genuine. Probably the former.

Most of us wandered over to the Martyr's Monument to look around the structure which reminded me of the city's minarets and prayer towers. Looking up at the massive dome, I admired the architect. He was a talented man and the monument's workmen were obviously skilled. I'd read once that Saddam used the same man to design this structure as he'd used to recreate Ishtar's Gate in the ruins of old Babylon. We descended a massive concrete spiral staircase to the levels below, where former shops and offices had been commandeered and occupied by the American admin and logistics machine. Some stood in line to cash their checks at the finance office, while others raided the PX for goodies they couldn't get elsewhere. I went in search of a western-style flush toilet. Few things say civilization to me like the feel of cool porcelain on my butt. The toilet. I didn't get much of that feeling at the FOB—or anywhere else in Iraq, for that matter.

There was a familiar Little Soldier's room at the end of a long hallway, and as I stood admiring the plumbing, I thought about a stop we'd made on the long convoy run from Kuwait to Baghdad. That was just five days ago, but it seemed like years. We been pissing into plastic bottles most of the way until the convoy finally stopped to refuel. At the site was a long line of military Porta-Johns for the use of travelers. We stood before the bank of green and gray plastic outhouses waiting for our turn when I noticed several of them were marked as "Arabic Bathrooms." Never having seen an Arabic Bathroom and curious about potential differences, I pulled a door open and inspected the interior. The first thing I noticed was no toilet seat. In its place was a pair of molded plastic foot impressions on either side of the hole. Treaded grooves were built in to the foot rests to provide extra traction for those awkward mornings after a fig binge. Apparently, the evacuation procedure involved placing your feet in the indicated position, squatting over the hole, and letting it rip.

There was none of that in the Little Soldier's room here. Angels sang and cherubs capered as I scrabbled at my belt and gazed at the glory of a modern, American-style bathroom complete with firmly attached plastic toilet seats. It was bliss. And so what if I'm that easy to please.

----

Later in the day, we were back out in the city turning just shy of Route Silver and weaving through some of the sewage-infested back streets. So many people had spliced into the main power line that our vehicle gunners had to carefully lift the tangled wires over their turrets as we passed. We went slowly, leading an ever-growing crowd of singing and clapping children through alleys full of excrement. They walked along boards that had been placed on bricks as a makeshift sidewalk, laughing and oblivious to the stench. After several minutes, the platoon leader announced that we had reached our second destination and called a halt.

It was a school of some sort—a two-story seafoam-colored building that rose above a high concrete wall covered with red and black Arabic writing. Other buildings, taller and dressed with drying laundry, stood nearby. As we dismounted, a crowd of about 100 people materialized from various alley outlets. There were older men, boys and teens dressed in the black shirt and trousers that composed the uniform of the Sadr Bureau. In the mix were some women in black *burqas*. They all gathered around our position. Either they wanted something from us or they wanted to give us something, and neither seemed promising. We spread out on full alert and waited to see what might happen.

Lieutenant Aguero led his usual contingent forward to find the person he wanted to meet. Those of us delegated to tag along included our interpreter, Staff Sergeant York, Specialist Tyrell, Specialist Perry, the black musician from College Station, Texas, and me. We formed a tight ring around Aguero as he charged toward the walled compound. The crowd gave us a fairly wide path until the lieutenant found an older man who seemed like he might have some authority, and used our translator to ask for the Moqtar. The gray-beard assumed an air of great importance and gave rapid Arabic instructions to a boy at his side. The kid disappeared through a metal gate in the compound wall. We followed the chosen elder—and several undesignated people who decided to tag along—toward the door.

"Sir, what is this place, and who are we meeting?" I had my notebook out ready to record whatever was about to happen.

"This is a boy's high school that's in our platoon's sector. I'm supposed to show my face to the local Moqtar and the Headmaster to let them know that we'll be helping them."

"Very good, Sir. And what's a Moqtar?"

"He's the guy elected by the people to represent them at the District Area Counsel—some Grand Poobah type that likes to act important."

Aguero stopped to wait for his contacts and asked several of the usual word-on-the-street questions of the elder he'd spotted in the crowd. There was a lot of give and take through the interpreter, but it all boiled down to something like, "Gosh, Americans, everything's just swell here."

Aguero crushed his cigarette as another old man dressed in gray and black robes with an impressive black turban entered the street from the school's green door. When he saw us, his eyes opened wide with surprise or delight. He opened his arms wide as if he were receiving a long lost relative. "Peace be unto you," he said in Arabic.

"And unto you, peace," said Lieutenant Aguero in the pro forma Arabic greeting we'd all learned in pre-deployment training. There was a burst of laughter and chattering from the assembled crowd who were apparently surprised to hear Arabic spoken by foreigners. The old man who greeted us identified himself as Ahmud Ishani, school proprietor, and said he was anxious to talk to us. The crowd crushed in to listen to the exchange and a clear pecking order took shape as the Lieutenant spoke. Every time Aguero asked a question through the interpreter, all the men in the assembly pressed closer to hear what was being said. When things got too tight, an elder among them would establish his seniority and start shouting for the younger men to back off. This was occasionally accompanied by a swat aimed at one of the boys in the crowd. The jockeying for position and prominence went on until we were surrounded by concurrent rings of male Iraqis with the eldest inside and the youngest standing on tip-toes on the outside. It was apparently standard operating procedure, as it happened everywhere we stopped to confer with Iraqis.

Eventually, it got so tight out on the street that our security detail was about to be overwhelmed. Amid all the babble, Aguero couldn't hear the answers to his questions. Frustrated by a crowd he couldn't control, the lieutenant finally asked for a tour of the school. He didn't wait for permission or cooperation. While the interpreter was translating his request, Aguero rushed us toward the compound gate. We pressed through a smelly phalanx of unwashed flesh and entered the school grounds. By the time we reached the door to the school, our interpreter caught up with us.

"Sir, please, he say that school is closed for now, and could you come back again when it is open so that you can see the children, too."

The lieutenant looked around at the smiling proprietor and then at the crowd still gaping at us from the street. He shrugged and then began to work out a date for a later visit. While they went over details, I sidled toward the entryway and took a look inside the building. In an open courtyard inside the structure, I could see what looked like some kind of karate class. There was a formation of kids dressed in black and wearing green bandanas around wrapped around their heads. The bandanas were marked with Arabic writing that I couldn't read, but I recognized the guy out in front doing the instruction. He wore the uniform of the Sadr Bureau. On his command, the assembled kids began to perform punches and kicks that I thought might be Tae Kwon Do or a similar martial fighting style. The kids were disciplined and focused. As their sensei began a lecture, they paused in the ready position, one fist extended to block and the other tucked in tight to their bodies ready to strike. The instructor caught me looking, but didn't pause in his harangue. I turned to catch the lieutenant's attention.

"Looks like they've got some kind of after-school program going on, Sir."

Aguero broke off from his scheduling conference and took a look. "Yeah, whoop-de-doo, kids. Don't do drugs and remember to anni-hilate the infidel." We were getting nowhere with this public relations stop. The vaunted Moqtar was nowhere to be found, and the school principal was not what you'd call a fount of information. Aguero thanked him for his time and led us all back out to the street where he signaled for everyone to load the vehicles.

"What did you make of that little karate class back there, Sir?" I climbed into the Humvee and settled as Aguero began to study his map and the GPS fixed near his seat.

"So what? They want to prance around in ninja suits and kick each other silly that's their business." He handed me the GPS as our drivers cranked up the engines. "Take this GPS and write down the coordinates whenever we come across any large shit puddles. We've got a mission coming up to suck sewage, so we need to know what locations need the most attention."

As we got rolling, I toyed with the GPS and tried to put what I'd seen at the school out of my mind, but it nagged at me. Clearly there was a lot more going on at that school than reading, writing, and arithmetic.

----

At the corner of the north-south route Delta where it intersects route Copper, almost exactly in the center of Sadr City, we ran into some-thing that looked like a carnival crowd milling around an Iraqi Police Station. We headed for the station gate where a skinny little sentry stood behind a wall of concertina wire. He quickly realized that the American convoy was bound to enter without his permission and pulled aside the wire to let us roll into the station. As we parked, the sentry scampered away to alert someone more senior that they had American visitors.

The lieutenant dismounted and lit a cigarette while he waited for someone to confront. He took little irritated puffs as he stared across the intersection at the crowds outside the police station. It was a busy place. Busses and vans arrived at regular intervals, dropping off more and more men to join the throng which stretched south as far as the eye could see. There were those familiar red, black, and green flags everywhere poking up through a sea of people. And there were pictures of the dark-eyed Muqtada al-Sadr plastered on practically every vertical surface. Somewhere off to the south, we heard the thump of drums and a chorus of shouting. We couldn't see it, but the crowds were there for some kind of rally or celebration.

"The natives are restless." I crawled out of the vehicle and checked the safety on my M16. From what I could see, we were in the middle of something between a militia gathering and a monster-truck rally. Aguero watched it all with a critical eye while our apprehension mounted.

"What do you reckon they're doing, Lieutenant?"

"Don't know," he said. "Why don't we go ask?" He called the usual crew to accompany him and charged out into the street. Staff Sergeant Davis, Staff Sergeant York, and Sergeant Fowler fell in with me, Rogers, and Denney as we strolled out of the police compound and crossed the busy street. We tried to maintain as much of a non-threatening posture as seven heavily armed soldiers can, and ran up on a contingent of people that outnumbered us about ten to one. Amid the crowd was a man speaking into a hand-held radio. This guy had some authority, or at least was in contact with someone who did. Aguero went right up to him and offered the standard greeting which was idly returned to include a limp handshake. We could tell he had zero enthusiasm for the encounter even as he patted his chest to let us know he was being sincere. We were quickly hemmed in by curious onlookers.

Through our interpreter, Aguero asked the man if he was in charge. No, he replied, but he could use the radio to ask for someone who was. He turned his back and gabbled into his handset. Within minutes, a man wearing thick bifocals over a well-trimmed beard pushed toward us through the crowd. He returned Aguero's greeting, but there was no offer to shake hands. While Aguero asked questions, the guy just stood there with his hands clasped behind his back trying to look wise and pensive. The crowd pushed and shoved closer, trying to monitor the conversation. I suspected an informational pamphlet was circulating Sadr City: "Fun Ways to Annoy American Soldiers."

The man who said his name was Assad Abed al-Hussein indicated that the Mahdi Army was having a rally, and it had all been approved by local authorities. I could tell from the lieutenant's body language that he found that particular bit of Intel dubious. Aguero told the man we had a mission and needed to pass through the crowd to make a meeting on the other side of the rally. There was no way that was going to happen right now, according to Assad Abed al-Hussein, but they rally was set to conclude shortly anyway. Aguero just nodded and asked him to keep the intersection clear. It was a matter of waiting a little while or creating a confrontation that might get ugly.

We headed back across the street, but soon found our way blocked by several busses that arrived and parked in the middle of the intersection. The drivers were going nowhere and neither were we. Aguero glared at the drivers for a while, willing them to move—but no dice. There were no passengers getting on or off and the drivers just sat there with their hands folded. The lieutenant stormed back toward the man in charge, and we followed in his wake. As we approached, we were confronted with a line of men standing shoulder-to-shoulder with their arms linked. They didn't want us to go any further.

Aguero was trying to get someone to move the buses when the Iraqi Police arrived. Two blue and white IP trucks pulled into the intersection and a senior policeman dismounted to investigate. He was a lean man with an impressive mustache, wearing an immaculately pressed uniform and the rank insignia of an IP colonel. He was a big wheel, Col. Hussein Jadoa, the Sadr City Chief of Police, and he was concerned that our presence there in that intersection might serve to agitate the crowd. He told Lieutenant Aguero that it created the potential for danger.

"What danger?" Aguero asked looking around at the crowd. The Chief of Police was about to explain when Sergeant Fowler interrupted.

"Gun—in that van!" he shouted and pointed at a shabby Nissan van full of chanting Sadr Bureau youths wearing black shirts.

We jostled for position, keeping an eye on the vehicle as the Police Chief tried to calm our fears. "Let me investigate this," he said, and sent one of his cops to take a look at the people in the van. The cop walked up and shouted something at the driver. There was some back and forth before he returned to make his report. The Chief listened for a while and then smiled. "My man said that he is an off-duty policeman. He was warned to keep his weapon concealed."

"Colonel, gatherings of this sort have to be approved through the proper channels. Do you know who sanctioned this?"

"It is most certainly the District Area Council who approved it."

"The DAC? I'm trying to get there for a meeting with my boss. Could you escort us through?"

"It would be impossible right now as it would make problems with the people. But please, wait for this event to pass and then please come to my office after so that I may show you better hospitality."

"Rollings!" Aguero snapped, "Get up in that IP tower with a pair of binos."

Specialist Rollings and his battle-buddy Briones snatched a pair of binoculars and trotted to the walled police compound where a sentry pulled aside the gate. The tower rose about 20 feet above the wall that surrounded the police station. The pair of soldiers scampered up a ladder and began scanning the crowd. The Lieutenant let the pair look for a while as we made our way back to the vehicles and then asked for a report.

"How many people do you see, Rollings?"

"A whole shit-load, Sir."

"Is that a metric or a standard shit-load?" The lieutenant smacked his helmet in frustration. "Give me a number, you jackass!"

"I don't know, Sir. Maybe eight or ten thousand."

"Keep monitoring. Let me know if you see any weapons."

We leaned against our Humvees and watched the crowd. More busses and vans arrived to discharge people, and the ranks at the intersection were steadily growing. They were all chanting by this time, and we could feel tension in the air. I looked over at Aaron Fowler who had more time in Iraq than the rest of us. He'd come over with the ADVON, the advance party, and was the answer man in our platoon when it came to weapons and tactics. He was also an amateur gunsmith and read the Ranger Handbook like it was gospel. Fowler was eyeing the crowd with one foot cocked up on a Humvee bumper and one hand caressing the safety switch of his rifle. If he was uneasy, it was a sign that the rest of us should be more alert.

Fowler had spent some time riding along on patrols with the 2nd Armored Cavalry Regiment to get the lay of the land in Sadr City and learning their effective tactics, techniques, and procedures. I plied him for information at every opportunity, and he generally gave me useful tips or background on our AO.

We'd been watching developments in the streets for about half an hour when Rollings alerted us from his perch up in the police tower.

"It looks like a brigade-size plus marching up the street toward our position. About eight-hundred meters out." I did the math and understood he was telling us there were about 2,000 to 5,000 people approaching. That's a good size mob and potentially very dangerous, depending on their mood and inclinations.

"Do you see any weapons?" The lieutenant wanted details.

"I can't tell." Rollings reported after a while. "There's a whole bunch of dudes waving swords around."

It looked like there was a parade approaching up the street with people in blocks like human floats. We could hear drums and cymbals getting louder, but we couldn't see the musicians. The ceremony was supposedly over, but that didn't do anything to decrease the ardor of the people we saw filing by the compound.

"Hey, look…" Bourquin pointed at the passing parade who glared at us as they passed. "I didn't know we'd get to review the troops today. They're even doing an eyes-right."

"More like the stink-eye," said York. The militia was chanting a Sadr City golden-oldie that began with "Allah…Mohammed…" and ended with a rousing chorus of "MOOK-tada, MOOK-tada, MOOK-tada—something—something." It was becoming a familiar refrain. As they passed our position, they waved flags and brandished old ceremonial scimitars. We didn't understand the shouts, but there was no mistaking the evil glares. I caught the eye of an older man in the passing mob and he gave me a nice throat-slicing gesture.

I just smiled and that apparently was not the reaction he wanted. He fell out of ranks and stormed toward me. As he approached, I made an obvious effort to switch my rifle from safe to semi-automatic. Either he saw the move or he felt close enough to make his point. He stopped within a few feet of my position and gave me the old "MOOK-tada" a couple of times followed by a maniacal "Down USA!"

"*Salaam a lechum,*" I said amiably. He headed back to rejoin the crowd and I slid my weapon back onto safe. It was a relatively mundane confrontation, but I didn't turn my back on the demonstration until the last of the crowd passed.

We finally reached the District Area Council after the melee at the intersection cleared and met up with Captain Denomy. While he and Lieutenant Aguero conferred on the demonstration, I stood security, staring at a bombed-out structure next to the council building. It was just a shell, victim of skillfully applied high explosive in earlier fighting. The shadows and rubble provided plenty of good sniper hides, and I scanned it carefully from top to bottom. Almost all of the walls were missing in the top five or six floors, exposing rusting iron skeletons. Near the top someone had hung washing to dry. It was obvious that someone lived in that shattered structure. Likely several someones, given the amount of laundry flapping in the breeze like tattered, shell-shot flags over the battlements of a besieged castle.

Movement on a ground floor caught my eye, and I saw the little kid with the injured foot that we'd treated yesterday. He advanced toward me smiling and limping. He was still shoeless. We greeted each other and he called me "Good Mistah." I felt a sudden urge to scoop him up out of the mess and mail him home where he could have shoes and wouldn't have to live in a bombed-out building or beg for food from strangers. Of course, I couldn't do that, so I just smiled at him and wondered if he'd want to slit my throat when he got old enough to understand his situation in this war-torn country.

After a while, we departed for a meeting with the Sadr City Chief of Police. Captain Denomy's vehicle slipped seamlessly into our convoy, and we steered through the Sadr City streets until we reached the IP compound where Police Colonel Jodoa was apparently waiting to show his visitors the promised hospitality. At the station, a smiling sentry lifted a bar to let us enter and we drove in to park and sort ourselves out for the visit. While the Captain gathered us to outline his plans, Swope had the drivers maneuver around the parking lot until they had all the Humvees facing the gate. It was what we called combat parking and made for a quick exit if required.

"This is the Chief of Police Headquarters," Captain Denomey said. "I just need to introduce us, find out what their needs are, and see what he has to say about this morning's demonstration." He pointed a finger at Aguero. "We don't need a lot of people. I'll take my RTO and whoever you want to go."

"Sir, I'll go with you on this one." Swope stepped toward Aguero.

"Good. Fisk, you'll go, and also Staff Sergeant York."

A police guide led us to an office in one of the compound's two buildings. We passed groups of Iraqi policemen in clean, well-pressed uniforms, clustered in small groups and whispering as we walked by, smiling and nodding. Colonel Jadoa Hussein stood to greet us as we entered his office. His quarters were spacious but unadorned, like most Iraqi public offices. His desk was clean and there was no evidence of the paperwork piles that surround most American bureaucrats. There was an old rotary dial phone on the desk, a few pens, and an overused notebook, but not much else. There was no computer, no bulletin board or maps bristling with marker pins, no copy machine—not even a coffee pot. We were invited to find space on a clutch of old chairs that looked like they were flea-market purchases.

While the officers went through the greeting rituals with Colonel Jadoa, I found a seat and pulled off my helmet, letting a cool breeze blow over my bald head. It was nice to be off my feet, to give my body a break from the weight of my gear. The palaver with the Company Commander was mostly conducted using his interpreter, and I tried to catch what I could of it from a distance. The subject at hand was the demonstration. "Tell him," the Captain said to his interpreter, "that he has to report requests for gatherings like that through the liaison at the DAC." There was more, but I couldn't hear much of it. I kept my eyes on Colonel Jadoa. While our officers were speaking, he leaned forward, squinting as if he was painfully trying to comprehend the English phrases. I'd become convinced that he knew more about what was being said than he let on during our visit. He was acting like an ally and a gracious host, but Colonel Jodoa, the Iraqi Police Chief of Sadr City, betrayed us the very next day.

# April 4th, 2004

IT SEEMED LIKE just another day in the combat zone. I had break-fast, shaved, and was contemplating a game of spades when I saw the platoon sergeant speed-walking toward the platoon area leaving a small plume of dust in his wake. Since I happened to be the first swinging Richard that he encountered, I caught his initial blast.

"Fisk, go get your goddamn P-L—and I mean right now!" Swope's tone and the ugly look on his face promised some sort of up-coming shit storm, so I hustled away wondering where to find the L-T and what sort of orders we would get when I did. Riddell was nearby and hustled along with me indicating he knew where the lieutenant was at the time.

Our platoon leader slept in the Advance Party area, which was a large maintenance bay that had a roof and cots. That's where we found Aguero crashed and sleeping soundly. We stood there for a while, wondering how much physical contact was appropriate in waking an officer. The way Aguero was sleeping, a polite request to wake up wouldn't do much good. His cot was wedged tightly among a host of others containing sleeping soldiers and men who were al-ready up and banging around, but Aguero was oblivious. He escaped it all by stuffing plugs into his ears. Apparently, he didn't think that might cause him to miss his morning alarm.

"Sir!" I leaned in close and shouted. "Sir, Sergeant Swope wants to see you!"

Lieutenant Aguero's head snapped up and he took a close look at his watch. We stood there listening to him curse the makers of Japa-

nese time-keeping instruments while he swung up into a sitting position and scrabbled around for his boots. "OK," he said waving us
away. "I'm up."

That was the start of a less-than-stellar day for Aguero and the
rest of our platoon. Once he heard what Swope had to say, he became
philosophical. Aguero had learned through long experience as an officer that no plan of his survived first contact with reality—and the
day's mission was as real as it gets. He had wanted to spend some time
getting to know the AO and the people who inhabited it so we'd be
ready and able to fight when the time came, but higher command
seemed to have other ideas about more mundane missions.

About a week before, Aguero had been told that we were to take
two jet trucks—Iraqi sewage-suckers, if you will—along with us on
some patrols to clean up all the filth and garbage that littered the
streets. Those trucks had never showed up, so the lieutenant assumed
he was free to carry out his more pressing plans. That morning, he
was told the shit-sucking mission was back on for his platoon.

When Riddell and I made it back to the Comanche Company
area, the NCOs were busily arranging the vehicles in the proper order
and assigning duties. While we waited to hear what was in store for
us, I spent time watching the men who had become my brothers. We
were an interesting and diverse group with all sorts of divergent paths
that brought us to an infantry platoon in a combat zone. While Specialist Jon Denney helped Specialist Carl Wild prepare his M240B
machinegun for action, Staff Sergeant Darcy Robinson and Staff Sergeant Trevor Davis—professional soldiers—were huddled around a
map that listed all of the street names and points of interest in Sadr
City. Davis had felt a little disoriented since we arrived in Sadr City,
and he was trying hard to learn the geography of our AO, as local
street signs in Arabic were no help. The lieutenant had yet to formally
brief his NCOs, but they'd heard from Swope that the shit-sucking

escort mission was on, and they wanted to be ready for anything. And Swope was in no mood for nonsense.

Corporal Shane Coleman, a slight, sinewy man with numerous tattoos, was cleaning the .50 caliber machinegun on one of the vehicles. He was from a little suburb of Houston called Friendship, Texas and a big fan of punk-rock, heavy metal, and rappers like Tu-Pac. Coleman was a 20-year-old former druggie who would celebrate his 21$^{st}$ birthday in Iraq, where alcohol was not allowed, even for a soldier who'd just became eligible to buy a drink. He told us that he'd joined the Army to keep from winding up in a jail cell. Coleman was always smiling. He had an unsinkable positive attitude that never changed, even later in the day when he took a bullet in the leg.

Coleman often reflected on the path that led him from wild-child to warrior. He told us basic training had been easy. He was used to yelling and violence. Coleman was with his training platoon on the bayonet course when the Drill Sergeants called a formation, and their Company Commander announced that terrorists had struck the Pentagon and the Twin Towers in New York. It was a shocking revelation, and everyone knew it might mean war. Shane Coleman knew at that moment that he'd likely wind up in a combat zone. And here he was in Iraq, prepared to test himself in the ultimate crucible yet assigned to help escort some lowly shit-sucker trucks. How could you do anything but laugh at that?

Private Derrick Perry performed maintenance checks on one of our Humvees. Next to him was Sergeant Justin Bellamy, a slender young man from Warsaw, Indiana, who would ride as gunner on Red 3 that morning. He was the fastest guy in the platoon, and he'd been something of a star at track and field in his hometown. If he'd managed to work things out with his wife, they would have been celebrating an anniversary that morning, but Bellamy was in Iraq and separated from his wife by circumstances beyond his control. He told me the story once, all about getting married at 19 to a woman four years older than he was and planning a long life together. Money was tight, but he had a good job with prospects in a grocery store where he'd been promoted to assistant manager. His family had the means to help, but Bellamy wanted to be his own man and make his own way. He enlisted as a part-time soldier in the National Guard for some extra income, and decided he liked it. He talked his wife into agreeing that he should go on active duty even when that meant a cut in their income. They agreed to a temporary split while he soldiered at Fort Hood and she lived with her parents. It inevitably led to divorce, but Bellamy still considered his ex-wife a friend.

Bellamy was nearly through his enlistment and looking forward to a possible reconciliation when he discovered that cynical soldiers were correct: US ARMY stands for Uncle Sam Ain't Released Me Yet. In the middle of a final training exercise, he was notified that he was a "stop-loss" and would be retained in uniform beyond the end of his enlistment. He would deploy with Charlie Company to Iraq. So there he was, smoking a cigarette, talking to Sergeant Chen and waiting for the order to move. The order that would send them to suck shit off the Sadr City streets.

There was a missing man on Staff Sergeant Davis' crew that morning. Wild would ride behind the machinegun today, replacing Blake who was suffering from a bad case of what we called Sadam's Revenge, an attack of painful diarrhea that keep him chained to the latrines. We'd all come to suffer that same malady at one point or another during our deployment, so it was considered no big deal. Other than Blake's absence, there was nothing that morning to indicate we were getting ready for anything but a routine mission.

----

We finally got our collective crap together and rolled out the gate for our very first humanitarian mission. We had all four trucks loaded down with almost everyone in the platoon, including Monsoor and Sala'am, the two interpreters. The platoon leader's vehicle—often called a *victor*—led as usual with Riddell driving and Chen up on the .50. I was stuffed in the back beside Sala'am. Following us in trace was Staff Sergeant Davis and his crew in a victor of the type we called a Mad Max Machine—no top and a gun mount jury-rigged by the welding shop. Staff Sergeant Haubert was in the third victor, another Mad Max. He and Davis carried the majority of our dismounts piled tightly into any and all available space. Those were the guys who would get out at stops to provide perimeter security. I spent the time trying to remember who was where, but it was difficult. It didn't take long for things to get confused with stops, dismounts, and remounts as we patrolled.

We picked up two pristine white sewage-retrieval trucks just outside the FOB, where they'd been waiting for escort. Monsoor spoke briefly with the Iraqi boss-man, and we were rolling toward the city in a few minutes. The Honey Wagons slid into the middle of our convoy, and we set a rapid pace. Riddell had shed the last vestiges of civilized driving and was now in the aggressive, pedal-to-the-metal mindset of a combat driver. Lieutenant Aguero occasionally had to tell him to back off as the heavy trucks fell back and the formation began to spread.

We turned right off Route Copper and pulled into a neighborhood we'd patrolled on foot the previous night. There had been crowds then, but today the area was nearly deserted except for the usual crowds of kids begging for goodies. As we maneuvered into our first stop, they chased us down shouting for chocolate or anything else they thought we might spare. There were so many kids in the area that I wondered if this neighborhood even had a school to keep them off the streets. Our route was interrupted by a huge pool of reeking water that surrounded the neighborhood like a moat. Riddell pulled forward and positioned the victor so that we could dismount without having to stand around calf-deep in the muck.

The dismounts piled out of our vehicles to set up a perimeter as the Iraqi sewage workers hopped down into the goo-making splashes with their rubber boots. I spotted one guy wearing galoshes festooned with little colorful flowers that would have been a big hit in any gay pride parade as they went to work stringing hoses from the trucks into the sewage water. One man—likely the junior member of the team—waded deep into the cesspool with the open end of a hose while his senior buddy manned the pump controls. It was fairly efficient, and the Iraqi crews finished sucking up the mess sooner than any of us expected. It took them about 20 minutes to clear the water, remount, and let us know they were ready to roll on to the next scheduled stop.

It was just a block or two distant, so Aguero ordered us to walk while the trucks rolled behind our formation. We were led by a pack of kids who skipped along piping that golden-oldie refrain: "Good, good Mistah! You give me shock-o-lata." We strolled on full alert through a neighborhood lined with mud-brick structures, individual houses intermingled with a few shops. Power lines in the area were fairly high over the roadway which made things easier on the gunners riding along in the victors ready to engage if we ran into trouble. There wasn't much traffic. We could see Iraqis hanging out windows and watching the passing parade, but none of them seemed threatening. Some of them even waved, especially to the shit-sucker crews who were apparently a welcome apparition in a neighborhood without much in the way of plumbing or drainage.

Eventually, the street ran into a big vacant lot amid a nest of multiple-story apartment buildings. The lot was swamped with sewage: our next objective. We spread out as the vehicles approached, checking out a narrow alley that we thought might intersect Route Copper or some other major east-west thoroughfare. Off to our left was a small convenience store operating out of what looked like the shop-keeper's living room. As the sewage crews dismounted to do their thing, Aguero greeted the shopkeeper, and we were pleasantly surprised when the man's teenage daughter responded in British-accented English.

"We are very happy to have you here," she said while we stood and stared. She smiled brightly with dark eyes shining from the *hijab* that covered her head. He father puffed on a cigarette and asked her a question. Whatever it was she responded seemed to please him. He nodded and offered his two cents. "Good Mistah. Thank you very much."

Tyrell was impressed, but he didn't engage beyond a few muttered comments. Perry, who considered himself a player with the ladies, waded right in and began to chat with the girl. She giggled like she was talking with a rock-star when Perry handed Tyrell his camera for a quick snapshot with his new-found fan. That was too much for her father, who said something to her and then began to close shop. She gave Perry a wave as she climbed into a white hatchback next to her father. "We must go now," she said. "Nice to meet you."

It was time for a comm check with our highers, but Riddell was having problems. "Sir, I can't reach anyone on the radio," he said, extending the handset in the lieutenant's direction. Aguero tried to communicate with battalion and had the same luck. He switched to the platoon internal net and discovered he could at least communicate with his own vehicles. Swope came up to confer, and they decided to escort the sewage trucks back to dump their current loads. When they were in the area of the FOB, they could enlist a tech to check the radio. We remounted and rolled, splitting with the Iraqi disposal crews after making arrangements to meet up with them again when they'd disposed of their first load and were ready to go back out onto the streets. We led the patrol back to FOB War Eagle and turned the malfunctioning radio over to maintenance and split up to grab some lunch.

Deaver, Rusch, and I sat weighing the pros and cons of another MRE versus crunching on a camel spider. I listened casually to Carl Wild gabbing with York about Texas. They were a mismatched pair. York was tall and rangy at six-five while Wild was a foot shorter, but they both adhered to the notion that the Great Republic of Texas would someday conquer the world. Wild once told me he planned to become a Texas Ranger when and if he ever got out of the Army. As a Texan, he was big on spicy chow.

"Carlito," I called, pulling a tube out of my MRE. "You want my jalapeno cheese spread?" It was rhetorical. Anything containing jalapenos was good with Carl Wild. I tossed the tube full of cheese at him, but York stretched out a long arm and intercepted. That was too much even among fellow Texans. Wild said a few disparaging things about York's mother and then jumped on York to wrestle for the prize. It was like watching a poodle attack a mastiff, but it went on until York gave up the cheese spread. Wild was a hard man to ignore. When he wanted something he went after it and refused to quit until he got it.

At that point in the day, I didn't care much about the missions, the radios, or the lunch. It was enough that we were back inside the wire and able to drop our gear for a while. Little things mean a lot in a combat zone. The main entertainment as we waited for orders was watching Sergeant Bellamy trying to make the radios work. Apparently the problem was software and not hardware. The radios worked fine but the Tactical Operations Center or TOC had changed the Communications Security codes while we were out, and didn't bother to tell us about it before they made the switch. If two radios in a network are not using the same COMSEC codes, they can't talk to each other. That was our problem, and it did nothing to improve the mood of our leaders. Both Aguero and Swope both loudly wondered what the hell else could go wrong, even though they both had soldiered long enough to know the answer. It was the familiar Murphy's Law at work. Anything that can go wrong will go wrong at the worst possible time and under the worst possible circumstances.

Around this time, as Aguero and Swope stood cursing and waiting for the radios to come back on line, one of those strange strokes of fortune happened that either bless or haunt an infantry soldier's existence. Swope left the platoon leader to watch the radios and called a meeting of his NCOs. It was a significant event for some soldiers in our platoon, and I'll never be convinced it was just dumb luck. Fate or God or something beneficent had to have taken a hand.

I could barely hear the details from where I sat, but Swope had decided that having so many soldiers around, packed into unarmored vehicles on a shit-sucking escort, was counter-productive. We were offering too many easy targets if something went wrong outside the wire. Swope wanted his squad leaders to make decisions and leave some of their people behind when we went back out on the mission. Staff Sergeant Robinson walked over to his crew and told Tyrell he would be staying. Tyrell was more than a little happy to catch up on his sleep, and retired to a stack of duffel bags where he stretched out with a grin on his face.

"Wild and Arteaga." Robinson pointed a finger at the pair. "I'm only taking one of you. Who's it gonna be?" Rafael Arteaga just shrugged and looked at Wild who volunteered with a smile.

Robinson nodded and pointed at his vehicle. "OK, load up. You and Denney can take turns on the gun."

Carl Wild shrugged into his armor and walked to the Humvee. He wasn't a particularly bloodthirsty guy, but if there was going to be a fight he wanted to be in the thick of it. Carl would soon get his wish.

I piled into the lieutenant's vehicle and scrunched up next to Sala'am, the younger of our two interpreters who had lost the toss with Monsoor and would go along on the second shit-sucking foray. It was fine with me. Sala'am was young and full of energy and was usually happy to help me with my Arabic vocabulary and pronunciations. He was surprised that I had an interest in his country and culture.

"You like Iraq?" he asked in Arabic as the drivers cranked the engines.

"Yes, I like Iraq," I replied in kind, noting that I had learned to lie in two languages.

We formed up and rolled through the gate with Staff Sergeant Trevor Davis following us in the second victor with Perry driving and Wild on the gun. Denney was in back ready to relieve Wild as required. Staff Sergeant Stanley Haubert commanded the third Humvee, with Specialist Taylor driving and Sergeant Bellamy on the gun. They had Staff Sergeant Robinson and Doc Guzman in the back of their vehicle. Bringing up the rear was Swope with Rogers driving and Corporal Coleman on their .50 caliber. Sergeants Bourguin and Hayhurst were in the back seats.

The doo-doo wagons were waiting for us outside the gates and fell into our formation without discussion. They knew what the game was by this time, and the first mission had given them some confidence about working with Americans. I sat conflicted behind the lieutenant. On one hand, I was hoping we'd get more opportunities to interact with locals. I was fine with that—I actually enjoyed it unlike some of my platoon mates. On the other hand, there should be a better way to do it than walking along through piles of poop. This was literally a shitty mission and the sooner we got it accomplished, the better I would like it.

We ambled down Route Silver as quickly as a snarl of donkey carts and rusty automobiles allowed. This was a bad road, full of huge potholes, lined with piles of rusty I-beams and scrapped sheet metal that made great IED hiding places. As we rolled past a line of workshops. I noticed a man welding something. He was doing the job without a mask. Apparently in Sadr City, a squint and an old shirt wrapped around the head were sufficient safety precautions.

Our objective was near the neighborhood we'd left earlier in the morning. It was flooded ankle-deep with foul-smelling sludge that rose as far as the curbs all along the streets. It was a formidable job for the Iraqi crews, but they parked their trucks and got to work. We pulled our vehicles into a loose perimeter and dismounted, taking up security positions that gave us a good view of the area in all directions. It wasn't long before the neighborhood kids started crowding around to watch The Amazing Infidels and The Flying Shit-Suckers. We were quite a show, not to mention a shot at getting a little free candy. We kept them at a distance, focusing on the rooftops and windows of the surrounding buildings. The older people who bothered to approach mainly talked to the sewage crews. Could be they were thanking them for doing such a great service, or it could be they were asking about job opportunities in the shit-sucking industry. I never got close enough to ask.

Sergeant Chen shouted from his vehicle and got the lieutenant's attention. "Sir, Lancer Mike is asking for you." Aguero nodded and broke through the circle of kids with whom he'd been exchanging high-fives and walked over to the radio. He took the handset and slumped down in the driver's seat to take the call. While that was going on, I wandered over to watch Sala'am in discussion with the senior sewage man. Sala'am had a hand on the man's shoulder, reassuring him about something. I started to move closer, hoping to pick up a little of their conversation, when Aguero bolted out of his vehicle and motioned for me. I followed him, trying to pick a semi-dry path across Crap Creek where we could confer with Swope.

"I just got a call from Lancer Mike," Aguero grumbled. "They said that there's a lot of activity down by the Sadr Bureau on Delta and they want us to drive by and report once we go drop this load off. After that, we are supposed to go by every hour as long as our patrol lasts."

"I heard," Swope said pointing at his own radio. "Any idea how much longer this deal is going to take?"

Aguero fired a few epithets in the direction of the disposal crews as he estimated progress on the job. "Beats me. Maybe another fifteen minutes if it goes like it did this morning. Anyway, Sala'am says they haven't eaten yet and they want to take a break once they drop off this load."

Swope gave his assessment of the situation in typical fashion. "Well, they should have sat there and frickin' goddamn done that while we were sittin' there gettin' our comm squared away. How do you want to play it?"

Aguero eyed the workers and thought it over for a few minutes. "We'll cut them loose to eat once they've filled their tanks and dropped their load. Meanwhile, I'll stop by the house of this local sheik I'm supposed to meet. Then we link up with the trucks again and they can suck some more shit. Fisk, go get Sala'am for me."

When I returned with the interpreter in tow, the lieutenant outlined his plans. "Sala'am, I need you to tell them that they can eat once this load is dropped off. You need to find out where to meet them. We'll give them a time once the down-load is complete."

I noted Sala'am's concern about passing those precise instructions along to the disposal crews. He tried to buy some time. "Sorry, Sir. You give to them time when they what?"

"Once they have emptied the tanks," Aguero said patiently.

"Oh, yes. I will do this. But sir, the man say that some people are giving to him problems."

"What do you mean by problems?"

"He say that some people are saying to them why you do this for coalition forces? Why you do this for them? It makes the man nervous to hear these things."

"Tell him to say that he's working for the people of Sadr City. And not to worry; we're here to keep him safe."

Sala'am trotted off to pass the word, but he didn't seem happy with it. There was something wrong here, something lurking beneath the surface—something that did not bode well for the remainder of the day. I tried to get a grip on what it might be as the crews finished and we fired up to escort them to the dump site.

----

The dump site was on the south end of the city within sight of the fire station that we had visited a few days earlier to retrieve expended ordnance. Lieutenant Aguero charted a course along Route Delta, which gave us the opportunity to collect some eyeball Intel for the TOC. We blew past the Sadr Bureau where there was a crowd milling around that looked to be several hundred men and boys. That didn't seem very unusual. There were always crowds around Mookie's headquarters. Staff Sergeant Robinson reported that several men had caught his eye and made the throat-slitting gesture. Whatever was on the minds of the people in that crowd, it wasn't good will toward Americans.

The contractor crews quickly pulled their trucks into the site and began pumping as we got parked and out of our vehicles. We set up our security perimeter, and I looked around trying to orient myself. We were north of Route Pluto and parked near an open field with jerry-rigged soccer nets and goal posts. There were no holding tanks for the sewage. The crews just uncoiled their hoses and let the sludge flow where gravity took it. The soccer field was going to be a very smelly place very shortly. When the download was complete, Sala'am got his orders from the lieutenant and trotted off to tell the workers where to meet us for the next run at 1430. That should give them time to get something to eat, and give us time to drop in on the local sheik that Aguero wanted to meet.

We left the sewage crews and rolled into a tightly packed neighborhood a few blocks south of Route Gold. That's when the streets got seriously narrow and crowded. Our drivers were forced to slowly thread through a maze of squalid alleys and backstreets. What made it tougher on them were the long lines of dilapidated or abandoned civilian vehicles parked haphazardly all over the area. The slow speed and jerky maneuvering made us all nervous and kept everyone scanning high for snipers or random grenade throwers and low for signs of IED.

Several times during the trek, Chen—who was gunning the lead victor—had to climb out of his turret and clear antennas from low overhead wiring. Normally, our antennas could be secured in a low position using tie-downs provided with the vehicle. Our tie-downs were missing, naturally, so Chen had to hold both antennas down by hand which left him only one hand free for the machinegun—and a .50 caliber can't be fired accurately with one hand. It was an aggravating situation, but Chen never bitched about it or swore. He just grimly put up with it, hopping in and out of his turret, managing the antennae, and clearing low-hanging wires until the lieutenant indicated that we'd reached the location he wanted.

When we stopped, Aguero checked the grid he'd scribbled in his platoon notebook and motioned for us to follow him. Sala'am and I trailed him while he walked up to a door and knocked. After several minutes, a young man in his early teens cracked the door and Sala'am asked to see the Sheik. There was a conversation that told us the Sheik was elsewhere and would not return that day. Aguero took it stoically and began the standard game of 20 Questions regarding how the young man thought things were going in his neighborhood. He knew where all this was going. He'd have to come back tomorrow or some other day. That was the bottom line as we went back to the vehicles and began a roving patrol of the area. There was still a good deal of time to kill before our scheduled reunion with the contractors.

Finally, the lieutenant decided we should find some place to park and save fuel. We pulled into the parking lot of an abandoned school, and Swope got the vehicles in position to provide 360 degrees of observation and security. It was a great spot; likely the only place in Sadr City where we wouldn't be mobbed by kids wanting hand-outs or adults wanting to give us the evil eye. We sat around smoking, joking, and looking at watches until a few local kids finally ambled up to beg for chocolate or MRE remnants.

With nothing particular to do, I engaged the kids and practiced my Arabic. The oldest one was about ten and dressed in loose, dirty garb that looked like it had been plucked from a rag pile. I ran out of vocabulary in about 30 seconds and we defaulted into the standard *Mistah, you giff me* routine. I tossed them a roll of Charms, an MRE confection with a passing resemblance to candy, and then chased them off. We got no further visitors, and the lieutenant finally ordered us to mount up for the meeting with the sewage trucks.

They were waiting for us at the designated time at a little open-air restaurant on the far west side of Sadr City. We got some interested looks from civilians sitting at white plastic tables, eating or smoking, but the crews were aboard the trucks and ready to roll. We jockeyed for position a while and then led the jet trucks toward our next assigned area. That turned out to be a return to the area that we'd been working before lunch.

We pulled the vehicles into position around the designated cesspool and sat scanning the surrounding buildings as the sewage workers went right to work. There were a few locals who sauntered by to observe, but none of them approached or showed any particular interest in the trucks or their American Army escorts. I didn't much miss the standard *good, good, Mistah.* I was getting more than a little tired of that. I felt that if I could make an effort to learn a little Arabic, the locals could do the same in English.

Ignoring the images and the stink, I stood behind the open door of our vehicle which I thought might provide some little protection if somebody took a shot at us. Lieutenant Aguero sat inside, scribbling in his notebook with the radio mike held against his ear by his helmet chinstrap. Behind me, I heard a commotion and spun to see what was happening out in the center of the sludge pool. The Iraqi workers were furiously retrieving their hoses and packing up gear. I glanced at my watch and noted that we'd been onsite less than ten minutes. The cesspool was still at a reeking level with no signs of decrease.

"Hey, Sir…" I tried to get Aguero's attention and let him know the contractors were about to bail, but he was listening to the platoon net with a look of shock on his face.

"They what?" he shouted into the handset and rose to look around at the sewage trucks. He was too late. Both vehicles were speeding down a nearby alley. "Hold your position," he said to whoever was on the other end of the communication. "Hold your position! Fall in behind Davis when we pass you." Aguero tossed the handset and signaled for us to mount up in a hurry. "Crank it up and haul ass after those damn trucks!"

And so began the Great Sadr City Honey Wagon Steeplechase. Riddell had us rolling before I was fully seated, and I struggled to pull the door closed. Aguero apparently saw some humor in the business of Army Humvees conducting a high-speed pursuit of fleeing shit-suckers. He began to laugh maniacally.

"They just took off!" he laughed when I asked him what we were doing. "Jesus Christ, these guys—you gotta watch 'em like a hawk or else they'll just up and leave." It was the first and only time I'd ever seen Aguero laugh, and he was nearly in tears as we flew down the streets in pursuit of the shit trucks. I tried to imagine how he was going to brief this aspect of our mission to highers. "Riddell," the lieutenant said as he tried to regain his composure. "You're gonna pull around them and set up to block their route."

Specialist Riddell was into the game by now like an excited cop chasing bank robbers in some mob movie. He whipped the wheel hard right around a corner and mashed the accelerator with a big grin on his face. Chen took a more stable stance up in the turret trying to keep his balance, as Riddell shot the Humvee around slower traffic. The trucks were setting up to make another turn and Riddell made his move. The engine was screaming as he closed the gap and swung into a left turn gaining on the desperados. Aguero broke out in another laughing fit as he reported the situation to battalion. In a side-view mirror I caught a glimpse of the other Humvees racing to keep up with the pursuit.

We were on a straightaway now, and Riddell had the victor gunning for all the engine and transmission would take. About 100 meters into Route Echo, we managed to pass the Iraqi contractors and maneuvered into position to block their escape. He swerved in front of the lead truck and stood on the brakes. I swung out the door and crouched with my rifle aiming to the rear as the trucks hit their brakes in tandem and rolled to a stop. I could see the crew in the cab staring wide-eyed as Aguero and Sala'am stormed toward them yelling for the boss man.

Maybe I had lived a sheltered life, but I realized right then—watching the boss man climb from behind the wheel on rubbery legs—that I had never before seen another human in a state of abject terror. He waved his hands in front of his face and shouted the only English he knew. "Sir! No, Sir! Good, Sir! No, Sir!" He was trembling and on the verge of tears as he spewed a barrage of Arabic at our interpreter. Sala'am listened to the harangue for a while as the boss man continued to tell us by body language that he was scared shitless. When there was a break, the interpreter turned to Aguero with concern in his expression.

"He say that men at that place want to kill him. They kill his family if he work for coalition forces."

Aguero frowned and considered the revelation. "What did they look like?"

"He say he doesn't know. Only that they wore black clothes and that he has quit. He will work no more today."

"Tell him that if he doesn't work today, he'll probably lose the contract."

"Sir, he says he does not care. He will work no more today."

"Tell him to wait here." The lieutenant walked back to our vehicle and snatched at the radio handset to let battalion command know we were at a shit-sucking impasse. It took the TOC a while to digest that, and while we waited for instructions, we noticed a long line of civilian vehicles all headed south. They were full of people and giving us a wide berth, but a crowd of pedestrians was beginning to gather. These people knew a confrontation when they saw one and weren't about to miss the entertainment. My Spidey Senses began to tingle, and I got a firm grip on my weapon as the lieutenant acknowledged orders from battalion.

"Roger, Comanche Red One out." Aguero just stood there tapping his helmet with the handset as he contemplated the orders he'd just received.

"Hey," he shouted to get Sala'am's attention. "Just tell him we'll escort him to dump this load and then he can go home." The grateful Iraqi boss man vaulted into the cab and ground the truck into gear. Apparently this day's shit-sucking was at an end.

Our route to the dump site took us past the Route Georgia intersection, which featured a huge portrait of Mookie glaring directly at any and all passing infidels. We blew past a crowd gathering near the portrait and approached the Sadr Bureau where things got a little more ominous. The whitewashed building that housed the Sadr Bureau was crowded inside and out with men and boys in black uniforms. Busses and vans were arriving and departing, urgently picking groups of Sadr loyalists. Riddell crept by so we could get a look at what was happening.

The crowd waiting for transportation looked to be about 200 to 400 people. Some radio traffic from people who had a better view said it might be as many as 1,000. As we rolled by at ultra-slow speed gawking at them, several people in the crowd gave us the two-handed shooting-you-with-an-AK gesture. A few leaders in the crowd dispatched stuffed vehicles with a resounding slap on the roof and signaled for the next one to approach. They glared at us as we rolled by the bureau.

Like a good infidel, I just waved and smiled. When Carl Wild's Humvee rolled past he blew a few kisses from behind the armor shield surrounding his machinegun. He caught a few rocks tossed his way but he knew—and so did the people gathered outside the bureau—that if it went any further, they would die in a hail of fire. Rocks are one thing. An M-240 machinegun is another thing entirely.

Our orders did not include antagonizing a crowd. We did that for free and without any orders, so we picked up speed and headed for the dump site. I jotted down a few observations in my notebook, hoping we'd just leave the jet trucks to their environmental mayhem and head back to the FOB.

Since the sewage trucks didn't have a full load, it only took a short time for the nervous crews to empty their tanks. The lieutenant checked his watch and decided there was plenty of time left in our day. He made another try to get the Iraqi crews back on the job. It was no use. After a quick conversation with Sala'am, they indicated that they would be more than happy to suck shit anywhere we wanted, but they were done in Sadr City.

"They just keep saying over and over that people said they were going to kill them," Sala'am reported. "And there were guys in black making this…" Sala'am mimicked the throat-cutting gesture. "These men say to them that anybody working with the coalition was an enemy of Sadr City."

Swope and Aguero called the sergeants for a quick conference. I wasn't invited, and I didn't bother to eavesdrop. Most of us who were along for the ride, and didn't have life or death decisions to make, understood there was something serious simmering in Sadr City. Taken out of that context, the events of a day of shit-sucking didn't amount to much, but when you thought about the crowds and all the anti-American attitude out on the mean streets, sometime soon unsucked shit was going to hit the fan.

I remembered a line from Sioux Chief Crazy Horse's biography. His tactical skill was one of the reasons that the Sioux and their allies wiped out Custer's 7th Cavalry at Little Big Horn. The descendants of that storied unit were currently operating as a modern Army unit just across the Euphrates River from Sadr City. Our unit was part of the same division, the 1st Cavalry. I wondered if a sort of historical parallel between the Little Big Horn and Sadr City lay just over the horizon. What was it Crazy Horse said as he led his warriors into battle?

*Hoka hey!* It's a good day to die.

----

Once the leadership had agreed upon a plan in lieu of the sewage mission, the order was given to mount up and move out. I was ready to go back, take off the gear, and grab some nasty chow. The day had grown warm and as we turned around on Route Florida, buildings drained of color flashing by outside our vehicles, and I wondered how hot it would get. Riddell had the air blowing, but it wasn't pushing anything remotely arctic against the muggy heat.

"What's the plan, Sir?" I asked.

"We're going to do a quick presence patrol around here and then one more drive-by en route back to the FOB. Riddell, take us back out to Florida and turn left. Go to the far western edge of the city where Grizzlies intersects and come back on the other side of Florida."

"Roger, Sir."

The ordered route was arrow-straight, but I couldn't see much beyond the first mile as traffic was stacking up in a hurry. I began to relax a bit and reconsider earlier misgivings about the situation in Sadr City. On this end of our AO, there was no outward sign that anything was cooking below the generic surface tension of a turbulent Iraqi suburb. Just another normal Sunday in an abnormally shitty city. Maybe I'd just let myself get spooked by a bunch of random inconsequential circumstances and cultural biases. I tried to think of other things as we roared through the traffic snarls and shifted around to relieve the bite of the driver's seat frame on my shins.

In our vehicle's turret, Chen was focused on threats to the front, so he missed some potential trouble. Wild, who was in another vehicle and oriented toward the left of our route, spotted it first. We had just rolled past a mosque near the intersection of Routes Arizona or

Texas—or some such route that none of us recognized beyond map references—when Wild came up on the net.

"Gun!" Wild yelled to Staff Sergeant Davis as he swiveled his machinegun toward four men standing on the sidewalk. "Nine o'clock at the mosque!"

Chen checked the indicated direction. "I just saw somebody with an AK...left side...behind a barricade!" We all strained to look left and caught sight of Red 2—Staff Sergeant Davis' vehicle—jumping a curb to turn around and orient on the threat.

"Red One, this is Red Two. My gunner just saw somebody flashing an AK." Trevor's excited voice blared through our speakers. "We're turning around to intercept."

"Roger!" Aguero snatched at the radio handset to call it in to battalion and ordered Riddell to change direction. "Swing back around and get in behind them." As Riddell gassed it to find a turning space, Aguero called the TOC and told them what we had seen. "Lancer Mike, this is Comanche Red One." The lieutenant was calling in a situation report when Riddell found his space and hooked a U-turn that nearly put us up on two wheels. As we reversed, I caught sight of the following vehicles also turning and stacking up about 100 meters beyond the mosque.

As Chen struggled to maintain his footing behind Ma Deuce, the muzzle of the big weapon swept the road and that brought all civilian traffic to an immediate halt. Chen was giving all nearby drivers the Italian tasty cuisine gesture that meant *stop* in the Iraqi scheme of traffic signals. As we roared toward the mosque, I was expecting incoming rounds, but we got nothing but stares from the people watching along our route.

By the time we rejoined, the platoon had stacked up with all three of their vehicles parked beside a row of four-foot-high T-barriers. Riddell nosed us in behind Staff Sergeant Haubert's Humvee, and

Chen swiveled his machinegun to six o'clock so he could guard the rear. The rest of us were out of the vehicle before it was fully stopped. Aguero eyed the street up and down and then focused on the Iraqi civilians standing outside a fairly nondescript building.

Specialist Wild was covering three men standing outside that building with his machinegun. One of those guys, lurking around behind the other two, had an AK-47 slung across his shoulders. I took a quick look at Wild and saw the intensity in his eyes. His expression was neutral, but I could tell he was ready and willing to blow away all three of the Iraqis in a heartbeat. None of them seemed particularly intimidated as we approached.

"Great," Lieutenant Aguero muttered. "It's a mosque." I don't know how he knew that. The building didn't have any of the familiar trappings like an onion-shaped dome or minarets. Regardless, we were forbidden from entering without a compelling reason—and an Iraqi sentry with an AK likely didn't constitute due cause.

As we tried to decide on an appropriate course of action, our vehicles maneuvered around into a herringbone configuration that would provide all-around field of fire. Traffic was beginning to jam up on the main thoroughfare, and a glance at my watch told me we were approaching Sadr City rush-hour. It certainly looked like a bunch of irritated commuters were all trying to leave this part of the city. Swope came trotting up to make his report with Davis trailing him.

"Sir, Davis' gunner spotted one of these shitheads who sat there and had an AK. So we sat there and turned around to find out what's going on." Aguero just nodded and eyed the trio of Iraqis who were eyeing us and making no move to leave their post.

"Sir, what's the restriction on weapons?" Davis pointed at the guy with the AK. "I know every adult male is allowed to have one in his home, but how this guy…"

Aguero interrupted Davis with a wave of his hand. "Yeah, I know. Everybody can have one, but as far as having them out in the open— they have to be registered. They've got to be registered with the Iraqi Police, Force Protection Services, or Iraqi National Guard, something like that." He turned to our interpreter and pointed at the trio. "Sala'am, ask them if they are registered in any of those capacities. They'll have to have the card with them if that's the case."

While we deployed our dismounts into a security perimeter, Sala'am strolled over to consult with the guards. They spoke with our interpreter but never quit giving us the evil eye. After a few minutes, our interpreter returned with a report. "They don't have these card. Only they are here to guard the Imam for some special meeting they are having."

Aguero shook his head and chewed on his lip for a while. "Did they say who they are affiliated with? Are they Sadr Bureau, SCIRI, KDP? What are they?"

"He say they are for SCIRI. They need guard to protect from Sadr Bureau. He say there was bomb last week, and they are nervous." It took me a few seconds to sort through the acronyms. SCIRI was supposed to stand for Supreme Council for Islamic Religion, or Islamic Relations—or Islamic Religious Idiots for all I could recall. Whatever their affiliation was, it didn't involve openly flashing an AK on the streets of Sadr City as far as Aguero was concerned.

"Tell them they can't just walk around outside carrying weapons without a badge or uniform or anything. Tell them that it's illegal."

Sala'am was about to carry that message when a blue-and-white painted Toyota pick-up rolled to stop bearing a pair of Iraqi Police officers. They unloaded and adjusted their uniforms, taking in the situation. Both cops were probably in their mid-30s and clearly concerned with both the standoff and the traffic snarl it was generating.

They ignored us and strolled toward the mosque guards where they had a quick conversation replete with nods and sweeping gestures.

Sala'am caught the gist of it. "He say they have the permission from the Chief of Police for Sadr City."

Aguero wasn't buying that. "Listen, you tell them that Colonel Hussein does not make the law. The Iraqi Provincial Government makes the law." He sent the interpreter into the fray and reached for a radio handset. He was going to get guidance from higher authority before we gave up on this situation.

The problem was clearly a matter of interpretation. During his orientation with the departing unit, Aguero had learned that the law permitting every male Iraqi to keep a weapon in his home had limitations. Open carry was granted exclusively to officially sanctioned personnel such as soldiers, police, or uniformed force protection guards. The guys in question didn't seem to be affiliated with any of those organizations, which made them lawbreakers. On the other hand, I realized as Aguero contacted the TOC, there was the possibility that regulations had changed or exceptions had been made. And we all knew that as the new guys on the block, we were bound to be tested by the locals to see how far they could push the rules.

While Sala'am talked to the cops and the guards, I listened to Aguero trying to outline the situation and get the necessary guidance. "Lancer Mike, this is Comanche Red One. I've got a request for information regarding the situation here at the mosque. The guard here is saying that he has permission from Colonel Hussein and the Second ACR commander to display these weapons for this meeting they're having between the SCIRI Imam and a rep from the Badr Corps. Can you confirm that? Break—also can you tell me what is the minimum distance from a building under protection a guard or FP is allowed to go? Standing by for further guidance."

While we waited for the requested guidance, I kept my eyes on the confab outside the mosque which appeared to be turning ugly. There was also a gathering crowd of frowning spectators that was gathering and required our attention. The crowd seemed to be wondering if the infidels would have the balls to do something stupidly infidel-like—such as conducting a raid on a mosque. As the crowd began to murmur and mumble, I could see danger signals all around, as if someone was out there in the distance warning us to leave it alone and clear the area.

Sala'am seemed to be making some progress in calming the guards and reassuring the cops, but I didn't like the vibes we were feeling. What did the lieutenant expect? Was he waiting for one of those sentries to approach wearing a smile and letting him know they had no idea they were breaking a law? So sorry, infidels, it's just a big misunderstanding. Why don't you folks just come on inside the mosque here and we'll all drop our guns and maybe drink some tea? Of course, nothing like that happened.

"Sergeant Swope!" Coleman yelled at our platoon sergeant. "I just saw a guy in a man-dress that looked like he was carrying an MP-5—or some kind of compact weapon!"

Swope rushed over to take a look as Coleman pointed up the street. "He came from around the far corner of the building on the right there. Then he walked into the mosque and I lost track of him."

This new wrinkle caused Aguero to confer again with Sala'am and the cops. He wanted them to go into the mosque and check it out, but they didn't seem to want to be bothered. There was a lot of murmuring and tongue-clicking, which usually meant they were either unwilling to do what was being requested or just generally displeased about a situation. There was a lot of body language in the back and forth between the lieutenant, the cops, and the sentries, and I tried to interpret that since I couldn't understand much of the Arabic conversation. As a long time student of languages, I know things—often important things—get lost in translation. The key is to catch the nonverbal cues and context, but that takes total immersion in a culture, and we were a long way from that in Sadr City. It seemed fitting that it would play out this way in the land where the Bible says the tongues of man became confused.

Finally, one of the cops reluctantly agreed to enter the mosque and check for a visitor carrying an illegal or unauthorized weapon. A few minutes later, he strolled back onto the street with a little machine pistol slung over his shoulder. Since he had nothing but a pistol on his hip when he entered, I presumed the little sub-gun was the one Coleman had spotted.

I was getting hungry for some subpar Army chow by this point, and so was everyone else. And adding an edge to my attitude was the fact that Sala'am was beginning to make me nervous. He radiated unease until I began to feel my own skin prickle by simple proximity. Lieutenant Aguero had zoned out from frustration and was no longer talking with anyone, neither police nor civilian. He just stood outside our vehicle smoking and casting irritated glances at his watch.

After a while, Sala'am reappeared and walked up to make his report. "Sir, just take their weapons or leave because people are getting irritated." Aguero nodded silently and crushed out his smoke. He'd been told by the IP who arrived to try and take an edge off the tense situation that security guards were allowed to have the weapons outside because of a deal made with the base commander. That permission, if it was indeed given by an American Army official, had to have come from the CO of the 2nd ACR who was still nominally in charge of the area. There was some exchange between Aguero and Sala'am, but I missed it as I floated between vehicles in an attempt to make myself a less-inviting sniper target.

I was sure of only one thing: you could bet your sweet military assets that we were headed for trouble on this excursion. The Iraqi Police were attempting to contact the Iraqi Liaison on our FOB so that they could find someone to corroborate the alleged permission for the guards to brandish weapons. They must have called during high chai-time because they couldn't find anyone who would respond. As a secondary course of action, they called in the big gun himself, Colonel Jaddoa Hussein.

While we sat there waiting for some sort of decision or explanation, the dispute over permission from 2nd ACR was about to become moot. The commander of the outgoing outfit was just then turning over his responsibilities to our own battalion commander, Lieutenant Colonel Gary Volesky, at a formal Transition of Authority or TA. Minus the Army acronym, the rub was that after a brief orientation with only a relative handful of people from our own Task Force Lancer, the 2nd Armored Cav troops were leaving. At that point they had just one remaining company of tanks to pack up, and then they'd be gone. As we milled around hungry, nervous, and irritated, an entire planeload of our predecessors was already overhead in an aircraft headed home. At 1730 on that very day, TF Lancer would officially own the AO, warts and all.

It was something that all of us were vaguely aware of. We were about to discover that some 10,000 militia fighters were a little less vague about the situation. In fact, they not only knew the details of the change in American units, they had been eagerly anticipating the shift for days. We were the new kids transferring in, and they were the bullies all set to let us know who ruled this schoolyard.

----

Colonel Hussein strode to meet Lieutenant Aguero with the air of a diplomat greeting an unruly foreign despot. The L-T gave him the standard *peace unto you* greeting that, by now, had become second nature. The good Colonel was all smiles and conciliatory gestures. He and Sala'am had a long exchange before the translator began to tell the L-T what was transpiring.

"Sir, he say that they have agreement with the base commander that they could have weapons like this."

I could tell that Aguero was completely incredulous by the look on his face. "Tell him that I'm not aware of any kind of deal like that."

A longer exchange this time. The Colonel did not appear to be offended by the L-T's words or mannerisms, so either Sala'am was playing the role of peacemaker very well, or the colonel was willing to overlook minor slights in return for the possibility of a longer-term objective. The police chief listened with his hands behind his back, squinty-eyed smile affixed to his face like a brittle layer of stucco. I heard him say *Na'am* which I knew meant *yes*, but also seemed to be a typical way to begin a sentence in which they slightly disagreed with another's point of view. He spoke for a minute, all the while with his hands behind his back, slightly bent at the waist. He was tall for an Iraqi.

"Sir, he say that he will take these weapons himself and will go with you back to the base to speak with the commander, if you wish."

"Tell him that will be fine."

Colonel Hussein relaxed visibly when Sala'am relayed the L-T's concession. He spoke a brief word of thanks and went straight away speaking with his subordinates as he walked. They began to load up into their pickup trucks even as Aguero gave the command to mount up. We all moved quickly, eager to leave what had become a tedious and failed promise-of-action for the dusty motor pool in the FOB that was our home. My mattress of duffle bags shimmered in my mind like a vision of El Dorado in the distance.

We approached Route Delta and the snarl of traffic ahead was the worst I had seen yet. Roughly 2.5 million people seemed determined to turn south at the intersection. We arrived at the Delta intersection in under a minute, but the mass of traffic stopped us dead. I could see COL Hussein's truck ahead of us. As our large vehicle slowed, his small Nissan darted around the orange-and-white taxi in front of him, shoved in between two other vehicles and, blue lights flashing, shot the gap in between a microbus and a bongo truck. After that I couldn't see him.

Aguero was non-plussed. The plan was to follow COL Hussein back to FOB War Eagle. But where were they now? They had artfully dodged the traffic jam ahead and left them in the dust. Was he deliberately trying to lose us or what?

"Riddell, can you see where they went?" demanded Aguero. He was craning his neck back and forth, trying to spot the truck through the grinding traffic.

"No, Sir. What do you want me to do?"

"Get us through this shit," he said, and we turned once more toward the Sadr Bureau for one last look.

----

I would not have been surprised to see a tumbleweed or two go rolling across the deserted street, a Sergio Leone western set in the Middle East. There were several vehicles still crowding the southbound lane of Route Delta. There were none heading north, except for us. Out of my window I could see several full color posters of the man, the myth, the legend Mookie Al Sadr plastered on the wall. On most of the high-gloss depictions, his chubby little finger jutted out at us with a warning. His body language read, "One of these days, Alice! Pow! Right in the kisser!"

We cruised up to the next block, passing the Sadr Police Head-quarters on the left just shy of the Route Georgia intersection. The guards must have been inside their little shack, perhaps playing pinochle, for there was not a soul around to man the drop gate. *How's that for security*, I thought. *Must be about quitting time.*

I saw one woman in a black burqa pulling a Red Flyer-type wagon with several butane tanks in it. She could have been old or young, and she had no concern for us, lost perhaps in mental preparations for the evening meal.

Sadr Bureau. The L-T picked up the horn and called for Lancer Mike, his eyes locked onto the crowd of people on the right. Only three or four microbuses remained waiting next to the curb. A few hundred people watched us approach with eager eyes. "Go slow past here, Riddell."

A beep and crackle of static, "Go ahead, Comanche Red One."

"Roger. We got a couple hundred people massed in front of the Sadr Bureau, time now. Activity…"

"Sir!" called Chen. "They're running away!"

I glanced around Sala'am and could see several dozen people sprinting away from the street in all directions. It reminded me of a school of tuna fleeing a shark.

Aguero had taken it all in from the moment we had drawn even with the Mookie Central. There was a big group of Iraqi men on the south side of the Sadr Bureau, 200 or so. They were just sitting there standing and talking. And then as we rolled up they looked confused and guilty as if we had caught them in their dad's porn stash. They all fled in different directions. Some of them ran to the east, some ran to the west across the road. Maybe ten or fifteen remained in front of the Sadr Bureau on Route Delta, gesticulating and shouting. Some were trying to wave us away and some were beckoning. "Roger, Lancer Mike, approximately fifty to one hundred personnel fleeing the Sadr Bureau."

Relatively safe in the enclosed cab of the up-armored M114, I nevertheless gripped my rifle tighter. Not afraid—more like a novice opera singer about to take the stage in front of a packed house. As a guitarist, I have often played to entertain people and, no matter how many listen, I always have a brief attack of the butterflies before I strike the first chord. That was exactly how I felt in that moment. Ready to play, nervous that I'd play the wrong tune.

"Fisk, be sure you're writing this stuff down," the L-T called, hand-mike dangling from the helmet strap on his left side.

I was trying to decide how to phrase what I was seeing. "Roger, Sir!" I dropped my head to the page with the black pen between my teeth, considering. In scrawling letters made jittery by the bouncing vehicle I wrote "1730hrs…"

I noted the abrupt decrease in traffic and also noticed that there were far fewer pedestrians around this side of Delta and Gold. Odd. There were always people out and about around here at this hour.

A big bump, jostling my arm. I steady the pen, pause for a second, and then wrote, "Pass by Sadr Bur. Large Crowd immediately scatters away from us…"

We kept going, and in the next 30 seconds, nothing but wind filled the streets. I glanced up, left, then right, noting the absolute calm in the neighborhood. No living thing stirred. I had never known such palpable tension in my young life until then. I bent back to my notebook and wrote, "No traffic to our front…"

At that exact moment a young man named Hashimi fired his AK-47 from the west side of the street. I glanced casually at my watch and noted that the time was 1734. Back home in Texas, it was Sunday at 0834. Many would be getting ready for Sunday school and church or perhaps sleeping off a bender from the night before. Without knowing why I said it, I cried, "Here we go!"

## SO note by Gordon, Francis @ 23 MAY 2008

*Chief complaint—Was in an ambush with my platoon, It was pretty bad. Become anxious esp when I try to write it down. Memory problems, problems with concentration...I think I have flashbacks, nightmares very frequent until last year. Pretty much the same nightmare. Later on had a mortar land very close. It hit from behind and could have taken my head off. We got evac'ed and when I stood up I couldn't stand up and I couldn't hear. My equilibrium was off for about a week. I don't know how long I was unconscious. My wife says I have become short of temper, irritable, snappy...*

**Assessment: ADJUSTMENT DISORDER**

# ACT II: INNOCENCE LOST

# Ambush

RED 1 HAD ALREADY cleared the traffic circle at Route Gold as the gigantic painting of Muhammed al Sadr stared down with stern disapproval.

"Contact left!" cried Chen.

"Stop, Riddell. Chen, do you see where it's coming from?" demanded the lieutenant. The streets were still empty as the victor lurched to a halt. Aguero had heard the shot behind them, and was scanning both sides of the street to gauge the scope of the attack. Would there be more than one gunman? He vividly recalled his week of riding with the 2nd ACR guys. Then on several occasions, shots had been fired while their patrol was in the vicinity. Each time the shooter had merely been engaging in that peculiar Iraqi custom known as 'celebratory fire.' Either their favorite soccer player had scored a goal or there was a wedding or some other event that required a festive bout of gun play reminiscent of a Wild West saloon. None of his counterparts had seemed overly concerned. They had merely dismounted, found the elated gunman, and arrested him. He was deposited at the nearest Iraqi police station for them to deal with. One time, the culprit had even been falling-down drunk. No alcohol in Muslim countries, indeed.

Aguero didn't want to overreact now. Let the situation play out a second longer. Could just be an over-zealous idiot.

----

"Hey! Where did it come from?" Bellamy called out from behind his 240B. The echo effect from the surrounding brick buildings masked the shooter's position. "I just heard small-arms fire!"

The convoy slammed to a halt behind the L-T as everyone tried to identify the location of the shooter. Staff Sergeant Stanley Haubert ordered Guzman, who was completely exposed in the rear, to dismount and take cover on the vehicle's right flank.

----

Red 4, at the rear, estimated that they had traveled maybe 200 meters from the Sadr Bureau. The platoon sergeant whipped his head to the left. "OK, was that gunfire?" knowing full well that it was.

"Roger," answered Bourquin from behind him.

"Where did that come from?" Swope asked.

To Shane Coleman, the rapid pop, pop, pop of the Kalishnakov rifle seemed to come from behind him—he was facing the rear—and to his right. He called down, "Contact! Small arms off the nine o'clock!"

Swope, a veteran of the first Gulf War and the only one among us to already have his Combat Infantryman's badge, felt the familiar red fury settle over him like a cold, burning blanket. His eyes relentlessly scanned the buildings next to them, and he began to develop a plan about how best to maneuver his men into that urban labyrinth to kill the sons of bitches that had dared to throw lead their way.

----

Davis, the self-described cowboy from North Dakota, at first confused the sound of gunfire with some ambiguous mechanical sound coming from someone in the vehicle behind him. Although closer to the gunman than anyone else, he found his echo-location foiled by the poor acoustics. He saw the L-T come to a screeching halt in front of him, but didn't see him getting out. He cast a glance behind him and noticed that everyone was bailing out of Haubert's truck. He wondered why everyone was outside their vehicle. Must have had contact, he decided. Davis began to bark orders in rapid progression.

"Wild, Contact left. Denney, dismount, take cover on this side. Rob! Hold it down until I get back." Davis was left guessing at enemy locations based on the direction everyone in the truck behind him was facing. He heard nothing on his radio, but couldn't afford to stay in his seat to listen. The L-T, to his front, still hadn't dismounted, which meant that the best source for information was Red 3. Davis sprinted back to Haubert's truck to find out what was happening.

----

Wild, Staff Sergeant Davis' gunner, had heard the shots and was momentarily stunned with disbelief. He knew that this had been coming, but now that the moment was upon him his mind refused to accept that someone was actually trying to kill him. He picked up movement behind one of the numerous tin-metal vendor stalls popular in the markets that reminded him of a mailbox or trashcan. The man stood up, no weapon evident, and threw his arms up over his head in a kind of double wave. Wild, mindful of the rules of war, waved the man off of the street. Even though the sudden rush of adrenaline had him on a razor's edge, he was anchored by his training.

"Oh shit, we're about to get hit with something!" Wild exclaimed to no one in particular. The streets were now as quiet as a tomb. It was silent just long enough for his heart to sink into his combat boots.

----

Aguero dismounted and stood with the door to his back as he peered back at the convoy, trying to decipher what was going on. I opened my door and put one leg on the ground. He hadn't given the dismount order, and I wanted to be able to get back in quickly. If this was an ambush, then our drill was to just push through, so it wouldn't do to get left behind. I brought my rifle up and scanned rooftops, looking for a threat. Most of the buildings here were the bland three-to four-story tenements that afforded plenty of high ground to a determined enemy. Chen still had the .50 cal oriented to our front but was casting nervous glances to his left from where we had received fire. "Sergeant Chen, I've got your nine o'clock!" I yelled.

Chen kept the .50 cal pointed forward as he twisted left in the turret, left hand supporting his weight as he tried to identify a target. There had only been one burst of three to five rounds and then silence. We all knew from the start what type of weapon was being fired at us. An AK-47 had a unique sound: a loose, metallic rattle like it was about to fall apart when fired, quite unlike the M16 or anything else in the U.S. arsenal.

Our next course of action would be dictated by the situation. We were only taking fire on one side from one or two hostiles. If that was all that it turned out to be, we would follow standard react-to-contact drills and eliminate the enemy. Half the platoon would fix the enemy in place by directing so much fire their way that they wouldn't be able to move. Meanwhile, the other half of the platoon would move to the left or right using available cover—anything that will stop a bullet—and concealment—anything that will hide you—to close in and kill or capture them. The L-T and Swope would be the ones to make that call. However, if it turned out that we were in the middle of a complex ambush in spite of the low initial volume of fire, our move would be to get the hell out as quickly as possible.

----

Like individual musicians adding their instruments to a rising symphony of destruction, the enemy began to fire. Most of the contact came from the left side, but soon from the right, front, and rear as well.

Justin Bellamy stood dazed behind his machine gun. While everyone else had dismounted to the right of the vehicle for what cover they could find, he remained standing out in the open, manning his weapon. He was keenly aware of how exposed he was and wondered if he was about to make the last down payment on the proverbial farm. "God!" he cried, "I'm coming home. I'm going to die."

Specialist Taylor, his driver, reached across the vehicle and struck him in the leg and said, "Sergeant Bellamy, get down!"

As if Taylor had hit Bellamy's power switch, the gunner's mind snapped into focus. He saw a flash of weapons fire coming from a second-story rooftop and drew down on the man who was trying to take his life.

----

Specialist Wild heard Bellamy's machine gun open up behind him with a long burst of fire. He felt a sick surety as he heard a bullet whiz over his head that he was going to die a twisted heap in the dirt of an ungrateful city. He was scared plenty, almost to the point of paralysis, but the Bellamy's return fire goosed him into action. It was time to fight.

----

Bourquin and Hayhurst took shelter on the right side of the Platoon Sergeant's vehicle and desperately tried to find a target.

"Hey, where are they at?" called Coleman from the gunner's turret. He had the best vantage point but could not positively ID a bad guy.

"Shoot!" cried Bourquin.

"At what?" Coleman said indignantly. "I don't see anybody!"

"Just lay down suppressive fire," meaning that Coleman should fire off rounds in the general direction from which they had been fired upon in order to keep the enemies' heads down. Until they knew what was going on, suppressing the enemy's ability to shoot at them was their top priority. Just then Bourquin saw a small figure dressed in black leaning out to fire at them. "Up there in the window!" he yelled.

"All right. Roger!" Coleman knew in an instant that was the heavy machine gun could not elevate high enough. He traded it for his M16 rifle and managed to drop the man in black with two well-aimed shots.

----

The sounds of machine gun fire saturated the air. Black-garbed figures scurried to and fro across alleys and streets. Swope saw a near-magical transformation take place in his soldiers as the initial fear and shock gave way to training, and the young men became professional killers methodically plying their trade. His men began to call out the familiar litany of distance and direction to each other.

"Shit-head in the open to your seven o'clock, seventy-five meters!"

"Roger, engaging!"

"Second-story building to your left, first corner window. Guy in black with an AK."

----

Sergeant Chen yelled down from the turret. "Sir, they're firing from everywhere!"

A round hit the windshield of the lead Humvee and cracked it. Aguero snapped off a splendid malediction and then said, "Well, just shoot back!"

Chen repeated, "They're everywhere!"

"Then shoot everything!"

The L-T was on the radio yelling at Lancer Mike, "We're in contact!"

Another round hit the windshield as Lancer Mike asked, "What type of contact?"

"Heavy contact!"

----

York and Fowler were sitting around shooting the breeze, both feeling equally pleased that their Platoon Daddy had told them to stay back. The whole escort mission had been tedious, and, to their mind, a quasi-insulting use of a hard-core Infantry Soldier. Swope had left York in charge as the senior guy, so the gigantic redhead chose a quiet spot in their motor pool-slash-hotel where he could manage the guard tower his Soldiers were manning while keeping an eye on their baggage. As he and Fowler sat talking, Corporal Erwin—a guy from another platoon—pulled up to them in a Humvee, dust billowing behind him.

"Hey, Sergeant York. I think your boys are under contact. Listen."

Erwin had his radio set to monitor the battalion frequency. What York heard next would haunt him forever. Swope's voice, usually so quiet and monotone that you had to strain to hear him, was blaring across the speakers, frantically calling that they were under heavy contact.

Hardly daring to believe his ears, York thought, *Wow, they're really in something deep. They're in bad, bad shape.*

York heard the battalion commander, Lancer 6 himself, break across the transmission and urge the NCO to take a deep breath and repeat their grid location. Lieutenant Colonel Gary Volesky had been in charge of this wonderful city for a whole ten minutes. Now the Battalion net was awash with confusion as either Red 1 or Red 4 tried to transmit their situation. In the background was the ever-present roar of machine gun fire.

----

### SO note by McGowan, Doris @ 28 APR 2008

*SM seen 50 minutes at CTMC. Patient reports being in an accident couple of weeks ago. He reports driving and having a flashback. He states that he released the brake in his car and rear-ended another driver. Per self-report he began writing a book in 12/07 about his 03/04-03/05 deployment. Since that time spouse has stated within the last few months he has been distant and withdrawn, inc irritability, possible anxiety related somatic complaints such as inc heart rate and chest tightening when recollecting events, dec concentration, and reexperiencing reported. SM stated prior to starting the book he had no problems. He expressed skepticism toward therapy/counseling, as well as psychotropic medication use.*

*Psychological Symptoms: Anxiety...Feeling guilty and disturbing or unusual thoughts, feelings, or sensations. Nightmares related to deployment and/or violence, less frequency since beginning book, possible flashbacks, intrusive thoughts.*

### Assessment: 1. ADJUSTMENT DISORDER: R/O PTS

----

THE SITUATION WAS getting ugly quickly. I still could see nothing, but the volume of AK-47 fire rose like a the voices of man and wife locked in a domestic squabble over which way the roll of toilet paper should face. The L-T was talking rapidly into his mike to someone as he stood outside his door. My heart was pounding hot blood through my veins. There were so many windows, so many doors and rooftops and alleys to cover. Anyone could pop out at any minute and begin spraying us with lead. My adrenaline-fueled mind suddenly flashed back to playing a game called Hogan's Alley on the early Nintendo System. I could remember how fast my heart would beat as the 32-bit hooligans jumped out to take their shots at me. A mad desire to burst out laughing gripped me even as my head darted from side to side.

I caught the L-T hurling himself back inside from the corner of my eye. Taking the cue, I pulled my legs in and shut the door. I dropped the window down half-way and stuck out the barrel of my rifle. My field of vision was limited, but I still hoped to keep the heat off of Chen as much as possible.

----

Lieutenant Aguero's mind raced through everything he had studied about leading men in a fire fight. Uppermost in his mind was the only aggressive act committed in Sadr City against Coalition Forces during the past year: the enthusiastic young scout platoon that had pissed off the locals by removing a flag of religious significance. They had shortly thereafter been hit by a hasty ambush that was about 300 meters long conducted by approximately 50 angry Muslims.

Was it possible that they were using the same tactic now? He thought it likely. The ever-escalating volume of fire told him that this was indeed a deliberate, well-planned ambush. He realized that the hundreds of people that had been loading onto buses all day long at the Sadr Bureau were most likely the same ones positioned against them right now.

Hundreds. All out here to kill them.

They had to get off this damn street. He hoped that it would be as easy as tucking their heads and barreling through the kill zone, maybe, hopefully only three football fields long. If all went well, they would just drive like hell until no one was shooting at them anymore, hang the very next right, and beat feet to the FOB. He was aware that the Iraqis outside the Sadr Bureau had seemed surprised, like they had been caught flat-footed before they could fully set the trap. He held on to the glimmer of hope that once they made it three, maybe four hundred meters that they would be in the clear. Surely they couldn't have prepared much more than that.

----

I began to hear what sounded like rocks hitting the sides of the vehicle. There was a sound of shattering glass as a stray bullet hit the L-T's side view mirror. We were now taking fire from both sides. Aguero gave no sign that he noticed. He spoke quickly into the handset to the rest of his platoon, "Get everyone mounted up. We're leaving time now!"

"Sir," Riddell said calmly, "we've got to get off this fucking street." I marveled that he could sound so tranquil. As if to punctuate his sentence for him, Chen opened up with the Ma-Deuce. The roar of the .50 caliber rounds spitting destruction left my ears ringing, a not-so-subtle reminder that I wasn't wearing my hearing protection.

I fumbled with my ear plug case and belatedly shoved the soft plastic deep into my badly abused auditory canal with trembling hands. I wasn't afraid yet, but the adrenaline coursing through me made my fingers shake. In fact, I felt a rush of exhilaration. I reared my head back gave voice to the rebel yell peculiar to the land of my birth. "Get 'em, Sergeant Chen!" I cried.

"Fisk!" yelled the L-T. "Shut up." He was talking on one of the radios, but I couldn't tell which one. I wanted to yell and cheer, excited as I was, but I realized then that the L-T was having a hard enough time hearing without my shenanigans.

"Give them a second to mount up," Aguero yelled to his driver. He picked up the hand set for battalion and relayed, "Lancer Mike, this is Comanche Red One. We are in the middle of a complex ambush just south of the intersection of Gold and Delta. Enemy fire is heavy and sustained. We are returning to base time now. We need QRF support. I say again, we need QRF support." He picked up the platoon mic and snapped, "All Comanche Red elements follow me out." He shouted to his driver, "Riddell, let's go!" Riddell pulled out as if the demons of Hades were nipping at his nethers.

I remember taking a communication class in college. We learned all about the sender, receiver, and message elements. We also learned about the role interference can play in disturbing the receipt of the message. It could be that the interference takes the form of people talking, music playing, background noise, or even racial prejudice. However, we never got to the chapter on the effects of heavy enemy contact and machine gun fire on receiving a message. I'm sure that if Lieutenant Aguero had been considering these practical matters rather than the more abstract matter of, say, surviving, then he would have been aware of the possibility that the rest of the platoon never heard his transmission.

A few hundred meters farther north, our vehicle was taking a beating. Bullets were striking the sides like a flurry of rocks. A slug struck my door so hard that it stung the side of my leg. I jerked my leg back, feeling for blood. The bullet hadn't penetrated the thick armor, but it was enough to flip my perspective. I was suddenly not as excited about combat as I had been. In fact, I had my fill at that moment and would fully support the slogan: Make Love Not War. I raised my window up another notch so that my barrel barely stuck through.

Chen had his work cut out for him and wasn't complaining one bit. He unleashed volley after volley from the Deuce. I could only see him from his waist down. He appeared to be doing some exotic sort of dance as he repositioned himself time and time again to take shots from different angles.

We passed the traffic circle on Route Gold which was a good 800 meters, or half mile, from where we had first received contact. The angry-looking old man whose mural was painted there on a mint-green concrete slab stared down at us as we rounded the deserted circle and continued north.

No sooner had we hit Delta again when I noticed that there was a lot of junk strewn across the road. A whole lot. Sadr City was a filthy trash pile to be sure, but I couldn't recall seeing so much of it littered across the street. Then it struck me that these were obstacles deliberately placed to slow or stop our forward movement. This was where they planned to pin us down and finish the job. Riddell drove like a man inspired. He wove the heavy vehicle around metal poles tipped with spikes, large piles of rusty metal, old air conditioners. He powered through refrigerators and vendor stands. He drove over anything that wouldn't move.

Before we had gone another 100 meters, Chen started yelling something down through the turret. I was so deafened by the gunfire that I couldn't understand him. The L-T was giving a SITREP to battalion when Riddell picked up the platoon mike. He said something that I couldn't make out, then handed the handset to the P-L.

"Sir! It's (inaudible to me). They (something, something) back there."

"What?" exclaimed the lieutenant. No problem hearing that.

Then I could finally hear what Chen was saying, "Sir! No one is behind us. They're still back there!"

Up until that moment I had never heard a mortal swear as elegantly as did my fearless and profane leader. "Riddell! Turn us around!"

Riddell screeched to a stop, did a quick two-point turn over a pile of rubbish, and sped back toward the platoon. He managed to find the exact route he had carved through the piles of garbage and hastily strewn obstacles. The enemy was only too glad to take their shot at us again. I was reminded of what it sounds like to be in a car during a bad hail storm.

Within a minute we had regained the traffic circle. The rest of the patrol came quickly into view. They were firing on both sides of the street but had moved for the most part to the driver's side of their vehicles. As we approached, the L-T directed his driver to go down the side where everyone was taking shelter, wearing looks of disbelief, shock, anger, and fear.

----

When we pulled even with Swope's truck, the L-T jumped out and told Riddell to get us turned around. Aguero hustled over to confer with his senior NCO while Riddell did another two-point turn and slid to a stop.

Aguero and Swope had a brief discussion about the situation. The L-T told them about the obstacles that had been emplaced up ahead and what he intended to do. The Iraqi Police station—from which we had watched the Mahdi Militia demonstration—was about a mile down the road, just past Route Copper. He said that we would bust through this ambush and take shelter in the station until reinforcements arrived and higher had a chance to figure out how they wanted to play this.

Swope nodded his agreement. "Good. We're sitting ducks out here. We've got to get off this damn street!"

Aguero hustled back to his vehicle while Swope relayed the plan to his section leaders over the net. He had told Davis to keep an ear to the radio, and Davis passed that up to Haubert. Red Two and Red Three acknowledged the transmission, and Swope saw that everyone was loading up. He turned to his crew and shouted, "Hey, get in the vehicles! We're getting out of here!"

----

Specialist Rafael Arteaga had been with his platoon earlier that morning. He was one of several who were told to stay behind when the mission continued after lunch. He had been lounging on his mattress of lumpy duffel bags, talking to his friend Specialist Miranda from another platoon, and enjoying the lazy afternoon when he had heard the call from his platoon leader come across the radio. He rushed over and crowded around the makeshift company command post with others who couldn't at first comprehend what they were hearing. Could this really be happening?

----

Time flowed like a lazy old man on a Sunday drive. The moment the ambush was initiated until the L-T returned to the platoon had been just over five minutes. It took less than a minute for Aguero to realize that we were in a complex ambush and order everyone to plow through it. It took two minutes to clear through the traffic circle while the rest of the platoon engaged an ever-increasing number of insurgents. It took a little over two minutes for us to get back. The subjective experience, however, was much, much longer.

Now it only took about 10 seconds for everyone to load back up, probably less since they were highly motivated to leave. As we pulled into the front, I perceived the devastating effect the enemy fire had wrought when we passed the gauntlet in our heavily armored vehicle. With mounting horror, it dawned on me that we had to now try and get everyone—even the lightly armored Humvees—through that hell and to the other side. We passed first Haubert, then Davis, and I tried to imagine those unarmored trucks going through all that. They would never make it. A wave of relief washed over me that I wasn't sitting in one of those combat convertibles. And then came the guilt.

As the L-T led the mad attempt to break through the ambush, things went from bad to worse. I heard an explosion to our rear. A loud whoosh filled the air somewhere behind and to the right. It was followed almost immediately by a loud cracking boom. That was my introduction to the RPG, or rocket-propelled grenade. I don't know where exactly it hit or how far back, but immediately following the explosion came a smell that has stayed with me. I've never smelled anything like it since. The bouquet could best be described as a combination of acrid dust and burning brake pads with a hint of ammonia.

Riddell had a good feel now for the best path through the obstacle course set up for our amusement by the Mahdi Army. We roared through the deserted traffic circle again, and the volume of RPG attacks exploded as we crossed Gold and continued north. At speeds approaching 40 miles per hour—which feels damned fast in a M1114—he slalomed back and forth through the path he had already carved out. The L-T cursed as he was tossed mercilessly about the cab while he tried to use the radio. Meanwhile, bullets bounced off the armor like a shower of gravel.

I felt like a pin ball in a machine headed toward *tilt*. No one wore a seatbelt. We never did, since they were so hard to get on over our armor. Since every second counted when responding to an attack, the need for speedy egress trumped all else. I saw that Aguero was having the Devil's own time trying to communicate on two radios while being slammed around in his seat. He looked out his window then suddenly let go of the radio, dropped the window, and stuck his short M4 carbine out. Without any hope of hitting his target, he fired off several rounds at a figure dressed like a ninja with a green bandana. I was astonished when the insurgent fell backwards and did not move.

----

Behind us, the others fell farther and farther behind. The whole street burned. Thick smoke billowed from tires that the enemy had set on fire to either channel our movement or obscure theirs. The L-T could not see behind him anyway, as his mirror had been shot off. Riddell tried to glance back at the rest of the convoy and discovered that his own mirror was also destroyed. The volume of fire that we were wading through was insane, and I worried for the soldiers in the two unprotected vehicles.

"Sergeant Chen, can you see them back there?" yelled the lieutenant.

"Yes, Sir!" Chen unleashed another long and deafening burst of fire from the deuce. I whooped and hollered my encouragement to him.

"Are you OK, Sergeant?" I called.

"Yeah, I'm good!" He was in the middle of a steel rain that I couldn't imagine weathering and wasn't even breathing hard. Another fusillade rapped against the side of the vehicle, and I heard the big warrior behind the gun let out a sound like a cross between a weak cough and a whoosh. Chen's legs unhinged and he dropped straight down then straight back, face up on top of the olive-green ammo cans.

"Chen's hit!" I screamed. My heart turned inside out and time froze. I put my weapon muzzle down into the floorboard of the seat and twisted sideways onto my knees to begin the process of casualty evaluation. This precise battle drill had eight distinct steps—at that time—upon which we are rigorously trained. I had attended the Combat Life Saver course several times and had performed well. I could start an intravenous feed and knew how to treat everything from abdominal gunshot wounds to insect stings. I remember learning CPR on the plastic dummy the medics called Andy. Andy was made of soft plastic, cold to the touch, and left the student feeling slightly dirty after practicing the artificial breathing and chest compressions. Academically, I was well-versed—for an infantry guy—on any medical issues that would cross our path. Or so I thought.

Lieutenant Aguero turned around to look at Chen, "Where's he hit? How bad is it?"

I was searching for a sign of blood, entry wound, trauma, something. "I can't see where he's hit!" I called. Panic began to settle in, leaving me cold and numb.

Sala'am leaned over him from the other side, searching. "There is no wound, no blood," he said. "He has a pulse!"

"He's not breathing," I noted. His eyes were closed. Chen had a prominent jaw with just the suggestion of an under-bite. His lips were parted, revealing a neat row of teeth stained with blood.

Riddell, still roaring down the street and swerving hard right and left, glanced back once. He reached across with his right hand and pulled out a Combat Life Saver bag, our standard issue first-aid kit, plus an IV starter bag. Without taking his eyes off the road he un-zipped the bag and felt around until he found what he was looking for. He produced a white piece of plastic that resembled a question mark. He handed it back without looking. "Use this!"

It's called a J-tube, made for insertion into the throat to keep the airway open during CPR. The vehicle was still bouncing and bucking like a rodeo bronc as I put my thumb on the fallen warrior's chin and pushed downward and prepared to insert the tube with the hook side down.

Blood poured out of his mouth, along with something else. I noted a small piece of pinkish, bloody meat that landed on his chest next to his jaw. Revulsion, horror and panic struck me at once when I realized that he had bitten off the tip of his own tongue. His face was rapidly turning pale, and he still was not breathing. I put the index and middle finger of my left hand over his left carotid artery. Nothing. Absolutely nothing. Not even a flutter. He must have been shot through the chest, and now his lungs were filled with blood. Without being able to clear out all that blood and with a hole in his lung, CPR suddenly seemed like a useless endeavor.

I was half-right. He had been shot through chest, the bullet enter-ing just under his right armpit and piercing his chest cavity, maybe even one or both lungs. If I had been taught lifesaving techniques that became standard in 2006, then I could have possibly saved his life.

When the sac surrounding the lungs is pierced, it fills up with blood and other fluids until the pressure is too great for the lungs to work against. They usually collapse, with death following close behind.

But the Army had yet to experience the vast number of casualties with this signature, not-necessarily-fatal, injury. Within a year, they would notice the alarming trend, and within two years they would add side armor to our vests and training to line soldiers on how to drain off fluid in this sort of wound. So, in a sense, Chen's death was not in vain. Lessons were learned and other lives have since been saved.

Yet the 2004 very frightened version of me was sitting in the middle of a fire fight with a good man's blood on my hands, struggling with an interior debate. Should I invest time into a most likely futile effort, or should I get up and man the now-silent gun? Chen's life was important to me. All of our lives were important to me. Years of training for this moment already dictated the answer: when in contact, security remains the priority. Rendering first aid to friend and foe always happens once the objective is reached. I never thought I would have to apply such a clinical doctrine while staring at the dying face of a friend.

I sat back and exhaled a ragged breath. "He's gone." Above me the gaping hole in the roof—the gunner's turret—sat empty. The big gun was silent, perhaps mourning the fallen.

Riddell heard me and I could hear the disbelief in his reply. "Give him mouth to mouth!"

"It's no use," I said, my lips numb. My eyes never left the turret. "He's got blood coming out of his mouth. He's dead."

A silence like the grave filled the truck.

"Lancer Mike, this is Comanche Red One. We have one KIA. I repeat, we have one KIA." The L-T, his ashen face furious, handed the platoon net to his driver. "Tell Red Four."

----

### SO Note by Fields, Boyce @ 10 NOV 2011

*Chief complaint: depression, anhedonia, nightmares, feeling on guard, avoidance and feeling numb or detached*

*Patient … is married and has deployed twice to Iraq. Patient is from Arkansas. SM is a college graduate…His parents divorced when he was 14yo. He was the only child. SM stayed with his mother. Denied having any family history of alcoholism or mental illness. Patient does drink on occasion. Stated he has never had an alcohol incident or been to ASAP. His religious preference is Protestant. SM said he [did] not have any financial or legal problems. Patient is having some marital problems. He has been seen by a mental health provider in the past for depression. He has taken Prozac. Patient said he had suicidal thoughts while taking the medication.*

### A/P: 1. Adjustment Disorder

----

York heard Riddell's frantic voice coming over the radio screaming that someone had been hit, was bleeding out of the mouth and had fallen down into his truck. His heart sank as fear for his brothers' safety gripped him. He was overcome with a mad desire to rush out of the gate in the nearest vehicle. He began to shake and couldn't stop.

----

"Sir, we need somebody on the gun," I heard Riddell say, calmly, as though discussing interior décor options.

Lieutenant Aguero looked back, twisting far enough around to see Sala'am sitting behind him. "See what you can do for Sergeant Chen. Fisk," he said to me, "get on that gun."

"Roger that, Sir!" As if I hadn't already thought of that. My eyes had not left the turret. I could see a beautiful blue sky through the round hole in the roof. A calm sky with not a cloud to be seen, unaffected by what was going on beneath. Chen was dead. For all I knew, others were joining him, even now. The thrill that I had felt at the thought of being a warrior had left the moment that my Asian buddy had collapsed in a heap with a bullet in his chest. That was the reality that awaited me behind that gun. The peck-peck-peck of the bullets striking the vehicle had not let up in the slightest, and spoke to me like Morse code. Stand your ass up and see what happens. Stop. This is not like you thought it would be as a snotty-nosed kid playing army with toy guns. Stop. We're all real out here where there is no *I got you first; No you didn't* bullshit going on. Stop. You'll end up just like him in nothing flat if you stand up now. Stop. Your breathing, your pulse, your life will also—stop.

I was afraid. This was not how this was supposed to be. In the stories the hero always runs toward the battle with a knife between gritted teeth, both guns blazing. Unafraid. Well, I realized I'm not that guy. But there were people, my brothers in arms, depending on me to do my job. Echoing in my mind were my father's final words when we parted ways, "Son, do your duty."

Drawing in a deep breath, I got my feet underneath me and yelled. Shouted. Terrified, I sprang up like a jack-in-the-box and seized the double grip of the Ma Deuce, expecting at that second to be cut down. Maybe the bullets were still striking our coach, but I could hear nothing except my own guttural, enraged voice.

The buildings here were very tall, mostly four- and five-story apartment buildings. Riddell juked sharply left at that moment, throwing my right hip into the side of the turret. I growled, completely pissed off and afraid. A round zipped past my nose. The displacement of air startled and focused me. My eyes darted right and left looking for movement. I saw someone dressed in black 100 meters to my right, what would be the two o'clock position. The vehicle bounced as I tried to engage him, missing badly. I don't think I was even close enough to make him mildly concerned. He ducked down an alley and disappeared.

Lieutenant Aguero slapped my leg. Only then did I notice that he was yelling at me. I squatted down so that I could hear him. "Are they still behind us?" he yelled.

I stood up and looked over the round hatch that doubled as a rear shield. About 300 meters back I could see one of the unarmored vehicles. They weren't moving. "Sir, they've stopped way back there!"

The vehicle slowed. The L-T opened his door while we were still rolling, one leg hanging out. I jumped, surprised when he fired his weapon. Glancing right I saw the same guy I had missed with my .50 fall dead. What in the hell? How could I miss with a solid wall of lead, and he nailed the guy with a pop gun? The HMMWV stopped and Aguero stepped out, craning his neck to peer around and over mounds of trash and metal. Cursing, he lunged back inside. I realized that the fusillade of fire had ceased. We were out of the kill zone.

----

Meanwhile, a few hundred meters south, Private Perry was having the worst day of his young life and it was about to get worse. He watched in dismay as the L-T's vehicle left him in the literal dust. His M998-variant Humvee could not keep up with the super-charged engine powering the M1114, although Perry was trying his best to keep up without flipping the vehicle. He saw a few metal poles placed in his path that had metal spikes protruding in all directions, created for the specific purpose of popping a tire. He dodged the jagged scraps of metal as best as he could at high speed, but quickly felt one tire then another give way. The L-T's vehicle was almost 100 meters in front of them now, and he couldn't squeeze any more speed out of the tortured engine.

Why, oh why, had he joined the infantry? He was a musician rapper with a poet's soul. This was a scene straight from *Blackhawk Down* that would make the hardest thug from the hood cry for their mama. He knew, though, that he could not afford to give in to fear, even as round after round impacted against his door's bullet-proof glass. He was the driver and would ram his vehicle through the fires of hell because he it was his duty to do so. How many of his old friends from high school understood what that meant? That life seemed to belong to someone else. Someone whose largest concern had been to make sure that his numerous girlfriends didn't meet each other. Would he ever be the same person again? His thoughts were focused on his new-born son. He now wanted nothing more than to live long enough to be the kind of daddy that such a beautiful young boy needed.

If he was going to survive, he had to focus. His vision narrowed until it seemed that Route Delta had shrunk to a tunnel littered with scrap metal. All that existed in the world was this road and the wheel gripped in his hands. His vision sharpened and he could almost see the displacement of air caused by the bullets as they zipped by in front of his windshield. At least his doors were armor plated—or this would have been a very short ride.

----

Davis saw that the L-T was pulling ahead and desperately tried to reach his officer on the radio. "Red One, this is Red Two. We can't keep up with you! I say again, we are falling behind." He heard no response and wondered if he would be able to even if Red 1 was broadcasting. His gunner, Wild, was throwing out a deafening volume of fire from the belt-fed 7.62 mm machine gun, and everyone else was adding their two cents to the fight. The doors were holding up well against the determined assault of the enemy. He was so glad that Swope had made the call to leave the extra personnel back at the FOB. Anyone sitting in the rear cargo area would have been chopped to ribbons. The fact that Wild was still standing, and uninjured, testified as a scathing indictment on the enemy's marksmanship.

"Perry, you've got to keep up with him!" cried Davis, who shared his platoon sergeant's concern about being left behind. He could barely hear himself talk over the ringing in his ears. He doubted that the L-T would be able to hear them at all over the puny radio speakers.

"I'm trying, Sarge. There's shit everywhere!"

"Just hit it," yelled Davis, "Ram through it!"

Robinson cried, "RPG! RPG!" just as a rocket whooshed a few feet over their heads.

"Perry, stop!" roared Davis. "Dismount and engage!"

----

The rocket-propelled grenades began to fly from everywhere, one striking Red 4's left flank and exploding harmlessly. No one really thought about why they were stopping. They just knew that they weren't going to be a target in a turkey shoot any longer. Davis knew that they had to methodically clear out the route. The volume of fire was so heavy that unless they did a mounted version of a break-contact drill, where one element moves out of enemy fire while another element provides covering fire, they weren't going to make it out alive.

Everyone was out of the vehicle except for Wild, who stopped firing only long enough to reload, the brass links hanging out of the left side of the gun like the golden tongue of some starving carnivore. Robinson threw himself down in the prone even as he saw a small, black-garbed target at least 250 meters to the east and rear. Bullets were coming close enough to kiss him, but he hardly noticed. He had an M4 carbine with an ACOG sight that allowed for a small bit of magnification. Rather than cross-hairs, the scope had a small white arrow in the reticle. Rob put the tip of the arrow right on the insurgent's chest, drew in a breath, exhaled slightly, held his breath and squeezed the trigger. And just like that, Darcy Robinson, a soft-spoken gent from the country whose greatest joy was playing Call of Duty with his son, killed his first man. He felt no joy, no loss of innocence. He merely sighted in the next target.

----

Swope barely had time to comprehend what was taking place. He was well aware that this little ambush was developing into a battle they could not hope to win with their scant numbers and unenviable position. He had realized with mounting frustration that they were going too slow to keep up with the L-T. Now he saw Davis' vehicle stop. Everyone in his vehicle got out and began firing in different directions. What were they doing? He tried to call Davis on the radio, but then saw him out of the Humvee alternately firing and shouting orders to his crew. *Shit!* Hoping that the L-T could hear him, he radioed that they had stopped. He thought about dismounting his vehicle to see what was going on, but if he left the radio, that lack of communication would be more likely to kill them all. He had to get in touch with the L-T or Battalion or both—and right now.

He frantically called to his P-L to get them to slow down, that they were pulling too far ahead. Quickly he realized that either Aguero wasn't getting his transmission or—more likely—the heavy metal singing of the machine guns was drowning everything else out.

A bullet ricocheted off the back of his vehicle, and the platoon sergeant swore with conviction. Little puffs of dirt were erupting everywhere in the street around them as the enemy attack grew more emboldened. What they needed was more firepower and quickly.

"Coleman!" Swope said. "What are you doing with that M16? Use the fifty."

"On what?" Coleman demanded. "I don't see a target!"

Sergeant Bourquin called, "There! There's a guy right there by the green car, running towards the green car!"

"All right. Roger!" Coleman hit the trigger. His shot went wide as the man dodged behind the trunk of a car. He put a volley of lead into the vehicle's cab and adjusted fire right slightly. Swope saw the insurgent collapse.

Swope felt as busy as a one-legged man in an ass-kicking contest. He was constantly scanning for enemy threat, listening to his crew call off targets and listening to the radio traffic over the small speakers mounted to the middle console. He was delighted to hear first one big crew-served weapon and then another throw their harsh language into this insane conversation. He heard the lieutenant's frantic call to higher that they were in contact. During the short space of 30 seconds or so, four or five black-garbed insurgents fell dead to the lethal fire of his crew. He watched as some fell—the ones he didn't see were called out gleefully by his men.

"Got you, you son of a bitch! Target down."

"Get that shit-head by the car."

"On it—he's down!"

"Sergeant Swope," Bourquin called out to him, "Four insurgents down." Then five. Six.

Swope heard Lancer Mike request their location. He was still really new to this place and couldn't think of what street they were on. He thought that this one was Delta. They had passed what east-west route? Was it Florida? Georgia? It was one of the states. He knew basically where they were in his mind and could have pointed to it on the map. He ducked in the cab and fished out the bulky military-issue GPS called a Plugger or PLGR. He had been using the stupid thing not long ago when they were at the Mosque—God, that seemed forever ago—and was chagrined to discover that it had shut itself off to conserve battery power. He pushed the power button again, knowing that it would take several minutes for it to initialize and acquire a grid, and threw it on the seat. This was a well-planned and deliberate ambush. There was no way they would be able to successfully defend against the number of enemy that he knew must be engaging them right now. They would have to blow through this ambush time now.

----

Coleman was in a target-rich environment. Heads and rifles poked over the roof tops like evil Whack-a-Moles. As quickly as he sighted in on one target, it would disappear to be replaced by another on a different building. All the while, the steady dull thud of bullets against the vehicles armor told him how close he was standing to death. He smoothly transitioned back to his M16 and shot one more on a roof and then another who popped up in a window just below that.

----

Just ahead of Coleman, Bellamy was firing at anything that seemed remotely suspicious. He couldn't yet spot a solid target, but he fired anywhere he could hear the report of a rifle or catch the tell-tale flash from a muzzle. He quickly realized how dire the situation was when he heard machine gun fire *behind* him. This development threw the notion of *sectors of fire* right out the window. His weapon was mounted on a simple pole jutting from the middle of the vehicle allowing the 240 Bravo machine gun 360 degrees of movement. He made good use of that flexibility, spinning around to engage enemy contact to his rear. His dismay grew when he realized that he might have more targets than ammo.

A few times, he had to lay across the roll bar and canopy over the driver's seat to fully line up his sights on a target. He found it easier to distinguish targets on the east side. The buildings were further back from the road, at least 200 feet away, and that open space extended further to the north than he could see. The lot was full of parked cars in different states of operability—some dented and battered and others pristine. They were mostly of the obscure foreign make and model unfamiliar to most Americans but punctuated here and there with Mercedes and BMW brands. A few concession-type carts dotted the field as well. Most were painted a pale blue. All were stripped of their merchandise and abandoned by their merchants. Now Bellamy could plainly see men dressed in black, and a few with white *didashis* and matching pants, darting for cover and firing at them as they moved.

A white sedan charged toward them from an alley to the east. The battered car, an Astra or Seneca or God knew what, was hurtling directly toward them at a speed that made the front end bounce up and down as if on hydraulics. The driver was the only passenger, and with his heightened senses, he could see the man's lips moving as if in prayer from 150 feet away. A mental klaxon alarm sounded in his head, *V-BIED, V-BIED*. Vehicle Borne Improvised Explosive Device. Had to be. Bellamy unleashed a burst of fire, saw the rounds kicking up dirt in front of the car, and walked the next burst directly into the engine block. Dust and paint chips flew into the air as holes appeared in the hood, the spider-webbed windshield obscuring the driver. The car coasted to a halt. Before Bellamy had time to wonder if he had killed the driver, the man lunged from the car with an AK-47. The idiot, dressed in a new, white man-dress, was charging toward him. Justin Bellamy was determined that he would not be killed by a man in a dress. He put his weapon's front sight post on the man's hips, knowing that the muzzle would lift as he fired, and squeezed the trigger. A dozen holes peppered the would-be martyr. The man collapsed in his tracks.

Someone—he thought it was Taylor, maybe it was Guzman—called out, "Van from the south. East side!" Bellamy could see at least four heads in a silver mini-van. He didn't notice weapons, but he knew that no good could come from someone who would drive a minivan alongside a bunch of soldiers with their guns blazing. Was mom dropping off the kiddies at soccer practice? Unlikely. In unison, everyone around Haubert's vehicle opened fire on the van. The windows exploded, the passengers danced a little number in time with the bullets, and the minivan slowed to a stop. No one got out.

Specialist Pete Guzman, the medic, was armed with only a 9mm Beretta pistol and felt suddenly underdressed for the day's festivities. He slapped Bellamy on the leg, "Hey! Let me use your rifle. All I got is my pistol."

"Sure, go ahead!" Bellamy said without ever taking his eyes off of a small man with an RPG. He sprayed him with an unhealthy layer of 7.62 mm. Then he realized what Doc had asked. He was shocked. *If things are so bad that the Doc needs a bigger weapon, we're all screwed*, Bellamy thought.

----

Fire was erupting all around Trevor Davis, and he was trying to get a handle on the situation. Once everyone started firing, he was no longer able to hear anything coming across his radio, as their volley was deafening. He looked south and saw Haubert's vehicle about 100 feet behind him, and his platoon sergeant's victor another 100 feet beyond that. They were all on the right or east side of their Humvees and were firing at targets to the west. Davis yelled for Perry and Denney to get the hell over to his side. Darcy Robinson had been sitting behind him and was now by his side, scanning for targets. Wild began firing at one of the windows to the southwest. Almost immediately, he heard weapons fire behind him. He whirled and realized that they were surrounded. He saw figures dressed in black, green bandanas rolled up and wrapped around their heads, darting furtively from car to car in the open field to the east.

This activity all happened in the space of less than a minute, but to him, time had lost relevance. Denney called out, "Hey! Where's the

L-T?" Davis looked at the big man, saw his large, young eyes brimming with near-panic, and swallowed the first comment that came to his mind. *He's right there in front of us, duh.* He whipped his head right and then noticed for the first time that the platoon leader's victor was no longer in sight, as if they had evaporated. The colorful old infantry interrogative rose to his mind. *Whiskey Tango Foxtrot?*

He heard Wild, his gunner, call out, "Denney! I need you to cover my back! Pick up those roof tops to our three o'clock. I can't see over there."

"Roger. I got your back!"

Davis picked up the radio and called out to the L-T. Nothing. He called out to Red 4. Nothing. Shit. Either his radio was disabled, no one was listening or no one could hear. Or all the above. Double shit.

"Rob!"

"Yeah!"

"Hold it down. I gotta find out what's going on." Davis took off at a run for Haubert's vehicle. He asked if anyone knew what the hell was going on. Where did the L-T go? Did he know that they were still here? No one had any answers. He looked further south to where Swope was alternately firing his weapon and shouting at his gunner. Davis noticed with clinical detachment that rounds were ricocheting off the driver's side of the up-armored Humvee. Coleman, heedless of the near-hits, was responding vigorously with the .50 caliber machine gun. All five, Swope, Coleman, Bourquin, Hayhurst and Rogers were actively engaging.

Davis didn't really consider that he was charging toward the hottest part of the fight, though he was keenly aware now of the tactical situation. He just knew that he had to link up with the platoon sergeant. Find out what's going on. Develop a plan. His soldiers were in extreme danger, and they were depending on him to see them through. This was why he joined the Army 15 years ago. This moment.

Davis ran at a dead sprint toward the trail vehicle, toward the high volume of enemy fire. He never felt the added 40 pounds of his gear's weight. Swope sensed his approach and whirled to make sure that he wasn't being attacked. His face was the same red that Davis had come to expect when a man was about to thoroughly ream a soldier's ass for doing something stupid. The platoon sergeant's lips were pulled back from his teeth like a rabid wolf looking for blood.

"Where did the L-T go?" asked Davis.

Swope's grimace was replaced with genuine puzzlement. He craned his neck around his door and noticed that Red 1 was gone. He snatched up his handset and shouted over the volume of fire on the Platoon internal net, "Red One, this is Red Four. We have not moved. What is your location? Red One, this is Red Four. Do you read me, over?"

The response came almost immediately, "Red Four, this is Red One Delta. Actual is on the battalion net. Hold one." That was the L-T's driver, Specialist Riddell. What was going on?

He heard nothing but static on the platoon net for tense seconds, but then he thought he heard, "…one KIA. We have one KIA, over!" It sounded like Riddell. Shit, this was bad. The worst thing a leader could ever face.

Not knowing if the TOC received the report, he picked up the battalion frequency and sent the message again, "Lancer Mike, this is Comanche Red Four! We are under heavy fire, taking casualties. We have one KIA, over!"

----

Everyone in the company was, in short order, trying to crowd around the radio, fascinated by the sounds of gunfire coming across the background of each transmission. The voices sounded excited, tense, almost panicked. Swearing to himself, York followed Fowler over to Captain Troy Denomy's Bradley. They would be leaving shortly to go help. At least they had better be, or York would grab a vehicle and go himself.

York saw several of his soldiers already gathered around Comanche 6's victor. "Get it on!" he shouted. "Get your gear on and get ready to roll!"

Fowler swore vigorously and said, "York, I've gotta grab my stuff. Don't let 'em leave without me!" York nodded as Fowler left at a dead sprint.

----

As Swope was attempting once more to contact his platoon leader, a huge explosion off the left side rocked their vehicle onto two wheels. Coleman, facing to the rear, cursed as the RPG hit. Swope scrambled to hold on, thinking that the vehicle might rollover onto its side. He felt a momentary disconnection, his head ringing. He fought to clear his head and realized that they were still OK. Another rocket went wide and exploded 100 meters in front of him. He ducked and cursed again as another projectile sailed over his head.

"Coleman, are you hit?" he shouted up to his gunner.

----

"I'm good." Coleman sounded almost cheerful. He saw another RPG team approaching from the south, drew down on them, and pulled the trigger. Nothing happened. The .50 caliber machine gun had been in the military's arsenal continuously for over 60 years, and sometimes the ol' gal seemed to feel her age. *Shit. Shit. Shit.* Coleman grabbed the charging handle with his right hand and pulled hard. A new round seated; he felt it. He put the advancing rocket team in his sights and pulled the trigger, grateful that the temperamental gun worked this time. Both of the approaching figures were cut to pieces.

Coleman cut his victory dance short as three rounds impacted the small shield in front of him, *ting, ting, ting*. His heart skipped a beat and he felt the keen edge of fear for the first time.

*Wow. I'm glad that thing is bulletproof,* he thought.

He saw the guy who had shot at him, another rooftop jockey. Coleman levered the M2 up to engage, pressed the trigger, and was dismayed to find that the gun had jammed again. About every three to ten rounds it would jam, because the ammo can that he had bolted to the swing arm as a make-shift belt holder wasn't lined up right to feed into the 50 cal. He picked up his M16, eyes never leaving the target, brought the rifle to his shoulder, and brought down the man who had given him such a start.

----

Everyone was firing now at the enemy that had engulfed them. Later, the news agencies would declare that 10,000 insurgents took part in that fight. It seemed to that small, determined band of men that all 10,000 were firing at them now.

----

Alpha Company had been tasked with providing the on-call QRF. No more than 20 minutes after the first report of trouble, they rolled out with two Bradleys and two Light Military Tactical Vehicles, cargo trucks full of soldiers that fairly bristled with weapons. York watched them pull out and had a momentary feeling of panic that he would be left behind. Bourquin was like a brother to him and needed his help. Nothing mattered more to him now than getting out there to bring them home alive. He would not be left behind to watch the baggage.

----

Wild was peripherally aware of his leaders' conversations, but he was so deep in the zone that they might as well have been on another planet. He had never known such a sharpening of his senses. His eyes were drawn to a figure appearing on a second story building's roof with an AK-47. The enemy raked the platoon sergeant's Humvee with fire, rounds impacting around Coleman yet leaving him unscathed.

The insurgent was so ridiculously close that Carl could have looked into his eyes had not the westering sun washed out the man's features, turning him into a retail-store clothing dummy—a perfect target. As he placed his weapon's sights on the man's chest, Wild experienced a surreal separation from reality in which his mind, realizing that he was about to take his first human life, began to whisper to him, *This is just like a movie*. In movies, the hero always said something cool or brutally hard core before he dispatched someone. A myriad of clichés and theatrical catch phrases rattled around in his head. But which one to choose? He fussed over it like a debutante anxiously trying on dresses, looking for that perfect one, as his finger tightened on the trigger. Carl screamed a terse profanity and followed it with a long burst of fire, dropping the man cold. Not perfect, but it would have to do. He found that the act was over quickly and heralded no acute twinge of consciousness. It was no harder than swatting a fly.

Before he had time to reflect further, a small man stepped out of the alley on the far side of the two-story building and raised an RPG in their direction. Wild, still trying to process the combat experience in terms he could understand, was struck with comparison of an old West shootout. Time became saturated and slow. His imagination transformed the outlaw's green bandana into a black cowboy hat, the theme to High Plains Drifter filling the air. The outlaw brought his trusty RPG to his shoulder in slow motion even as Wild shifted his balance to bring his weapon to bear. Wild felt sickeningly sure that he wasn't going to be fast enough. His front sight post centered on the man's hips and he squeezed the trigger. *Got ya', ya' dirty varmint. There's only room enough for one of us in this town.* Black Bart's chest caved in as the 7.62mm rounds ripped through him. As he fell backward, his dying finger convulsed on the trigger and he fired the rocket straight up into the air.

Before Wild could celebrate, he heard a buzzing thrum in the air below him and looked down in time to watch with complete fascination as he saw a flurry of bullets zip by underneath his gun. He was so dumbfounded by his brush with death that he almost didn't hear Robinson's M4 carbine sounding off as the dead-eye NCO took the insurgent out.

----

They had won a momentary respite now, but none knew for how long. Perhaps they had defeated the ambush. Swope agreed to take over point while they walked everyone forward, clearing and engaging as they went.

"All right, we're walking out of here." yelled Davis. "Perry, go at a good walking pace. Use your doors for cover. Engage at will."

Perry scrambled back into his seat, switched on the accessory power, and turned the ignition switch hard to the right. The engine failed altogether to roar to life. He twisted the switch again, harder, as if the vehicle just needed a little reminder about who was boss. No sound came from under the hood.

"What are you waiting for Perry? Start the damn engine," cried Davis. Then everyone—quite understandably eager to leave—began shouting at him to start the engine.

"Start it. Let's go."

"It won't start." Perry yelled. "They shot the engine."

Davis' eyes went wide. *Please be joking.*

Perry tried frantically again and again to crank the diesel engine. Nothing. It was dead.

----

Specialist Jermaine Tyrell had his battle-rattle on in nothing flat. They were all ready within seconds, but the leaders were still trying to understand the situation and develop an appropriate plan. Only after Red Platoon had radioed that they had lost two vehicles and were seeking cover in an alleyway did the magnitude of the event begin to register. Tyrell stood, helmet in hand, trying to hear what was going on. Swope relayed a grid to their location. Tyrell could hear it clear as day, along with the accompaniment of weapons firing in the background, but the Battalion TOC seemed to be having a difficult time. They asked him to repeat—say again, over—no less than five times before they acknowledged his transmission.

----

"Riddell," shouted the lieutenant, "Who's behind us? Are they still back there?"

Riddell took his eyes off the road briefly. "Sir, I can't see. The mirror's blown off."

Aguero spared a glance into his own and saw that it was gone, too. He could not stop himself from thinking, *Can this possibly get any worse?* Either no one was listening, or they could not hear his radio call. His gunner was dead and they were cut off from the rest of their platoon. They had made it to relative safety. He could hear gunfire to the south, but since he had shot that one shit-head—and the second one from a bouncing vehicle, he thought with only a touch of pride—the bullets had stopped pinging off of the M1114's tough hide. Now, as he stood outside his vehicle, much too pissed to be scared, he could barely make out the rest of the platoon stopped behind him about 400 meters. He yelled and waved and screamed at them to come on, get moving. He saw that they had dismounted. Something must be wrong. Well, wronger.

"All right, Riddell. Turn around."

Riddell, distressed by the news, asked, "Why?"

"Because they're back there."

"Well, they'll follow. They'll catch up." Riddell seemed concerned for the first time since the fight began.

"No, we're going back." Aguero snapped, all too prescient of the cost. He knew that he was safe now, but he also refused to put his own safety over those he had chosen to lead and serve. He could smell the blood of Chen filling the vehicle, an aroma strong, unsettling, and full of reproach. *I'm sorry, Eddie*, he thought, *I'm so very sorry.*

----

Riddell turned the vehicle sharply around to the right and took to the sidewalk, which had little or no trash blocking it. Realizing that we were heading toward a friendly element now, I released the turret lock and twisted around to face north. The turret was not mechanized and took considerable muscle to turn it. I was careful not to step on Chen but found it impossible to avoid. I had hoped that he would pull out of it, or that maybe Sala'am could resuscitate him, and didn't want to bruise him unnecessarily.

And, oh Lordy, did we ever go back through the shit. Because I was facing the rear, I couldn't see where we were headed so each bump caught me by surprise. Dirt and pavement began to puff and pop in front of me. I heard a bullet whine by my head, buzzing like an angry wasp. It bore no resemblance whatsoever to a movie sound effect.

----

SO note by Davis, Asha @ 22 July 2014
Chief complaint: [intake]

*Appears to be fixated on focus concerns despite negative work-up, questionable validity of the extent of his memory loss given tendency to contradict himself. Also inquired about MEB which brings up potential of secondary gain. SM is a transfer from Dr. Gorton. Most recently prescribed Celexa; reports he was 'unable to function, dropping things at work' on this medicine. Notes he initially saught [sic] treatment for concentration concerns, but also had anxiety. This has been worse since 2008. Currently reports feeling flat, depressed most of the time. Wife recently became pregnant, yet he is 'scared of kids.' Says he did not recall he shot kids until someone else wrote a book about it. Feels guilt from this, as well as '7 men died trying to save me.' Has constant anger, felt more anxious related to the active shooter drill on post today. Sees 'shadows or shapes out of the corner of my eye.'*

**Assessment: Anxiety Disorder NOS.**

----

Robinson and Denney frantically waved for Red 3, Haubert's vehicle, to come closer. Taylor pulled up to within a few feet and strained to hear what they were saying. Why weren't they moving? At first he didn't want to believe his ears, ringing as they were from Bellamy's gun. They were saying, "It won't start. It's dead."

He turned to look at his vehicle commander Haubert for guidance, then realized with a start that he had been hit. When had it happened? He couldn't say for sure. Blood was leaking from one corner of his mouth and he was cradling a bloody hand to his chest and rocking back forth. His eyes had the glazed and far-away look of someone in shock.

"Sergeant Haubert," Taylor yelled. The wounded man turned slowly to look at him with eyes that did not seem to comprehend his own name. Ah, great. Their leader was catatonic and the only other non-commissioned officer was too busy keeping the bad guys off of them to do anything else. Shit. Jon was not ready for this. He was too young, too inexperienced to handle this responsibility. But who else would do it? Taylor opened his mouth to say something else, realized that it was a waste of time, and turned his focus back to the more pressing issue. Red 2 was out of commission. They had trained on performing vehicle recovery under fire before using towing cables, but they had no such cables now. They had worked out a recovery method using ratchet straps and had tested it out at the National Training Center in Fort Irwin, California. It had worked just fine. The problem was that it took a couple of minutes to get the straps hooked up. A couple of more minutes in this mess, and they would all surely die. His mind hit on a more practical solution. He decided to…

"…push you. Hold on," he shouted. Denney and Robinson nodded understanding and enthusiastically agreed saying,

"Yeah. Push us. Push us," they cried in frantic chorus.

Davis twisted around and shouted at Rob and Denney to get in Haubert's vehicle. With the speed borne of panic, they both rushed Red 3 and vaulted into the bed.

Taylor eased the vehicle forward until he felt the bumpers connect and then rammed the accelerator to the floor. To his delight, both vehicles lunged forward, and they were off again. They were going to make it.

----

Perry, his power steering completely gone, was using every ounce of strength he had to steer the dead Humvee around the largest obstacles. Bullets zipped by from everywhere competing for his attention. It looked like an actual hail storm. Round after round hit Perry's window and whizzed by in front of him. His mirror shattered. An RPG whooshed over his head. Perry flinched, keenly aware that he was in a convertible and living on borrowed time. *I don't think I'm gonna make it.* His father was a pastor back in Texas and Perry shared his faith in God. He prayed now as he never had.

----

Sergeant Tuan Le was the training room NCO, the commander's secretary and adjutant. He had earlier stretched a tarp from two Bradleys that were parked side-by-side in order to provide some relief from the noon-time sun and serve as the Comanche base of operations. Now dozens of men were gathered around listening. No one made a sound for almost five minutes as they listened to the drama unfolding as if on an old-timey radio broadcast. Surely this was a joke. Some sort of War of the Worlds broadcast just for funsies. Maybe it was a small ambush and Red platoon would plow through it. They were American infantry soldiers, after all. What could these illiterate goat herders do to them anyway?

Then the paralysis broke like a bad fever. Someone started yelling, "Headquarters Platoon, we're moving out. Break everything down. Let's go." Le began frantically tearing the CP down, getting the tracked vehicles ready to move. He knew that they were going to need all the armor and firepower that they could find. Charlie Company had only the vehicles that they had driven from Kuwait, a collection of Humvees and LMTV cargo trucks with sandbags lining the bed and thin sheets of steel bolted to the side. There were only four Bradley Fighting Vehicles to be had now in this heavy mechanized company. They had been told to leave the rest in Fort Hood because that would send the wrong message to the Iraqis' hearts and minds.

----

**SO note by Rodgers, Renee @ 29 April 2014**

*Patient is a 41 year old male Army captain. SM reports chronic feelings of anger. Episodic rage. SM describes what appears to be emotional numbing. Recalls falling in love with wife (intensity of feelings at the time) and more difficulty sensing feelings now, other than at very high levels. History of homicides while in combat and feelings of anger he now has in retrospect. SM has deficits in self-regulation skills, coupled with problems related to emotional numbing and finding himself in emotional extremes, primarily panic and rage states.*

### Assessment: Anxiety Disorder NOS: R/O PTSD

----

Movement caught my eye. I looked up to my two o'clock and saw three small figures dressed in black, huddled together on the roof of a four-story building. Yellow-orange flame exploded from the midsection of the one in the middle. Muzzle flash. These sons of bitches were shooting at *me*. How dare they? I was about to be killed by some a-hole wearing cliché black. I mean, if I've got to go, please God, don't let it be at the hands of one with neither style nor imagination. Something about the scale bothered me. The tiny figure holding the flashing RPK—for it was undoubtedly a heavy machine gun—was less than 150 meters away. A man-size target at that distance is bigger. I knew this as a jeweler who doesn't need his loupe to tell a real diamond from zirconium. That meant that the target was sub-man sized, or as we say in the business, child-sized. My blood froze.

The child pulled the trigger again, angry flashes of flame signaling his intent to take my life. *RPK*, I thought again. Heavy machine gun. The kid on his left is his ammo handler; on his right is the spotter. My eyes, sharpened by impending death, saw that they each wore a karate-kid style green bandana. I could see clearly the formation of kids in the school lot we had visited yesterday. Black clad, green bandanas.

Holy shit, they were training little mujahedeen fighters. How many more? The kid was closer this time, two shots from his burst pinged off of the rear of the Humvee.

*Don't make me do this*, I silently begged. It was the voice of the teacher. I had worked for a year at a ranch for troubled teenagers. I had taught Spanish in their high school and led the younger kids in a daily physical fitness program that emulated military basic training. After school the younger ones liked to play army. I taught them basic drills like movement-to-contact or react-to-contact. I could hear their laughter now, transposed eerily like a psychotic soundtrack over the gunfire and shouts. The teacher in me, the one who loves kids and longs to bring healing to injured young hearts, was pleading with my hands to stand down. Let them take your life, just don't kill them. The warrior in me, the one who wanted to survive and see my wife and family again, said, *Sit down, Teach. I've got this.*

Time seemed hardly to pass, those thoughts racing through my mind in less than a second. I squatted a little lower in the turret to super-elevate the gun. I put all three small figures within the iron, unforgiving circle of my front sight post. The vehicle bucked once as Riddell ran over something. I paused. The platform steadied. I reacquired the target and depressed the butterfly trigger with both thumbs. The Deuce roared as bullets licked the wall greedily just below the children, climbed quickly and devoured them all. There was dust and there was blood, a fine red misty cloud of it. With half-inch slugs I had killed forever the better part of my soul.

Introspective self-flagellation would have to wait. If I did my job today, I would have years for it. I continued to scan for targets as we hurtled south, engaging anything that moved. Bullets continued to snap and whine past my head and careen off of the armor. The Deuce, hungry as ever, continued to feed.

----

Perry knew their luck couldn't last forever, but he was surprised that they had made it as far as they did, perhaps 200 meters or more. He saw a large pile of busted concrete in their path and turned the wheel hard to miss it. Their bumper lost contact with Red 3 for just a second. When they re-engaged, Taylor's truck hit the right rear and sent Davis and his crew spinning. Every fan of the show *Cops* could tell you that this is called the PIT maneuver, used regularly to put a fleeing felon out of commission. It worked like a charm—or curse—on Red 2. They spun around a perfect 360 degrees and went sailing over the pile of concrete.

----

Taylor was able to muscle his vehicle to the left at the last second without slamming in to them and came to a stop even with Perry. Their gaze locked, both of them staring with wide eyes. He looked over and could hear Davis shouting at him to keep pushing. Taylor nodded and threw the victor into reverse. Within a few seconds, they had locked bumpers again. His foot was heavy on the gas, but this time they were going nowhere.

Shit, what now?

Taylor backed up a few feet and then tried to ram them off of whatever had them high-centered. The bone-jarring crush of metal had no effect on their forward movement. He kept his foot on the pedal, engine revving, working his steering wheel back and forth.

Taylor spared a glance at his vehicle commander and saw that the man was dazed and unresponsive. He turned back to Bellamy and cried, "We ain't going nowhere. This Humvee is dead."

"Keep trying," shouted Bellamy as he continued to fire his weapon.

The tires began to smoke with the effort and then, suddenly, nothing. The engine still roared, but his vehicle was not moving at all. Jon Taylor was aware of Swope pulling up on his side.

"What's going on?" his platoon sergeant yelled.

Taylor turned to him, eyes wide with terror. "It won't go anywhere. We're dead."

----

The only two Bradleys without a dismount squad attached belonged to the commander and the executive officer, Lieutenant Clay Spicer. York seized his chance. "Hey, Mike Golf." The Mike Golf, or master gunner, was busy getting Captain Denomy's track ready for battle. "We're getting on with ya'll whether you want us or not."

The Mike Golf looked out and waved them in. "Get on. Let's go."

York eagerly piled in and took a seat on the bench closest to the turret so that he could put on the CVC, a combination light helmet and radio. Lovett, Rusch, and other soldiers eager to help also loaded into the troop compartment. Winkler, a mild-mannered Kentucky native, wanted to squeeze in, too, but room was scarce.

As York adjusted his microphone and began to listen to the frantic radio chatter, he called out, "Winkler, there's no more room. Just go jump onto that LMTV. Tyrell, you and Arteaga go with him." As the trio hustled over to the cargo truck without complaint, York realized for the first time what they were about to do. A city-wide ambush was in progress, and they were about to attempt to ram several unarmored vehicles through it.

*I think I just sent those guys to their death.* He suddenly felt really selfish for jumping in the back of a fully protected Bradley while he sent his soldiers to ride in the open air. As the ramp closed, sealing them inside, he wished that he could take it back.

----

Riddell quickly found that his way forward was blocked by a cul-de-sac of scrap metal walls at the intersection of Colorado and Delta. The

L-T smacked my leg. I dropped down on my haunches to hear what he wanted.

"Can you see them over this shit?" he demanded.

I popped back up and twisted to my left. At first, I found it difficult to pick out anything other than trash and wrecked cars, but suddenly movement a little further south caught my eye. "Sir. They are almost a hundred meters south of the intersection," I yelled.

----

"Push us. We're dead." Jon Taylor could hear Denney yelling desperately to him. He had the accelerator mashed to floor for only acoustical effect, it seemed. Robinson dismounted to inspect Taylor's undercarriage. "What's going on, Taylor?"

"We ain't going nowhere. We're not moving." Taylor mashed to gas as punctuation.

Robinson lay down on his belly to look as Taylor continued to gun the engine. Fluid was spurting from the transmission in an arterial spray. Not good. "Dude! Your transmission is gone!"

----

Red 4 pulled up on the right side. Swope was talking rapidly on the radio. Rogers leaned across, eyes full of worry, and demanded, "What's going on?"

"Both trucks are dead," yelled Denney, "We can't go anywhere."

Swope told Rogers to back up and attempt to push both vehicles forward. The ad hoc train wouldn't budge. Just then Coleman saw a man pop out of an alley to their south with an RPG. As the man brought it to his shoulder, Shane Coleman laid him out. He saw movement from a rooftop directly above where he had just killed the rocketeer. Quick as thought, he snatched up his M16, drew a bead on the black-clad figure, and shot him center mass.

Rob jumped up and ran over to Swope's window. "Hey, the transmission on Red Three is shot, and Red Two done caught up on something. What you want to do?" Rob's normally soft Southern drawl had disappeared. Swope told Rogers to stop pushing lest they disable another vehicle. Swope knew they had to get off the street, vehicles be damned.

----

Joe Thompson tried to prepare himself as he watched the vehicles in their own company begin to line up. Without waiting to be told, he went to the lead vehicle—a cargo truck operated by the headquarters section—and waited to load up. He had volunteered for duty during the initial invasion of Iraq as a truck driver. He had never taken part in a fight, but he was used to the adrenaline rush one felt before running in to a hot zone. One by one, other soldiers made their way over and gathered around the truck. Tyrell—the tall black kid from Brooklyn—joined Justin "Timberlake" Rowe, Arteaga the reformed gangbanger, Kentucky-born Tim Priddy, and Deaver, who had doom writ large across his Nordic face.

----

Wild heard the unmistakable sound of a .50 caliber machine gun approaching from the north. He could make out Red 1's victor now appearing from behind a pile of metal, Chen facing north. Wild shifted his sector of fire to the left even as his heart began to swell with relief. Red 1 stopped on the far side of the intersection beyond a wide median and a wall of junk. He could hear the L-T shouting, "Come on. Move!"

Wild yelled back, "The Humvee's down, the Humvee's down."

----

The L-T ordered Riddell to turn the vehicle around and pull up next to the disabled vehicles. Riddell executed a 23-point turn to accommodate both the numerous obstacles and the wide turning radius of his victor. Aguero, impatient in the best of times, growled, "Meet me over there when you get out of this mess." He opened the door and quickly began picking his way around, over and through everything that stood between him and his men.

----

Denney saw the L-T sprinting toward them on foot, puffs of dust and chunks of concrete exploding all around the man's feet, as the enemy continued to display their lack of marksmanship. He felt a burst of hope that they might just make it after all.

----

As Shane Aguero waded through enemy fire, he had time to think—even as his lungs seemed to fill with lava from the effort in dashing about in full gear—that this was pretty damned cool. He was suddenly the star of the best first-person shooter game ever. It was so surreal that it might as well have been a game. He saw as he approached that the lead vehicle was caught on something. Several people, including Robinson and Davis, had dismounted and were in various stages of problem solving, to include Stage 0, completely clueless. Red 3 and 4 were pooling their efforts to push him off. Swope, red-faced, was screaming something at the drivers. What the hell?

Sprinting full out for 150 meters with an extra 40 pounds of gear is not an easy feat. Lieutenant Aguero, a very fit man of 30 winters, was winded when he reached his platoon sergeant. "Why...aren't...we moving?" he panted. *Oh, Jesus, this sucks.*

Sergeant Davis yelled, "My vehicle won't move and Red Three just lost a transmission."

Alarm rising in his heart, Aguero cast a glance to Haubert's vehicle, wondering briefly where he was. At that moment, as if the Humvee had been waiting for the L-T to witness the event, he saw the transmission pan drop out of the vehicle. *Oh. Shit.*

Robinson, having long decided that the vehicle was a lost cause, sprinted over to his L-T. "I don't know what you're going to do, but we better get the hell up off of this road."

*Oh, to have the luxury of time to properly respond with the necessary sarcasm*, Aguero thought. "Good point," he said.

Aguero took a deep, calming breath and said, "All right, pull all the sensitive equipment and ammo of the Two and Three, cram everybody into whatever still rolls, and we'll duck down an alley until help comes." His eyes darted around, looking for the most defensible position. His gaze locked on to an alley just to the south. The entrance was commanded by a large three-story building that he thought would make a good base of operations. "There, we go there," he said, indicating the ground that he hoped would not become their Little Big Horn.

"All right, you heard him. Get everything off Two and Three and load everyone into the eleven-fourteens," yelled the Platoon Sergeant.

"Ain't no way we're all going to fit," Davis responded.

"Squeeze everybody you can, then. Last few we'll cover. It ain't that far to walk," Swope drawled.

"Who's walking?" laughed Davis.

----

Davis and Robinson ran back to their soldiers, shouting as they went for everyone to grab their gear and get into a vehicle. Trevor Davis had decided that he would remain behind to make sure the radios were disabled and everything that could be an advantage to the enemy was pulled off.

----

Wild grabbed his CamelBak and pulled the machine gun from the mounting bracket, hardly feeling its weight. A belt of six or seven rounds of a 200-round belt dangled from the feed tray, testifying to number of targets he had engaged already. He ran over to Taylor's Humvee, hurled the 240 in the back, and jumped over the spare-tire rack. He popped up and screamed, "Let's go."

Taylor looked back at him with pure terror. He said, "My Humvee's broken, it won't move. They shot the transmission."

Wild, who had been too busy to keep up with current events, was stunned. Every expletive he had ever learned or heard flashed through his mind. Unable to find one that adequately expressed his dismay, he said nothing. Davis, erasing the commo codes from the radio, looked back and noticed where his soldiers had gone. "Not there. Get in one of the up-armors."

*Now you tell me,* Wild thought.

He grabbed his M16 and jumped to the ground, moving quickly toward Red 1 as Riddell pulled up opposite the platoon sergeant to provide them more cover. Too quickly, as it turned out. As his hand grabbed the door handle, he had a nagging feeling that he was missing something.

----

Davis finished purging the encryption data. As he waited for the blinking LED that would tell him that he was successful, he felt a jarring impact to his weapon as his hand went numb. Cursing, he let the rifle hang by its strap and looked at his gloved hand. He saw no holes, blood, or missing digits. He tried to wiggle his fingers and could manage to do so only with effort. No time to worry about it now.

The radio LED blinked one final time and winked out. Task complete. He looked up as Wild ran across and piled into the L-T's vehicle, newly returned as they were from their romp up north. He cast his glance into the bed of the Humvee and noticed that Wild had left his machine gun.

----

*Stupid. Stupid. Stupid.* Wild cursed himself roundly as he turned back to the Humvee he had just abandoned to retrieve the weapon. Davis waved him off. *I've got it already*, the gesture told him. The young soldier hadn't felt so inept since basic training. Mentally smacking his forehead, he vowed to pull his head out of his own fourth point of contact.

----

Coleman, still rattled by the numerous rounds that had ricocheted off of his turret shield, felt something bump his legs and he jumped involuntarily. He glanced down and saw Private Perry looking up at him. Shane adjusted his legs so that Derrick could squeeze into the middle. He was peripherally aware of others piling in, but did not dare take his eyes off the road for another second. The young NCO tried to slow his breathing and racing pulse. This was actually kind of fun, when you got down to it. Fun for someone familiar with the extreme-sports-skater-punk lifestyle he had joined the Army to escape. Terrifying—but fun just the same.

----

Fowler sucked on a cigarette as though it were his last as everyone clambered aboard the LMTV, those with longer limbs assisting the vertically challenged. Fowler had never seen any of them move so fast. He noticed that people he didn't even know were asking if they could come, too. They were told, sometimes impolitely, to go somewhere else. He was peripherally aware of Specialist "Ski" Wodarski in the turret—in between the driver and shotgun seat—attending his M2 .50 cal while Sergeant Hunter, the supply NCO and driver, performed last-minute checks to his vehicle.

----

Bellamy knew they were bugging out, but he wanted to stay on the gun as long as possible to cover everyone. He had already killed nine people now and didn't mind if the tenth never showed up for the party. In the back of his mind, he heard a voice reminding him that today was his wedding anniversary with his ex-wife. He continued to wonder if they were going to survive and relished the hope that he would be able to consider life's regrets in the morning.

Behind him, Bellamy heard someone shout, "OK, get in this one. Everybody get in this Humvee." He looked back and realized he was going to be late for the ball, perhaps even as in the Late Justin Bellamy. He saw nobody near him except Davis and that Swope's vehicle was already packed with soldiers, their faces almost comically distorted against the bullet-proof windows.

Wasting no time, Bellamy jumped down and ran toward Red 4 as Red 1 took off for the alley. A red-faced and clearly angry Swope yelled, "Where's your weapon?"

"Doc's got it. Let me in."

"Your 240."

Bellamy looked back at the vehicle he had just left which now seemed eight miles away rather than eight meters. Yep, there it was, all right. Big, healthy machine gun sitting there in the dying sunlight. Justin took a deep breath and dashed back. He leapt up onto the back with unconscious grace and plucked the weapon from its mount. He also snatched up a can of ammo. His eyes danced over the few re-maining items, an AT-4, someone's shotgun, bottles of water. He looked up and saw that the platoon sergeant was advancing south to cover their retreat. He only had two hands and couldn't carry it all, so he jumped down and beat feet toward the alley behind Red 4. As he ran, he stepped on the ammo belt that hung from the gun like a long brass tongue. The belt disconnected, but not before sending him sprawling into the dust. Bellamy was back on his feet so quickly that one might have mistaken his fall as an optical illusion. Feeling only terrified, and not even remotely embarrassed, he snatched up the partial belt of ammo and kept running.

----

Deaver eagerly yearned for the fight and was completely sure that they were all about to die. He noted the truck's thin aluminum sides that protruded barely three feet from the floor, which was lined with a single layer of sandbags. He helped Tyrell and Thompson roll the tarp off the top so that they would have better visibility. Deaver desperately wanted to draw their exposure to someone's attention, wanted to shout that 40 men were about to die instead of 20. His fatalistic nature took over, though, and he knew that no one would—or could—pause long enough to listen to reason. Besides, his friends, Fisk and Denney, were out in that mess.

----

Trevor Davis noticed movement on a rooftop to the east. He smoothly took up aim, waited for the natural pause in his breathing, and pulled the trigger. Nothing happened. He went through the process of correcting a malfunction to his weapon that all soldiers learn in basic training. This so-called remedial action will correct 90 percent of misfires, allowing the return of the joyful sounds of 5.56 millimeter death. Davis felt no joy in that moment of awful silence. He cocked his weapon to the left as if to say, "What's wrong? Did I hurt your feelings?" That's when he noticed that his rifle had a gaping hole in the receiver, just above where his right hand squeezed the pistol grip. No wonder his hand was numb—he was lucky to still have one.

*That's just great.* He threw his weapon down in the bed and plucked the large machine gun from its mount. *Hell, maybe I like this better*, he thought with a grin. You couldn't help but feel like a bad-ass while holding such a beast. He spied the AT-4 rocket launcher behind the back seat and slung it over his shoulder. For good measure, he grabbed a can of 7.62 mm linked ammo. Still grinning, he jumped down with the 240 at the ready position, the brass ammo belt flapping. He sprinted after Bellamy, the fastest runner in the company, who had caught the platoon leader's truck at the mouth of the alley.

He could hear the L-T yelling to him, "Let's go. Let's go. Let's go," as if he weren't motivated enough to hustle. Hell, even with the extra 45 pounds of weight he was carrying, he couldn't remember ever running faster.

----

Swope knew they were in a pickle. His mind raced as he watched Davis extract the equipment and destroy the radios on both vehicles. Who was the KIA that he had heard reported over the radio not five minutes earlier? He tried to count the soldiers as they all scrambled to load up on the remaining trucks. Who was missing? He realized with a start that of all his squad leaders, he hadn't seen Haubert. There he was, sitting in the Humvee in front of him, not moving. Was he dead? Bellamy was hopping down from Red 3, shouting something at Haubert as he did. Haubert didn't move. Shit. Bellamy opened the TC's door and shook the man, shouting something laced with an obscenity that cut through the clamor and smoke. Haubert jerked and bolted from the seat, running back toward Swope's truck. Not dead then. Swope saw the ashen complexion and a copious amount of blood running from the NCO's mouth. He cradled his hand to his chest and ran stiffly, eyes wide.

*That must be who they were talking about as the KIA*, he thought. *They just thought he was dead. Good.* Swope felt a surge of relief and hope.

----

We approached the entrance to the alley, the gaping maw of some ravenous beast welcoming us with gently smiling jaws, and stopped short at the entrance. The L-T hopped out. "Riddell, pull in the alley and dismount. Find a door, kick it in, and clear the building."

"Roger, Sir!" Riddell interpreted the L-T's command to mean that he should pull as far in as possible.

I stared down the deserted alleyway as Jon Riddell squeezed the wide vehicle past one sedan and then another. Buildings of different heights crowded the narrow residential street, jostling with each other for a better view of the carnage to come. The street itself was relatively clean and uncluttered. A small air-conditioner condenser unit lay lonely and neglected on the left, about 10 feet short of where another small street crossed our path. The street was less than a 150 meters long from where we pulled off of Delta to the next intersection. Beyond that was another crossroad about the same distance, where I could see quite a few people milling about and, presumably, peering down the lane toward us. My hands tightened on the twin wood grips of the machine gun.

Our vehicle was crowded. Wild sat on Denney's lap in the seat I had previously occupied, his upper body leaning against my legs. Chen lay motionless on the ammo cans. I twisted to the right to track what I thought was movement on the rooftops. I inadvertently stepped on Chen's legs as I turned. The feel of his inanimate flesh beneath my boots unnerved me. I felt a lifetime's worth of revulsion and pity in one moment. I still felt that I needed to be careful not to bruise him just in case—just in case Guzman could…could do something.

At the precise center of the alley, about 60 meters in, Riddell slammed on the brakes. I cursed as momentum threw me painfully into the gun, but I didn't take it personally. This was all business.

----

Aguero waved Swope's vehicle in with exaggerated gestures that were completely unnecessary. Red 4 pulled to a stop beside him almost as soon as Red 1 had cleared the second sedan. Through the window, Aguero yelled, "Pull in behind Riddell. Enter and clear a building for our CP and set up a defensive perimeter." The L-T glanced up the alley and noticed that Riddell had gone much further in than he intended.

*I guess I should have been more specific, but that should do.*

Rogers threaded the large vehicle expertly past the cars clogging the entrance. He slammed on the accelerator and managed to catch up quickly with Riddell who was rolling on four flat tires. The L-T looked back at the immobile Humvees and saw Robinson and Bellamy running toward him with Davis bringing up the rear. Good, everyone had made it. Aguero waited a second longer to cover their approach. The firing had stopped. This pause wouldn't last long, the L-T knew. The Jihadists were just leaving their positions to get a better shot at the infidels.

----

Coleman worried about the rooftops in the tight alley. Actually, he worried about a great many things informing this jacked-up situation. There were so many people packed into their Humvee that he couldn't move his legs. When Rogers stopped the vehicle, someone popped the door latch, spilling soldiers out on the dusty lane like a platoon of clowns from a Cooper Mini. Coleman cast a nervous glance upward. No, he wasn't worried at all about defending the entrance to the alley. *Ain't nothin' coming in that I ain't gonna take out,* he thought. But he couldn't use his big gun to ward off targets from above. He couldn't cover both the entrance to the alley and the roofs at the same time, so he would focus more on the threat from above until the situation changed. Perry and someone else, Davis maybe, were covering Route Delta. With at least a quarter-eye to the alley entrance, he picked up his M16 and began to scan the heavens. *We're about to have all kinds of stuff come up on top of us.* Coleman glanced left and saw a window. It was a glass-paned window that was opaque because of a glare that allowed the young gunner to see only his reflection. The window also troubled him. He was currently of the opinion that the whole city had turned on them. He knew that every Iraqi household was allowed to have an AK-47 for home defense. He thought, *they're going to shoot me right in the face because I am so open to this window right here.* For the first time he was truly afraid.

----

I glanced left and saw that we had parked next to a blue metal gate set into a bland wall. I craned my neck to peer over into the small courtyard and could see no one. Rogers was moving so fast that he beat everyone to the entrance that they meant to breach. Riddell, Wild, and Denney were out of the vehicle in a flash and lined up behind him. I could dimly hear Robinson calling for others to stack up behind him. Taylor jumped in line behind him. Although occupied with securing our front, I knew that they meant to breach, enter, and clear the building.

----

Bellamy, faster than any other man in the Battalion in a pair of running shorts, felt the extra weight of the heavy machine gun and ammo pulling him into the earth. He saw Robinson angle left and fall into line behind Bourquin, preparing to enter a doorway. Bellamy knew that his superior firepower would be useless at close quarters and decided that he should help defend the alley until further notice. He dodged around Perry, ran about ten more paces and hurled himself to the ground on the right side of Red 1. Sala'am the interpreter, still sitting in his seat, jumped nervously as the NCO seemed to fly through the air next to him. Bellamy cocked his body on his left side, dropped first one bipod leg and then another on the machine gun's barrel, and then shoved the stock of the weapon into his shoulder. Bellamy was breathing hard from the two hundred yard dash and could barely keep the gun steady. *God, don't let me die yet,* he thought. Over his shoulder he shouted, "Sir, we need to get in somewhere."

----

The L-T saw Davis bringing up the rear and knew that everyone had made it in from the street. At this point, he knew, the possibility of losing control of the situation was very real. *Losing control!* He snorted to himself. They had lost two vehicles, probably one Soldier, and were cut off from escape by a force that outnumbered them about 500 to one. A surfer had as much control of the ocean.

----

Rogers rocked his body back into the men stacked up behind him signaling that he was ready. A moment later, he felt a tap from the man behind him, signaling that everyone else was ready. *Go.* He thumbed the safety off of the 12-gauge pump-action shotgun and put a round through the locking mechanism. With the roar of the blast still ringing in our ears, he planted his boot into the blue door, sending it flying open. Maintaining the kick's momentum, he lunged forward into the doorway.

The courtyard was empty as they moved in. Rogers moved to the nearest corner on the left. No target. Immediately he swiveled right even as he kept moving forward. "Stairway on the left!" he shouted.

He reached the corner in less than a second and continued to travel up the wall halfway to the next corner.

Hayhurst split to the right corner, saw no target, and immediately swiveled to the left. "Door on the right! Door far corner!" The door closest to him was closed, so he moved past it, leaving it for the fourth man to clear. He trained his weapon on the doorway in the far right corner. He could see into the sparsely furnished room, noted a TV and a couple of chairs, and pegged it as a family room. He could see no one yet, but could sense—something. He moved half the length of the wall toward the den and stopped, finger on the trigger.

Rob split left on Hayhurst's heels, noting the open stairway Rogers had called out. He swept his M4 carbine up and right, following a second story L-shaped walk way that led to an upper-story room. The catwalk ended in a door locked with a brass padlock. Taylor had entered and now stood opposite from Rob, his wide, young eyes scanning the roof of the three-story building that loomed over them on their left.

"One, up!" Rogers cried, indicating that he was OK. "I've got movement in the next room."

"Team two, move through and clear!" yelled Robinson. Team two emerged almost immediately from the alley and stacked up on the wall in front of Hayhurst who shifted his weapon left to help Taylor cover the three-story roof to their east. Riddell led, followed by Wild, then Denney. Bourquin brought up the rear. Without hesitating, Riddell burst through the doorway, hooked right and then began to shout.

"Get down, get down, get down!" He cursed and swore and yelled, introducing himself in no uncertain terms to the family unfortunate enough to be in the wrong house at the wrong ambush.

"Short room!" yelled Wild, who had hooked left. There wasn't enough room to fit the entire team and everyone else should hang back. Denney stopped short, and Bourquin bounced off of the large man.

As Riddell continued to yell, replacing Arabic vocabulary with English volume, Bourquin pulled back to a closed door between Hayhurst and Taylor. "Denney, kick this door in and I'll clear it," he said. "Doesn't look like the room's very big."

Denney, pale-faced and wide-eyed, nodded but said nothing. The big man squared up on the wooden door as Bourquin prepared to go in. Bourquin nodded like a cowboy ready to go a full eight seconds on Ol' Widow Maker, and Denney fired his size-13 boot into the door, sending splinters and dust everywhere. Bourquin was in the room in a flash. Before Denney could enter, the heavily tattooed NCO yelled, "Room clear!"

The room held a propane cooking apparatus and a bag of rice or flour—the kitchen, if you will. Riddell and Wild emerged from the den with a very upset Iraqi family marching on trembling legs before them. The father was a balding man dressed in modern clothes who looked to be in his early 40s. His wife, a weathered woman who could have been anywhere from 25 to 50, was weeping and pleading. Her eyebrows had been plucked out and replaced with the ornate prison-style tattoos that the Sadr women favored. The children, a young boy and girl, both around six years old, were sobbing. Riddell forced them all to sit in the dirt in the middle of the small courtyard.

Robinson sensed that innocent lives hung in the balance. He told Rogers—the man who seemed least likely to execute someone for sneezing—to put the family into the small kitchen and watch them carefully. He turned his attention to the second-story walkway that framed the back side of the court. The high ground is what they needed right now, and he meant to get his boys on top of that roof.

"Hayhurst, up the stairs," Rob said.

----

Ben Hayhurst climbed the dozen or so stairs that led to the walkway. He glanced right and was glad to see that a low wall on the roof of the kitchen was actually the wall and roof of the next house, and no one was waiting on the roof to kill him. Even better, the next house was taller than the buildings beyond and provided good cover to the west. He reached the corner, turned right, and ran to the door. Taylor followed close behind him to provide suppression against anyone foolish enough to pop up on the other side of the alley.

Hayhurst noticed two things that didn't make him happy: the door was constructed of heavy gauge metal, and the padlock may have been made in Taiwan, but it wasn't cheap. He tried to hit the lock with the butt of his rifle, a move that usually seemed to work in the movies but failed miserably in practical application. He delivered a savage series of kicks to the door but realized the futility when he saw that it was hinged to swing out. He pointed his rifle briefly at the lock as if demanding its surrender. Wouldn't do any good to fire a bullet at it. It might ricochet and kill someone.

"Rogers!" he called. "Bring your shotgun up here!"

----

Rob nodded for Rogers to move out. As the former volunteer firefighter trotted toward the stairs, the Iraqi man began to speak rapidly and loudly as if trying to make his captors understand some great and important truth. Rob regarded the man warily. Then the light went on and Robinson understood. "Hold up, Rogers!" Robinson motioned the man forward. Their host walked forward, his nervousness receding, pulling something from his pocket. Rob was not concerned because he knew what it was.

"What's he saying?" Hayhurst called.

"He's got the key," Robinson laughed.

Their gracious host opened the padlock and motioned Hayhurst inside with the universal *mi casa, su casa* gesture. Inside was a steep staircase that ended in a ceiling trapdoor. "We've got roof access!" he called.

----

Everyone in Red Platoon who was not either manning a guard tower or already trapped in an alley were loading onto the two Bradleys, an LMTV, and an unarmored Humvee that now stood ready to enter the fray. The vehicles were lined up and ready for the go command. Bradley Fighting Vehicles armed with 25mm belt-fed guns and co-axially mounted M240C machine guns took up the point and rear positions. Captain Denomy had elected to ride in the Humvee. His armorer, a weapons repair specialist, was manning a machine gun mounted in the same Mad Max fashion as the vehicles that had just been lost in sector. Behind him the LMTV was as ready as it would ever be. What the rear compartment lacked in armor they hoped to compensate for with firepower. In the cab, Hunter sat in a pool of his own nervous sweat. Winkler had mounted the passenger seat and cracked the window so that he could engage as needed. In the bed, the soldiers had spread out—Tyrell just behind the cab on the driver's side and Fowler to his left. Priddy faced off the rear corner next to Fowler. On the TC's side was Le, Deaver, Thompson, Arteaga, and Rowe. They were locked and loaded and awaiting their first fight.

They rolled out within minutes. Two Bradleys from White platoon led the way, followed by the CO in his add-on-armor Humvee, the fresh meat in the back of the LMTV and the two headquarters company Bradleys bringing up the rear, commanded by First Lieutenant Spicer and First Sergeant Carson. The Bradley gun crews were still going through their pre-combat checks as the soldiers in the back—the dismount infantry squads—tightly gripped their weapons and prayed for courage in their own ways.

----

"Hey, they're rolling the QRF," yelled Swope from his seat. A Quick Reaction Force was a platoon designated to respond to crisis situations during the course of the 24-hour duty.

"That's great," exclaimed Aguero. The sooner the better, too. The L-T was standing between the two vehicles trying to decide his next move. They had been here less than five minutes, and he knew that every minute that passed brought the enemy closer to massing their full might on the Americans' meager defense. The L-T could see a large group gathering down the western end of the alley about 200 meters away. He couldn't tell how many, but the swarm seemed to number in the hundreds.

He saw red, black, and green flags unfurled from the previous day's demonstration. Now he remembered one of the Iraqi's they had questioned saying that the event was a Mahdi Army training exercise. Obviously so. How long had they been planning this? The obstacles they had emplaced so quickly, the organization, the sheer number of people they had witnessed loading and unloading, all bespoke a well-planned and executed trap. His platoon had just been the first fly to become ensnared in the web.

----

I accidentally stepped on Chen again as I traversed my weapon back and forth. Knowing that someone would have to get him inside soon if he stood any chance of resuscitation, I made a choice. No one was threatening us from my sector. The nearest human presence was almost 200 meters away. I climbed out of the turret and vaulted to the ground with the ease of a monkey. I yanked open the armored door and grabbed Chen's arm pulling him closer to me. Chen was a very big, muscular, Asian man, and—if I had been prone to introspection at that time—probably would have thought that pulling him out would have been hard. It wasn't. I grabbed his ballistic vest by the shoulders and pulled. I would be willing to do a TV infomercial on the strength-inducing benefits of combat on the adrenal gland. My fallen brother felt no heavier than a sack of potatoes.

With as much dignity as the situation allowed, I lowered him to the earth by the rear wheel. He never opened his eyes. Never breathed.

"Goodbye, Eddie. I'm sorry." I didn't know if he could hear me. I'm not even sure what I meant by it, because I hadn't meant to say anything. The words fell out of me and lay with Eddie on the ground.

I quickly climbed back up on top of the Humvee feeling ridiculously exposed until I dropped down into the turret. Even though there was no imminent threat from my sector, I turned my attention back to the lane and waited. Whatever surge of Viking fortitude I had felt earlier was gone. Seeing Chen laid out lifeless upon the ground reminded me that I, too, was mortal. I was afraid again.

----

### SO Note by Rodgers, Renee @ 21 March 2014
### Chief Complaint: Anxiety. Alcohol abuse.

*SM and this provider met for 30 minutes during Walk In Clinic hours at 2:30PM at BJACH BHD. SM states he wishes to establish mental health services at this time following recent PCS to FT Polk two weeks ago. SM started TBI assessment in January 2013 while stationed at FT Benning, GA. SM wishes to continue assessment process at this time. SM states he's having problems with anxiety currently and that this time of year is an anniversary period of loss for him related to his service. SM made contact with a SM recently who shares this same anniversary period and was emotionally triggered by it. Anger and aggressive urges are also a concern. SM states he's also received mental health care in Iraq. He is having sleep problems and currently uses alcohol to aid with this.*

## Assessment: ANXIETY DISORDER NOS

----

Mere minutes away from our imperiled group, York could see everything that the Bradley gunner saw, thanks to a closed-circuit screen in the troop compartment. In shades of thermal gray, York saw another Bradley sitting alone at the corner of Aeros and Silver, the area we called Home Depot because of the mounds upon mounds of gravel, sand, and other construction material for sale. No other vehicles were in sight.

York could hear conversation in his crew helmet between 1SG Casey Carson, commander of their Bradley, and the BC of the lone track. They were with Alpha Company whose vehicle had lost power. They sent their dismounts with the rest of the QRF and stayed back with the vehicle—driver, gunner, and Bradley commander—to secure it. Would they mind towing them back to base? Not at all. To York's frustration, he found out that Denomy was tasking Spicer and Carson to recover the vehicle and tow it back to the FOB while the rest of the convoy pushed onward.

The driver and Bradley Commander or BC of the inoperable vehicle dismounted and quickly attached a heavy tow bar to the back of Carson's Bradley. Within five minutes they were on their way. York gritted his teeth, impatient to join the fight. He felt like he had been tricked. Horribly, horribly tricked. He had jumped into the first available seat, rearing to go, and had, as a bad joke, been stuck towing another Bradley back into the FOB. Another five minutes and the Alpha company victor was safe inside FOB War Eagle.

Once at the FOB, he heard 1SG Carson say that they would be waiting in the base until the CO or someone else called them out. Fratricide happens, York knew, when friendly pieces move around the chess board without the other pieces knowing about it. The battle was moving too quickly and they had to wait until they were inserted into the plan again. York knew this made sense but hated that he was now sitting on the sidelines. Then the Bradley stopped and the ramp went down.

Pandemonium. That was the first word that came to York's mind. Soldiers and vehicles were dashing madly about. He looked up and saw that the soldiers manning the towers were firing at something over the wall that he couldn't see.

----

This wasn't Swope's first rodeo. He had seen combat before as a private during the first Desert Storm and was inured to the shock that most felt. As we set up the defense, the feeling that gripped him the strongest was pride. He saw his soldiers, many of whom he knew despised him for his detachment and relentless commitment to training, performing at a jaw-dropping level. He felt that swell of delight that a father feels when he lets go of the back of the bike for the first time and the child, laughing with delight, says, "Dad! I'm doing it!"

Swope could not keep up with how fast his soldiers had stacked up outside the door and then burst through to clear the building. He listened to the chatter on the radio and tried to discern how long it would take for the Quick Reaction Force to reach. As he listened, he watched Chen jump from the top of the vehicle in front of him. Wait, glasses—that was Fisk. Where? Fisk tugged open the door and reached inside. A second later he pulled the limp body of a large soldier. Chen?

Shit.

He could tell by the way that Chen's body hung that the man was dead. They had a KIA after all. Swope felt his stomach sink and convulse. The coldness that swept over him covered up the instant grief and sorrow that threatened to undo him. It washed away the sadness and filled him with something useful. Something that would help him get his men out alive. Something that would get him back home to his wife in Texas.

Rage.

----

Aguero knew that several things had to happen at once. First they had to secure their battle space. He felt confident in their command of the alley. Just like the Spartans at the pass of Thermopylae, they had a good chance holding off any advancing horde that attempted to cram any number of people through either entrance. As long as their ammunition held. Second, they had to establish and maintain comms with the cavalry. Unless the good guys knew where to find them rescue was unlikely. Then they had to make sure that the injured were treated and that Battalion was ready to evacuate them for treatment as necessary.

Aguero's thoughts turned to Chen, his gunner, his soldier. His eyes were drawn to the body of the fallen warrior as he lay in the dirty street. He wondered if he had failed him, if he had done something wrong that had caused this tragedy to befall such a decent young man. *No, not me. THEM!* The Lieutenant's mind filled with a buzzing, glaring rage that blotted out thought and reason. Aguero had long been an angry man, but now he was a man possessed. He turned back toward Delta, the street where a good soldier had fallen, where even now a large number of people were gathering to kill the rest of them. His teeth clenched in a savage grin that lit his face for the rest of the battle.

----

Swope sat in his seat with his foot propping the door open. Aguero stood by his own vehicle with one arm draped on the open door and one on the roof of the vehicle with his head hanging inside the vehicle. They were both listening to the radio chatter. Everyone was trying to talk at once. Men, confused by the sound of it, were trying to get the "SITREP," plying each other eagerly for more "INTEL," and generally seeming to be running around in "CIRCLES."

Volesky, call-sign Lancer 6, had received authority and responsibility for everything that happened in Sadr City at exactly the same moment that Red Platoon had been ambushed. The new field commander was just now getting a sense for the plight of the stranded platoon. He passed word through his operations center to Red 1 that he wanted Comanche Red Platoon to pull off of the alley and into the nearest house. They would have to defend themselves until he could leverage his assets to pull them out.

Swope shook his head as he heard the L-T acknowledge. "Did you hear that?" Aguero asked as he trotted up to his Platoon Sergeant.

"Roger, Sir, I heard it. But we can't sit there and do that."

"Why not?"

"If we pull out of these vehicles then we're not going to be able to sit there and talk to Battalion."

"We've got a man-pack don't we?" The L-T had performed the Pre-Combat Inspection himself and knew for a fact that they had a portable radio with antennae and batteries in a backpack. He thought it was either in his vehicle or in Swope's.

"Roger, we've got the man-pack, but it doesn't have a power amp. Without that amp, the output wouldn't be enough to sit there and talk to Lancer Mike. Hell, that's several miles back and the range just won't cut it, especially with all these buildings in the way."

Aguero cursed silently to himself and then not so silently. "Well, looks like we're stuck in the alley then."

"Roger, but we need to get somebody on a high OP right away. Once these shit-heads figure out that they can't sit there and get in this alley, they're gonna try to come across the roofs."

----

Robinson appeared in the doorway, looked left then right, and trotted over to the L-T. "Sir, the courtyard is all clear. We got the family inside detained. They ain't got no weapons. We've also got access to the roof."

"Good. Get a crew-served weapon up there then."

"Hooah." Robinson glanced left and saw Bellamy lying in the alley behind the 240B. Rob ran up and kneeled beside him. "Hey, man. I need your 240."

Bellamy glanced over his left shoulder at him. "I wouldn't have a weapon then. I gave my rifle to Doc."

"Here, take mine." Rob extended his M4 carbine. Bellamy climbed stiffly to his feet and exchanged weapons with him, glad to have the lighter weapon for a while. Robinson disappeared back inside the courtyard while Bellamy opened the L-T's door to provide a little more cover, grateful for a lull in the fighting that was not destined to last. Robinson dashed back inside without ever having noticed Chen, his friend and former gunner, lying beside the Humvee.

----

Swope leaned out of the window and said, "Hey, Sir! I need to get a status on our wounded to send up to higher."

Lieutenant Aguero turned in time to see Wild emerging from the courtyard. His eyes had a distant, far-off look—ye olde thousand-yard stare. "Wild, consolidate the wounded inside. Have Doc see what he can do. Let me know who's been hit."

Wild looked down at Chen and nodded. He went back inside and emerged with Riddell and Doc. Doc Guzman went to the back of Red 4 to check on Haubert, who was sitting in his seat cradling his hand and rocking. Riddell and Wild managed to lift the large Asian warrior by his arms and legs and carry him to the kitchen now designated as the CCP or Casualty Collection Point.

----

Robinson climbed up to the roof to get the lay of the land. White-washed buildings of varying heights stretched in all directions. Most were two stories or less, but some rose a few stories taller. To the south, he could see black garbed figures swarming the rooftops a few hundred meters away. There was very little action to the west. Route Delta was clearly visible to their immediate east. A tall, slender building at the mouth of the alley obscured part of the sector, but not by much. A four-story spire immediately adjoining the courtyard to their east kept them from seeing the entrance to the lane they defended, and Rob thought that that was probably a better place to be right now. He would say something to the L-T. He couldn't see very much north of the alley; could not, in fact, see their disabled Humvees. Rob was satisfied, though, that they could make anyone approaching from the south end of Delta pay dearly for passage.

As the soldiers mounted the steps, Robinson gave them sectors of fire. He placed Hayhurst on the northeast corner, Taylor on the southwest while Rob himself covered the southeast with the heavy machine gun. He couldn't see any targets yet, but he knew that it would only be a matter of time before he saw the enemy approaching from rooftops to the south—just your friendly, neighborhood Shiites. Behind him he heard Hayhurst engaging someone out on Delta and smiled.

----

Hayhurst had a narrow vista of Route Delta from his position. He could see people running toward them. People with weapons. He began to engage with lethal precision. He was able to shoot five of them before they reached the mouth of the alley that Coleman held.

Hayhurst was awed by the reckless courage displayed by the enemy. Awed and enraged. He was an even-tempered, gentle guy, but he could feel nothing but hate and rage brewing inside him now. He saw a child step into the street from a side-alley doorway to the east with an assault rifle in his hands. The child could have been no more than eight or nine years old and wore black pants and a black top that was reminiscent of a martial arts *gi*. The child began firing at them, spraying the gun back and forth, barely able to stand up under the weapon's recoil. Ben took aim and with a single shot the boy's body crumpled like a large doll. The weapon clattered to the earth beside him.

A man wearing a *didashi* emerged from the same doorway. He was bent over with grief. His hands held no weapon, and were stretched palm outward in front of him. He walked slowly toward the body, weeping and uttering words Ben could not hear from the distance. Hayhurst was transfixed by the drama unfolding in front of his eyes and had a good idea how this particular tragedy was going to end. The father—for surely the man was at least a close relative—bent and picked up the rifle his son had hoped would be a one-way ticket to paradise. *Don't do it*, Ben thought. *Don't you do it, you stupid son of a bitch. Don't.*

The father did. He raised the rifle toward the infidels with a defiant, mournful cry that was drowned out by the sound of Hayhurst's weapon putting the man out of his misery. The rifle once again clattered to the earth.

Immediately another figure emerged from the same doorway at a sprint and snatched up the weapon. *Damn it*, Hayhurst thought, *when will this end?* He dropped the man with another well-placed shot. The rifle clattered to the earth once again, awaiting another hand to continue the endless cycle of violence and vengeance.

The rifle waited not long at all. Hayhurst was dumbfounded to see another man emerge from darkening doorway. He grabbed the leg of the man most recently shot and began to drag him back inside.

As almost an afterthought, the man bent down and retrieved the AK-47 that had caused so much trouble. Hayhurst fired again, but his aim was fouled by some random act of chance or the intervention of a higher power. The bullet struck the man in the thigh, but he still managed to drag the corpse inside.

*Well, you sure paid dearly for that crappy little weapon,* he thought.

----

Guzman was not a doctor, not even a Physician's Assistant, but the common protocol was that medics assigned to a line platoon were inevitably called "Doc." Doc Guzman was an experienced medic who had never seen combat until that day. No amount of training could have prepared him for this. As he led a nearly catatonic Haubert to the newly established Casualty Collection Point, he knew that the NCO was edging into shock. Guzman himself had been so frightened by his ride in the unarmored Humvee that he would be surprised if his underwear was unstained. His hands were still shaking. He sat Haubert down in the corner and tried to calm his own nerves. His knowledge and skills would be desperately needed very soon, he feared, and he had to get a grip on himself.

Then Wild and Riddell brought in the limp form of Chen with small, shuffling steps as they labored under his weight. They laid him down slowly, as though not to hurt him, and then Wild ran out toward the stairs. Riddell looked at Guzman, and said, "What can we do?"

Guzman took a deep breath, and, just like that, felt the shakes depart him. "Help me get his gear off."

Doc held the man in an upright position while Riddell pulled the ballistic vest off of him. Guzman saw immediately that Chen's entire right side was drenched with blood and the sick, coppery odor of it washed over him. Working quickly, he opened Chen's shirt and felt the man's neck for a pulse. Nothing. He wasn't breathing and his skin was cool to the touch. Doc could see a small hole between Chen's fourth and fifth rib, and he knew that he could do nothing for him. Guzman began to treat him anyway, not with any hope, but rather to give himself something to do that he understood in this madness. He removed a J-tube from his medic bag and started to insert it. When he opened the man's mouth, more blood issued forth. Doc reached in with two fingers and swept the air way clear. He inserted the J-tube, wishing that he had a suction apparatus with him to clear his lungs.

"Riddell, we're starting CPR. Give him three short breaths in cycles of two when I tell you. Begin now."

Riddell bent to the task. He puffed three times, paused, turned his head to watch the chest rise as he had been taught, and then repeated. The chest did not rise and, Guzman knew that was because no air was making it to the lungs. The airway was clogged with blood and/or the lungs were surrounded with fluid by now that was squeezing them like a huge fist. Guzman placed one palm on top of the other, laced his fingers together and with his arms locked pressed firmly down and up on Chen's sternum once, twice, three times. Pause. Riddell gave three more breaths then three more. More blood oozed from Chen's mouth. His chest did not rise.

"It's not working!" gasped Riddell. "I can't get any air in him."

"He's gone," said Guzman. "He's dead. There's nothing we can do. I don't have the right equipment to help him." Guzman stood shakily, looking down at the body.

"You're not going to give up," growled Riddell. "We've got to help him."

"It's over. He's dead." *We're not God*, he thought. *We're not gods.*

Wild was descending into the courtyard to join a newly erupting battle in the alley when he caught a glimpse into the kitchen of a Soldier bent over the body of Chen. It was Riddell. The battle outside forgotten, Wild was drawn almost against his will toward the CCP. As he approached he saw that Riddell was attempting CPR. He rose from giving rescue breaths and began to beat wildly upon the fallen Soldier's chest. Riddell's fists landed with a sickening thud on the warrior's sternum.

----

Wild stood in the doorway, wishing that he would stop so that he didn't have to hear that awful sound. Doc Guzman was standing opposite Riddell, his medic bag open, arms hanging at his side like the limp banners of a defeated army. Haubert sat in a corner with his back to them, rocking. Wild looked up and locked eyes with Guzman, whom he had never gotten along with very well. Why was he just standing there? Why didn't he help Riddell? Why was he giving up on Chen? Wild's heart filled with rage and disgust. He spun on his heels and went to look for something to kill.

Wild joined his friend Denney above the CCP. Whereas Denney had to stoop to support his firing arm, Wild was too short to see over the wall. He pulled up a wooden crate and stood on it to get a better view. Denney, he noticed, was shaking badly. He was still scanning, looking for a target to shoot, obviously rattled. Wild was not firing on all eight cylinders, either. He couldn't remember how he had come to be standing on a box on top of this roof. Everything seemed fuzzy to him, like he had just awakened from a bad dream to a worse reality. Suddenly, he felt a strong urge.

"Denney?"

"Yeah?"

"I've gotta piss!"

Denney looked at him and smiled. His eyes never lost their glint of terror, which made the smile haunted and tragic. "Yeah, me too."

Without another word they both unbuttoned and released their bladders on the wall in front of them. The rush of their first combat pee was glorious. That wonderful sense of golden, full-bladder-first-thing-in-the-morning urinal release, combined with the euphoria of a pre-death adrenaline rush—the makings of Olympic-caliber urination. They began and finished as one, then resumed their post, looking for anyone stupid enough to cross their sights. Wild couldn't help but wonder, though, if that phenomenal piss hadn't been their version of a blindfold and final cigarette.

----

"We got somebody peeking their head around the corner!" yelled Coleman.

Aguero whirled around in time to see the silhouette of a small man's head appear and then pull back. A second later, a figure sprang full into the mouth of the alley, legs spread, assault rifle aimed from the hip, and fired his weapon in a short burst, raking it from side to side. He disappeared just as quickly behind a flurry of returned fire that kicked up dust and chunks of brick. The head appeared again, and this time Coleman fired immediately but without hitting his target. The little bastard was slick. Then two small figures popped into view, firing AK-47s. Aguero heard bullets whiz by as he ran to the left and stood beside Perry to add his fire to theirs. When their volley had ended, only one child—for so his size would indicate—jumped back out to fire as if this were a game for which he was waiting his turn. Aguero had anticipated it and dropped the kid with a single shot. The child in the black karate suit fell straight down as if he were a puppet and someone had just cut his strings. The L-T watched, completely engrossed as a small hand appeared and grabbed the dead kid's leg. With apparent difficulty, the young child was pulled out of view by his playmate.

----

I crouched in the turret, .50 cal at the ready and scared to death. Someone tapped my leg. I ducked my head inside the vehicle and saw Sala'am's young face staring at me. I wondered if I looked as scared as he did.

"Mr. Mathias, I have no weapon. Can I please use yours?"

"Absolutely," I said without hesitation. "It's in the floorboard there." It never occurred to me that the translator could take that weapon and turn on us. His fate was connected to ours. He would live or die as we did, so why not let him fight with us?

And he did. He grabbed my weapon, opened his door for cover, and stood with me against the enemy. I glanced down at him and realized that I was having my first taste of war fighting alongside a man who, in Arabic, was calling himself "Peace." I had to chuckle at the irony.

Time for some truth in advertising here. I would like to say that I conducted myself as fearlessly as an Arnold Schwarzenegger action hero with his frontal lobe removed. My grade school daydreams always involved me strutting through 1,000 bullets and a forest of arrows without flinching, winning through impossible odds to save a fair damsel. When I get my time machine invented—patent pending—I swear I'm going to go back to that Arkansas playground in the early '80s to kick my own ass for getting me into this mess.

The only resemblance my current situation had to that old daydream was the 1,000 bullets part. When everyone opened fire behind me, I utterly failed to utter anything remotely swashbuckling. What came out of my throat more closely resembled a teenage girl gargling her surprised shriek after spying a rat. My heart hammered in my chest as I tried to compose myself. Just as I almost had it together, there was another burst of gunfire from my rear. I yelled, most unmanfully. A single gunshot this time. I yelped. God, this was killing my macho self-image.

----

### SO Note by Karimkhani, Valeh @05 JUN 2010

*Chief complaint: SM presents for medication eval after his intake. He describes being unable to concentrate and this is effecting his work. He is clearly uncomfortable in the office with his back to the door and he is fidgety. He describes that at home his being on edge is affecting his marriage. He feels ok here, because "looking out for snipers and being alert isn't weird." He his hypervigilant, anxious, has nightmares, near panic, intrusive thoughts. He has tried Wellbutrin in past but I am thinking an SSRI will better serve this SM.*

**Assessment: 1. ANXIETY DISORDER NOS**
**COMMENTS: CLASSIC SIGNS OF PTSD. R/O PTSD**
**AS HIS PRIMARY DX**

----

Aguero, satisfied for now that we weren't in danger of being overrun, returned to his post between the vehicles. As he took a moment to calm his nerves and consider options, Doc Guzman approached him from the shadow of the courtyard gate.

"Sir, there's nothing I could do."

The P-L eyed Guzman uncertainly. "What do you mean?"

"Chen's dead."

Aguero let out a single, vehement expletive. "Who else is injured?"

"Just Haubert that I know of. He got shot in the finger. Took some shrapnel to the face."

"What about you?"

Doc looked at him quizzically, uncomprehending.

"What happened to your face? It's all cut up."

Guzman put a hand to his cheek and was surprised to see a little blood. "Huh." Without saying anything more profound, the Doc walked back inside.

Lieutenant Aguero looked around him to see how everyone was doing. The confirmation that Chen was dead rocked him to his core, threatened to push him over the brink from pissed into the land of totally insane. Davis and Perry were helping Coleman defend the east. Bellamy and Sala'am were assisting Fisk to the west, which was still quiet except for a roaring crowd, now a little closer than it had been before. Wild stood by Sala'am for a moment, grew bored, then moved to the other side. Sala'am looked small and somewhat naked compared to his heavily armed and armored warriors. Well, if the scrappy little man was going to act like a soldier, Aguero was going to make sure he looked like one, too.

"Sala'am! Come here!" The thin Iraqi looked back over his shoulder and then trotted up to the L-T. Aguero motioned for him to follow and led him into the court. Aguero, with his heightened sense of awareness, immediately saw Hayhurst and Taylor on the roof across the courtyard. He took in each doorway and window. Riddell and Denney defended from a rooftop to his immediate right. In the room underneath them, he spied Doc Guzman and then Chen's body. Without slowing, he burst into the room and swept the ground with his eyes. He bent down and picked up Chen's helmet and armor.

He rushed over and handed them to Sala'am, saying, "Here, wear this."

"OK." Sala'am saw the blood covering the inside of the vest but did not mind. He quickly donned everything. Aguero helped the man correctly fasten the straps to make the gear as comfortable as possible. Chen's vest hung loosely on the translator's skinny frame, and the helmet sat askew on top of his head. The total effect would not soon inspire fear in the enemy but would keep the brave man a little safer.

Aguero knew that there would likely be a counterattack, so he began to prepare his men to take the fight to the enemy. He assessed the situation and took mental note of who was still in the fight. Their casualties had been miraculously light. Riddell was using his driver's door for cover with Sala'am on the other side and Fisk manning the gun. Swope was maintaining contact with higher while Bellamy, Wild, and Coleman shot everything that was stupid enough to step into view. The L-T glanced up again at the soldiers providing security from the rooftops. Even from his vantage point on terra firma he could tell that there was no way that they were covering a 360 degree perimeter. There were too many buildings in their line of sight. The next building to the east, however, was much taller.

"Rob!" Aguero called. The NCO's head appeared immediately from the second story roof. "Come down here. I got a mission for ya."

The L-T pulled Robinson, Bourquin, and Rogers into the alley. He pointed out the black door on the front of the four-story building and said, "Get me on top of that roof."

Without another word, the soldiers stacked up on the wall behind Rogers. He put a round from the shotgun into the lock, but the door wouldn't budge. He cursed and fired a second slug into the door which finally decided that it had had enough and seemed to open on its own. Rogers kicked it wide and they charged the roof.

----

"Sir," Swope called to his P-L. "What's the status on our casualties?"

Aguero trotted across the alley and told him, "Chen's dead. Haubert's walking wounded. That's all."

Swope couldn't believe his ears. Had they really driven two combat convertibles through a literal hail of bullets and sustained only two casualties? He remembered rounds striking his vehicle with the frequency of rain drops. How was it possible that no one else had been killed? He called Lancer Mike and reported the latest casualty report and requested a location on the QRF. Lancer Mike said that their front line trace was approximately Silver and Aeros. Home Depot as we called it. Good. This hell would be over soon.

----

The roads traveling north to south were labeled—in order from FOB War Eagle—Aeros, Alpha, Bravo, Charlie, Delta, Echo, Fox and Grizzlies. Silver, the northern boundary of Sadr City, was completely free of obstruction and yielded no portent that evil was afoot. Specialist Rafael Arteaga, known as Puppet in the streets of L.A., huddled with his brothers in the back of the LMTV. They gripped their weapons tight, eyes scanning for threats. In the distance rang the constant din of battle.

AK-47s fired from nowhere and everywhere. Even in the light of day, Puppet had trouble discerning a target. The Rules of Engagement lay like lead on his trigger finger, aware the consequences should he decide to fire blindly into a city of 2.5 million people—massive loss of innocent life and an extended stay in Leavenworth prison.

The initial panic that can freeze a man the first time he's shot came and went. Everyone began to fire, and the rescue force kept rolling. Arteaga noted small groups of people in the narrow alleys, a group of five or three then five more, all firing at them from a range of less than 50 meters. He kept his Squad Automatic Weapon or SAW talking, but was never sure if he had hit his mark. They were going too fast. Bullets pinged off of the armored cab as Ski attempted to suppress the enemy with a weapon that jammed again and again.

Arteaga saw a man pop up from the roof of a two story building, flames flashing from his rifle. Rafael raised his point of aim and squeezed the trigger. A fusillade of bullets put holes into the roof's low wall then climbed up and punched the insurgent in the chest.

The convoy reached Delta, still under heavy contact, and turned left. As soon as they hit the road, the attack stopped cold. Everyone blinked in surprise with the echoes of gunfire still in their ears. What the - ?

----

Hunter followed the Commander's Humvee closely through a slalom course of jagged scrap metal and piles of rock. The constant sound, like a gravel storm of bullets hitting the cab, had left everyone on edge. Before they reached the second intersection, the Bradley leading them stopped. Then he heard that they were to turn the vehicles around—and go back the way they came! Captain Denomy was telling them that Delta was blocked further south and that they would have to find a bypass. Rather than chance the unknown further west, or risk getting stuck in a smaller side street, they would have to go back to Aeros and try Route Copper further to the south.

As the vehicles began to make three-point turns to point north again, everyone in the back of the LMTV began a philosophical debate. The "f" word was commonly combined with the words "what," "are," "we," and "doing." There was no radio in the LMTV, so the reasons for heading back into the ambush they had successfully broken were lost on Hunter. All he could do was pray and drive.

----

"What's our ETA on the QRF?" Swope asked his higher command while trying to mask his anxiousness. He hunched over with a finger in his other ear, listening carefully to the response as his gunner continued to engage. "Say again all after 'ambush,' over!"

Swope sat upright, staring ahead into nothing as his thoughts raced. He acknowledged receipt of the transmission and set the mike down. *Bad. This is bad. We're in a damn city-wide ambush that we just happened to be lucky enough to set off. We're it, good God A'mighty. We're all going to die out here.* As soon as the thought rose to his head, he squashed it.

"What's wrong?" asked Aguero. They had been partners in leading the Platoon for months now, long enough for the L-T to know when the Platoon Daddy was troubled. "What's up with the QRF?"

Swope said, "QRF just got ambushed on Bravo, man. It's going to be a while. We're in for a long night."

The Lieutenant again displayed a complete lack of originality at finding words that rhyme with "duck."

Swope started laughing.

----

Coleman watched as a large mob gathered directly across Delta from him. Men, women, and children amassed quickly, shouting and pumping their fists in the air and waving flags of various colors. He watched as the crowd, children first with women following after, approached the alley at a deliberate pace. Coleman saw no weapons being brandished and no shots were fired from the group, but they obviously meant to overwhelm them by sheer weight of numbers.

"Holy shit. They're stupid," Coleman shouted. The Iraqis weren't charging, weren't madly dashing forward, just walking. Now he could see some rifles being raised skyward along with a few swords.

----

As I watched the noisy mob approach, an SUV roared into the alley from the right side of the near intersection. It turned away from us and lurched to a stop maybe 50 meters farther up the street. It backed up to a gate like the one by which we were parked. The vehicle wasn't an overt threat yet, but I trained the .50 cal on it in case that changed. The driver and passenger jumped out quickly and ran to the door. The driver opened up the rear hatch while the passenger took something from a man inside the doorway. They were loading small bundles of something into the bed of the vehicle. I didn't know what I was seeing. Maybe they were preparing some sort of deadly surprise for us. They weren't facing down a cornered American infantry platoon to load up their groceries. I hesitated, locked in an internal debate: to shoot or not to shoot, that is the question.

The crowd was close now, less than 50 meters away. I saw rifles, but no one was shooting. Why weren't they shooting? They meant to either take us alive or rip us limb from limb with their bare hands. This was before the days of the internet when beheadings became commonplace. Perhaps they meant to set our severed heads on pikes at the outskirts of their fair city as a warning to infidels who come to their country offering freedom of religion and freedom of thought. Even at their slow, methodical pace they would be on us in a few seconds. God, this was a nightmare.

----

Aguero, his mind aghast at what was coming, stared in disbelief at the approaching crowd coming from Delta. He turned toward the west side and saw that the mob at that end was also approaching them at the same deliberate pace, now about 75 meters away. With the sudden realization that the crowds were coordinating their movement, his paralysis broke. He yelled, "Shoot. Just shoot them."

----

My mind went truly and deeply blank. I honestly don't remember what happened. Martha Raddatz wrote a book about this very battle called *The Long Road Home* back in 2006. I read it, curious to see what she had to say. When I at last came to this part of the book, my heart racing as if I were still there, I became enraged at the horrendous lies she told. What crowd? What slaughter? I wasn't there! I would never do that!

The mind is perhaps God's finest invention. It has a mechanism that acts like a breaker switch in an electric panel. When you come dangerously close to overload, it can shut down the parts that threaten well-being. This switch-off happened with my memory. The whole episode, beginning with the appearance of the SUV until the deed was done, had been missing from the otherwise crystal-clear recollection I have of the battle. Missing, until I really began to poke and prod and try to recall. With great effort, I have been able to remember as far as changing magazines.

I have been poking my brain with a metaphorical stick, replaying events before and after in an attempt to jumpstart the old noodle. I saved this part for last, hoping that it would come, praying that it wouldn't. I know that God will not allow you to be tested beyond what you're able to endure, so that must mean that I'm not ready.

I remember gunpowder. It's actually cordite, but it's the smell associated with gunpowder. What is that alluring fragrance you're wearing, Specialist? Why, it's Gunpowder 5.56, all the rage with ignorant buffoons marching to their doom. The way that cordite smells when it bakes into the dully gleaming brass casing conjures the memory of the first life I ever took. I was eight years old in southern Arkansas. My father had raised me to respect the rifle that would one day be my inheritance. We are in a small wooded area on the back side of my pawpaw's pasture. It's autumn and the leaves are off of the trees. I have had a gun in my hand since I was five years old, dad always close by. He's close now, watching me as I point the rifle toward my target. The rifle, a bolt action .22, is heavy and my little arms shake with the effort. Dad is so close that I can smell the Old Spice aftershave he wears, a smell I often associate with death. I aim as he has taught me, wanting with all my heart to please him. I squeeze the trigger (you must never pull it) and wince at the sharp report, and there's that smell (gunpowder) that's darkly exciting. My target falls; my aim was true or lucky. I cheer, delighted, and run to where the squirrel has fallen to the earth. It doesn't move but stares back at me with eyes of glass. I see what I have done and tremble, confused. The squirrel's mouth is open, teeth stained red, and from its mouth issues

Blood.

I remember the smell of blood mixed with gunpowder. The smell often described as having a coppery quality. I sometimes use that adjective myself, though not because I'm sure that I agree, but because it seems a convention. A convenient way to describe in a word the horrible, urgent, and necessary odor of a substance most primal. Blood always smells like blood to me. I only experience the smell as memory, as if some sort of synesthesia, or swapping of senses. I breathe in the smell from the corpses that shadows them like the memory of the squirrel looking up at me. The smell coats the back of my tongue with a miserable sweetness.

Blood and gunpowder is what I remember. Death.

I'm told that the mob only made it about ten meters farther after we opened fire. The L-T estimated that we killed about 40 people before they thought better of it and retreated. They left, pulling their dead and dying behind them. At least the ones without weapons did.

Here's what happened as best as I can remember:

I saw the children approaching, the women. Madly tumbling toward us like street urchins in a maniacal Macy's Parade. The Dia de los Muertos march as interpreted by angry Iraqis who refused to be occupied like the Palestinians. I leveled the huge gun at the crowd and pressed the trigger with both thumbs.

Click.

Nothing happened. Wild and Bellamy opened up on my left. Lieutenant Aguero joined Sala'am on my right as they, too, began firing. My heart skipped a beat as I grabbed the charging handle with my right hand and hauled back on it. Chu-chink. A live round dropped out of the bottom as another took its place in the chamber. I squeezed the trigger again only to be greeted with the sound of nothing happening. Shit, the timing or head space had been thrown off. Probably as we had been bouncing madly through the gauntlet of trash and metal to get back to our platoon, and I had given my weapon to Sala'am. Wait, where's Chen's? I twisted around and saw Chen's M203—a combination rifle and grenade launcher—hanging by its strap from the rear turret shield. I plucked it off and placed the barrel on top of the turret shield to stabilize my aim. I stared down the M68 optic sight at a young boy who had no weapon.

Bullets were ripping through the crowd, dropping people by the handful. This wasn't war. This was a damn slaughter. Up until now I had killed children with guns, children intent on rubbing me out as if they were doing no more than playing laser tag or Play Station. Most of this crowd had no weapons except their deadly resolve to come down the alley and snatch us up. Now they were dying for making the assumption that we were too weak, too noble in that foolish Marquis of Queensbury fashion, to defend ourselves. Well, we had all made our choice. We were going to fight so we could live. And damn them all for testing our resolve.

They were so close that I didn't need to aim. Not for this. I left the red laser dot on a man's chest, dropped my head, and began to pull the trigger. I made small, groaning noises, drowned by the roar of our weapons, as I pulled the trigger twice a second until the bolt locked to rear letting me know that the magazine was empty. Now I looked up at the carnage as my hands went through the autonomous action of reloading. Fifteen seconds of bloody work and they were still coming. Broken and bloody bodies piled in the street as hundreds of the insane steadily plunged forward.

----

SO note by Aycock, Lisa @ 24 June 2014

### Chief Complaint: concentration

*Patient reported minimal progress. Pt did not automatically pull down shades upon entering provider's office. Pt stated he made a conscious effort not to pull the shades. Pt reports he continues to be successful not consuming alcohol. Pt disclosed he has 2 primary stuck points. Pt engaged in discussion regarding being on patrol & being ambushed. Pt stated the "gunner" in his vehicle was killed & he was required to take over his position. Pt stated his stuck point is the enemy placed women & children in front of themselves & marched toward pt and his battle buddies. Pt reported they were forced to shoot & the result was that a significant amount of women & children were killed. Pt disclosed the anger he cont's to deal with. Pt able to discuss/process his feelings/emotions. Discusses pt's guilt; discussed pt's ability to forgive himself.*

### Assessment: Anxiety Disorder NOS

----

When the mob began to retreat, our weapons fell silent. Aguero spared a glance heavenward as if seeking guidance or demanding an apology. Through a haze of gun smoke he glimpsed a small bird gliding above the fray, unconcerned with the scene below. He felt a surreal wave wash over him, leaving him adrift in the notion that he was in some sort of war movie and not actually trapped behind enemy lines. The bird floated over the pile of bodies and out of sight behind a building where someone's brightly colored laundry fluttered in the breeze. The sudden silence gave a fleeting sense of peace that did not exist.

----

Even as we repelled the macabre parade, the QRF was attempting to find a bypass around the obstacles meant to keep us in the ambush kill box. Route Silver had been a clear shot going out. It was full of pot holes, though that was normal. Now, just five minutes after having turned on to Delta, the landscape had completely changed. The enemy had used the scant few minutes that it had taken for the cumbersome LMTV to turn around to great advantage. Route Silver was now littered with impromptu barricades and obstacles. Scrap metal, steel I-beams, vehicle parts of every type, and piles of concrete blocks had been strewn about to fix the infidels in place long enough to deliver a killing blow.

Hunter managed to dodge the myriad of obstacles laid out for them so hastily on Silver. He was still able to see, even though the sun was starting to sink below the line of buildings to the west. They were taking fire from everywhere now, mostly to the south, but also from across the canal that was the northern border of Sadr City. Just shy of Aeros, they turned right on Alpha. Contact was not heavy to the east, which was mostly open field, but gunfire was in abundance from the buildings and alleys to their west. On their first jaunt down Silver, only the soldiers sitting on the left side had been busy. Now, since they were going the other way, the right side had their turn at all the fun and frolic. By the time they had traveled almost a mile and turned on to Copper, every one of them had learned what it meant to take another man's life.

Specialist Jermaine Tyrell was no exception. Movement drew his eyes to a balcony. He saw a little kid, maybe 12 years old, wearing a blue shirt and wielding an AK-47. Fire flashed from the muzzle as the boy sprayed the weapon from side to side. He was surrounded by older men and younger children who were cheering him on as though he had just smashed a slow pitch and was rounding third base toward home. Tyrell had no time to contemplate this odd behavior before he unloaded the last of his 5.56 mm belt into the kid. He saw the kid fall and was glad that he didn't have time to feel bad about it. One of the bullets struck an old man dressed in a white *didashi*. With an almost superhuman clarity of vision he could see the individual black and white checkers of the man's headdress and the blooming red flower on the man's chest. He didn't want to think about it. The young kids cheering, the old men clapping their hands. The world no longer made sense.

----

Having failed to overwhelm our defenses with the patented Iranian tactic of sending weaponless women and children ahead of the courageous men, the insurgents wasted no time. They gave the kids weapons and sent them back after us. Coleman saw them first.

"Hey, guys," he called. "We got more peekers, left side."

At the northern corner, Coleman saw a small head just barely reveal itself and then disappear. A second later a small figure emerged, only half exposing himself this time, and fired a short burst before vanishing. Instead of following the last guy's tactic of popping out after the infidels had fired, this kid learned from his dead playmate's mistakes. He alternated popping out in full profile with just sticking his rifle around the corner and squeezing off a few blind shots. At least Coleman thought it was the same guy. Maybe there were two and one was more timid than the other. Whatever, Coleman thought, doesn't matter. What did matter was that he was completely irritated that he kept missing the little bastard. He had been using the .50 cal when the angry mob had tried, quite unsuccessfully, to storm their position. He was using it now in the hope that the rounds would penetrate through the corner and take out the stupid SOB.

After a few failed attempts, Davis said, "Coleman, hold up. Let him go; I've got him." Davis was on Coleman's right side with the

240B. To Coleman's amusement, Davis brought the 24-pound machine gun up to his shoulder like a hunting rifle and waited. Coleman was impressed that he could keep the heavy gun up like that without his arms shaking. Davis only had to wait a few seconds before the little jihadist popped into view again. He squeezed off a burst that threw the kid backward before he could fire the AK.

Another barrel poked around the north-side corner and fired blindly. *Crap,* thought Coleman as a bullet zinged off of his turret shield. *They're just as likely to hit us without looking. These guys really suck.* He felt like laughing, but he still didn't relish the thought of being offed by some little turd that wasn't even shaving yet. The dark humor seemed to help, though. The laughter was building up inside him, more madness than frivolity, but it felt good. Hell, bring it on, why not? Everyone's gotta die, and this was kind of fun. He sent another burst of half-inch diameter bullets after his would-be killer. *Choke on it.*

----

I heard everyone around Red 4 begin to fire in rapid succession. An angry bullet went by my ear close enough to make me swat the air as if to be rid of a winged pest. I was so scared at that moment that every time a bullet was fired I uttered a single, staccato profanity like a man with Tourette Syndrome singing along to bad karaoke. I couldn't stop myself from saying, *Shit. Shit. Shit. Shit.*

I saw a sneaky little face appear from the southern corner of the intersection in front of me. I tucked the rifle into my shoulder and yelled, "I've got a peeker on the left, fifty meters." Two small heads peeked out next, and I held my fire. I saw no weapons yet, and after what I had just been forced to do, felt no desire to shoot a non-combatant. Both black-clad children jumped defiantly into the alley and began to spray our area with 7.62mm contempt. I hesitated as a couple of lucky rounds hit my turret shield. Wild and Bellamy returned fire, and I joined them a split second later. The kids were quick, though, melting back out of sight.

----

### SO note by Rodgers, Renee @ 16 April 2014
### Chief complaint: periods of anxiety

*SM reports chronic feelings of anger. SM states he is hyper-alert much of the time. He notes increased heart rate; signs of paranoia when anxious. Problems with concentration. SM states he struggles to stay focused, even with simple tasks. Poor sleep quality: delayed onset, disruption, nightmares. SM uses ETOH to cope at times. Drinking 2-3 times a week, up to 5-6 drinks. SM shares how the reunion and wedding service for he and his spouse went at FT Hood over the past weekend. SM says both events were meaningful to him. Provider and he also discuss post combat stress related to killing children and adolescents in combat. SM shares how impact of this trauma effects his feelings about having kids now. SM referred to Acute Stress Reaction Group.*

### Assessment: Anxiety Disorder NOS: R/O PTSD; R/O Panic Disorder

----

Eric Bourquin appeared at Coleman's left, drawn by the gunfire. "Hey. You want any HE put somewhere?" The young NCO held up his M203 grenade launcher for emphasis. HE stands for High Explosives and Bourquin was just itching to make something highly explode.

"Hell, yeah," Coleman cried. "I've been trying to get these little bastards on the left side at the corner. Put one right at the end of the alley."

"All right, I've got you." Bourquin's heart thrilled with excitement as he prepared to fire his first live 40mm grenade in combat. Yes. This was going to be sweet. An imaginary MP3 player in his head cued up a slammin' track from Shai'Halud, one of his favorite emo metal bands. He plucked a blue-tipped grenade from a pouch on his vest. The grenade launcher, attached to the bottom of his rifle, was little more than a black tube with its own firing mechanism. With his left hand he thumbed the release lever and pushed the tube open. He slid the bullet-shaped grenade all the way into the barrel of the launcher and then pulled it shut. The launcher sealed with a satisfying click as the trigger armed. He tucked the 203 under his arm and put the building's corner in the quadrant sight attached to the weapon's side. It had a ferocious kick that would break your nose if you tried to fire it like a regular rifle, which made aiming at and actually hitting your target awkward and difficult. Bourquin pulled the trigger and saw the grenade slam into a white car in front of them. The hood flew open; windows shattered.

Coleman roared with laughter. "What the hell are you shooting at?"

"It broke," Bourquin said with disgust. Coleman glanced over and saw that he was holding his rifle in one hand and the grenade launcher in the other. The weapon had come apart in two pieces.

Coleman laughed harder, tears squirting from his eyes, "Oh, my God, you have got to be kidding me. Why did you break it?"

"Shut up," muttered Bourquin, who was thoroughly disappointed. "Made by the lowest damn bidder." Coleman couldn't stop laughing, even as the little peeker fired at them again.

----

Bellamy, Wild and Sala'am had opened the doors of the Humvee and used them for cover like large, armored wings. Wild, on my right, rested the barrel of his rifle on top of the door to assist his aim.

Sala'am was by his side, kneeling in the dusty road. The pair of murderous children lunged out again and raked their rifles left to right. Sala'am felt a small, hot sting as a bullet grazed his leg. He said nothing about it, but answered their fire with a burst of his own. We all joined him, our accurate fire sending chips of brick flying in all directions. The kids didn't reappear as I waited tensely, the red dot of my scope anticipating their return.

----

Bellamy heard the guys behind him continue to fire and dashed over to see if they needed help. He regretted now giving up the 240 to Rob because he couldn't use Rob's scope. Something had happened to the M68; an oily film covered the lens that rendered it opaque. It was like looking through a glass of milk. He tried to wipe it off with no luck. He was literally shooting from the hip. He saw that Coleman was rocking the .50 cal, Davis was shooting his 240B like a squirrel rifle, and Bourquin was walking toward him with his M203 in two pieces and a scowl on his face.

"Don't ask," he said, and walked into the courtyard shaking his head.

Bellamy saw Lieutenant Aguero's face frozen in a hideous smile. He walked slowly past Swope as he sat talking on the radio, rifle hanging limply from its strap. At the rear of the Humvee he paused, hands on hips. Bellamy saw the barrel of an assault rifle edge around the north corner. He ducked instinctively as flames flashed from the muzzle. Small, white puffs of dust exploded first from the south wall, then north, then south again as the slugs ricocheted toward them. Aguero never moved, never flinched. He extended both arms forward, as if to make a conciliatory *let's hug* gesture, then extended both middle fingers skyward. The L-T took about five steps forward, shouting profanity with such vehemence that Bellamy had no trouble hearing him over the roar of the Ma Deuce. The Lieutenant continued to hurl insults at the mothers of his enemy, daring them to take their best shot in language guaranteed to melt their faces off if they had courage to show them.

"Sir," Bellamy shouted, "What are you doing? Get back here." The dismayed NCO ran forward to stand beside his leader, intent on making him seek cover, when he saw movement on the other side of Delta. A man with a rifle scurried from a pile of broken concrete to a junked out car. Bellamy brought the rifle up to his waist, feeling ridiculously like an action hero cliché, and lined up a shot. Without a sight he had no hope of hitting the man, but wanted to try and keep his head down while they pulled back a little. Bellamy was surprised and delighted when the unlucky insurgent dropped after three shots. *That makes ten.* Bellamy put a hand on the L-T's shoulder, who was still breathing fiery vows to the enemy. "Come on, Sir. Let's find some cover." Aguero followed, turning his back to Delta with deliberate scorn.

----

Lieutenant Aguero stood between the two Humvees now, facing to the east, trying to calm himself down. He had never known such blinding rage in his life, but he knew he had to master himself in order to give his platoon a fighting chance at survival.

As he stood taking deep, calming breaths, something like a small rock struck him on top of the kevlar. He caught a peripheral glimpse of a dark sphere bounce against the wall and then roll behind him. It was a smooth Russian grenade. He wanted to keep watching it, fascinated by this object from the heavens, this escapee from a war-movie prop closet. The explosion propelled Lieutenant Aguero forward on to the hood of Red 4. The world was at first nothing but noise and light, then all sound abruptly ceased. He slid to the ground and wondered if he had just been killed.

His ears rang and he couldn't move his right arm and leg. *Oh, this is not good.* Aguero stood up and began to evaluate himself to make sure he still had all his parts intact. He felt his head. *Spinning, but still attached, good.* He held up both hands in front of his eyes and shook them. *Can't feel the right. Not good. Can't feel my leg or my ear. Also not good. Well, they're still there, at least. Just not working that well.*

His hearing began to come back. Davis was saying something to him. What was it? He squinted, concentrating intently. "- see the Doc."

Aguero shook his head. "I'm fine."

Davis shrugged and walked toward the black door to the four story building.

Bellamy, who had caught some of the blast without injury, said, "Sir, you're bleeding. Let the medic take a look at that."

Aguero shooed him off with a dismissive, impatient wave, "I'm fine, I'm fine, I'm fine." He leaned against Swope's Humvee and tried to collect his senses.

----

Bourquin tried in vain to put his broken weapon back together. The rifle component was fine and the grenade launcher component was also intact; they had simply separated. Perhaps it was missing a nut or something. Inspiration struck him. Chen also had an M203. He would be too busy using the .50 cal to need a grenade launcher. He would go ask if he could switch weapons with him. The rifle was still good if Chen needed something smaller.

He trotted out to the alley and was a little puzzled to see the L-T staggering around. The P-L's trousers looked as if they were stained with chocolate milk. What happened to him? Bourquin looked up and opened his mouth to get Chen's attention. He paused, confused, when he caught the profile of the gunner. Chen wasn't a long-nosed Caucasian with glasses.

"Fisk. Where's Chen?"

- - - -

I turned to Bourquin, my heart heavy. "Chen is dead."

Bourquin was young, and in that moment he looked like a child. His lower lip quivered, his blue eyes filled with either fear or sorrow or both. "No," his voice was small. Then anger flooded his face and he shouted at me, "NO, HE'S NOT!"

"I'm sorry," I said quietly and turned my attention back down the alley.

- - - -

Bourquin whirled and saw Wild emerging from the gate. "Wild, where's Chen?" Bourquin's voice was deep, loud and thick with emotion.

"He's dead, Sergeant."

"No. No, he's not. He's not dead." The young NCO spat the words as if Wild had just questioned his mother's virtue.

"Believe me, Sergeant. He's dead. There's nothing we can do. He's dead."

An eerie change came over the heavily tattooed young man as if he had flipped the switch in his brain that controls sorrow. "OK," Bourquin said calmly. "Help pull security."

- - - -

Bourquin was silent beside me for a moment longer. "Hey, why don't you let me use your 203? You've got the .50 cal and my grenade launcher came apart."

"The deuce is down," I replied. "I think the timing got thrown off when we plowed through the debris, and I don't know where Eddie put the tool to fix it. I gave Sala'am my rifle."

"Well, dude, find it," he said. "Look around in the vehicle while I cover you."

I dropped down, glad to give my burning legs a break. Several frantic minutes of scrambling among the ammo cans turned up nothing. "No dice," I said as I resumed my post.

Bourquin told Wild to go search Chen for the tool.

----

As soon as Wild entered the CCP, Guzman spat at him, "Wild, I don't need your help."

*Like you were doing anything anyway.* Wild stopped and regarded him coldly, "I'm not here to freaking help you. I'm here to get his stuff." Wild rifled through the dead man's ammo vest, pulling out some 40mm grenades and all of the magazines. However, the tool was AWOL. He stuffed everything into his cargo pockets and went to relay the bad news.

----

Doc turned his attention to Haubert. The man was in shock but not badly wounded. A bullet had penetrated the windshield and taken off the tip of his ring finger. Flying glass shards imbedded in the man's face caused, he assumed, only superficial injury. Guzman fished through his aid bag and pulled out a "two-by," a two-inch square gauze bandage, and secured it around the missing fingertip with a Band-Aid.

"How are you doing, Sarge?"

Stanley Haubert muttered unintelligibly. His eyes stared into the far distance.

"Think you can still fight?" Doc knew that the man could technically still use a rifle if his trigger finger was OK. He could tell by Stanley's unresponsiveness, however, that the man was out of the fight. Probably for good. He looked up from his patch job and saw Perry in the doorway staring down at Chen's body.

----

Private Perry had the deepest respect for Chen. He saw most NCOs in the infantry as blustering, arrogant a-holes who loved to throw their weight around. Chen had always been gentle and unassuming with Perry. He never pushed the issue of who outranked who which bought instant credibility with the young man. They were often paired together for Charge of Quarters (CQ), a duty that entailed spending a solid 24 hours together manning a desk in the company Area. While they sat together, Chen—with his unique quiet humility— would teach the young private about military issues he thought the young man should know. Or admonish the private when he had been acting foolishly.

Now that gentle voice of wisdom was forever silent. Chen was gone and Perry felt the loss keenly. He couldn't bear to look at the body and his eyes began to burn. The Iraqi man under their protection stirred quietly, shifting his position to relieve discomfort from sitting on the concrete floor. The movement drew Perry's eye. Robinson had asked Perry to come inside and guard the family. Now that he knew that Chen was dead, he was struggling to subvert his base impulses to what he knew was his clear duty. He wanted nothing more than to kill them. Execute them. Make them pay for what they did to Chen. His chest heaved with the effort of suppressing his desire to exact retribution. He had been a preacher's son, a gangsta' thug and a soldier, and now all three personalities were battling for his soul. Forgive the family for a crime that others had committed, assassinate the family for being party to Chen's death, or guard the family because that was the Law of War. A mad drum beat resounded in his brain, near his temple, as the voices of who he had been, who he was now, and what he would become shouted to be heard.

Private Perry looked away from the Iraqis under his protection and relaxed his finger, only now aware that it had been on the trigger.

----

On the roof above them, Riddell and Denney finally had some eager customers looking for lead at bargain-basement prices. Rooftops to the south and west were mostly one or two stories, with a three-story building or two thrown in for flavor. After they had been defending this dismal piece of Iraqi soil for almost 20 minutes, he saw a dozen figures clothed in black karate suits trotting toward them across the rooftops, jumping from one to the next like a platoon of comic-book villains. Denney saw heads popping up closer to them. Riddell went through two magazines in short order as he attempted to halt their progress.

"I got one," cried Denney as one of the attackers fell.

"You'd better shoot faster if you want to keep up with me. I've got three."

----

Denney climbed down the stairs on trembling legs and stopped briefly in the middle of the courtyard to glance in the kitchen at Chen's body, plainly visible. *That's going to be me soon.* But something kept him moving. He couldn't quit, not while his brothers needed him. Not while his family waited for him to come home. He stepped out into the alley to see how he could help.

----

Davis couldn't remember a time when his arms had ever been so tired. He had been using the heavy machine gun as an assault rifle for a half an hour past the point where his body told him he was exhausted. He was not built like a professional wrestler. He didn't power lift or spend much time seeing how much he could bench. He had developed toughness growing up on a farm in the Dakotas. He could chop wood or use a shovel all day long. Now that endurance was being tested. His biceps and forearms burned with the effort of using the big gun in a way that doctrine had never intended. Davis managed to take out a few more unlucky souls who attempted to storm the alleyway.

Davis had the driver's side door of Red 4 open to provide cover as he continued to light up every dumb son-of-a-buck who set foot in their alley. With the door open, he could hear the radio traffic on the speakers when either he or Coleman weren't making a racket. He spoke briefly with the platoon sergeant, noting number of kills, number of personnel they were still attempting to engage, so that Swope had a clear picture of the battle to communicate to higher. When they had been defending the alley for 30 minutes he heard a welcome sound: the thumpa-thumpa of approaching helicopters.

----

Swope heard one of the pilots call to confirm their location. The call sign they used identified them as Kiowas, known also as "Little Birds." Armed with machine guns, Hellfire rockets, and serious attitude, the choppers were as welcome as water to parched lips. However, the Kiowa pilots would not engage the enemy until they knew exactly where the platoon was defending. The lessons of fratricide prevention from the first Desert Storm had been well learned. Three days in sector had not been enough for Swope to learn all of the Route names in the City. He knew the major routes. Delta, of course, Gold, Silver, Aeros, and a few others. He even knew exactly where they were on Route Delta, but didn't know the name of the next street up. Finally, he coaxed a grid coordinate from his large military GPS device and read it off to the pilot. The pilot repeated the grid exactly and was silent for a moment. Swope and Davis looked at each other as the helicopters passed overhead, moving quickly in order to evade a massive volume of small-arms' fire. Over the speakers he heard, "Cannot identify. Cannot identify."

----

Lieutenant Aguero was hobbling around from one vehicle to another. He could definitely feel the pain from the grenade blast settling in deep into his bones. He knew that if he gave into the notion of being wounded, if he sat down and let someone treat him, he would lose momentum and freeze up. He had already lost one soldier, and he would be damned if the enemy thought they were going to take another. So he kept moving, relentlessly, denying his body's strident demand to stop. He looked up as the Kiowa attack helicopters passed over them.

Swope leaned out of the vehicle and said, "Hey, there's birds in the air but they can't locate us. We need to mark our location for them."

Aguero thought quickly. We could use yellow smoke grenades; I think we have some of those. Or- "Listen up," he called to everyone around him. "I need a VS-17 panel, time: now. Who's got one?"

Bellamy called out, "There's one in Swope's vehicle."

The L-T limped over to Red 4. He wasn't feeling much pain, but his body was slowing down. No matter how much he wanted to, he just couldn't move quickly. Coleman told him that the panel was under the rear driver's side seat. A VS-17 panel is a large swath of extremely durable material—something like the lovechild of silk and vinyl—one side of which was subdued olive drab and the other a two-tone hot pink and hunter orange. The express purpose of the cloth was to serve as a marker or beacon for aircraft. They were a part of a vehicle's basic load and usually kept folded up and stuffed away in some dark corner collecting dust.

Aguero removed the seat cover revealing a compartment full of stuff, mostly large heavy tools. The panel, of course, was at the very bottom. Aguero grabbed the corner and yanked on the material, struggling to free it. His right arm was not cooperating. He felt so tired.

"Coleman, a little help."

Coleman bent down and grabbed the material to assist. The two of them began to pull until they were red-faced, frustrated and swearing profusely. They gave a final, herculean heave and the signal cloth came free, unfolding into a cumbersome mass as it did. Aguero gripped it with his right hand and turned to walk away. He dropped the panel from his numb fingers. He indulged, at high volume, his penchant for variations of the f-bomb. He bent down wearily and began to gather the yards of cloth together with his left hand. *Gotta get this up there quick.* He started to run toward the stairwell to the tall over-watch building. *I'm not going very fast. Why can't I go faster?*

He staggered to the doorway and took the stairs three at a time. At least that was what his mind told his legs to do. His body offered the compromise of one stair at a time. His mind kicked it around for a second then made the counter-offer of two steps. The body, having made the down payment of a single flight of stairs, told the mind in no uncertain terms what it could do with its offer and walked away from the bargaining table.

His bold plan to storm up the stairs with the life-saving signal panel met with the crashing reality of only being able to take one step at a time and that with only his right foot. He could only use his left foot as a stabilizer, a prop to keep him vertical against the wall, while the right power-hopped to the next step. Aguero was left standing on the first landing, sweat pouring from his face. A daunting pile of old window-unit air conditioners, chairs, and other junk blocked his path forward. He had absolutely no strength left to climb up and over the mound to get to the roof. *Screw it. This blows.*

"Rob. Sergeant Rob."

A second later the Georgia gentleman's head appeared at the next landing.

"Hey, take this VS-17 panel and lay it out for the choppers." Aguero drew back and threw the panel with all the strength left in him. It failed to travel three feet. *Damn it.* "Never mind." He spied Bourquin in the courtyard. "Hey, Bourquin."

The lanky NCO trotted over quickly. "Put this out where the birds can see it."

"Roger, Sir."

Aguero turned around and limped back down the stairs as quickly as he could. He managed to hobble over to the driver's side of Red 4 and tapped Davis' shoulder. "Take the 240 upstairs and help provide over-watch. We can handle these turds down here with the fifty. When you get up, there make sure they have the man-pack radio set up and give me a radio check."

"Roger, Sir." Davis disappeared up the stairs with a speed the L-T now envied. Aguero assumed the spot Davis had occupied, both doors open to provide cover fore and aft. He looked around to assess their situation. He wanted, needed, to move about more. A leader was supposed to circulate the battlefield tirelessly, keeping the ever-evolving picture of the fight clear in his mind. His leg was betraying him. He could hardly stand now on his stupid numb foot.

----

Bourquin ran into the courtyard with the signal panel. He saw Wild ascending the courtyard steps leading to the lower roof. Yelling to get his attention, Bourquin explained what the L-T needed—what they all needed. Get the panel set out so the Birds could see it and not kill them by mistake. A fine plan, indeed.

Wild ascended to the first rooftop that the platoon had occupied and quickly stretched out the large piece of fabric, colors to the sky. He found pieces of broken brick and cinder block to weigh down the corners. Wild looked over the edge and asked Bourquin, "You think that will do it?"

"You've got a 203, right?"

"Yeah." Wild waved the grenade launcher at him.

"Here, use this. Mine's broke." Bourquin pulled a 40mm smoke grenade from his Load Bearing Vest and threw it up with a gentle underhand pass. Wild caught it dexterously, so thrilled to shoot the M203 in combat for the first time that his hands were shaking. So excited that he didn't think about where he was aiming. He pointed the grenade launcher at a high angle, tucked the weapon under his armpit, and pulled the trigger. The weapon bucked hard and spit the projectile far out of sight.

"Uh…Got another one? That one didn't work."

Bourquin threw him a small olive-drab cylinder. The pull-ring indicated a smoke grenade; the purple top indicated the color of smoke that would emanate from said grenade. Wild grinned. This day just got cooler. He looked down at Denney and Riddell, who were engaging from the CCP rooftop, and called down in a loud voice, "Guys, I'm getting ready to throw a smoke grenade. Don't freak out."

Apparently, with their attention focused on feats of marksmanship, or perhaps because of the rising wind, they heard nothing he said before or after 'grenade.' They both immediately screamed, "Grenade!" and dropped down with their ears covered.

"SMOKE grenade, guys," yelled Wild. "Smoke." He laughed hard as he pulled the pin and rolled the smoke canister next to the signal panel. There was a small pop as the fuse ignited the minuscule charge. Purple smoke began to trickle out of a small hole in the top of the can. The trickle grew to a jet to a plume as purple smoke issued forth as if for a Prince concert.

----

The rooftop OP was about 10 feet wide on the alley side and almost 15 on the side facing Delta. A demi-wall about four feet high made of mud brick was their only protection. Robinson had carefully placed his men so that they were evenly spaced and covered the surrounding neighborhood. They were in the perfect position to rain down devastation on the enemy. All nine of them were busy picking off targets.

Robinson looked over the edge of the roof and saw the panel was laid out and visible on their original OP. A palm tree provided a little bit of shade for the roof, which he had enjoyed earlier, but it probably wouldn't obscure the view from the air. He saw Bourquin toss up a grenade, laughed to himself when Denney and Riddell hit the deck, and nodded approval when the purple smoke began to flow. As he started to turn back to the business of directing his troops, however, he noticed something wrong. A strong wind was gusting now, had been for a few minutes. The smoke, instead of rising to the heavens as sign of their deliverance, was being forced down off of the roof by the atmospheric pressure. Not good.

Robinson strode to the middle of the roof and snatched up the radio. He informed Red 4 that they had deployed the VS-17 panel and a smoke grenade. He asked if the Birds had seen their display of plumage. Stand by. Negative. No ID.

They needed to think of something else, and quick.

----

Both ends of the alley were blocked effectively and were quiet for the moment. Justin Bellamy pulled off the line briefly to say goodbye to his friend and former roommate.

He walked into the CCP and saw Chen's lifeless body lying on the concrete floor. It was him. It was not him. He couldn't have thought of a better way to express it than that. His life force, that insubstantial quality that made Eddie who he was, was missing. Bellamy didn't need to check for a pulse—he could tell. His armor suddenly felt too heavy, too hot. A wave of nausea swept over him. He stumbled out of the doorway and threw up. He began to weep uncontrollably. His vision blurred as he stumbled back into the room that held all that was left of his old friend.

One of their Iraqi family hosts stirred in the corner. Bellamy whirled toward the movement and pointed at them, tears streaming down his face. His outstretched hand balled up into a fist as Bellamy tried to convey in universal sign language the extent to which he held them responsible for the death of his friend. The message was clearly received—the man and woman moved their hands back and forth in front of their face even as they said over and over again shouting, "*La. La. La.*" No. No. No.

Bellamy felt detached from himself, a disembodied spirit, and wondered what his body was going to do next. *They knew,* he thought. *They knew what was going on just like everybody else in the damn city and did nothing to stop it. They're just as guilty for Chen's death as the guy that pulled the trigger.* He felt as if he were teetering on the brink between madness and sanity. Grace and murderous restitution. Good and evil. His hands shook with desire to extract payment from their Arabic hides. The power of life and death was his to command. Tense seconds passed as he weighed their fate. Life. Tick. Death. Tock.

An eternity later he decided. No. He wasn't going to waste his soul on them.

He stood glowering at the family a moment longer, letting the anger and sick hatred wash over him. It filled him like infernal fuel, driving out sadness and fear. Someone was going to pay. At length he spun on his heels and stormed out. Bellamy had mastered his emotions and decided instead to redirect them before he did something that would land him in front of a war crimes tribunal. Someone would pay, though.

Looking left as he returned to the alley, he saw that Fisk and Sala'am were engaging a single target. Let them have it. He looked right and could see that the hunting was much better. Insurgents dressed in black as well as older men in white dresses darted from place to place. Much better. Riddell was on the left and the L-T on the right side of the vehicle. Bellamy took up a spot beside the Lieutenant and began to exact payment.

Bellamy was lethally accurate. One target after another fell, and he began to count each one out loud as they fell. "Eleven. Twelve." The shakes were gone. The fear was gone. He felt cocky beyond measure. Immortal. He felt totally comfortable now in the skin of a legalized killer.

"Worry about the kill count later," growled Lieutenant Aguero. "Just keep killing them."

----

The L-T realized that he needed a cigarette. He decided that a smoke could wait at least until he killed the guy across the street who began firing wildly at them. That target fell to his M4, but another scampered into view, trying to pick up the rifle his comrade had dropped. Geez, were these guys ever going to let him light one up?

Bourquin's young face appeared in the doorway to the stairs. "Sir, they're massing on the rooftops to the south, east and west." Above them, the machine guns erupted with the fury of guardian angels to underscore Bourquin's message.

"Continue to engage. Don't let them get close." Aguero turned away as movement caught his eye across the street in front of Coleman's position. A piece of sheet metal appeared from the right as an insurgent seemed to be preparing cover for a fighting position. The L-T couldn't tell if he was trying to be sneaky, but he could see the man's shadow as he continued to throw out random pieces of steel.

*I see you, dumbass,* Aguero thought and grinned. The man had finished with his fighting position and was surreptitiously peeking around the corner as he prepared to run for cover. The L-T's finger tightened on the trigger as he put his sights on where he expected the target to appear. He prepared to squeeze off a round.

A little girl appeared in the round glass of his target reticle and stood facing him motionlessly. What the--? Aguero eased the pressure from the trigger and angrily motioned her away, unsure whether she could see him or not. "Stupid little girl. Go away." He felt sick thinking about how close he had come to killing her. Her attention was diverted by something to her left, presumably the man who was casting the shadow. Son of a bitch. He had told her to step out into the street to see if he would be able to make it. Aguero vowed that this low-life would die today.

The insurgent, not content with the results of his human experiment, stuck his weapon around the corner and sprayed a full magazine at nothing in particular, which is exactly what he hit. The L-T's discipline and training kept him from foolishly returning fire. He was trying the old Mohammed Ali rope-a-dope technique. Let the man feel more comfortable, let him feel a bit more at home with the idea of coming out into the open. Aguero sighted his weapon in again.

The coward peeked around the corner and ducked back. He repeated this three more times, psyching himself up for the lunge. It was enough for Aguero to sense the man's rhythm. The man stuck his head out one final time just as he squeezed the trigger. The insurgent's head exploded in a red mist and his body collapsed forward into the street.

*That is the coolest thing I have ever seen*, Aguero thought. He stood at the driver's side door laughing and celebrating the greatest shot of his short career when a giant snuck up behind him and hit him over the head with an enormous mallet. Something struck his helmet so hard that his legs buckled and consciousness waivered.

"Oh, my head," he started screaming.

Coleman laughed, "What are you doing? Sir, are you OK?"

The L-T kept screaming, "My head." He managed to crawl partially inside the Humvee. Without removing his helmet he cradled his head in his hands and rocked silently back and forth, trying to collect his senses.

Something about the situation struck Swope and Corporal Coleman as funny, not the least of which being that the platoon leader was still alive. "Look at this guy," Coleman jived like a goombah mobster, "he's got a headache." They roared with laughter.

Eventually the L-T was able to collect himself and stand up again. The laughter at his expense was completely lost on him. "I'm all right. What the hell hit my head?" It would not be clear to him until later at the aid station that he had been shot.

- - - -

### SO note by Rodgers, Renee @ 06 May 2014
### Chief complaint is: periods of anxiety. Anger.

*Behavior demonstrated no abnormalities; Attitude abnormal. SM asked this session and last if this Provider felt uncomfortable with him. Dysthymic anger is prevalent. Focus of session today is initially regarding how he is adjusting to antidepressant. He is noticing feeling "zombified" on the medication as he adjusts. Cognitively impacted. SM is not using alcohol and notes no other changes. SM returns to issues related to the therapy relationship and discusses his experience of provider being "uncomfortable". SM discusses his anger; he notes that it rises after session and that he has the expectation he'll progress in treatment but is frustrated by the process. Progress will mean "I won't feel like a powder keg that's about to go off."*

### Assessment: 1. Anxiety Disorder 2. Panic Disorder

----

Wild, drawn to the sound of battle, appeared next to Denney and climbed on top of a crate for a better view. Denney, glad for the respite, took a knee and leaned against the wall.

"Oh, hell yeah," Wild exclaimed as he observed the advancing enemy. Heart pounding with dark excitement he began to engage. Although he was thrilled to have such a wealth of targets to choose from, he was still aware of the need to use target discrimination in accordance with their Rules of Engagement. Running to and fro didn't necessarily signal bad intent. Wild did, however, send his warmest regards in the form of 5.56mm slugs to anyone with a weapon in their hand.

Wild observed a small man looking back at him from a rooftop almost 150 meters to the Southwest. He could hear the roar of an angry crowd in that vicinity, a bubbling cauldron of outrage in the street that intersected the alley they defended. Wild couldn't see a weapon in his hand, but the man was pointing right at him and shouting at the crowd below. The man walked to one corner of his roof and craned his neck, then walked back and pointed at Wild again, chattering at people below that Wild couldn't see. Then the man's left hand came up for a brief second and Wild saw that he gripped a rifle by the barrel.

Close enough. Wild felt threatened. He saw the man point at him again through the lens of his M68 sight as he put the red dot on the man's head and pulled the trigger. The shot was perfect and clean. A red mist appeared as the man's head whipped back and he fell over. It was the coolest thing that the young warrior had ever seen, if not the coldest. He felt no remorse over taking the man's life, just a sense of professional accomplishment like a corporate salesman who just closed a huge account or a firefighter who just saved a life.

"Denney, I just got a head shot."

If Denney heard him he didn't say a word. Wild looked down at his friend and saw that the young man's face was pale white and he was shaking. He told Denney to go downstairs and take a break.

----

Jon Denney was indeed deeply shaken. He had been convinced several times over that their lives were forfeit. First, they had sped through the ambush, bullets striking their vehicle with the frequency of popping kettle corn. Then their vehicle had died. Then the recovery vehicle went down. He had ridden in the Lieutenant's Humvee as they retreated into the alley and was face to face with Chen. That's when the reality of death struck him with the full force of inevitability. He was very intelligent and had instantly understood what was happening even as they had tried to bust through the hastily emplaced obstacles. The thousands of people they had seen at yesterday's rally were now trying to kill them. Thousands. If help didn't come soon, they would run out of ammo and then be overrun. He was becoming more and more convinced that he would never see his wife and child again.

----

I was aware of very little happening in the alley except for when the L-T was shot in the head. I heard his shouts and turned momentarily to see what was wrong. Seeing him collapsed halfway in the Humvee worried me. "Are you OK, Sir?" I yelled. I saw him stand up and wave me off.

Soldiers, insubstantial as ghosts, brought me news from the other fronts like fully armed war correspondents. Riddell was with me briefly. Wild continually appeared and vanished like a death-dealing genie. He stood briefly at my left-hand side as we watched for a target, then he casually told me, "I got a head shot." He delivered that tidbit with the same sort of inflection one might use when soliciting someone to see their new tattoo. The totally dead way in which he made the statement froze my blood. I looked over at him and noted that he was completely relaxed, much unlike myself.

"Cool," I said. This was a line of conversation that I had never pursued and was unsure what the proper protocol might be.

"Want a cigarette?" Wild was pulling out a cig from a pack of cheap, Iraqi-made smokes that could be had for a dollar per pack.

"Naw, I don't smoke. That stuff will kill ya." We looked at each other and laughed. Something about making that simple, corny joke in the middle of the worst day of my life turned a corner for me. I relaxed a little. Death suddenly didn't seem so scary.

One small head, then another, comically stacked on top of each other, peeped out from the south end of the intersection. I tensed and prepared to fire. Sure enough, both of the kids put their rifles around the corner and fired. They had learned better than to jump out like mini-commandos. Their small heads didn't present much of a target, and they were as quick as snakes. I tried to anticipate when they would pop out. They alternated the timing of their attack, and even switched up the tactic of peeking around to fire with just poking the rifle out blind.

Then there was a pause that was a little longer than the rest. What were they cooking up now? I tried to think like a homicidal child; tried to anticipate their next move. I kept my sight trained on the spot where their heads had been emerging, eyes unblinking, finger tight on the trigger. A silhouette emerged from hiding and, I held my fire at the last instant.

A woman, ancient in years, shuffled from the very spot where the two youngsters were hiding. She was carrying a paper sack full of groceries, apparently taking advantage of the fire fight to get in that last-minute shopping. I let out a ragged breath. I had almost greased someone's grandmother. What was she thinking walking out into my line of fire like that? Her progress was agonizingly slow, one plodding footstep after another.

Those kids are going to use her for cover, I thought. I aimed at the south intersection expecting the little creeps to pop out at any second. The old lady, either blissfully ignorant of her imminent doom or completely blasé about it, continued trudging across, a journey of ten seconds drawn out to an eternity.

C'mon, move, move, move!

During her entire epic travel across the 17-foot wide alley, she never once looked my way, and, thankfully, the kids waited for her to get across.

But the moment that granny reached the other side, my old friends were back at their usual antics. They picked up the tempo as they alternated turns to hit the infidel and win a prize. I began to curse each time they popped out and I missed them. At least I wasn't squealing with fright again each time someone squeezed a trigger.

I emptied my magazine again and reloaded. After a few more shots I could now see a baseball-sized shot group on the wall beyond where my nemesis kept peeking out. My marksmanship was great, but my timing sucked. Having almost killed some centenarian for picking the wrong day to stock up on milk made me even more cautious about positively identifying my target.

Sala'am tapped me on the leg to get my attention. "Mr. Mathias, can you show me how to make..." Under stress he struggled to recall his English vocabulary. He showed me my own weapon and pointed at the magazine. The kids down the hall unleashed another volley— one of the rounds struck the shield and made me jump.

"You need to change mags? You're out of ammo?"

"Yes, that is it!"

"Turn the weapon on its other side. See that round button? Push it. OK, just let the empty magazine hit the floor. Take this and slide it in. Tap it real good on the bottom. See that small lever? Push it." The bolt slid forward and Sala'am thanked me. I wished that I had hundred more like him right then.

Denney emerged from the courtyard and replaced Wild at my left side. I glanced over once and saw that he was shaking badly. "Matt," he said, "I'm scared."

His vulnerability touched me deeply, but I didn't know what to tell him other than the truth. "Yeah, me too, brother." Then I added a lie, or at least an uncertainty that I didn't believe. Our small force of 16 combat-effective soldiers and one untrained Iraqi were squaring off against what had to be the entire Shia Glee Club from yesterday's parade, which had numbered in the thousands. Half our vehicles were destroyed, my heavy machine gun was a sexy paperweight and God alone knew when the cavalry would arrive. "We're going to be fine," I grinned. "Don't you worry."

I spied Guzman looking out at us from the gate. "Hey, Doc. Come give Denney a break for a sec; he needs to take a knee." Denney tensed up as if I were banishing him from the tribe rather than giving him a moment to gather himself. "Denney, go rest a second. We've got this. Come back out in a minute and we'll swap."

Denney nodded his head and reluctantly stepped inside. Doc stepped up to take his place. He usually carried a 9mm pistol, so I was surprised to see him with a rifle. I gave him a brief rundown of the enemy and friendly situation. Two dirt bags 12 o'clock, 50 meters at the left side of the intersection and all that. Guzman nodded as he shuffled quickly from one foot to another, a sort of modified pee-dance. The latest craze, all the kids are doing it. I imagined that he felt like I would if I was suddenly ordered to stop an arterial bleed. He was staring through the optic sight just above the Humvee's armored door, nervous but ready to engage the enemies of his country. I saw one thing wrong with that picture.

"Doc."

He looked up at me, eyes glowing white in the fading light. "Yeah."

"Raise your barrel up a little or you're going to kill both of us." The tip of his barrel was pressing into the armored door.

"Oh." He giggled and I laughed along with him.

Another salvo pinged off of my turret shield, but it didn't faze me anymore. I got back behind Chen's rifle, growing angrier by the minute. I still had not been able to coax the .50 cal back to life. Meanwhile, the neighbor kids and I continued to play catch with hot lead. I think I must have clipped one, or at least scared the Shi-ite out of them, because they resorted to a new tactic. They allowed only the tip of their barrel to protrude into the street and fired volley after volley into the opposite wall. I watched in awe as bullets struck the north wall then south about 10 meters closer, then back to the other wall, bouncing madly toward us like deadly billiard balls. The rounds struck the windshield and glanced off my turret. Damn it, that was annoying!

Chen had been a solidly built guy, but I was a lot taller. He had made a platform out of extra ammo cans that I now found uncomfortable. I did not dare stand up to my full height to face down the enemy—those little brats would have already cut me to ribbons. In order to keep as low a profile as possible, my eyes just barely over the shield, I had to stand at a half squat. I had been in this position for so long that my legs were exhausted. The exertion combined with frustration about those darned kids pushed my temper into the red zone. Me! I have, or at least had, no temper to speak of. I never got mad at anyone, yet here I was, feeling an emotion with which I was wholly unfamiliar. Rage.

----

SO note by Aycock, Lisa @ 14 July 2014
Chief complaint: concentration

*Pt reports minimal progress. Pt reported his spouse is preg-
nant. Pt stated this news is a shock b/c they have had significant issues conceiving & were considering adoption. Pt stated
the pregnancy has created significant triggers for him as a result of the experiences he had while deployed involving children. Pt stated he feels like he will be a failure, fears he can't
bond with the child, has a slight phobia of children due to his
experiences.*

**Assessment: Anxiety Disorder NOS**

----

Corporal Coleman was having a similar experience with those pesky
insurgents at his end of the alley. The day was dying when a figure
peeked around the corner on the right.

"Guys! We got a peeker, right side!" Coleman called. The skinny
Houston native was peripherally aware that Bellamy had joined him
again at his right side, a wolf eager for the hunt. The figure's head
appeared then quickly disappeared again.

"Hey, he's peeking again, you see him?"

Coleman said calmly, "I know, and when he pokes his head
around one more time I'm taking it off." Under his breath he dared
them, "Peek around the corner again."

Coleman had the .50 cal aimed exactly where the target kept appearing. He had carefully memorized the precise spot and anticipated
that the man was likely to pop out a third time with a gun. There!
Coleman saw the familiar silhouette of an AK-47 with its curved magazine and pressed the trigger with both thumbs. The Deuce barked
once and the man's head was gone. The body dropped to the ground
like a sack of potatoes.

*Nice!* Coleman thought.

The headless man disappeared quickly as his comrades pulled him back by the ankles. The rifle remained clutched in the corpse's lifeless hands.

His death did nothing to diminish the enemy's determination. They redoubled their efforts to avenge their fallen comrades. Coleman had taught them the foolishness of attempting to fully expose themselves to fire off a volley. Instead, they stuck their rifles around the corner and fired blindly. This was just as effective as their previous attempts at aiming—which is to say not very. Coleman's nerves were tested as the 7.62mm rounds buzzed around his head like angry hornets. The rifle and arm appeared around the corner again to fire off another wild volley, but Coleman was faster. The .50 sent forth one quick burst that severed the arm from its owner and blew the AK into several useless chunks.

On the far side of Delta, he spied a pair of black-clad insurgents dashing across the street from the left to the right. He fired on them and thought that he might have winged them both. Maybe. They fell down out of his sight behind a small pile of trash. A second later he saw one of them crawl behind an old car. Coleman raked the vehicle from side to side with lethal fire. He couldn't tell if he hit his intended target, but he was pretty sure that said target wasn't having a good day.

----

Riddell picked off any stragglers that Coleman missed. He saw two young men dressed in black trotting toward them along the side of a building on the right side. They moved quickly at a crouch, one behind the other, with their Russian-made rifles held low. Riddell put the red dot of his M68 laser sight on the lead man's chest and squeezed the trigger. He had expected to fire two shots for two targets.

Both men fell in a heap. A common complaint about the 5.56mm ammunition that the Army used was that it tended to over-penetrate rather than provide knock-down power. Riddell wasn't complaining now.

"Holy crap!" crowed Coleman who saw the whole thing. "That was awesome!"

Riddell was about to agree when he saw another man dart from a doorway to grab the fallen duo's weapons. Quick as thought he aimed and fired. That man fell, too, never to rise again.

----

A brief silence fell, and Lieutenant Aguero took advantage of the lull to pull out a battered cigarette. Before he could put the cancer stick to his lips, a long stream of tracers zoomed down the alley at them from 200 yards west. Everyone hunkered down behind cover as the swarm of ammo fell around them. Aguero looked up to identify the source. He saw another flash from a two-story house in the same vicinity as where the mob had gathered. Another frightening volley kept our heads down briefly. Tracers flew by like laser beams.

Aguero felt a rush of excitement that momentarily blotted out the pain in his head, leg, and arm. That had to be an RPD or RPK, Aguero knew—the Soviet version of an American M60 or M240 heavy machine gun.

----

I could hear the L-T behind me telling me to *take him out, take him out*. I put the red dot on the window where I could see a weapon flashing fire. Two hundred meters? No problem. I sent a single shot his way. The RPK answered my shot with 30 of its own. I aimed carefully and fired again. Nothing. I was unlikely to hit anything at a distance with Chen's weapon since the optic was calibrated to him. Without a spotter or a scope with any kind of magnification, I couldn't even tell if I was aiming high or low. I gave up after a dozen attempts and passed the torch to Denney and Bellamy.

----

The L-T watched from behind, impatient for the RPK gunner to go down. He sat down in the driver's seat next to his Platoon Sergeant to rest his throbbing leg. He was about to get up and try his own luck when he saw several tracers flash by out of the corner of his eye. One round hit the wall next to him, but three slammed into Red 4's windshield. Little chips of glass fell from the star-burst holes.

Sergeant Swope tapped him on the shoulder and said, "Still bulletproof, hum?" Swope picked up a map and placed it over the bullet holes, as if to reinforce the window.

"Oh, that's funny," laughed Aguero.

Aguero pulled out his Marlboros. *Please, God, let me have just one*, he thought. He had lost track of the times that he had almost managed to grab a smoke. Expecting some new attack, he flicked the flint wheel of his lighter with a shaking hand. The paper caught fire and retreated into an angry orange circle as he pulled smoke into his lungs that tasted like Olympian ambrosia. Aguero savored the smoke.

By the time he finished the cigarette, the ass-clown with the RPK was still annoyingly not dead. *If you want something done right...* Aguero stood up and propped his M4 on top of the armored door. He shot once, twice, thrice, and did not win the stuffed animal at the carnival. Cursing with each miss, he fired off half a dozen more shots before his bolt locked back to the rear: magazine empty. Aguero brought out a few curses he saved for special occasions as he reloaded. One expended magazine later he was bringing out the very rare epithets. A few rounds into the next magazine, he was spared making up entirely new words when the RPK gunner at last fell. The L-T didn't know whether to celebrate victory or slap himself for expending so much ammo. He supposed that the early or late arrival of the QRF would decide that for him.

----

Once the RPK gunner was down, I returned my attention to the jokers at the first intersection. They had been cowed by the sheer number of us firing at the same time, unaware that they weren't the target. As soon as our guns fell silent one of the boys fired again, only the barrel visible, sending out bullets as if he were attempting a difficult corner bank shot. I saw the round bounce right, then left, then right, then left each time kicking up a small poof of dust from the wall it struck. Then my luck ran out.

The bullet struck me in the left thigh, having snuck through the small gap between the bottom of the turret shield and the top of the Humvee. My leg collapsed and I fell into the Humvee.

"I'm hit!" I yelled.

I heard someone yelling for Guzman, saying that I'd been hit. My leg stung, felt like it was on fire. My eyes were winced shut and I didn't want to open them for fear of what I would see. I put pressure over the wound, expecting gouts of blood. My gloved hand still felt dry. I tilted my hand over and peeked with one eye open at my thigh. No blood. No hole in my pants. Smiling, I rubbed my leg and immediately cursed in three foreign tongues at the pain. I checked for blood again and found none. Puzzled to the extreme I grabbed the turret above me and pulled myself up. More pain. Still, I wasn't bleeding so I had to count my blessings. Two days later, when the adrenaline had tapered off and I found myself unable to climb a ladder when it mattered, I finally dropped my trousers to look at it. An angry bruise yelled at me in Day-Glo colors. The bullet had lost kinetic energy each time it struck a new surface until, finally robbed of most of its velocity and flattened by multiple impacts, it only had enough pepper left to knock me down. That's what I told myself, though I wasn't ruling out a guardian angel, either.

I stood up and yelled, "I'm good!" In fact, I was far from good. I was good and mad. I was growing enraged to the point of madness. If you've never gone Alice-in-Wonderland-Tea-party insane, you should try it once before you die. I began to breathe heavy, almost snorting like a bull about to charge. I wanted blood on my hands. A vision began to take shape in my head. I would pop down into the driver's seat and haul ass to that intersection and leap out at whoever was unlucky enough to be standing there. I would tackle them, pull out my knife, and just plunge that bad boy home again and again and again.

Fortunately, the rational part of me was still there and tried to talk the irrational part of me off the ledge. Unfortunately, I was unable to convince myself to abandon the plan altogether.

"Sala'am, close that door and go inside the courtyard," I said without taking my eyes off of my target. The translator looked up at me uncertainly, saw something he must not have liked, and hurriedly shut the door. I put Chen's rifle in the passenger seat and slid behind the wheel.

Denney was using the driver's door for cover. He had returned with a renewed air of confidence and had been acquitting himself well. He looked in at me now, surprised. "Fisk, what are you doing?"

"I'm going down there to kill those S.O.B.s. Now pull back inside." I managed to pull the door closed. I dropped the window so that I could stick my weapon through it, a little surprise for the neighbors. Through the window I said, "If I don't make it back, tell my wife that I love her." I wince now at the war-movie cliché, but the sentiment was real enough then. My voice trembled when I said it.

Then Bellamy and Denney saved my life. Denney reached through the window and opened the door. Someone else would have had a problem stopping me, but Denney is a pretty strong guy. Bellamy was saying something to me, trying to talk some sense into me, and I was trying to get his hands off of the door so I could go and get it over with. I don't really know if I said anything else, and I hope I didn't do anything physically that hurt him.

After a moment's struggle, I was aware that Bellamy's face was magically replaced by the L-T's scowling visage. He demanded that I explain myself. I'm not sure what I said, but he kept repeating "No, you're not. Stand down! That's an order!" until my rational brain was strong enough to regain control. My blood was still pounding, but the savage need to rend and claw and slash was abating. I wasn't going to disobey my leader. I wasn't going to throw my life away in my rage and desire for retribution. I resumed my post in the turret a little embarrassed for being so stupid. And a little disappointed that my plan had been foiled. The L-T stormed off growling something about, "...retarded Johnny-Ninja bullshit"

Stinging from the Lieutenant's rebuke and still glowing red hot from my own rage, I settled back into the turret and doubled my efforts to take out the threat at the intersection. A small hand popped out, and I sent several rounds at it with an enraged growl. A head popped out one more time, but I missed again. Aiming in the same small area where all my shots had previously gone, I unloaded the rest of my magazine as fast as I could pull the trigger, shouting as I did so. When I changed magazines, I heard a keening wail come from the vicinity of the junction. Had I hit them? Bounced *my* shot into them as they had done to me? I hoped so.

Movement caught my eye. The wall I had been firing into was part of a two-story residence with a door that opened into the street I was covering. From that door, two thin young men emerged. Between them they carried the bloody body of a man who had been riddled with bullets. He hung limp and lifeless as his friends or relatives carried him heedless into the path of our rifles. Their need must have been great or their courage born of love for a brother or cousin. The never looked our way, never cared that we were there. They only cared about getting help for their loved one. Several younger women followed them out into the street, weeping. The two little insurgents were silent.

I watched the procession move quickly away from us with a lump in my throat. The blood-lust, the killing rage was gone, replaced with heaping portions of guilt. I was in the process of justifying everything to myself when the ultimate repudiation of my arguments walked through the door. A woman dressed all in black, as if she anticipated mourning on this day, staggered into the street. She was the source of the wailing that I had heard. Her high pitched shriek of grief pierced my brain and lanced through my justifications. At first I thought that I had shot her, too, for she was covered in blood. Then I realized that the blood was only on her hands and that it didn't belong to her. She looked to be older than the man I had accidentally shot. By her sorrow, I deduced that she was the mother. Her hands were covered with blood.

Her back was to me; she stood in the middle of the street and watched them carry off (her son?) the man. Her shoulders moved up and down, jerking in rhythm with her sobbing wail. I willed her not to, but she did, she turned around slowly, inexorably. She does this in my dreams, my frequent nightmares. She turns around and there is blood on her hands. I know this because she is walking toward me now and her hands, bloody hands, are extended to me. The blood. She is reaching to me, perhaps pleading for me to take it back. Her hands with the blood. She wails, she weeps, she shouts to me in a grieving tongue that is foreign yet easily understood. I want to turn away, but I cannot help staring at how transfigured she is by grief. She has become terrible and beautiful and awful to behold. And still she approaches, one tottering step at a time, heedless of the sounds of battle, lost in sorrow. Her hands covered with that blood.

"*Y'allah!*" I shout. *Go away!* I wave futilely for her to turn back, turn aside. She is heedless; she has reached the middle of the intersection, taking each step with feet made of lead.

I use every last bit of Arabic that I have picked up, trying vainly to convince her to seek the answers elsewhere. "*Im'shi! Y'allah!*" I try telling her that she is not safe, combining disparate words into a sentence that I hope is intelligible. "*Y'allah! Ente la fi amen!*" I look over to Sala'am for help. "Tell her to get out of here, Sala'am! She's going to get shot!" That would be the absolute last straw for my current, very tenuous grip on sanity.

Sala'am begins to shout and yell and plead and cajole. The woman stops at least, but she is now directly between us and everyone who's been trying to kill us for the last two hours. I don't want her to die. I just want her to take her bloody, reproving hands and go. Her voice has grown hoarse with weeping and shouting. Her message is perfectly understandable: Why? We were doing nothing, minding our own business. We asked no part in this. Why did you take away what matters? Why? Why? Why?

My finger is on the trigger, and I am sweating like I wouldn't have thought possible. My eyes haven't blinked since this sorry game of charades began. My heart is broken into pieces and lodged in my throat. I aim to the left side of her, praying that the evil little brats don't decide to try and bounce more rounds off the walls. The poor woman would be cut to pieces. Oceans of time ebb and flow as the grieving woman pours out her travail. Eventually she turns and walks slowly down the street to be with her departed, taking her blood-stained hands with her.

At that moment, blindness struck me. My eyes stopped working as if they had seen enough and had decided on a sabbatical. One moment I was staring intently at the wailing woman's back, praying that she wouldn't get killed, the next I could see nothing except for a not-quite-total blackness that was like watching a television screen experiencing technical difficulties. I could see faint sparkles of purple and green.

"Hey! I can't see!" I called out, not remembering who was around. Leaving my weapon leaned against the turret shield, I sank down on my haunches, too panicked to care how badly my leg was throbbing. The world was totally obscured. I was close to hyperventilating and had to force myself to breathe deeply. What had happened? Had I been shot again?

Denney opened the rear left door and took me by the hand. He gently guided me out on to the ground where I stood blinking. I could see something now. It was as if I was looking down a long tunnel. The edges of my vision were the same blackness, but I could see blurry images in the center. Denney told me to take a break, that he had it. I left my weapon and stumbled in to the courtyard. After several minutes of blinking and straining and breathing my vision returned. I'm not sure what happened, whether the stress had talked my optic nerves into taking a hiatus, or whether I had simply forgotten to blink for several hours. As I paced around I was reminded of a bit from one of my favorite books, *The Hitchhiker's Guide to the Galaxy.* One of the characters wears a special pair of sunglasses that go completely dark in the face of peril. This helps the wearer develop a relaxed attitude toward danger. I always laugh when I read that bit, but it really is the best way to describe what I experienced.

Feeling refreshed, I went back outside and climbed back into the turret as the sun died before me. I was glad to be able to see it, especially since it might be my last.

----

SO Note by Flowers, Naomi @ 05 JUN 2010

Chief complaint: 1) Increase in anxiety related to in-
terpersonal worry. 2) Lack of concentration 3) Interrupted sleep pattern.

*SM states that he has moderate difficulty accomplishing
daily tasks, interacting with others. SM is a voluntary client of
the clinic.*

*Physical Symptoms: muscle tension, numbness, shortness of
breath, heart pounding, vision changes, choking sensations,
trembling/shaking, tics and twitches, rapid heartbeat.*

Assessment:  1.  MAJOR  DEPRESSION,  SINGLE
EPISODE

----

We were all aware of the setting sun, some more uneasy about it than
others. Bellamy called out to no one in particular, "Conserve your
ammo! Pick your targets. Leave everything alone outside of a hun-
dred-fifty meters."

Good advice, too. We had ammunition, but what we didn't have
was a single clue about how long we'd have to make it stretch. Where
was the QRF? And why weren't the Kiowas engaging? I kept hearing
them buzz overhead and wondered if they could see us.

Before we deployed, heck, even before I rejoined the Army in
May of 2003, I had sat enthralled before the movie *Blackhawk Down*.
The combat was so realistically rendered that none of us could help
but compare our current situation to that film. I heard Bourquin, perhaps rather optimistically, asking Bellamy who was going to play him
in the movie about *us*. Logic told me that we would first need to survive before anyone even *knew* our story. Unless the cavalry arrived

soon—1ˢᵗ CAV, that is—there would be no lone Spartan survivor sent from Thermopylae to sing our song.

Still, it was entertaining listening to the cheerful banter. *Me? Tom Cruise, probably. He's too tall. Screw you! I want Jamie Fox to play me. Dude, he's black. So? No one has to know I'm white!* Everyone seemed to be holding together remarkably well. We had taken the worst sucker punch the enemy could throw and then had come back swinging. The Quick Reaction Force was on their way—Swope hadn't let the cat out of the bag that they had been hit on Silver—and we would all be whisked to freedom soon.

But it was getting dark now, and I was reminded about *Blackhawk Down* for another reason. The Rangers in that story had brought gear with them with the expectation that they would be back before afternoon tea. No need to bring Night Vision Devices on a day-time raid, silly goose. They left water and night-fighting gear in exchange for ammunition. I certainly don't condemn the decision. I'm an Arkansas boy, after all; bring on the ammo! However, I did learn from their plight. Bring all of your gear, all of the time. Better to have it and not need it than the converse. Taking advantage of the lull in the fighting—my cross-road nemeses had not offered a peep since the woman with the bloody hands—I reached into a pouch and pulled out my AN/PVS-7B Night Vision Device and snapped it on to my pre-installed helmet mount. I didn't need it yet, but when I did need it I would only have to swivel the goggles down and power up.

I reminded others around me to go ahead and put their NVGs on. While everyone had seen the movie, not everyone had embraced the lessons learned. Most didn't have their NODs, as we called them, and many were running out of water. The ammunition was holding for now, but we didn't relish the thought of holding this alley against an all-out assault with black-garbed ninja wannabes swarming over the rooftops.

Swope was able to provide some good news. "Here comes the QRF down Delta!"

The news spread quickly as we began high-fiving each other. We were going back to that beautiful piece of dusty real estate that was looking better all the time.

----

From the moment the QRF turned left on to Delta, the volume of enemy fire steadily increased to a fever pitch. Bullets ricocheted off of the LMTV's armored cab and buried into the sandbags on the bed of the truck. Everyone fired in all directions, trying desperately to keep the enemy at bay. No matter how much they fired, though, it seemed that Mookie's men were turning up the volume.

Joe Thompson heard Arteaga scream, "Sergeant, I'm hit! I'm hit!"

Thompson cursed and said, "Man, screw this!" He scrambled over to Arteaga who had rolled on his back, both hands on his knee. "Where are you hit at, Rafael?" Even after Arteaga removed his hands, Joe could barely see the two small holes in his ACUs. Thompson plucked a knife from his belt and thumbed it open with a single snap. Carefully, because the LMTV was bouncing as they hurtled down the street, he cut away the fabric around the Puppet's knee.

"Hey, dog! Why you cuttin' my pants up? They're going to charge me for that!"

"Shut up, Rafael!"

When Thompson ripped open Rafael's trousers he saw what looked like a vampire's kiss just below the young man's knee cap. Arteaga looked up at Thompson, "They shot me, dog. They shot me. I can't believe them fools shot me."

Thompson felt the dark humor of the moment and would have laughed if bullets had not been flying so close that he could almost read the lot number stamped into the lead. Joe had pulled out a new field dressing that they had been given in Kuwait, which had been designed by the Israelis as some sort of super-bandage. It was composed of a combination of crushed shell fish, unicorn kisses, or some crap, that was supposed to work as a coagulant. Arteaga was hardly bleeding at all, but this was a good chance to use a new toy.

Thompson had never trained how to use it, had never even opened it. When he did rip open the brown, wax paper wrapping the whole bandage fell out on to the sandbags. Real sanitary, that. Thompson was lying on his side and found the position awkward for performing first aid, even if vital to survival. He scooped it back up, the cloth ends trailing out and snagging up on his gear. Since he was turned mostly on his stomach, Thompson felt keenly exposed. *I'm going to get shot in the ass.*

Thompson became so frustrated with trying to use the Israeli bandage with its built-in tourniquet that he threw it down in disgust. He reached up and snatched the old-school bandage from Arteaga's own vest. Within 15 seconds he had wrapped it in place on Arteaga's knee. "Keep pressure on that," Thompson told him, and rolled back over into position.

Rafael pushed down and winced. "Ah! It hurts!"

Thompson said, "Well, no crap. Hold pressure on it anyway."

Fowler crawled over to assess the situation. "It's all right, Rafael. It's all right," he said, "You're going to make it."

Arteaga seemed to take heart at the news. "All right, cool, cool."

----

Arteaga felt as if he had just injected Speed into his system. His pulse raced, his heart pounded in his chest, and he was more alive than he had ever felt before. He grabbed his weapon, rolled over to his good knee and raised up as high as he could, daring someone to take him out. He began to fire the SAW, raking it back and forth as the ammo belt disappeared.

Unleashing long burst of automatic fire, Arteaga screamed, "You can't kill me! You can't kill me! I'm a gangsta, dog! I'm a gangsta!" The young Latino was up on one knee, gun blazing, invoking the spirit of Tony Montana inviting his enemies to "say hello" to his little friend. Everyone laughed and kept firing.

Arteaga's arms eventually sagged and he lowered his weapon as a fit of nausea and weakness swept over him. He tried to bring the SAW back up, but it suddenly seemed so heavy. Fowler noticed the young man beginning to flag and told him to lay down and relax. Rafael slumped down to a reclining position and rested the barrel of his weapon on the side skirt of the truck. What was happening to him?

----

Justin Rowe noticed that Puppet had stopped firing and moved to take up the slack. No sooner had he settled on a comfortable posture when he saw a target running toward them off their eight o'clock. Rowe had no time to think as the insurgent raised an AK to fire at them. Just as the man started to take cover in a doorway, Rowe pulled the trigger and saw a splat of blood decorate the door. The man pitched forward, dead.

----

Le cried out, "I'm hit, I'm hit!" as he fell backwards. All sense of merriment fled Tyrell as he looked back at Le and saw smoke coming out of the hole in the man's inner thigh. Le was screaming. Fowler whirled around and assessed Le's injury. He was most worried about massive hemorrhaging from a femoral artery, one of the largest in the human body. He quickly enlarged the gash in Le's trousers and was relieved to find that the bullet had only dug a large furrow in the man's leg. No bullet, no gouts of blood. Fowler used Le's own bandage to bind his injury. Le quickly regained his composure and, ignoring the searing heat of the wound, resumed his post as if nothing had happened.

----

Tyrell was peripherally aware of how close the bullet had come to the NCOs groin. He felt queasy and convinced that he, himself, was about to be shot in the nether regions. Dust was thick in the air as bullets struck sand bags. He wasn't alone either. He saw Deaver pull sandbags on top of his own legs and groin.

----

Coleman saw the QRF. He knew when they were close because he saw 7.62mm tracers flashing down the street toward an unseen foe. That was the Bradley's coaxial machine gun, and it was gorgeous to behold. He saw the first Bradley pass the alleyway, heading south. Obviously they were going to form a defensive circle around the mouth of the alley to pull them out safely. Another BFV zoomed by, and Coleman wondered how wide their perimeter was going to be. When the third combat vehicle—an LMTV loaded with his comrades—rolled by, he realized that the rescue party couldn't see them and were going to miss their location. *How do I get their attention?* he wondered. *Do I shoot at them?* The .50 caliber rounds wouldn't hurt a Bradley's thick hide, but it might be a good way to get some very unwanted 25mm attention. He began to yell as loud as he could, hoping that the next vehicle would hear him. Futility. A soft-skin Humvee passed. Coleman saw Burkholder on the gun and called to him. Nothing. Another LMTV. The Soldiers facing him were barely exposed and had their attention focused on the rooftops. A fourth Bradley passed with its turret pointed over the rear deck a sign that it was the last vehicle in the group. They had passed them by! Coleman felt suddenly sick.

Coleman turned to Swope and said with a dismayed shake of the head, "They're gone. What's going on?"

----

Swope said nothing in reply as he continued to call desperately over the radio to his Company Commander. The radio was so clogged with chatter, however, that the Senior NCO couldn't tell if anyone knew that the rescue force had just passed them.

He tried again. "Comanche 6, this is Comanche Red 4, you have passed our position, how copy, over?"

A tense second passed then he heard Comanche 6's voice punctuated by small-arms fire, "Roger, Comanche Red 4. We are in heavy contact, taking casualties. We're going to push another unit over to you."

Swope sat in the vehicle with the mike cradled loosely in his hand as he absorbed the information. He took a deep breath. "Acknowledged, Comanche 6. ETA?"

----

The Light Military Tactical Vehicle had endured a whole heap of abuse. The tires were all flat from 7.62mm lead and an abundance of scrap metal in the streets. The engine made an awful racket. Winkler, riding shotgun, heard the driver mutter a single phrase over and over like a prayer, *Come on, come on, please just make it back, make it back; that's all I'm asking you to do.*

Then the Bradley in front of them stopped in the middle of the most lethal street in the world. The most popular topic of discussion among the very concerned tenants of the LMTV was *What the hell is going on?* They were stopped for about two minutes while Denomy tried to sort out the snarl of information coming from Swope, who was screaming that they had just passed by them, his other two platoons in sector, and a Battalion Commander directing a 1,000 piece running battle while simultaneously engaging bad guys from his Humvee window. The seconds passed grudgingly.

Winkler could hear someone pounding on the cab while shouting, *What the hell is going on? Get the hell out of here. Get the hell out of here.*

Finally, decisions were made and the convoy moved south. They hit Route Gold and turned left, noticing an almost immediate relief in contact. As fast as the tortured LMTV would run, they pressed on to Aeros on Sadr City's far eastern side then turned north. Within a few minutes, and only a few potshots later, they reached a convocation of American soldiers and vehicles at the intersection of Copper and Aeros.

----

The rally point was under sporadic fire when Denomy's convoy arrived. Second, or White Platoon had several soldiers on the ground attempting to suppress the enemy. From the condition of their vehicles, the other platoons had fared just as badly. Arteaga saw one of his closest friends, Miranda, pulling security from a Humvee mounted machine gun. Another comrade, Sergeant Garza, was putting his soldiers on line in preparation for a ground assault.

When they passed them by Arteaga called out, "Hey dog, I'm hit."

Miranda looked up and replied, "Hey, dog, I've got blood running down my forehead."

Rafael laughed, "We're both screwed."

----

It took a few minutes to consolidate all of the wounded from both Charlie and Alpha companies. Tyrell and Deaver, both SAW gunners, were told to escort the battered LMTV back to the FOB and assist with the MEDEVAC. The LMTV limped toward home, barely making it outside the FOB gate before the engine seized up. Hunter continued to chant his "Please make it home" prayer the whole way. Medics and other volunteers flooded in to help unload, prioritize, and then reload the more critically wounded onto an ambulance. Arteaga tried to walk, but Winkler made him sit down and wait. Tyrell and Deaver helped Puppet and Le down onto a couple of stretchers, preparing to take them inside.

A sniper opened fire from a good distance away. The rounds bounced off of the armored cab and further deflated one of the front tires. The personnel coming out to help flinched. The newly minted veterans of Sadr City barely blinked. Compared to what they had just gone through, a few pot shots were nothing. The FOB Mayor, Sergeant Major Garner, ran out of the gate yelling at everyone to get the wounded behind the vehicles before someone was killed. Tyrell just smiled.

----

Swope looked up as he heard the Kiowas pass over again trying to find us. "Comanche Red 4, still cannot identify, over," they broadcast, voices devoid of emotion. Swope knew soldiers. He knew that if he felt like his heart had turned to stone, then his boys were sucking twice as hard. The Kiowas were still blind to them in spite of the VS-17 panel and the smoke grenades. They simply had to fly too fast—swapping speed for armor—to spot a five-foot-square piece of fabric.

"Bourquin, why don't you get up on the roof and moon the choppers?" Swope drawled when the skinny NCO appeared to gather more ammo. "If that white heiny of yours don't sit there and flag them down, nothing will."

Eric prepared a witty rejoinder in defense of his alabaster posterior but was struck dumb by a flash of inspiration. He sprinted up the stairs.

Bourquin climbed on to the roof, breathless. "We need to start a fire!" he exclaimed.

"What?" Robinson looked at Bourquin like he was crazy.

"A fire! The birds can't make out our panel. We need to make smoke, a lot of smoke, to attract their attention."

Rob wasted no time. He, Rogers, and Bourquin began to gather up everything they thought might burn. There was a stick of some unknown wood that was dry and broke into kindling easily. Bourquin ripped off first one sleeve, then another and tore the cloth into strips. Rob, recognizing the utility of sacrificing a uniform for the greater good, followed suit. Within seconds, the materials they had gathered were burning brightly. Davis pitched over a couple of rubber flip-flops near his position. The burning rubber sent up billowing dark black clouds.

Davis called over the radio, "Red 1, this is OP 1. We got a fire going. Ask if they can see us now, over."

----

Swope relayed to the Kiowa pilot. He waited in tense silence as they heard the thumping of approaching rotors. *Please, please, please.*

"Roger, Comanche Red, I have visual. I repeat, I have visual of your location. Commencing run." Within seconds came the glorious sounds of heavy machine gun fire as the attack choppers moved in.

----

Denomy was nonplussed by their inability to find and extract his platoon. They had taken numerous casualties, though thankfully no one else in his company had been killed. A matter of providence or luck—take your choice. He was not going to send his soldiers back into that mess unprotected. They had so few armored vehicles, though. This was supposed to be a humanitarian mission, not the worst combat seen in a decade. Once he sent the LMTVs with his wounded back to the FOB he prepared to personally lead another attempt with White Platoon's Bradleys.

Denomy asked for volunteers to accompany him back into the city. Thompson instantly raised his hand. Dumdee, a squad leader from another platoon also volunteered. Rowe, too, started to climb into the open bed of the Humvee, but Fowler grabbed his arm. "No, you don't. I got this," he said. Rowe tried to get into the back seat, but Thompson grabbed his arm. "Sit this one out. I got this."

----

Ben Hayhurst was killing people in bunches on the rooftop. He had been pulling security off of the northeast corner with a clear line of sight on Route Delta for some time. After the action had died down, he let Taylor pick up his zone while he crouched down to rest for a minute and drink some water. Three kids suddenly appeared, one wielding an AK-47. Before Taylor could draw a bead on them and fire, the young fighter sent a wild volley their way, raking the rifle back and forth like a hero from a bad action movie. One of the rounds slid through a tiny crack in the wall and lodged in Ben Hayhurst's left shoulder. It felt as though a small rock had struck his shoulder followed by a sharp, burning sensation. As an added bonus, it blew concrete and plaster everywhere, fracturing his jaw and blowing out his eardrum. Taylor shot the kid and his friends scattered.

Hayhurst felt disoriented and confused. *What the hell just hit me?* he thought. He wondered how he had been hit when he was behind cover. Perhaps an RPG? As quickly as the pain came, it subsided as his adrenaline kicked into overdrive. He slumped down at the base of the low wall, growling and holding his shoulder. Davis ran to him, keeping a low profile. Hayhurst's eyes were shut tightly. "They shot me!" he exclaimed.

Davis told him, "Don't worry about it. It's just a scratch."

Ben felt his arm growing cold and his face was numb. He turned to Davis and said through gritted teeth, "What does it look like?"

"A scratch, I said. Quit being a sissy. Keep going, you'll be fine."

"Oh, OK then. No big deal." Hayhurst tried to shrug off the pain and numbness he felt in the socket of his shoulder joint. He rose above the wall, searching for a target, preferably the one who had sucker-punched him. He fired a few rounds at the corner of a nearby building where shadowy men emerged from time to time to rake the air with their indiscriminate marksmanship. He tried to lift his arm to support his weapon and felt it slip out of the socket. He bit off a yelp and squatted down again. This was not going to work.

----

Robinson saw that Hayhurst was going to be out of the fight for good. Plus, by wounding one man, the enemy had taken two soldiers out of the fight. Davis had to abandon his sector to give aid. Rob readjusted his perimeter quickly. He called Swope on the radio and informed him that Hayhurst was down and asked that they send Doc Guzman up to take a look at him.

In the meantime, Rob needed more men. He went to the west side and looked over. Wild and Riddell were standing on top of the CCP roof, rifles at the ready, but they weren't engaging. Perfect.

----

Wild was so intent on scanning for a target that he almost didn't hear. Then he thought he heard his name drifting down from the heavens. "Riddell, do you hear that?"

Riddell, whose face had a sickly cast to it, muttered, "I don't know."

Wild was sure that he heard something, "I think Sergeant Rob's calling my name. Cover my lane a sec." Wild walked back to the small entryway onto the rooftop. He looked up immediately saw Sergeant Rob; he was yelling, but Carl couldn't tell if he was yelling at him. He put a hand to his ear. *What the hell is he saying?*

Wild called back to Riddell, "Hey, I think Sergeant Rob's calling me; I'm going to go see what he wants. Are you going to be all right over here?"

Riddell gave a thumbs up and returned to scanning his sector.

Wild looked across and tried to figure out how to get over to Robinson. The rooftop he was on was at least as high as or a little taller than Robinson's roof. It didn't occur him to take the more pedestrian route. He looked over the edge and contemplated crawling. *Oh, screw that*, he thought. There was no ledge and crawling across would have left him exposed without being able to maneuver. Wild wasn't one to back down from anything and didn't plan to start now. He popped up, uttered the single vexation "Shit!" and sprinted across the rooftop. Painfully aware of how exposed he was, he jumped down to the roof below. He felt like Spiderman in DCUs.

It was maybe a seven-foot drop according to his knees. He looked down into the courtyard and saw that it was at almost the same height. He jumped again, barely feeling the impact, and climbed up the stairs to Rob's rooftop.

Slightly winded, Wild asked, "Sergeant Rob, what's going on?"

"Hayhurst's been shot. I need you to cover down on his sector."

"Roger, Sergeant." Hayhurst was Wild's friend, and he immediately felt a pang of concern. He saw that Ben was still at his position, nursing his left arm and trying to engage targets with his right.

----

Robinson took Hayhurst by the arm and moved him to the middle of the roof as Doc's head appeared in the spider hole. Ben was still protesting that he was fine, and that if they'd just leave him alone he'd resume his post. He rotated his left arm at the shoulder to prove his point. An audible popping noise made everyone that heard it wince.

Hayhurst's face paled and his knee's unhinged as he flopped to a sitting position. Nausea threatened to overtake him as a wave of pain rushed through his body.

"What happened to you? Did you forget to duck?" cracked Guzman as he cut the NCOs shirt away. He noticed right away that there was not very much blood at all. Good sign. Brachial artery still intact. Looks like he's not going to bleed out. Two holes, entrance and exit? Some kind of spalling on the back. Shrapnel?

Hayhurst explained that he had been sitting with his back against the wall when he was struck from behind.

"What, you were just sitting there?" Shrapnel must be brick fragments then.

"Yeah, must have gone right in between the mortar."

"Damn," laughed Guzman, "They got you good, huh?"

"Don't know that I'd call it good," muttered Hayhurst. "Still, if I'd been sitting a little further left…"

"Damn." Guzman didn't say anything else as he pulled out two gauze field dressings and applied one to each hole. The surgeons would have to dig out the bullet. It was lodged between the ball and socket of his shoulder joint, causing the loud, unnerving pop. And pain. Hayhurst traded sectors with Davis. Davis didn't feel that the south end was much of a threat now, and Ben was starting to look pretty rough. Hayhurst tried to stay alert but as the pain sunk deeper and deeper, concentrating on anything was becoming impossible.

----

Carl Wild, still brimming with restless energy, looked around the roof to see where he could best fit in. He wanted what he was doing to matter, to make a difference. Just standing or sitting around while there was action to be had somewhere was a gigantic 'no go' in his book. He saw Hayhurst, in pain but smiling, leaned up against the southern wall. Taylor was kneeling in the busy northeast corner with his eyes barely above the top of the wall. Davis was propped against the middle of the north wall with his head tilted back. It was the same spot where Hayhurst had been hit, but Davis looked too tired to care. Even the Doc managed to bag a bad guy. The medic picked out a gun-toting jihadist less than 70 meters away and pulled the trigger. No one was more surprised than Guzman when the man jumped as if stung and fell straight down.

Wild approached the heavy machine gun team of Bourquin and Rogers with an offer of respite. Rogers nodded and stretched out on the tar-covered roof.

"Watch yourself," warned Rogers, as Wild settled in. "That wall won't stop shit."

"Yeah," agreed Bourquin, "That's how Ben got tagged. Round came right through."

"So basically," Wild said with a wry grin, "you're saying…"

"Yeah, we're pretty much screwed!" laughed Bourquin. Wild joined him in round of manic laughter that was devoid of the shaky tone that one would attribute to a nervous person fighting for his life. The laughter was cleansing, like a man facing the gallows who had come to terms with his maker and then asked the executioner to pull his finger.

Wild was disappointed to have nothing to shoot at. All was quiet below. For a time, he, Bourquin, and Rogers took turns behind the gun, each hoping for a little action, a little chance to pay back some for their fallen. They stalked from position to position like hungry lions, each quickly growing bored and swapping out with each other wordlessly.

Wild realized that their field of view was much better here than it had been in the other spot. He yelled down to Riddell that he should go downstairs to help out in the alley. "I can cover your sector better up here," he added. Riddell didn't even bother acknowledging. He moved quickly and disappeared back down the stairs out of Wild's sight. The sun, he noted, was beginning to set.

----

Thompson was the first person injured in the vehicle, though not the last. They had just turned down Delta into the mass of obstacles set out to slow their progress. He was firing left-handed from the window behind the CO when a stray bullet hit the door. The round fragmented, pieces flying in all directions. Two of the fragments lodged into Thompson's right hand. The metal bits burned, and Joe shook his hand as if to extinguish flames. He shone a flashlight on it, fearing what he might see. It wasn't bleeding and he could still move his fingers, so he put it out of his mind for the moment. He would take care of his now throbbing hand later, should he survive the night.

"Thompson, what's wrong?" Dumdie called over to him.

"I'm hit, but I'm OK. I'm all right." Indeed, he felt more than all right. He felt almost immortal.

----

Denomy knew that they were getting close to his embattled platoon. He glanced down alley after alley as they flashed by, hoping to catch a glimpse of American soldiers. Instead, he saw large groups of people huddled down each lane. He couldn't see any weapons and they weren't shooting at his convoy, so he let them be. They had plenty of work firing at the insurgents who were using the rooftops to rain metal down upon them. His gunner, Specialist Craig Burkholder, was engaging rooftop targets on the left and right, but there were too many. The doors were lightly armored, and there was no cover of any kind on his vehicle. The noise from the crew-served weapon was so deafening that the commander's numbed ears could hardly hear anything now over the radio. Suddenly, Denomy felt a burning sting in his left shoulder and swatted it as if he were shooing a fly.

----

Thompson was also hit again, this time in his right shoulder. It was superficial, although it stung like bite of a burning wasp. He saw his commander flinch in front of him. Thompson was able to make out blood coming from the CO's left shoulder. Thompson, ignoring his own wounds, leaned forward and pulled out Denomy's own field dressing from the case on the CO's left shoulder. Joe began trying to apply the bandage to his commander's shoulder as the vehicle bounced wildly over debris, and the commander attempted to contact Red 1 on the radio. Thompson felt like he was trying to put socks on a restless toddler while riding a roller coaster.

Out of the corner of his eye, Thompson saw the smoke trail of an incoming RPG from the left. The rocket sizzled as it sped toward them out of the growing darkness, hit a piece of garbage ten feet away, and exploded. A large chunk of burning frag ripped through the door and took a chunk out of Dumdie's shin. The NCO began to scream as he bucked wildly in his seat. Thompson grabbed the man and pulled him toward the center of the vehicle so that he could assess his injury. Joe had to lay sideways across the middle to get a look at the injury. He was concerned once again that, with his ass pointed toward the rooftop snipers, it would be too juicy a target to pass up.

Dumdie groaned and cried out as Thompson shone a light on the man's leg. A huge piece of the man's shinbone was missing, and he was gushing blood. Thompson retrieved Dumdie's field dressing and slapped it on the wound. He held pressure on the leg even though it made the NCO writhe in pain. It wasn't enough to kill him, but the shock certainly could if they didn't get him help soon.

"Sir! Dumdie's hit bad! He's bleeding heavy from the leg!"

----

"Roger that!" Denomy yelled back. He had been mulling their situation over. They were heavily outnumbered by a determined and prepared enemy. He had a nebulous picture of his combat strength. Hell, the wounded in his own vehicle were stacking up. The pitiful groaning from Dumdie was enough to override the last reservations he had about violating the Rules of Engagement. The ROE, particularly the limitations on the types of ammo that could be employed, had been directed for use in a humanitarian relief setting devoid of a persistent threat. The situation had changed and he was ready to lay his career on the line to make a tough call. He picked up the radio and said, "All Comanche elements, this is Comanche 6. Twenty-five millimeter High Explosive rounds are authorized. I say again, go hot on 25mm HE. Engage at will!"

Denomy wasn't entirely sure that they heard him until the heavy whump-whump of the Bradley Fighting Vehicles' main guns began to beat the air. It was one of the sweetest sounds he had ever heard. Between salvos, Denomy heard his boss—Lieutenant Colonel Volesky—over the radio. "Comanche 6, this is Lancer 6. Go ahead and authorize HE on your Bradleys."

Denomy casually replied, "I've already done that, Sir."

----

Captain Denomy looked to his left and noticed that his driver, Specialist Seth Weibley, had been wounded. Now everyone in his vehicle, including himself, was a casualty, though none as severe as Dumdie. The NCO had quieted but was still rocking with pain. Thompson tried to keep him talking. If he lost consciousness, he could easily slip into shock and die. "Stay with me, Sergeant!" Denomy made the call to abandon the rescue attempt and push south down Route Delta to link up with the rest of Task Force Lancer.

By this time, the Battalion had gained control of the southern end of the city. Just outside the District Area Council building, the government edifice at the corner of Florida and Delta, they had established a hasty Casualty Collection Point. Alpha Company had been hit hard and they were still trying to load out the wounded and dying.

Here, Troy Denomy put a badly wounded Alpha soldier in his seat and told his driver to follow their escort back to the FOB. He then dashed off for a face-to-face with his boss.

----

Thompson didn't see him again until much later that night. JT called back to Fowler, who had been in the open for their entire jaunt down Hell's Alley, worried that it was too quiet back there. At first he heard no answer. Panicking, he looked over his shoulder. Aaron Fowler was sitting calmly, a self-applied pressure bandage over his bloody knee, smoking a cigarette.

"You know you can't smoke within fifty feet of a military vehicle, right?" Thompson was grinning. Fowler offered him a few anatomically impossible pass-times for his consideration and continued to puff. They both laughed.

----

Each soldier on the roof shared the same thought when Robinson told them that the QRF had again been repelled: *are we screwed now or what?* Then everyone laughed. They had no idea of the horror that the convoy was plowing through, but would have laughed just the same had they known. Not from cruelty—that their brothers were experiencing the same baptism by fire into the fraternity of warriors—but rather from an acceptance that their fate was still in the balance. They could all yet die, so they laughed and laughed to keep the fear at bay.

Riddell appeared with two boxes of 5.56mm ammo. He moved to the middle of the roof and told everyone to throw him their empty magazines. Everyone gladly complied; multiple mags clattered to the ground around him. Rob, noting that Hayhurst was no longer able to focus on anything but pain, told him to pull in and help Riddell. Between the two of them, they completed the task quickly, making good use of the speed-loaders included with each box of bullets.

Wild retrieved enough magazines to replace his expended basic load of seven. As he began stowing each gray metal magazine into an empty pouch, he noticed that every bullet that he could see in the mag's opening were tipped with orange

"Tracers?" Wild groaned. "You idiot, you brought all the tracer rounds."

"They'll kill just the same," Riddell said with a touch of defensiveness.

"Yeah," conceded Wild, "And melt the barrel down, too." He shrugged. At least it would be one hell of a last stand.

"Christ, I need a cigarette!" sighed Bourquin.

"Here," said Wild, "They're Miami's, but better than nothing."

"Let me get one of those, man," said Riddell. Wild ended up passing a smoke to each man on the rooftop except for Rogers, who declined. They shared the tobacco without saying anything, wondering how long they would have to hold on until help could find them. Hayhurst puffed on the Iraqi-made cigarette with his back to the very wall that had ejected the bullet that hit him. Doc had cut his sleeve away to the shoulder. Two tiny dots of red could be seen through the white of the bandages. Wild sat beside him and told Bourquin to snap a picture.

Eric Bourquin saw the white edges of Hayhurst's bandages were beginning to turn red. Each time he moved his shoulder the wrong way, the sickening pop made Bourquin wince as though he were watching someone get kicked in the gonads. Bourquin picked up Roger's shotgun—unused since breaching the door—and handed it to Ben. "Why don't you take this and trade out with Perry guarding the detainees?"

----

Hayhurst descended from the LP/OP, easing past the blocked stairwell, bandaged and bloody, holding a shotgun. He walked across the courtyard and called to Perry so that he wouldn't be spooked. "Friendly coming in!"

Perry turned to him and nodded. The young private did a doubletake when he saw the Sergeant's bandaged and bloody shoulder. The family he had been guarding had been speaking to each other comfortingly in low voices until the wounded Arizona native entered the room. They fell dead quiet when they saw his expression and the large-bore shotgun in hands that trembled with rage.

Perry noted the look, too, and recognized it for what it was. He had felt the same thing earlier when he had been faced with the offensive sight of Chen's body and needed someone to blame. Almost everyone who had come in to pay their last respects—as if the tiny kitchen, reeking of stale cooking oil and blood, were a funeral parlor—had mirrored that same expression. Perry asked the NCO what he was supposed to do now. Hayhurst said nothing; his burning eyes locked on to the cowering family, but pointed up. Perry understood. He went upstairs to the LP/OP to see what he could do.

----

By happy coincidence, Aguero came limping into the CCP to pay his last respects to his gunner. He paused in the doorway as he noted Hayhurst standing watch over Chen and their involuntary Iraqi hosts.

The wounded man's posture told Aguero that the young lad from Arizona was considering Texas-style justice, holding a shotgun with one hand and cradling a bandaged arm.

Aguero stood over Chen's body, sharing Ben's anger. Anger and sadness and then more anger to cover up the sadness. He didn't know what to say, couldn't think of anything that didn't reek of sympathy-card insincerity. The only thing in his heart at that moment was, *I'm sorry.* The L-T caught movement from the corner of his eye and saw Haubert rocking back and forth in a dark corner. Aguero burned with rage.

"Get out there and fight, Stanley!"

Haubert held up his hand and muttered something that the L-T couldn't hear.

"Damn it, Stanley! Pick up your weapon, go out there and fight!" Aguero knew what shock was, and he knew about Post Traumatic Stress Disorder. He was so angry at the moment, though, that he honestly didn't care how bad Haubert's injuries were—he was on the verge of grabbing the NCO by the collar and throwing him out into the street.

Stanley Haubert turned his back to the lieutenant and sat down, mumbling something over and over that was not quite audible. Aguero hurled a curse at him and spun around.

Guzman appeared behind him. "Yeah," said the medic, "He's pretty much gone."

"Screw him." The L-T walked out, searching for something to kill.

----

Break time was over. The Jaeesh Al-Mahdi fighters had returned from the momentary distraction by the rescue team. Another squad of insurgents attempted to storm Coleman's side of the alley while a small group traveled from roof to roof on the southern end. As the militia once again tried to assault their position, rifle fire began to kick up dust and chips of brick and mortar.

Doc Guzman and Taylor called out to Robinson as if reciting lyrics to their least favorite song, "I've got enemy movement over here!"

Robinson moved to Taylor's corner first and yelled, "light 'em up. What are you waiting for?" He turned away, running crouched over toward the two when a bullet knocked him down. Rob thought this might be the end. He didn't feel anything and worried that shock was already taking hold of him. He felt his hips and nearly panicked when his hands encountered a spreading wetness on his backside. "I'm shot!" he exclaimed.

Rogers scrambled over to him and assessed the wound. "Rob, I've got bad news. You're canteen is not going to make it."

Rob looked over his shoulder as Rogers tossed his canteen in front of him. Water poured from a hole near the bottom. "Dude! That had me scared as hell!" Rob chuckled at himself and got back up.

----

Rogers and Bourquin were back on the machine gun. A sudden burst of return fire from the street kicked up dust obliging them both to duck. Rogers rolled over to his knees and yelled, "Shit!"

"What's wrong? You hit?" Bourquin asked as he kept firing.

"No, man. I gotta shit!"

Bourquin laughed hard. "Go right over there then and try not to get your ass shot off!"

Rogers scuttled over and dropped his pants. "Damn," the former fire-fighter said. "I need something to wipe with."

Bourquin threw him a cloth bandoleer from the ammo packaging. "Don't squeeze the Charmin!"

----

### SO note by Rodgers, Renee @ 2 April 2014

### Chief complaint: periods of Anxiety

*SM is groomed for session. He is Caucasian, dressed in military clothing; he is tall and has a large build; he is mildly overweight. The SM is balding; he wears glasses and appears slightly older than his stated age. SM and this provider met for 50 minutes at BJACH BHD. SM describes panic yesterday evening as he read interviews he conducted of fellow SMs who spent time together in combat. SM states he is writing a book about related events and that this is also the anniversary week of that combat experience. Provider reinforces idea of adaptive vs. maladaptive coping methods. SM has plans to meet friends from prior service at FT Hood this weekend. He and his spouse are also repeating vows in front of friends and family.*

### Assessment: Anxiety Disorder NO

----

Since the woman with her damnable bloody hands and my brief foray into blindness, my end of the alley had been quiet. I imagined that the little kids who had been so doggedly trying to kill me had been overcome with remorse at the consequence of their actions and decided to go home. Or maybe I had managed to take them out. Either way, I was grateful for the quiet. Darkness was almost complete and I had my NVGs at the ready. The illumination was good, however, and my ability to see in the dark is excellent.

Behind me, I kept hearing people swapping battlefield rumors. Soldiers in combat are worse than housewives in a beauty salon for gossip. *Yeah, the tanks are at the police station. No, the tanks are turning back. The tanks are at the police station again. Charlie 6 can't make it back. They lost everyone in the convoy. The Mahdi Army is surrendering.* On and on.

About a half hour after darkness fell, the massive main gun of an Abrams tank shattered the momentary lull with a 120mm shell—a bunker buster. A column of M1 tanks were rolling toward us from the south. They weren't troubled by such things as obstacles or debris. The bunker buster round was designed to punch a massive hole through any obstacle.

We were happy as collective clams. I didn't even have to turn around to hear the tanks as they passed. One…two…three tanks rolled by, and I had a momentary feeling of dread that these guys were going to pass us by as well.

----

Attracting their attention was foremost on the Platoon Sergeant's mind. He tried to raise them on the net, but was unsure if his radio was transmitting. He could plainly hear them talking but could not hear a reply. He began flashing the vehicle's headlights and honking the horn.

----

High above them, Robinson and Bourquin were having an animated discussion about their fear of escaping discovery. The first rescue party had missed them in broad daylight even with the coordinates provided by Swope. The two NCOs determined that it wouldn't happen twice. The fire they had previously started to get the helicopter's attention had died. They hoped that if the idea worked once, then it would work twice. Bourquin tore off his other sleeve, revealing a second arm completely covered with tattoos. He lit the end of his sleeve with his cigarette lighter and let the flames build. He then stood up, exposing himself to enemy fire, and began to wave the improvised brand back and forth. He knew that the tanks had thermal sights that could detect even faint heat signatures, but they mostly looked out not up. He hoped that the waving motion would attract the attention of either the tank commanders or their loaders who often rode with the hatch open. Robinson ripped off his sleeve as well and added his make-shift torch to the effort.

Either the radio or flailing torches paid off. The third tank in the order of march stopped directly in front of the alley.

----

Speed was of the essence now, Swope knew. They had to break down their defenses quickly and get everyone loaded up. He was sure that he wouldn't have to cajole his soldiers to get them high-stepping. They would need to account for all their weapon systems. The wounded and dead would have to be loaded and the vehicles recovered. He was pretty sure that the M1114 Humvees would still roll, but they were banged up. It was great to see all that firepower out there, though he had no illusions about what lay ahead. They weren't home yet. He called up to the rooftop observation post on the radio and told them to break down everything and get downstairs on the double. He ran into the courtyard and shouted the good news to the guys in the CCP. "The tanks are here! Get ready to move."

----

Lieutenant Aguero left the preparations in his Platoon Sergeant's capable hands. He ran out toward the tank platoon, wounds forgotten, to have a pow-wow with whoever was in charge. A tall figure extracted himself from the top of the tank, M4 carbine in hand, and jumped to the ground. The name tape said 'Moore.' The rank said 'Captain.'

"Glad to see you," quipped Aguero, "Mind if we get a ride?"

"That's the point," said Captain Moore, "We're going to need your guys to ride on top of the tanks just behind the buzzle rack."

Aguero nodded sagely as the senior man spoke, but he was thinking, *I saw it in a book once. I don't have a clue what the hell you're talking about. I've never even been on a tank.*

He let the Captain talk a moment longer, going on about 'this man here' and 'that man there' before he interjected. "How about if I put my wounded on one tank and then I can just stuff everybody else inside two Humvees?" The L-T was keenly aware of how much his soldiers had endured just driving through the nightmarish ambush, especially the guys in the combat convertibles. He balked at putting his men out in the open unnecessarily. Aguero knew that they couldn't squeeze everyone inside two Humvees. He thought it best, even if cruelly pragmatic, that he keep his non-wounded guys healthy. In the days to come, he was sure that he would need as many able bodies as they could find. The tank commander agreed readily enough and ran back to his tank. The L-T ran back to his platoon to brief them about the plan and supervise the load out.

----

Robinson heard the Platoon Sergeant telling them to collapse down into the alley, even as everyone laughed and cheered when the tank column stopped at their front door. No one was about to argue. Soldiers can be lazy from time to time, and, on occasion, will brag about it. Those who achieve the rank of Specialist often talk about "shamming" and "getting over" on the same par as the seven Army values. Our guys were no different. This night, however, every one of them was a convert to the new religion of velocity. Those on the roof had gathered their equipment and ex-filtrated down to the alley within a matter of seconds. All, that is, except for Robinson, Bourquin, and Wild who were having a spirited debate.

The substance of the argument lay in who was going to be the last one off of the roof. The discourse was lively, cordial, and light-hearted. They were jockeying and jostling with each other to be the last one off the battlefield like Mel Gibson's character in *We Were Soldiers*. Bourquin attempted to settle the discussion by pulling rank. Rob reminded him with a cackle that he had more time in rank than Bourquin had time in the Army. Pushing each other and laughing like brothers—which we all were by that point—they joined the mass exodus down to the lane.

----

Riddell hurriedly took his seat behind the wheel of Red 1 and prayed silently that it would make the journey home. He noted that his baby was riddled with bullets. It had holes in the radiator hose, the transmission was done, all four tires were flat, and the air cleaner had holes in it. The exhaust line had been crushed by the debris in the road. Yet despite all that, it still managed to crank up. Hopefully it would run long enough to get them to safety.

----

I kept my rifle at the ready in case some misguided insurgent wanted to make a last minute bid for the 72 Virgin grand prize. Others were piling in to the vehicle now; I can't even remember exactly who. I was psyching myself up for the trip out, telling myself over and over that 'it's a good day to die' in the hopes that my mind would believe the hype. Davis postponed my chance at Valhalla and a warrior's death a little longer by ordering me to drop down and not to worry about pulling security. The tanks were firepower enough, he pointed out, and we weren't going to risk our lives needlessly. He got no argument from me, I can tell you.

----

Hayhurst left the terrified Iraqi family behind when Rogers and a few others came in to get Chen. In the alleyway, Comanche Red Platoon was collectively preparing to get out of Dodge. Swope saw Hayhurst standing in the gateway and told him to get in Red 4. Ben walked toward the front passenger door in a daze, shock from his wounds threatening to shut him down. He opened the door and climbed in.

"Not in my seat!" yelled Swope, "Get in the back!" Swope realized then that the man was wounded and seemed to not be all there. He opened the rear door for Hayhurst and hurriedly shut it for him as soon as the he was seated. Well, not quite. The door shoved him, shoulder first, into the rear panel of the vehicle, causing far more pain than the bullet had. His vision grayed out for a minute even as he called down curses upon the Platoon Sergeant.

----

Loading Chen was difficult in more ways than simply emotional, which they would all grapple with for years. A dead body has a weight many times greater than what a scale would read. The heavy man's limp form would not cooperate with their best efforts. They spent valuable time trying to perform a simple task that was like trying to thread a noodle through a needle.

Swope cursed, frustrated. "All right. Put him on the hood and we'll sit there and back out of here. Perry! Get behind the wheel, go!" Swope hated to do it. The dead soldier deserved to be borne off the field in honor, but if they didn't hurry, more would join the unfortunate man. Rogers and Coleman laid him as reverently as they could on the hood of the truck. Coleman remounted the gun turret even as Perry began to back the vehicle out under Swope's guidance.

Perry, with no mirrors and four flat tires, could barely maneuver the battered Humvee. He inadvertently hooked the bumper on the same vehicle that Bourquin had tagged with his defunct grenade launcher. Swope pulled him forward about ten feet and told him to ram that SOB through the car if he had to. Perry gunned the engine hard and plowed into it. The car turned sideways and was shoved into the street with such momentum that it came up on two wheels.

----

Davis stood next to Riddell's window as the young man followed in Perry's wake. I was squatting on my haunches, leaned up against Wild or Denney, I can't remember who. Coleman told me that he had seven people crammed into his victor and we had at least that many. This would be the first time in Mechanized Infantry history that you would never hear a grunt complain about being crammed into a vehicle.

----

Lieutenant Aguero reiterated the order for the wounded to ride on the tanks. Swope, recalling the bandage he had seen on Hayhurst, pulled him out of the Humvee and asked Bellamy to help him get on the back of a tank. Bellamy decided to ride with him. Robinson and Davis climbed aboard the tank in front of theirs in the order of march.

----

Bellamy and Hayhurst were just settling into their positions when they saw Swope, Bourquin, Denney, and Wild bearing Chen's body toward their tank. "Help us get him up on the buzzle rack," Swope said. Swope watched as his three soldiers pressed the fallen hero over their heads and gently pushed him onto the deck of the tank. Their hands dropped to their sides almost as if they were performing a funeral rite at Arlington National Cemetery. They all said simultaneously, as if on cue, "I'm sorry." It came out as if they were singing a song. A sad, simple dirge for a good man gone too soon.

Bellamy's heart went numb as he grabbed his dead friend's arm. Hayhurst couldn't use his wounded arm so he wrapped his legs around some unfamiliar protuberance and pulled with his good arm. With great effort they were able to place Chen behind the tank commander's hatch in the spot where Hayhurst had been. Ben laid across Chen's body. He felt so numb from the shock of his wound that the strangeness of laying on top of his dead friend did not sink in until much later.

----

"Swope, let me know when you have a hundred percent accountability of everybody and we'll roll," said Lieutenant Aguero.

Accountability. A very important word in Army parlance. Knowing where your people are is the most basic of leadership functions. Equipment and personnel must be accounted for before movement can begin. Under optimal conditions, this drill only takes a minute at most.

Ten minutes stretched into a seeming eternity as the leadership, nigh to panic, tried to figure out why instead of 20 soldiers—five per vehicle—they could only come up with 19. Did you count the interpreter? Yes. Did you count Chen? Yes. Recount everybody in the Humvees. I did. Shine a light in there, dammit!

Aguero swore violently and muttered, "What the hell is going on?"

Bellamy offered Aguero and Bourquin a smoke.

"Yeah, sure." Smoking within 50 feet of a military vehicle wasn't the most dangerous thing he had done all day long, and a smoke sounded pretty good right now.

Just then Sergeant Bourquin saw something on a rooftop, right above the alley they had just evacuated. "Sir, there's something up there! I don't know what it is but it keeps moving."

"Shoot it," said the L-T with no more concern than if they were discussing politics.

Bourquin sighted in on the target, aimed center mass and fired.

The Lieutenant laughed hard. He had donned his own NVD and saw the target clearly. "Congratulations, Sergeant! You just took out a really nasty insurgent flag. And it was heading right for us!"

"Sir, we're good!" Swope shouted over the roar of the tank engines. "I was looking for twenty soldiers, but I forgot that we left York in the rear when we changed the COMSEC at lunch."

"Lucky him," Aguero noted. "It's been a long day at the office, Sergeant. What do you say we blow this joint?"

"Roger that, Sir!" growled Swope as he climbed into his victor. "Let's roll!" he shouted.

Lieutenant Aguero gave a thumbs-up to Moore that they were ready as he ran to his own vehicle. Moore transmitted to his Battalion Commander that they were pulling out, time now.

----

Captain Moore twisted around and shouted at Hayhurst, "We're going to shoot the main gun like a mother! If the guy behind me has to shoot, you need to stay low because the blast could kill you. I say again, the concussion could kill you, so you need to stay low."

Hayhurst thought, *I'm going to die.*

----

As Lieutenant Aguero reached his Humvee, he realized that he had already put someone in his seat, and he didn't feel like kicking the soldier out. He just didn't have it in him to do that right then. As he looked around for an empty spot he heard Davis call to him, "Sir! Come up here with me!" Aguero sprinted to the Abrams tank and leapt up as nimbly as he would have done ten years ago, uninjured and with no gear.

The tank column pulled out, heading north toward a safety that was completely uncertain.

----

**SO note by Rodgers, Renee @ 31 March 2014**
**Chief complaint: periods of anxiety**

*SM states the 4th of April is the anniversary of his first combat experience. He recently reestablished contact with a tank commander by email. SM states he did not have a difficult anniversary period in 2013 but he has prior to this. SM reports anger, intrusive thoughts, and problems with sleep.*

### Assessment: ANXIETY DISORDER NOS

----

I don't remember much about our last flight up Chuwadr Street, or good ol' Route Delta if you prefer, except being uncomfortable. It was dark outside, and I was grateful that they had decided to button everybody up inside the vehicles. The sound of deadly pebbles hitting our armor was loud, but it no longer raised my heart rate even a little. Routine stuff. The mind can get used to anything, I guess.

Each four-seat Humvee was carrying six or seven soldiers, and everyone was getting to know their neighbor very well. Wild, Coleman, Rogers, Bourquin, and Haubert were engaged in a rousing game of combat Twister: *right foot, passenger seat; left foot, Coleman's helmet.* Before they had rolled very far, Rogers began to growl with pain. "Dude!" he said, "My calf is cramped up!"

"I got you, Bro!" said Wild. He began to knead Roger's leg to ease the charley horse.

The ride was rough. The tanks flattened everything in their path, and left a trail of debris that the armored Humvees had to either dodge or bounce over. With every tire flat and with maneuverability severely compromised, it was mostly bounce.

----

The men on the tanks were not having as much fun. In fact, both Hayhurst and Bellamy considered it to be the most traumatic thing that they had ever had to endure. Hayhurst's mind blanked out most of what happened. He could remember sinking as far into the buzzle rack as he possibly could as the bullets bounced off the side of the tank and the rockets sizzled over their heads. His good hand gripped the shotgun that he knew would be ineffective unless insurgents were stupid enough to attempt to board the vehicle. Where his rifle had absconded to he could not say. He felt Chen's dead body underneath him and shuddered.

----

Lieutenant Aguero, Davis, and Robinson were in the lead tank, which suited the Platoon Leader just fine. He would have a better handle on the unfolding battle as he was right next to the convoy leader's head. He didn't realize, however, just how loud a tank can be. He had never ridden inside an Abrams before, let alone on top of one. The 60 tons of rattling and roaring steel, on top of the ringing in his ears from the grenade blasts and machine gun fire, made him effectively deaf.

So when the TC—Tank Commander—began pointing something of apparent interest out to him and trying to otherwise communicate, all Aguero could do was shrug his shoulders. The tanker pulled off his CVC helmet and shouted louder. Aguero gave him a thumbs up so the guy would turn around and pay attention to the battlefield.

Behind the tank bearing the P-L rode Bellamy, Hayhurst, and the fallen warrior. The two battered and smoking M1114s were next with five more tanks pulling up a very heavy rear guard. Ak-47s rattled on all sides, bullets striking against armor like deadly gravel. Fortunately, a tank has an impressive amount of point defense weaponry. And they weren't stingy with the 120mm main gun, either. The thunderous boom of the silver-bullet rounds echoed into the night as the Crusader Company cut a bloody swathe through the previously impenetrable barricades.

Tracers crisscrossed the night in front of them like laser beams. Aguero thought it looked like a gunfight scene from the first Star

Wars movie. He wasn't sure what to shoot at or where. The flashes of light left his monocular PVS-14 Night Vision Goggles in continual wash-out. He fired in random directions, not caring what he hit, attempting to suppress whoever was trying to cut them down. When he fired the last round of his last magazine, he reached forward, tapped the TC, and yelled, "Ammo!" The TC disappeared into his hatch and reappeared with a whole bag of magazines like a merry ol' Santa. The L-T rummaged through the sack, slapped a new mag home, and continued dealing death at discount prices.

----

Davis and Robinson followed their leader's example and slung lead like there was no tomorrow, a suspicion they were beginning to think might prove true. Davis did a double take when he heard an extended volley of fire from Robinson. *How did he get the SAW?* Davis wondered. Deciding that it wasn't really important, he directed Rob's attention to a two-story building with darkened windows they were passing on the left. Orange flashes of fire erupted from a second-floor window. "Take 'em out, Darby!" Robinson raked the enemy position once, twice, and found his mark on the third attempt. The gun in the window fell silent. To add injury to injury, the tank behind them, having been drawn to the target by Rob's tracers, fired the main gun into the building. Davis' ears rang with the blast, but he couldn't stop grinning.

----

They reached Silver and swung right. Aguero noted a little white car of vague European make weave through their formation from the left. The daredevil driver matched his speed with the lead tank. The passenger crawled out the window with an AK-47 and began to fire. Aguero wondered if he had fallen into a bad action movie. *Who does something that dumb?* he thought as he shot the assailant in the forehead. The tank commander opened fire on the driver with his M4 carbine. Lieutenant Aguero was thrilled when the car swerved wildly to the right, plowed into a metal kiosk, and burst into flames. The Platoon Leader felt a surge of hope for the first time that they might actually survive the night.

----

Riddell should have felt secure tucked in as he was among the most powerful land combat vehicles the world has ever seen. The night had turned extremely dark as the full moon hid behind gathering clouds. The Abrams in front further obscured his vision as the treads kicked up a gray cloud of dust. Riddell could just see the tank's two tail lights peeking out. Red 4's vehicle, directly in front of him, had long since lost its tail lights to enemy fire. Riddell had managed to dodge the majority of the wreckage even with four flat tires and a desire to stay close to the man in front. Riddell matched the tank's right turn on to Silver perfectly. "Awesome! A straight shot to the FOB!"

Riddell saw a spark come from the under carriage of the Abrams tank and had only a split second to wonder what it was. Perry swerved quickly left then right, but Riddell was following so close that he wasn't able to dodge the hidden obstacle. The vehicle suddenly lurched to a stop as if a giant hand had exploded from the ground and grabbed us like an insect.

"Riddell, what happened? Why did we stop?" cried Guzman.

"We bottomed out on something!"

"What?"

"I don't know! We're not going anywhere!"

Riddell looked up and saw the tail lights of the lead tanks disappearing into the darkness.

----

Lieutenant Aguero had no idea that he was leaving his platoon behind for the second time that day. The two lead tanks kept rolling, oblivious to the platoon's plight. The tanks bringing up the rear had no idea that the rest of their element kept going because of the dark and dust.

Crusader 6 stopped outside the entrance gate to FOB War Eagle where a massive casualty collection operation was underway. Moore called over his shoulder to Comanche Red 1, "You boys are good! Tell everyone to dismount; we're going back out in sector."

"OK!" Aguero yelled over the engine's rumble, "Thanks for the ride!"

The commander waved his arm dismissively as if he did this sort of thing three times a day before breakfast. Aguero, Robinson, and Davis alternately jumped and helped each other jump down. Aguero was beginning to feel a little stiff.

----

Medics and other soldiers were swarming around the other tank, helping Hayhurst descend. Bellamy stayed on board to make sure that his friend was unloaded with utmost dignity and respect. Chen deserved that. Once accomplished they began to walk toward the clinic as medics loaded Chen's body onto a stretcher.

"Hey, you're injured," someone called. "You can't walk. We need to load you out."

"Piss off," growled Hayhurst. "I've been fighting for the last two hours since I've been hit. It's not going to matter if I walk another hundred meters."

----

Aguero remained behind standing on Route Silver with Rob and Davis. They were looking down the road they had just travelled wondering when the Humvees were going to show up. He saw nothing on the road as far as the night would let him see. Feeling more than a little dazed and much confused, the three warriors looked back and forth at each other.

"Son of a bitch." swore the L-T. Aguero ran to the FOB entrance where he encountered a large Staff Sergeant who was coordinating the medevac.

The medic looked at him with no comprehension. "I don't know what you're talking about," the man said.

"My platoon, asshole," Aguero was shouting now, almost blind with fury, "Where are my two Humvees? And where did those two tanks just go?"

The NCO was so dumbfounded by the question and the raw emotion in the Lieutenant's voice that all he could do for a moment was gape like a newly caught fish. "Sir, I don't know."

----

York would have been relieved to know that as his group pulled out of the FOB a very battered and very relieved platoon was returning through the entrance gate. York still felt the keen sting of worry, though, as he continued to wonder who had been killed.

His team watched the gunner's view on the monitor in the Bradley's troop compartment with fascination. It was like watching the best movie and the best video game all rolled in to one. As they neared the corner of Delta and Silver, York saw the gunner acquire a target and dispatch it with clinical precision using a single burst from the 240 Coax.

The turret door swung open and the Bradley Commander shouted down to them that they were dropping the ramp so that they could dismount. York couldn't tell who it was and didn't even know what vehicle he currently riding in. It looked like the XO, Lieutenant Clay Spicer, but he wasn't sure.

York's impromptu squad was out of the vehicle before the ramp hit the ground. The streets were empty and quiet. He had no clue where they were, but tall buildings rose on all sides. They were in the middle of an intersection with a Bradley Fighting Vehicle covering each avenue. York saw Specialist Holbrook and Lovett several meters away behind cover. Tyrell moved to an empty vendor stall.

York squinted as his eyes adjusted to the gloom. Darkness was gathering close and clouds obscured the moon and stars. Clouds or smog. York guessed that they were probably staring south down Route Delta. Maybe this was the corner of Copper and Delta, but he wasn't sure. He saw in the very middle of the intersection a door-less Humvee. York ran over to them.

"Hey, who are you guys?"

"We're 2nd ACR," said a wide-eyed young Sergeant.

"OK," said York, "Well, we're going to secure this side of the intersection. Let us know if you need any help." York glanced and their completely unarmored Humvee as he said this, shaking his head.

The red-headed Texan ran back over to his men and began to assign sectors of fire. Specialist Bo Roth—pronounced as one name, Boroth—was a gangly red-head from Minnesota and a perpetual clown. York liked the kid. He was easy to work with.

York told him, "You watch here and here."

Roff gave him a thumbs-up. "Roger, Sergeant."

York turned around to give directions to Rusch, but before he could move, a rocket roared between Roff and himself at eye level and slammed into the Bradley behind them. York cursed and dove for cover. He was up in an instant and sprinted to the side of the vehicle away from contact. Specialist Rusch pointed his SAW in that general direction and sent for a long volley of fire in response.

York rounded the far side of the Bradley just as Roff appeared from the other side. Bo's face appeared absolutely transfigured with glee. He was laughing as if he were playing tag with the neighborhood kids. York didn't know whether to be pissed or impressed.

"Sergeant York, did you see that?" Roff was practically gushing, "What do I do?"

"Shoot back, dumbass," yelled York, but he was laughing now, too. The kid's attitude was infectious. The BFVs also joined the fight, throwing hundreds of rounds down range. York felt his heart pounding and his Irish temper rising. His fear flew away, replaced by a sudden urge to kill the sonofabitch that had dared to shoot at him. He thought, *Oh, my God, this is real, this is for real.* He wondered how his brothers trapped in the alley were going to make it back alive.

----

Those same thoughts were running through my head as we sat atop a massive bump going nowhere fast. Bourquin called out to make sure that we were OK. Fortunately, we had wedged ourselves in much like proverbial sardines, so it was almost as good as a seatbelt.

We untangled ourselves and exited the vehicle. Riddell was peering under the vehicle to find out what happened and how we could quickly fix it. The headlights of the tank behind us revealed that we had fetched up on top of a massive rock and were now high centered and immobile. It also looked like the axle was sheered in two.

Riddell picked up the radio, frustrated but calm, and called, "Red 4, this is Red 1; we just lost a wheel."

Swope's swift reply was incredulous and quite explicit.

"I say again, we just lost a wheel. We're stuck on something."

----

Swope stopped his Humvee at the Home Depot intersection. The two tanks in front of him, the one in the lead carrying the L-T, continued without slowing toward the FOB. Another Humvee platoon—a group of four—was sitting at the intersection to claim ownership of that piece of land. Swope left his Humvee and ran to one of them.

Swope yelled up, "What unit are you in?"

"Second ACR."

"Hey, can you run me back down Silver about two-hundred meters? I've got soldiers down there. I've lost two vehicles tonight, and I ain't losing another!"

Swope pulled up in short order riding in a Humvee with no flat tires. He was on the ground before the victor stopped moving, assessing damage to Red 1. He peered under the vehicle and asked the guys from 1st AD if they would back up to our front bumper. Taylor and Riddell worked quickly together to release the cargo straps they had previously attached to the grill. These straps were part of a redneck solution we had developed in the gentle sands of the National Training Center as a method for self-recovery. Actual towing cables were hard to come by, and the more desirable tow-bars a thing of myth. The two expert drivers had the straps attached in less than a minute, just the way we had trained for in the Mojave Desert. The good Samaritans from 1st AD powered forward and the straps snapped as though made of toilet paper. Pulling out of sand, it seemed, is vastly different than trying to miracle yourself off of a rock.

After some creative swearing, Swope ran back to the L-T commanding the tank behind us. "Hey, Sir." Swope had to shout loudly to be heard over the roar of the tank engine. "Can you sit there and use your tank to push the Humvee?"

"What?" asked the tanker. Swope explained his plan at high volume. The tanker, of a mind that infantry guys must be half insane, said, "Uh, OK."

Swope looked up and saw Taylor, the young kid who had kept his head and drove so brilliantly when his leadership had been taken out. "Taylor, can you steer this thing? I ain't gonna make you do it, but I'm going to have this tank push the victor off and back to the FOB."

Taylor looked at him soberly and nodded, "Roger, Sergeant." He crawled behind the wheel as Swope motioned the tank forward. He got on his knees and peered under the vehicle to make sure that Humvee was being pushed and not crushed. It was working.

----

The tank made short work of liberating our vehicle. Swope wisely told the rest of us not to get in the back of that particular Humvee. If we snagged another quick stop like that, the tank would probably not be able to stop until it had crushed the rear compartment. Not odds any of us wanted to play. Riddell and Guzman alighted onto the tank pushing Red 1. I watched Sala'am and Denney load up into the 1st AD truck that had brought Swope. I went to load up with them but saw that they were ridiculously overloaded.

"All right," I told the driver, "I'll run beside you. It's less than a mile; just let me use you for cover." My leg was throbbing now, but I felt no doubt that I could run twice the distance if need be and gladly. I took off at a trot down Silver, not giving them time to debate it. I ran an entire 30 feet before I came to another Humvee parked across the road. The driver's door opened and I saw faces that I did not recognize. More 1st AD.

"Get in!" They called. I dove in the back, happy to oblige.

----

Aguero, not knowing where the rest of his platoon might be or what had become of them, was not going to sit around and wait. He would lead another expedition himself if he had to, but everyone was coming back. "Bellamy, Rob, Davis, let's go!"

Worried that the L-T was about to do something foolish like lead a three-man rescue team on foot back into the city, Davis said, "Sir, it's good. They're coming."

Before Aguero could protest, a Sergeant First Class trotted up to them. He had obviously been alerted by the rattled medic that an officer, newly arrived from sector, was about to go postal. In a placatory voice he said, "Hey, your men are on Silver. They've got five tanks with them. They're coming here right now. You need to go report to the TOC."

Mollified, the L-T said, "OK, cool."

Aguero slipped into a semi-conscious state of shock. He couldn't remember next if he walked or had caught a ride from the gate. He remembered telling Davis, "Make sure you get full accountability of all the people when they show up. We lost two Humvees, so go try to find another two. And get more ammo for when we go back out."

Then he went to find the TOC, or Tactical Operations Center. He found the building that their Battalion Task Force had been using when his platoon had left the FOB what felt like millions of years ago. When he walked through the door, he had a sense of disconnection most profound. He thought, *All these new people, I have no clue who they are.*

Aguero called out to a bustling Captain, "Where is the Battalion Commander?"

He turned around, "Who are you?"

Aguero, hurting and ill-tempered, shot back, "Who are you?

"This is the 1-12 TOC."

"Where is the 2-5 TOC?"

"Over there," the captain said with a disinterested wave.

"Where is 'over there'?" The L-T was alarmed at how quickly his temper threatened to take over.

The officer regarded him for a moment, "The big red building."

Aguero then recalled that the Change of Command had happened a few hours earlier and his Battalion's TOC had moved. Cursing in frustration, the battered L-T limped toward the headquarters building. He saw a familiar face along the way: Captain Gerhardt, commander of the Battalion's Forward Support Company.

"Lieutenant Aguero!" Gerhardt exclaimed.

"Hey, Sir. What's up?"

"What is wrong with you?"

"Nothing, don't worry about it."

"No, no, here, let me help you."

Captain Gerhardt tried to help support Aguero's weight with a side carry, but Comanche Red 1 was irate. "Get away from me!" Aguero limped toward the large, two-story structure in the center of camp. He opened a door leading into a room and hallway on the first floor and found no one. He called out and heard nothing in reply. He stepped outside and ran into a face he vaguely knew.

"Where's the TOC?" he asked.

"It's upstairs."

"Upstairs?" The L-T looked up the abnormally tall flight of steps attached to the outside of the building. A door at the top of the landing had a small window from which glowed a faint light. Of course, upstairs. Cursing his luck and his aching leg, he grabbed the railing and took the steps one at a time.

He saw the familiar face of Captain Battle—the Battle Captain by title—who greeted him with warm surprise, "Lieutenant Aguero, holy crap. You're here!"

"Yeah, where's my platoon?" He didn't feel like exchanging pleasantries; he just wanted to find his men.

"What? You don't know where your platoon is at?"

"No. The tanks are supposed to bring them, and they hadn't arrived yet. I've got Davis, Rob, and Sergeant Bellamy looking for them. And some E7 said that you needed to talk to me and I'm supposed to be here. Where is my platoon?"

Battle said, "I don't know where your platoon is."

"Goddam it, where is my platoon?" The captain ignored him and walked off. Captain Gerhardt, who had never been far away, approached him. "Your platoon is inside the FOB."

"What?"

"They returned to the FOB. They're over there somewhere."

"Well, let me go see them."

The Operations Officer, a major, walked back over and said, "No, you're going to stay here. You need to tell me what went on."

So Lieutenant Aguero gave him the rundown, delivering it in a dead tone that belied the rage beneath. The Ops Officer made small vocalizations like punctuation. "OK, OK, uh-huh," while writing notes and shaking his head.

When Aguero finished, the major snapped his green notebook closed and exclaimed, "Great job. Now, go find your platoon."

"Captain Gerhardt, where is my platoon?"

He said, "I'll take you there."

They went downstairs slowly. Gerhardt took the L-T's weapon so that he could move easier. Aguero saw that they were heading to the aid station.

"Where are you going?"

"Your platoon is at the aid station."

"OK."

----

Swope had returned even as the crafty Captain Gerhardt attempted to lead the half-mad Lieutenant Aguero into a medical ambush. As soon as the battered remnants of Red Platoon entered the FOB, the NCO directing traffic at the entrance said, "Hey, man, you've got to take your vehicles over here for maintenance."

Swope took a look at the smoking wrecks that had been in great shape a few hours earlier and thought the man was having fun with him. He laughed to himself and said, "All right. I guess the paint could use a touch-up."

Swope ordered everyone out of the vehicles except the drivers. Medics swarmed the rest, asking who had been wounded. We walked through the gate, victorious and weary.

----

"You lied," Aguero accused Gerhardt, "My platoon's not at the aid station."

Gently, the good captain replied, "You need to see the Doc. You're all bloody."

"Screw you. Where is my platoon?"

The FSC commander sighed, "OK; hold on." Gerhardt produced an ICOM radio, a fancy, military-grade walkie-talkie, and made a call. A second later came the crackly reply. "They're all back. Your commander is consolidating everyone at the chow hall. Go check on them and get yourself seen, Shane."

Aguero nodded and limped toward the DFAC. It took a seeming eternity to cross a very short distance. When he arrived he saw that most of his platoon was indeed assembled there.

Captain Denomy saw him and waved him over. "Looks like you had a rough day, Shane," said the commander.

"Yeah."

Denomy said, "There blood's running out of your ear."

Aguero shrugged, "Oh, it's not mine. It's other people's blood."

Denomy half believed him for a second until he saw a little more blood ooze out of his ear. "You need to go get that looked at."

"I'll do it later."

"You're going to do it now, Lieutenant." The captain smiled and said gently, "Shane, that's an order."

Shane sighed, "Let me talk to my platoon first."

Denomy nodded, "You've got five minutes."

Lieutenant Shane Aguero, Platoon Leader and warrior, limped over to where his soldiers, his men, were gathered. Aguero felt a welling pride that left him in imminent danger of weeping over their bravery. He wanted to tell them something that conveyed how proud he was to fight with them; to what great extent they had kicked ass. Something cool like that. He stood in front of them and felt that any word that came out of his mouth would cheapen their gallant actions. He stood for a second in front of them and let the moment pass. He began to sway on his feet and was suddenly aware that he was no longer inside the cafeteria but was being escorted to the aid station by his company commander.

Denomy sat him down inside on a litter and caught the attention of one of the scrambling medics. "Take care of this man," he said.

All the lights were off in the clinic, presumably to remove a potential targeting method for the numerous mortar teams. One of the attendants squatted down and began to look him over, "Where are you hit?"

"I don't know," Aguero said truthfully. He hadn't had time to think much about it.

The Medic was incredulous, "How do you not know?"

"I don't know. My whole left side is numb and my head hurts. Let's start there." Aguero felt like he would rather have another cigarette right then.

"Take off your gear so we can evaluate you." Aguero began to peel off layer after layer of bloody equipment and clothing. The doc began checking the armor plating for holes with the help of a small, powerful flashlight. Finding nothing, they told him to take off his Kevlar helmet. When he did a fine powdery, white substance fell out onto the floor. "What is that?" asked the medic.

"I don't know, man."

"Dude, you got shot in the head!"

"Yeah, whatever," said Aguero dismissively. "It didn't penetrate."

The medic carefully felt around the L-T's cranium to see if that was indeed the case. "You've got a big lump right here. Do you hurt anywhere else?"

"My whole leg and arm."

By this time, another combat medic had joined the examination. They both helped the Lieutenant take off his DCU top and then his tee shirt. "You've got a small wound here." They put a Band-Aid on it. When the medic spun him around to examine his legs, he sucked in a breath.

"Whoa," they said. Aguero had blood all over his leg and rear end.

"Sir, you need to take your pants off."

"What, right here? I'm going commando today," said Aguero, using the common infantry euphemism of the underwear-less.

"Oh, OK. Hold on." They moved him into a holding area where two soldiers were both asleep. They were lying on the floor in the fetal position.

The Doc said, "Take off your pants in here."

Aguero stripped un-self-consciously, if a little stiffly. The medic left the room to gather medical supplies, leaving the L-T with his pants around his ankles. About that time one of the wounded soldiers awoke to find a naked man standing over him.

Aguero, aware of how he would feel in that situation, said, "I'm sorry, guy; the medics just told me to take off my pants."

"All right," the wounded man said groggily. Nevertheless, the man backed into a corner. Then the other man awoke and likewise noted the new, bare-ass neighbor. The soldier got up and left the room.

At about that time, the new battalion chaplain appeared in the doorway. "Well, how are you doing today, soldier?" he said.

"I'm pleased to meet you, Sir," Aguero said while shaking his hand. The L-T added, "I never thought I'd ever shake hands with a chaplain with my junk just hanging out."

"Yeah," agreed the chaplain with perhaps a touch of discomfort, "That's pretty unusual. That's pretty unusual, Soldier. Well…good job." The good chaplain turned on his heels and left.

Medics returned with antiseptic swaps and Band-Aids. "Sir, you caught a lot of grenade shrapnel, but you'll be just fine."

"Are you going to take it out or what?"

"No, it'll work its way out," the medic said.

Lieutenant Aguero was not at all pleased to learn that he would be carrying around more than the USDA recommended daily allowance iron and minerals. "Like when?"

"Don't worry, you'll be fine."

"OK," the L-T said dubiously and thought, *Easy for you to say*. He was amused to note that the entirety of his medical treatment consisted of Band-Aids and Motrin.

----

The Company gathered in the Dining Facility to rest, recover, and regroup. The 1SG, XO and the rest had returned after witnessing the destruction of Muqtada Al Sadr's headquarters building as M1 Abrams tanks rammed the building like bulldozers dancing on a concrete grave.

Denomy called us all together quietly. He was not a fire and brimstone kind of guy. He was solid, kind, and decent. He was the sort people listened to when things were tough. His firm jaw and honest Midwestern features lent an automatic credence to whatever he was saying. Now he was telling us that it was all right to be sad, to mourn. He explained what was happening outside the fence. He told us that we may have been kicked in the teeth, but that those responsible were going to know our names real soon. He didn't promise us that we would take some time off to gather ourselves or to lick our wounds. He promised us that we would soon go back out into the fight.

When he made that promise, a glad cry erupted from a hundred throats. On this day we had our first taste of battle and wanted more. Soldiers had fallen, never to rise again, but we would avenge them. War was no longer an abstract concept; it was our profession and trade. Bonds of brotherhood had been forged with blood and sweat. We had been made to bleed, but we could not be made to quit. This was our first day as true warriors.

After Captain Denomy said his piece, we bowed our heads to remember a good man fallen too soon. The macho sense of ego-preservation was markedly absent. No posturing. No pretending that we were too strong to need the comfort of another human being. Tough, strong warriors wept uncontrollably in each other's arms, grieving for a friend. Not all, but most. Others mourned in silence, content to take strength from each other's company.

Death is something that every soldier learns how to deal but seldom learn to deal *with*. It's hard enough steeling yourself to the act of taking a human life, no matter what any of these hard-charging knuckle draggers will tell you. It's a hard thing. Not hard to do. Hard to live with once it's done. It's even more difficult to process the simple fact that a man you have lived with, trained with, and fought with has gone to the long hall of his father's leaving you to grope about in the dark. He has become the gaping hole in your formation. He has become the letter home to grief-stricken loved ones. He has become the one you might have saved if you had trained harder, fought more ferociously, or made wiser decisions in the heat of the moment.

When I felt able, I went outside to the refrigerated van that was tasked to contain the last remains of the fallen until they could be sent home. Bellamy, Bourquin, and Wild were gathered around Chen's body, saying goodbye with words I couldn't hear. I was glad that I couldn't hear. I waited until they left and then said my own goodbyes, hoping that Chen could hear me. I told him that we were going back out soon and that I would try to make him proud when it mattered. I told him again that I was sorry. I was sorry.

I saw other bodies in the truck stuffed into their tidy black cocoons. In the gloom I couldn't make out exactly how many were there. Horror struck my heart when I realized that these were fallen heroes who had, no doubt, died coming out to our rescue. These men had died for our sake. For me. The weight of their sacrifice, the smothering nobility of it, was too great for my heart to bear. I turned away from them, appalled, and almost ran back inside. Of everything that I had endured that day, I had just faced the worst.

And our year-long deployment had only just begun.

----

### SO Note by Rodriguez, Jennifer @ 09 DEC 2010

*37 year-old Active Duty USA Captain currently assigned to HHC 3SB presented to CSC-JBB December 2010 reporting worsening of anxious and depressive symptoms related to writing a book about his first OIF deployment in 2004-2005. Several mental health evaluations in 2008, 2009 for similar symptoms with a diagnoses of Anxiety NOS and Adjustment Disorder. Psychological testing for reported concentration/memory problems with RBANS and CPT. Seen at old CSC-JBB June 2010 and diagnosed with major depressive episode and initiated on Celexa which patient discontinued after 2 weeks due to nausea/fatigue and general reticence of pharmacotherapy.*

*Patient states that his "flipping out" due to recurrence for the last several months of re-experiencing nightmares now occurring almost nightly (often alternated with anticipatory dreams), intrusive thoughts, hypervigilence, irritability, physiologic reactivity when thinking of past combat exposure. States that he has had these symptoms off and on since 2005 but would be able to suppress due to significant avoidance. However, with goal of finishing his book (300 pages complete) he is "having to pull things out I don't want to."*

*Reports depressed mood (described as "a dark weight settling on me" for the last 6 months with feeling like he could cry at any moment.*

### A/P: 1. POST-TRAUMATIC STRESS DISORDER

# ACT III: LANCER LEGACY RANCH

## From Under Fire: Haunted by Memories of War, a Soldier Battles the Army

*By Lynne Duke, Washington Post Staff Writer*
*Monday, November 1, 2004; Page C01*

An Army survey, completed last December, found that 17 percent of soldiers and Marines who'd returned from duty in Iraq reported symptoms of major depression, anxiety or PTSD. The number is expected to go higher with time, as more soldiers return from duty in this conventional war that has become a harsh counterinsurgency campaign. And Matthew J. Friedman, executive director of the National Center for PTSD, predicts that many more PTSD cases will go unreported; the Army survey also found that soldiers still are intensely reluctant to divulge their symptoms because of fear of being stigmatized as weak.

# April 9th, 2004, FOB War Eagle

IN THE EARLY HOURS of April 5th, we launched a counter-offensive to take back the city. I don't remember much of it except that I hardly ever felt tired and my leg hurt like the dickens. It took almost a week to put the enemy back on their heels and another 81 days of daily, sustained combat to bring the insurgents to the peace table. We stayed busy which kept us from imploding under the weight of our memories.

About a week after that first engagement, our battalion took a knee briefly to remember our dead and honor their sacrifice. It is tradition to erect a small monument to the fallen using their own personal effects. We attach the soldier's bayonet to their weapon and stand it up, barrel down, into a wooden base. The dog tags of the fallen hang from the pistol grip. We complete the memorial by placing their boots in front of and their helmet on top of the rifle. Perhaps you've seen pictures.

The day we paused to pay our last respects there were eight memorials, eight soldiers who had paid the final price for freedom. Most of them died on the 4th while trying to rescue our platoon. Trying to rescue me. We honored each one in turn, the First Sergeant of the dead warrior calling their name as part of a roll call that began with the two soldiers immediately preceding the deceased in alphabetical order according to their assigned company.

First Sergeant Casey Carson called out a name that I don't recall. He would have been the man in our company who immediately preceded Chen alphabetically. The soldier responded smartly, "Here, First Sergeant!"

The First Sergeant called out, "Chen." Silence.

"Sergeant Chen!"

"Sergeant Yihjih Lang Chen!" The silence was horrible.

Once all the names were called from the Roll of the Dead, the bugle played "Taps" while a detail fired three volleys of seven shots. To this day I can't bear to hear that awful, irrevocable song. We all bowed our heads as the chaplain led us in prayer. Many tough, tough men openly wept. When the "amen" was given we filed by the memorials one by one. I stopped at each shrine, held the dog tags in my hand and whispered, "Thank you."

I lingered long in front of Eddie Chen's boots. They were clean enough to make me suspect that they weren't his or that perhaps they had chosen another pair. Clean, without spot. I looked down at the blood on my boots. Chen's blood. Eddie was gone. All that I had left were memories and blood.

# Fort Hood, Texas – 2005

I HAD MY OWN demons to confront in the early part of 2005 after completing my first combat tour. I didn't see them at first. In fact, I was feeling downright euphoric. Our unit was home and the Army's 10th Mountain Division was dealing with our former AO in the Sadr City Shiite hole. My wife and I were getting to know each other again, and I had big plans for the future. We were moving back to Columbus, Georgia where I planned to complete my college degree and then move on to officer training. I was so caught up in plans that I failed at first to notice that there were some not-too-subtle changes in the way I confronted life's little problems.

There were nightmares, but I shrugged them off as just a fleeting legacy of my combat experiences. And it didn't seem at all odd that I spent time scanning the Wal-Mart rooftop for snipers before I entered to do some shopping. My heart-rate soared every time we drove along a crowded street, but that didn't seem too weird. Everyone is irritated by traffic, right? I was simply feeling what people are supposed to feel as far as I was concerned and any lingering doubts were erased by the booze that I was consuming at great rates. The booze was a celebration of survival and when I had a bellyful, I could ignore how little I felt about anything.

I was mentally numb and physically deteriorating. My two-mile run time slowed from 13 minutes flat to 14 and a half, but I put that down to the Iraq experience. Our FOB was so small that a guy couldn't really run far enough or often enough under regular rocket and mortar fire to stay in top shape. The Motrin I ate from a Pez dispenser every day numbed the painful twinge in my spine, a result of that close mortar round that should have killed me.

The possibility that I might have something more than a few physical problems occurred to me one evening when I offered to whip three dudes' collective asses if they didn't apologize to my wife for some snide comment made at a local watering hole. The details are blurred by the shots of Cuervo I'd been slamming, and it might be my wife had a hand in the confrontation, but that's not the point. I went from happy drunk to raging bull in a heartbeat. Not only was I demanding unconditional surrender by three pissed-off yahoos, but I recall hoping they would refuse my terms. Fortunately, my wife defused the situation and kept me from serious injury or possible jail time. Pondering the situation the next morning, I wrote it all off to the tequila and forgot about it. Nothing to see here, folks, just move on and ignore the drunk. So, I moved along and shoved Sadr City way down deep in my mental footlocker.

# Fort Benning, Georgia – 2006

Two years have passed since that first deployment to Iraq. I sit staring into a glass of Jack Daniel's whiskey and note the tremble in my hands. The whiskey is supposed to help with that, but it doesn't. What I see reflected in the liquid is a man I can scarcely recognize anymore. What happened to that jovial, wise-cracking soldier that patrolled Sadr City with Lieutenant Aguero and Sergeant Chen and all the other soldiers in his infantry platoon? Where's that guy with such an appetite for knowledge and such a zest for life?

He's sitting here toasting the dead; thinking about good men gone too soon. And this is the second year that he's done that, always on the same day, April 4. And on this night, unlike so many others since he came home from Iraq, this is the only drink he will have. Debauchery is now strictly for weekends. This guy needed to do well in his studies and that demanded a semi-clear head. Like it or not, this guy is me and I'm bound to finish my degree, get a commission, and get back to war. That's a goal and a promise I intend to keep—to myself and to those good men.

The first time I took a shot at getting an education, it was mainly to please my parents; maybe get some kind of degree and some kind of acceptable life. It didn't go well and that eventually led me to the Army, to war in Iraq. That was nearly a decade past and this time I had a goal, a mission, a purpose in passing my class requirements. Despite the motivation I didn't have on the first foray into academia, it's been tough sledding. I struggled every day to focus, to forget—at least for short periods—what happened in Iraq. The irony of chasing a degree in order to obtain an Army commission that would take me back to war wasn't lost on me. I simply ignored it.

The real challenge these days on a college campus in 2006 was suppressing the urge to kill the people who pissed me off. There were a lot of them, and my temper ran hot all the time. During the 20 minute drive to school every day, I imagined myself back in Sadr City behind the trigger of a heavy .50 cal, ready to use it on the idiots sharing the road. And every day it seemed like some slack-jawed snob in one class or another ran his mouth about "that unjust war in Iraq" which led me to daydreams in which I used the bastard's shaggy beard to scrub out an Arab toilet. Some days, the pressure was so intense that I had to just leave to avoid blowing a very violent gasket.

A detonation like that would mean the end of my ROTC scholarship and an insurmountable roadblock to the commission I wanted after graduation. I had to maintain and survive at least eight hours every school week in close proximity to young Americans who couldn't be bothered to occasionally stir the mush in their skulls. And, God help us, a number of those people were also pursuing military commissions. There were just two of us in the ROTC unit who had prior service. The other guy had never deployed, so I was the only one with combat experience. Since I'd spent an Iraq deployment in an infantry platoon, the NCO in charge of our campus unit often tapped me to assist in training the other cadets. I taught familiar stuff like squad tactics and tried to give the cadets—male and female—the occasional motivational lectures in between battle drills. Most of those inspirational talks began with "pay attention" and ended with "or you will die as a horrible failure." They seemed to get the message and I was proud of that. Maybe I had that rare leadership gene.

Other than that, I mainly behaved like an antisocial asshole. The stupid students in my regular classes just made me angry or elicited my sympathy for their ignorance. The men and women in my ROTC unit were mostly just as ignorant, and they made me fear for the soldiers they might lead someday. They were clueless about the sacrifice and bloodshed involved if and when they ever got onto a battlefield in charge of a unit. When I taught them or just talked to them about military service, I wanted to scare them; to get them to re-think the whole deal. When that failed, as it usually did, I was proud of them for ignoring the manic combat vet and sticking to the program.

I struggled to stay focused on the goals, the degree, the commission, the return to war as a leader in the mold of soldiers like Lieutenant Aguero. That required an effort so intense that I had no time for my wife, my parents, old friends or new acquaintances outside the ROTC unit. When I thought about my lonely life—and I didn't do it very often—what I really missed were my Army buddies from my platoon in Iraq. They were either dead, wounded, scattered to the winds chasing a life after the Army, or preparing for yet another combat deployment while I was safe on a college campus.

Sometimes I went through my notes and the tape recordings I had made in Iraq with the intention of writing a book about my combat experiences. My mother made good on her promise to have the tapes transcribed, and I had a pile of papers that contained lots of thoughts and memories about war. The problem was that I couldn't bring myself to begin writing, to turn those notes into something that might be useful or moving for others to read. I always seemed to be too busy with other things or just unwilling to resurrect the memories, free the ghosts, and try to make sense of it all. On the rare occasions when I promised myself that I would try, that I would just get started, I wound up frozen like a cliff diver staring down at surf breaking on deadly rocks. There was bound to be serious pain if I stepped off that cliff, so I procrastinated and justified my cowardice.

And then staring into that glass of Jack on the second anniversary of that April 4 ambush I decided the coward reflected in the whiskey needed to suck it up and honor his buddies by telling their story.

"Here's to you, buddies," I whispered and chugged the drink. And then I settled down to write.

# Columbus State University, Georgia – 2007

I sat in my car on a cool spring morning in Columbus, Georgia after an hour's worth of pushups, sit ups, and a brisk run listening to two journalists talk about the battle of Black Sunday—and lie about me. Martha Raddatz was the guest on some morning show where the host wanted to know all about her new book, *The Long Road Home*

I tuned in halfway through, mesmerized to hear familiar names coming at me in Dolby surround, "…rocket-propelled grenades are coming from everywhere. So they decide they'll get back in Humvees. Before they know it, two of the add-on armor Humvees are disabled. So they find an alley. Shane Aguero, the platoon leader, leads them into the alley. And they turn this small band of soldiers, nineteen soldiers and one Iraqi interpreter, and they walk down this alley. The alley's about ten feet wide. Concrete houses jammed together. And they look for a house to take cover. So they basically break down the door, go in, and they go to the roof. They put the remaining Humvees forming a box in front of that door.

"They've got wounded; they're getting more wounded. They have one soldier who is dead. They're in this house. They don't know where they are. The communications, because they had just gotten there, they didn't have GPS. They were trying to find these guys from dusty maps in the Tactical Operations Center.

"Lieutenant Colonel Gary Volesky started dispatching men, the Quick Reaction Force, to go out and try to find them. They line up all these vehicles. Of course, what was disastrous about these vehicles was that many of them weren't combat vehicles.

"Troy Denomy, who is the captain who is the company commander…those were his men out there. Troy Denomy jumps in a Humvee that has a canvas top and canvas sides. His gunner totally exposed in the back. These men thought they were on a peacekeeping mission. The Army, the Pentagon, did not send all the tanks, all the Bradleys that they normally would've, because they wanted this to be a peacekeeping mission, but they were unprepared for this combat mission. And the moment they go, every rescue company goes down, they immediately see the same thing that the pinned down platoon saw. Empty streets, people fleeing, garbage floating by, obstacles. And there's one point Troy Denomy said, 'It's going to happen now. Brace yourselves.' Then the gunfire starts again. And then these trucks…it was as one soldier described it: 'we were fish in a barrel.'

"The patrol is in the alley. So many of them said to me, 'When we were standing in that alley we just knew that we were in a bad movie and we didn't want it to end the way the bad movies had ended we'd seen before.'

"There were waves of citizens and Mehdi militia who approached both sides of that alley. Children in front, adults, Mehdi militia in back, teens in the middle. Old people. And they killed a lot of those people. They approached the Humvee. Lieutenant Aguero said at one point he just knew they could overrun them. A lot of the soldiers have children. And I asked him, 'What was that like, to face children and know that you were going to kill children?" And they said, 'In some ways having my own children, oddly enough, made it easier. Because it was kill or be killed. And if those men were so horrible to put children in front of them…' They said there was nothing they could do."

One of Martha's assistants had reached out to me long ago via email to ask if I would go on the record and provide my insight into what happened. She sent me a 20-page questionnaire to fill out and return that wanted to know what my nickname in the platoon was, and what pithy things I might have said while returning fire, and so on. I looked through the questions and pondered what response to make. On the one hand, I felt relieved that someone wanted to hear about what happened and flattered that my input could find life on the printed page. On the other hand, I distrusted journalists because of their disingenuous treatment of us during the deployment, and, unfamiliar with Ms. Raddatz world view and track record, was unsure how she would treat the story.

Still, in a moment of weakness, I briefly toyed with handing over more than 300 pages of transcribed interviews to the professionals to do with as they pleased. Over the course of six months, I had written and erased enough material to fill two books, but the project had me in the grip of a terror so profound that I couldn't write more than a paragraph without feeling the onset of panic. The problem wasn't writer's block but a simple matter of survival. My subconscious brain seemed to be shielding me from matters that it flatly believed would kill me if I tried to deal with them before their due. Therefore, every time I brought myself to the computer to write, my traitorous mind would turn on my adrenal gland to divert me from the task.

For reasons that remain unclear, I declined her offer. Apparently, they did just fine without me, because here was Ms. Raddatz on the radio plugging her book in a seven-minute rundown. The mere fact that she was able to condense what felt like eternity plus three hours—for me anyway—into seven minutes was nothing short of genius. For three and a half minutes, I listened as she spoke names from my past: Lieutenant Aguero, Captain Denomy, Colonel Volesky. It was a roll call of heroes that had me grinning like a jackass eating briars.

Then she lied.

Lied like a greasy politician. Lied like a criminal on trial. Lied like every parent who ever attested to the existence of Santa Claus and God in the same breath. Her lies awoke in me a rage too great to contain—the wrath of a titan caged. How dare her! I *love* children. I was a teacher for out Pete's sake. Under no circumstances would I slaughter unarmed children, piling up bodies like some barbarian king. Lies!

My chest was heaving, heart pounding. I wanted to kill something, anything, to appease the death angel with the blood of sacrifice that he might pass over me. There was no way that her allegations could be true. Lies!

Or so I desperately wished in vain.

# Fort Benning, Georgia – 2008

RIFLES THUNDERED to my left and I froze. Perhaps a dozen or more and all M16 variants by the sound. Even as my knuckles tightened on the wheel and blood began to pound like counter-fire in my temples I listened for the reply of AK-47s and RPKs, sounds that would tell me where to shoot. My God, was my heart pounding. And yet, I felt so alive in that moment that I couldn't restrain a fierce smile. *Here we go again*, I thought. It was a good day to die.

I reached for my rifle and my foot slipped off the brake. My eyes continued to scan my nine o'clock trying to pinpoint a target, and the vehicle eased forward until I felt a bump. My hand clawed desperately all about me looking for my weapon as a drowning man for a life line. C'mon, c'mon. I committed the cardinal sin of turning from contact, but I hadtofindithadtofindit. There was no rifle—only a pile of empty Burger King wrappers stacked in the passenger seat like the skulls of vanquished Whoppers. What the-?

I saw movement. My head snapped up. A large black woman dressed in a business suit was exiting the driver's side of a mini-van in front of me with government-issued tags. Rifles continued to blaze away off my nine as she walked toward me without the slightest hint of hostility or evil intent.

"Well, now," she said as I rolled down my window. She must have seen the confusion on my face and was very kind. "Everything OK?"

*No.* "Yeah, I just...I, ah, I just wasn't paying attention."

And just like that the voices sprouted, fully formed like the goddess Athena from the forehead of Zeus, whack-a-memories that would pop up at the most inopportune time and drown out everything around me.

*The dust drifts and Wild calmly says, "Hey, I got a head shot."*

That fender-bender was the first time I acknowledged that something might be wrong. The volume setting on my nightmares turned up a bit each day, week, and month that I spent at home, in school, in garrison doing mundane things in world that seemed drained of color. The adrenaline that I had marinated in for 335 days drained slowly from muscles and joints leaving me increasingly aware of injuries that I had previously ignored. I felt cut off from my wife, family, friends, and fellow soldiers by experiences and deeds that it seemed no one would understand. As these symptoms of what I knew was Post Traumatic Stress Disorder multiplied I felt that I had it under control. I had seen grown men cry, shit themselves, and devolve into madness under the conditions we endured day after day in the maniacal, bloody circus that was the Iraqi Insurgency, but I felt that I had handled it well. Was handling it well.

Until that day on Dixie Road in Fort Benning, Georgia waiting at a red light in the safety of my car next to a live fire range. What the hell? An honest-to-God flash back.

*"We're all gonna die in this shit-hole," Deaver said with quiet rage faded like his eyes.*

Three weeks later I found myself in a small, windowless office on the 4th floor of Martin Army Community Hospital speaking to a counselor with a thick, black beard and a merry sense of humor. *"Lancer Mike, this Comanche Red 1. We are taking fire. I say again, we are taking heavy fire. Vicinity Route Delta and Georgia!" the Lieutenant screamed over the sound of the .50 Caliber machine gun.*

The only way that I could have seen him sooner was if I had threatened to kill myself, kill someone else, or sprinted naked toward the general's command tent—which I've been known to do sane and sober. I can't remember the man's name or what we talked about. *Riddell glancing back, desperate to live, driving like hell. "Sir, somebody's gotta get on that gun."*

I had just commissioned as a butter-bar lieutenant and had serious concerns about what effect this trip to the shrink was going to have on my career. I saw him one more time and quit. *"Sir, he's gone,"* *I told the L-T.*

# Hamilton, Georgia – 2009

I've got Carl Wild's number, but I don't call. We've been texting back and forth, so I know where he's been and his assorted shenanigans. I know that he deployed to Iraq again from 2007 to 2008 and got hit with a rocket two months into his 2009 tour of Afghanistan. For some reason I can't bring myself to hear his voice. Maybe it's because I feel guilty for having spent the last six years in school and in non-combat units when I should have been watching his back. He asked how the book is coming, and I lied and said that it's almost done. Truth is I couldn't bear to look at it most days.

About that same time, I ran into newly promoted Sergeant First Class Trevor Davis while shopping at the Sam's Club in Columbus, Georgia. He looked exactly the same except more serious. We clasped hands vigorously while we congratulated each other on recent promotions. He called me "sir" which made me feel like an imposter. I would have been more comfortable going to parade rest while speaking to him. His words of congratulation were kind but they nailed me to the floor like accusations. Before we parted company he asked me how the book was coming along. I lied and said it was almost done.

The bright spot in my world was the imminent deployment of my battalion to Iraq. I had been languishing in a maintenance company for over a year, first as the executive officer and then as a warehouse supervisor. The gig out at the warehouse was not that bad. It was isolated, and I could shut my door when the anxiety started to overwhelm me, which began to happen more and more. I sat at my desk and tried to work as my racing mind attempted to fixate on shiny objects.

My commander at the time was also a prior-enlisted man who was a little older than me. He sported one of the new Combat Action

Badges that were created for all of the non-infantry guys who saw varying levels of enemy contact, which varied wildly from case to case. I asked him how he earned his and kept waiting for the punch line before I realized that he had finished the story. He began to exhibit PTSD behavior not long after and was eventually removed from command to seek further treatment. The whole affair left me shaking my head as I tried to envision how the events that he had described could have driven him over the edge. It made me wonder how close to the edge I might have drawn.

As my boss began the transition process with his replacement, a female West Point graduate, I was promised to the battalion headquarters for the upcoming deployment. Deep down in my bones I longed to return to the devil's sand box, even as I told my wife how upset I was at leaving again. The truth was that I couldn't wait to go. All of my old comrades had been at least once while I enjoyed the soft life. I was a junkie hooked on combat. A grave error had been made by the Death Angel, and I sought to give him a second go at it as though Death were a child who couldn't quite hit the ball off the tee. So I grabbed hold of the opportunity to go 'once more unto the breach' at the expense of my health, my marriage and—most likely—my sanity.

## Joint Base Balad, Iraq – 2010

Out of the darkness, a man's pre-recorded, metallic voice called the warning, "Incoming. Incoming. Incoming. Take cover. Take cover. Take cover."

I was back in Iraq and felt alive for the first time in five years. I threw myself into the gravel and covered my head. A rocket split the night sky and slammed into a concrete barrier in front of me. I waited briefly for a second or third strike before springing to my feet and sprinting toward the impact to help the wounded. In that moment, I felt buoyant as adrenaline, my long lost friend of battles past, slid through my bloodstream like children on a water slide. The complete absence of a weapon—checked into the arms room—and body armor—locked in my trailer—no longer bothered me as it had in previous days. I felt like taking on all comers with a spork if necessary.

A small group of soldiers had gathered around the point of impact. In the dim illumination of the portable lights, I could see plenty of dust though no one appeared to be hurt. I looked up with my fists on my hips searching the skies for more indirect fire. After a few minutes of silence, I threw my hands up in disgust. I stalked off toward the ops center where I worked to find out what was happening.

Nothing interesting, as it turned out. In fact, one could characterize the entire deployment to Joint Base Balad as such. That single incident on the third night in theater was the pinnacle of excitement. Although plenty more salvos were fired our way by the local model rocket enthusiasts, few caused any damage at all. A typical attack might follow this script:

Soldier 1 (lounging by the Olympic-sized outdoor pool): What was that?

Soldier 2 (also lounging, too engrossed in tanning to lift head and remove sunglasses): Indirect Fire. (Yawns)

Soldier 1 (sips from a can of Monster energy drink): Oh. Belch. Think we ought to go report in?

Soldier 2: If you want. I'm just getting crispy, though.

Joint Base Balad was like Candyland compared to Sadr City. Two swimming pools and a movie theater were just a few of the perks for living alongside the Air Force. I was continually thrown off balance by the memories in my head and the reality I was living. Danger was too bored to rear its ugly head. The only deaths that happened during that deployment was the accidental death of an Air Force demolition tech and an older National Guardsman who suffered a heart attack while walking around the track. I had fought so hard to return to this Allah-forsaken piece of real estate to find what my Viking ancestors called 'a good death,' yet I would have had better odds attending what my more recent kin called a tractor pull.

I must confess that I went a little crazy that year. Not crazy like your drunk uncle who tries on the lamp shade as a hat. I mean not right in the head. It began after that first hohum rocket attack and built in intensity the more I delved into writing this book. As I began to process my memories onto the written page, my mind began to kick and buck so hard that my body felt it. For years I had managed to keep the vehicle that was my psyche, if not safely in my lane, at least between the ditches. Now anxiety wrapped around me like a back seat-driving mother-in-law off her meds, threatening to squeeze my heart out of my chest. I was short of temper, withdrawn, and deeply depressed. When the stress levels began to redline, I developed a tick and would hear little noises escape my lips as if my subconscious mind was sending me Morse code messages. I sought the help of an on-base counselor several times until the Prozac quieted the voices

294 J. Matthew Fisk

enough to help me finish my memoir without undue collateral damage.

# Fort Benning, Georgia – 2011

The temporary euphoria of completing a task that I hoped would serve as a magic wand sort of treatment, banishing all my dark thoughts to the abyss, worked for a while. I finished the rough draft of our exploits in the early hours of New Year's Day. Redeployment a few months later helped, too. It's a really great feeling to return to the Land of the Free after a year in the Land of the Sand. I rode that emotional wave until the autumn leaves fell and the nightmares and depression returned. My marriage was washing up, so in a desperate attempt to save what was irretrievably broken—that was on the Petition for Divorce; a rare moment of poetry in the legal system—I called a military hotline to get a counselor.

Operator: Are you contemplating harming yourself?

The woman approached us, advanced upon me, with hands painted red by my will to stay alive.

Me: No…

Operator: Are you contemplating harming someone other than yourself?

Me: Not just right now…

Operator: OK, we'll try to get you in to see a counselor. It looks like their earliest appointment is six weeks from now.

Me: Ma'am, my marriage will be past the point of return by then. I can't sleep and I am so, so tired of living like an extra from a zombie apocalypse movie.

Operator: (Not without sympathy) There is a Family Life Center on Fort Benning. They have chaplains on standby that could see you with no waiting…

For a brief second I compiled a mental short-list of individuals to whom I wouldn't mind threatening bodily harm. Sensing that this would be a poor career move, I agreed and found my way the next morning to the counseling center. It was nested in a dilapidated building that was once a World War II barracks. I signed in on a clip board and sat in a comfortable chair next to a small, plastic Zen fountain. The water burbled at me cheerily and with sanguine assurance until I thought I must surely go mad.

Children in the alley who played at war with unparalleled enthusiasm. See how he dips his head into the lane begging for a baptism in lead.

A few toe-tapping minutes in the silence of the waiting room later, a large, slightly overweight chaplain welcomed me into his office. We exchanged pleasantries as he settled behind his laptop computer and began to build a file on me. "What are your goals for treatment? What do you want to achieve?"

"Let go of the goddam door, Denney! I'm going down there to take that little pecker out! Let go!"

"Well, Sir, my marriage is on the skids, I can't concentrate, can't sleep, I'm irritable and constantly depressed. I want that to all go away. I need help and quick."

The Chaplain observed me for a second over his glasses. "Yeah, we can help you but it won't be overnight. There's no magic bullet that will make it go away. You know someone who loses an arm in combat will never get the arm back. They just have to learn to live with their new normal. The best we might be able to do for you is help you learn how to live with it."

The bullet in a slow motion slalom from wall to wall like a living thing with metal teeth seeking me out; the dull impact.

"Anything is better than where I'm at now."

He continued to type for a minute longer then came over to a seat across from me with a pad of paper and a pen. "Tell me about your deployment history."

"Sergeant Bourquin, he's dead."

The tall, young man covered with tattoos. Too young to believe that we can die. "No, he's NOT!"

"I've deployed three times. The first was in support of Task Force Hawk during the Kosovo Conflict in 1999. We didn't see any action then. Most recently I deployed to Balad, Iraq when we turned out the lights and pulled out but that was quiet, too. A rocket landed about a hundred meters away from me, but that was it. Barely raised my pulse. Everything that's bothering me came from my first deployment to Iraq in 2004. Sadr City was—interesting."

Swope, the platoon sergeant who spoke so quietly that you thought he was slightly mad and, thus, terrifying. "Red 1, this is Red 4, Charlie one-two and Charlie one-three are mobility kill. I say again, both victors will not roll!"

The pen scribbled. "What was your job then? You were a lieutenant?"

"No, I was enlisted then. A specialist in the infantry. I'm in the Ordnance Corps now. Desk Jockey extraordinaire. Back then I was a rifleman, designated marksman and recorder for the Platoon Leader. We had a lot of interesting missions. On the same patrol we could hand out bread and lead in equal measure."

The never-ending swarm of Charles Dickens dirt-orphans always quick with a 'you giff me' this and 'shokalata' that until you wanted to gouge out your own eyes to quiet your heart.

The scribble of pen like rat claws scratching, scratching. "How often would you say you had an experience so traumatic that you try not to think about it?"

"I counted over two hundred and ten combat missions that I participated in over the course of a year. We left the base at least twice a day, sometimes three. Except for Thanksgiving Day. I remember we had that day off. I was shot in the leg, blown up by a mortar, struck by so many improvised explosive devices that it became mundane, hit in the head with rocks. A grenade once landed at my feet and exploded. But everything I'm dealing with today started on the 4th of April." In that damn street. In that damn alley.

The chaplain put down the pen and began to explain a procedure that he would like to try. It was called ERT which I think he said was Emotional Replacement Therapy or some such. It essentially used eye movement in coordination with sound and vibration while discussing a disturbing event. There was, of course, more to it than that. I had to construct an imaginary safe house that I could go to when I became overwhelmed. I also had to construct an imaginary container for the negative emotions in between visits. It struck me as bunch of New Age hippy crap, but I was at the end of my rope and willing to try everything up to and including coed naked bocci ball if it would work.

And let me tell you something; it worked. It worked like a charm in that the therapy replaced my typically emotionless state with good old-fashioned rage. As I began to recount for the good chaplain the sequence of events up to and including the children used as human shields, I felt the anger begin to well to the surface. On and on I went, my voice shaking, my heart pounding as I begin to tell about how I got shot.

# Completely Lost – 2012

The infantry soldier learns to fight on when everything around him says that the battle is over. He learns to ignore reality and continue to put one foot in front of another past the point where, to paraphrase Kipling, nerve and joint and sinew have long served their turn. This is a great mindset to have in the heat of combat. But when separated from wisdom, it can be a wrecking ball to your personal life.

My health was shot because I refused to hear what my body was telling me. The timeless exhortation of Drill Sergeants everywhere is to suck it up and drive on. Well, I sucked up the deteriorating vertebrae until I could barely tolerate standing. After pursuing physical therapy and epidural injections to no avail, I elected to risk a spinal fusion. I was fortunate enough to have Colonel Devine, the top spinal surgeon in the Army, successfully perform the procedure. In April of 2012 I began the laborious process of recovery. Drive on.

Then, after 12 years of marriage, I threw in the towel. It had been over for at least a year, but I couldn't allow myself to quit. Suck it up. I just put one foot in front of the other until exhaustion won out. If fault is to be found, I can definitely claim my portion. The decree stated that the bonds were irretrievably broken and that is apt in every way. Even without my confounded mental issues I'm not sure that we would have lasted, though I'm positive that my numbness, irritability, and anger hastened our relationship's demise. Drive on.

Now that I had a lot of alone time to contemplate life, the universe, and everything in it, I began to take inventory. As a husband I had failed. Surrender is not a Ranger word, but I was no Ranger. I was a quitter who couldn't hack it. As a soldier I no longer had anything to offer my country except my intellect. That was a painful admission to make. Not only was I pushing 40, but I realized that combat, my drug of choice, was forever beyond my reach. The very thought of having children terrified me, where it had once been a fervent hope. I could no longer look at a kid without remembering the ones I had put in the ground; I failed fatherhood before I even began. The math did not lie. I needed professional help.

How long had it been since I felt anything beyond the paralyzing numbness? Specialist Chapman, a Bradley driver in our platoon, lost his leg to an IED later on in 2004. He recounted what almost every amputee experiences, that he still felt the missing limb. PTSD is like that. Any emotion you express is not because you feel that emotion but rather you feel the ghost of it. The only exception would be rage. Rage is always there, separated by the thinnest layer of ingrained societal norms of behavior. My rage is a muzzled, rabid dog longing to be let off the chain.

My session with the chaplain had tapped into that fury so deeply that I decided not to try that route again. Instead I called up the Behavioral Health clinic and got on the waiting list to see a provider. Eight weeks later, I sat down with who I assumed was a therapist. After spending the first 15 minutes of our session watching her fiddle with her printer and listening to her prattle on about nothing, I asked to take a break so that I could walk off the frustration. When I returned she asked the normal questions I had come to anticipate: are you thinking about hurting yourself or someone else? How was your childhood? Did you get along with your parents? Do you have trouble sleeping? Did you ever experience anything so terrible that you can't stop thinking about it? On and on it went for half an hour as I relayed my first experience with combat and described the effect it was having on me currently.

The woman, though ditzy to a suspiciously high degree, was nice and informed me that their therapists were overwhelmed with large caseloads and wouldn't be able to see me for a few months. Apparently she wasn't a therapist but a social worker, another layer in the seemingly endless behavioral health cake. Suddenly I wondered if I had ever seen anyone qualified to deal with the issues I was experiencing. When I expressed frustration with the delays, the social worker was sympathetic and offered to enroll me for some sort of video-conference group therapy. In addition she recommended that I see the Traumatic Brain Injury clinic to receive a thorough battery of tests. They should be able to get me in sometime next year.

Apparently I had to try to kill myself or give in to my infrequent road rage impulses before I had any hope of receiving prompt treatment. The thought occurred to me that I could disingenuously claim to want to die. The sequence of events flowing from that would, I was sure, inevitably lead to summary dismissal from the service. I didn't want to quit being a soldier; it was what I had wanted to do since I was eight years old. For years I had avoided seeking treatment because I instinctively feared that it would end my career. I just wanted to get patched up and put back in the fight. They had repaired my spine, why not my mind?

# Fort Lee, Virginia – 2013

At about the same time as the beginning of the Mayan Apocalypse I sat with a yellow legal pad in front of me with a ballpoint pen clutched in my rebellious right hand. The fate of the free world was not in the balance, thank God, or all would have been lost. Recently I had watched a Science channel show about a German woman who had been awakened in the middle of a deep sleep only to find that her own left hand was attempting to strangle her. I was having a similar episode, though not quite so dire. My hand was refusing to write the letter 'L.' No matter how I pled, reasoned, and cajoled with what, up to this point in my young life, had been a generally reliable and subservient appendage, it simply would not commit the simple letter, a line bent in half, to the page.

Upon further diagnosis, I found the problem stemmed from a bit of confusion in my Parietal Lobe regarding which way exactly the letter 'L' should be facing. It seemed that the brace should face left, yet something about that didn't seem to jibe. Remembering my toddler days of the left versus right debate among my stuffed animals, which sometimes spun out of control, I held up both hands in the shape of the letter in question. No good, either might do. I had to find an example on a printed page and, even then, found the answer dubious.

The Parietal Revolt of 2012 continued to build momentum—the N was the next to fall along with the S—until I felt sufficiently concerned to seek medical assistance yet again. Fort Benning had a TBI clinic that was able to squeeze me in within eight weeks, and a few months later I had been diagnosed with a mild traumatic brain injury that had resulted from a mortar round explosion. At least I think so. I have yet to see the results.

While the doctors and assorted scientists were conducting this evaluation, I managed to contact my former roommate and Bradley gun mentor Ben Hayhurst on Facebook. The social networking site had proved useful in finding many of my old comrades. Now that the combat narrative of the book was complete, I endeavored to find as many from red platoon as possible to read the draft and provide feedback. Below follows a transcript of our conversation:

"Ben! What's up? How are ya?"

"I am re-entering society, I guess you could say," he wrote.

"What, did you rob a bank or something?"

"No, just was a little messed up for a while. I am back now though."

"Well, you're in good company," I replied. "I think every single person from the platoon has had to deal with things in their own time. I let it go so long that my marriage disintegrated. I've been getting help for the past year." I was going to quit there in adherence to my strict policy of avoiding deep conversations. Then I didn't. I felt at ease with this man, my brother.

"I still have nightmares but not as often," I continued. "I still check for snipers EVERY single time I step outside, but hell, no one is going to blindside me. I've lived with depression so long it just seems normal now. My drinking is under control...ish. My weight got out of control this last year when I had my spine rebuilt, but I'm on that, too. All in all, I guess we just can't be killed, beaten, or otherwise destroyed. I finished writing the book about us during my last deployment. It almost killed me. You might not be up to it, but I would like for you to read the draft, if you can."

"I would love to. I am writing a book right now about how I was kicked out with a personality disorder discharge."

Intriguing. "Ok, so how do you get chaptered with a personality disorder?"

"I was being treated for PTSD, was told that there was only one way to get help. It turned out it was a chapter for personality disorder.

So I got all my benefits taken away, and my bonus taken back. We lost everything. I have been fighting to get it changed now for about four years, but they just blow me off."

I read what he wrote and felt my blood boil. Sergeant Benjamin Hayhurst took a bullet for his country on April 4, 2004, spent a few months recovering stateside, and then pitched a fit until the doctors allowed him to return to fight at the side of his Army brothers. And in June of the same year, wounded combat veteran Ben Hayhurst was once again ambushed. This time he was the victim of a most unlikely foe: The U.S. Veterans Administration.

Back in Iraq, once again patrolling the mean streets of Sadr City, Ben couldn't stop thinking about what happened in April. His nightmares haunted what sleep he could find and bled over into his waking hours. No matter how hard he tried, no matter what he did, he could not forget how it felt to lie on top of a dead friend. He had tried to gut it out. He had tried to climb back on the horse that threw him by volunteering to return to his unit in Sadr City. He'd even sought help from Army professional counselors despite the silent contempt he felt from some superiors and fellow soldiers for not just sucking it up and driving on in the storied infantry tradition.

By June, the stress that haunted him became a heavier burden than he could bear and still focus on duty. He requested discharge and began the process of separating from the Army through appeal to a Physical Evaluation Board, a group of medical professionals who would evaluate his condition and aptitude for further active service. Ben's problem seemed to be a classic case of PTSD, but a counselor told him that a formal diagnosis of that condition would take quite a long time. He was faced with a large battery of tests and exams to determine his disposition and the board's resources were slammed with a large number of claims from the newly returned Soldiers of 1st Cavalry Division.

On the other hand, Sergeant Ben Hayhurst was told, if he was in a hurry to get out of the Army, things could be expedited if he would pursue an alternate diagnosis of his problem. Ben was told that an Army behavioral specialist could—and would without hesitation—officially diagnose Ben as suffering from Adjustment Disorder (AD), which amounted to the same thing. Or so he was told when he agreed to the deal as an expedited way to get out of the Army. He loved being a soldier, but he found himself thinking about death every time he put on his uniform. The only way out seemed to be no longer wearing that uniform.

What the helpful bureaucrat failed to mention was that although PTSD and Adjustment Disorder share similar symptoms, they differ in the time of onset, and that's all the difference in the world when it comes to seeking help or compensation. According to the mental health professionals, PTSD is brought on as a reaction to a traumatic event, which in the case of combat veterans is generally something they experience on the battlefield. Adjustment Disorder is often rooted in childhood or later experiences in life before the individual ever sees combat. Such experiences might include abuse, neglect, or other painful byproducts of a dysfunctional rearing. In other words, an individual diagnosed with AD was likely screwed up before he ever entered military service and his problems are considered not necessarily service-related.

Sergeant Ben Hayhurst didn't understand the nuances and he didn't much care if the AD diagnosis got him out of the Army and give him some breathing space to deal with the ghosts that haunted him. Like the good soldier he was, Hayhurst trusted those in authority to steer him on a true course getting out of the Army just as they'd done getting him into uniform. He was a long way from thinking about or understanding the realities of the diagnosis he accepted.

Only later would he discover the truth: Soldiers discharged with a diagnosis of PTSD get disability payments from the government scaled to the severity of their condition. Those who are discharged with a diagnosis of Adjustment Disorder get zip. They are presumed to be screwed up by life before the Army and the government can't be held responsible for that.

So haunted combat veteran Sergeant Ben Hayhurst found himself being told by behavioral health experts that his problems had nothing in particular to do with that day in Iraq when his unit was ambushed. No connection whatsoever to being shot. Nothing at all to do with escaping death on the back of a tank in the middle of a firefight. And certainly no connection to laying on the body of his dead buddy. His problems likely stemmed from something earlier and more traumatic—something like his mother slapping his hand when he tried to rob the cookie jar.

The behavioral health experts were not particularly interested in the facts concerning Ben Hayhurst's service. They didn't much want to hear about his combat experiences. They didn't care to know that he was an exemplary soldier, that he had a professional demeanor, and a level head in combat. They didn't care that he was selected as Noncommissioned Officer of the Month in his unit, or that he was selected to be the platoon leader's gunner, a position assigned only to the most trusted and reliable NCO. All of that was neither here nor there to the bureaucrats pondering Ben Hayhurst's official AD diagnosis when he applied for help with the ongoing psychological problems. They could have asked me and I would have reported that Sergeant Hayhurst was one of the most competent, intelligent, and steady leaders I have ever known. But they didn't ask me or anyone else about Hayhurst's combat experiences. They just scammed him out of his just compensation.

After our Iraq rotation, when I found out about what had happened to Sergeant Hayhurst, I began to look into the situation and ran across a quote often mistakenly attributed to George Washington that left me slack-jawed for a while: "The willingness with which our young people are likely to serve in any war, no matter how justified, shall be directly proportional to how they perceive how the veterans of earlier wars were treated and appreciated by their nation."

My research began to challenge the faith I maintained in my government and my service. I ran across an email sent by VA administrator Norma Perez to the staff of the Veterans' Center in Temple, Texas just a few days after I redeployed from the Middle East. Perez had this to say to the staff of mental health specialists and social workers at the Texas facility: "Given that we are having more and more compensation-seeking veterans, I'd like to suggest that you refrain from giving a diagnosis of PTSD straight out." She recommended as an alternative that they "consider a diagnosis of Adjustment Disorder" since VA staff members "really don't . . . have time to do the extensive testing that should be done to determine PTSD."

Of course, this could have been just one clueless administrator offering advice in a vacuum, a government drone ordering the worker bees to take short-cuts and never mind the real needs of the vets they serve, but that's not the case as later events and scandals proved.

Then a chilling thought rattled me. If the VA claimed that Ben Hayhurst—a man who was shot while defending against an ambush conducted by 10,000 socially disturbed bungholes—did not have PTSD, what about the rest of us? I thought back to the few times that I had sought mental health treatment over the years and wondered what had been written about one Captain Fisk.

The next day, I went to the Army hospital and put in for a copy of my medical records. The civilian told me that a doctor must approve to release the files on form such and such. This made no sense as the files were about me, but I submitted the request and waited. The request was lost. I returned to the TBI clinic, obtained the signature on such and such form and walked it over personally to the records department. They advised that I would be called when they were ready for pick up. When a couple of weeks had passed I stopped by only to find that the request had been lost again. This runaround did absolutely nothing to soothe PTSD-related symptoms. After returning to the TBI clinic for anger management counseling and another signature, I received the long-awaited documents.

My jaw clenched as I leafed through the chronological record of treatment. The words Adjustment Disorder jumped off the page. Really? If we could experience what we did in just one battle, let alone the 200 plus combat missions after, and fail the litmus test for PTSD, who exactly fit the profile? How many had been denied proper care simply as a cost-saving measure? Unsettled and angry, I began to reach out to other Black Knight alumni to find out.

# Fort Hood, Texas – April 4th, 2014

I haven't felt such nervousness in exactly ten years. Every eye in the church is watching me as I wait, sweating palms clasped in front of me, for my best friend of 32 years to walk down the aisle and become my wife. My father, an ordained minister who eagerly agreed to marry us, stands at my side. The best man, married to my future bride's mother, is a Vietnam vet who still won't talk about his tour. Today is his birthday. Earlier I had asked him how long it took before the nightmares stopped. "It gets better. Takes a good long while, but it gets better," he said.

A few months ago, while we were planning the wedding, my fiancé and I spoke jovially between shots of Jim Beam chased with Pabst Blue Ribbon. I can't recall what we were talking about exactly, but thoughts of the wedding had us in high spirits. Then we began to discuss what came next, our happily ever after. I had decided to leave the Army as my body could barely meet the physical demands, but as yet I hadn't decided on a new career.

Still laughing I asked, and slurring just a little, I asked, "You want to know why I'm getting out? I knew back when I commissioned that my body was getting worse, but I kept pushing and pushing. My boss wanted me to take a PT test before we deployed, but I dodged out of it. I knew I couldn't it pass it then, you see, because my back was that bad. I was afraid that if I failed it they would make me medically retire."

Shot. Swig of PBR.

"I knew I had one more chance to go back to Iraq, and I meant to take it. And then I was going to see if those sons-a-bitches could finish what they started back in oh-four."

Shot. Shot. Lisa moves closer and puts her hand on my shoulder.

"Because how in the hell am I still here? Shot at, shot, more IEDs than I can remember, a mortar round that should have vaporized me, a grenade at my feet that exploded around me. Why am I still here? Why Chen?

"Did you know I was the L-T's gunner before Eddie? I trained for it at NTC. They moved me when we came back to Texas. My ex-wife's ex-husband was in our battalion so I asked for a transfer. My platoon sergeant didn't want the hassle of a squeaky wheel, so he sent me over to the sniper section. They didn't have time to train me before deployment so they sent me back a month later. By that time they had put Chen in my place. In *my* place. Why? What am I here for? Why?"

Shot. Lisa pulls my head against her stomach as something unexpected happens. I begin to cry for the first time in well over a decade. It all comes spilling out, and I can't hold it back.

Getting married on the 4th was Lisa's idea. For years I had defined myself by one event. I was one of those guys in that alley who had to do nasty things to make it out alive. My vision was fixed in the past on the most horrible day of my life. She said that we could make the 4th of April a day I would remember with joy instead. She knew what she was in for and agreed to join her life to mine anyway. Talk about guts.

Now we stand ready to exchange vows in front of family and close friends. I've asked to speak before the ceremony begins so dad gives me the floor.

"I want to thank you all for coming out today as we exchange vows in the sight of God and men." I stutter a lot at first, but my mind clears and my speech becomes more firm as I continue. "It's important that I tell you why you're here on a Friday afternoon instead of a Saturday. Ten years ago today, I had the worst day of my life, and I was sure that I wouldn't live to see another."

My voice cracks. I pause for a second and continue, "I thought my life was over. But I'm reminded of God's promise to Jeremiah, 'I know the plans I have for you, says the Lord. Plans to give you a future and a hope…'"

I'm a crumbling dam holding back tears. Many seconds later I have regained enough control to choke out the rest. "…and not for destruction. Today I will marry my buddy in the very church we grew up in, so that when this time of year rolls around I will remember it as something good."

The ceremony began, and I forgot everything else in the world when I saw my bride coming up the aisle. We read the vows we had written to each other and were married before I knew what had happened. Not a dry eye was to be had.

A couple of hours later, my new bride and I drove to attend another ceremony, this one more somber. Members of Task Force Lancer, Operation Iraqi Freedom II, were assembling in Fort Hood, Texas to remember the fallen and commemorate ten years of life. The organizers had worked for a year to pull everything together, and anticipation ran high. What no one planned on, however, was another shooting in Phantom Warrior territory. The shock was especially great for a former member of Comanche Red Platoon. Former NCO Joshua York was now First Lieutenant (promotable) York of the Medical Services Corps and a member of the unit that had taken casualties. Once again the 20th man, the guy who was left behind and missed the ambush, he drew a lucky hand. Many of his fellow staff officers were injured. Josh left work two minutes before the rampage began.

On the 2nd of April, 2014 a troubled soldier named Ivan Lopez became distraught over the rejection of his leave request and opened fire on everyone who crossed his path. He killed three, wounded 16, and finally turned the gun on himself. Most of his targets were chosen seemingly at random after the initial encounter. Initial reports indicated that he was navigating the process to have himself tested for TBI and PTSD. Very little was forthcoming in the days leading up to our reunion about the gunman's motives. Some speculated that recent deaths in his family made him snap. Others hypothesized that TBI or war-related stress played a role, even though the Army stated that he saw no combat during his deployments. Whatever his reasons, the Black Knights were not deterred from honoring their fallen even in the midst of such tragic and senseless loss of life.

Several attended the beer-soaked gathering on the 4th but not the ceremony. John Deaver, for one. He still lives on the north side of Fort Hood and spends his days pummeling the young bulls at the local boxing gym.

Justin Rowe was another. He went through a long bout of alcoholism and made it through to the other side a stronger man.

Shane Aguero was also unable to attend the ceremony although he did make it to the informal gathering the night before. He is a major with the Intelligence branch and thoroughly miserable to be so far away from a fight.

The next morning, April 5th, we boarded a bus at the Fort Hood visitor's center that had been arranged to facilitate our movement past heightened security at the checkpoint. I sat behind a dark-haired man and his family.

"Hi. Who were you with?" I asked, unable to place his face.

"I am Hussein. I was General Volesky's translator."

God forgive me, but my heart began to race with suspicion. Did he have a bomb? Was he going to sell me out? I slapped my runaway imagination and combat-fueled prejudice. I spoke at length with him about Sadr City and how his life had been after. He had been forced to leave for fear of his safety and now worked at Fort Leavenworth.

The more I spoke with him the more embarrassed I felt about fearing this man.

His son was no more than five and bashful. I spoke with the child using all of the Arabic I could remember. In my mind, I couldn't help but see in him the little Iraqi boy whose foot I had once doctored. He would be a young man now. Did he grow up to hate me for my kindness?

Later, I sat in a fold-up chair holding a red, long-stemmed, thorny rose in my hand and watched the new generation of 2nd of the Fifth Cavalry Regiment soldiers approach the 1st Cavalry Division memorial in perfect lockstep. They are dressed in their best uniforms and look magnificent, young, and proud. Over 400 former Black Knights stand across from them like a mirror to the past, huddled with their families under a cold, steel-gray sky.

Lieutenant (P) York takes the podium wearing his dress uniform and black Stetson hat. Given the events of recent days, I can't imagine what's going through his mind. He reads from his speech with an emotion-laded voice that trembles like his hands. He gives the audience a brief rundown of what happened ten years ago and tells everyone how proud his is to call them brothers. I try but fail to hold back tears as he closes with the old motto, "Shoot 'em in the face." The thing about unbottling your emotions is that they often won't fit when you try to put them back.

A couple of the Gold Star family members, those who had lost loved ones in combat, stood to talk about the sacrifice made by the fallen. The names of the honored dead are read. A bugler plays "Taps." The mournful notes once again make my eyes leak.

At long last, Clay Spicer, former XO for Charlie Company, concludes the ceremony and invites everyone forward to pay their respects. A young soldier hands out a strip of white paper and a bar of graphite to make a rubbing of whatever name we choose. Everyone does. The line is long and moves slow. No one complains.

As I approach the marble wall carved with the names of the men who died while attempting to rescue me, I begin to see more and more of my old comrades. Some have put on weight, like me; others have grown long hair and beards; a few have weathered better, though the age lies hard around their eyes. One by one we join with each other, hug each other, and laugh. The laughter comes unbidden and seems more appropriate in that hallowed place than tears. We reminisce and ask about each other's lives.

Joe Thompson's marriage is struggling, but he is optimistic about the future. He was accepted at Texas A&M to pursue his degree.

Aaron Fowler has a regularly recurring role in the hit TV series Revolution. He dotes on his young daughter and has taught her to shoot well. He asks me how to get an Alligator tag in Louisiana so she can kill one. I laugh and say I don't know.

I see Puppet, good ol' Rafael Arteaga, and rush through the crowd to hug his neck. He limps a little and smiles a lot. He introduces me to his wife and children. The former juvenile delinquent works as a loss-prevention specialist for Home Depot.

Shane Coleman commissioned as an infantry lieutenant and married a fellow officer. He is the only one of us who hasn't changed a bit. He gives me Jermaine Tyrell's number, who was unable to attend. I promptly text him to question his manhood.

Justin Bellamy was there with his wife and young daughter. Still in a baby stroller, she tried to hand me her rose.

Jon Denney introduced me to his family beaming that infectious smile the whole time. He had spent many years with Comanche company after it was re-designated as Bravo Company under the new force structure. He actually went back to Iraq with them, a grizzled NCO able to say to his green soldiers, "You call this an ambush?"

Eric Bourquin still towers over me. He spent last summer after he left the service hiking the Appalachian Trail to raise awareness for PTSD. He came back looking like a mountain man with long hair and a beard. He and Fowler joke about buying land close by in order to start their own cult. At least I think it's a joke.

Ben Hayhurst stands next to Eric and sports an even longer beard. But he's smiling broadly. I ask him how he's doing and he answers, "I'm coming back, roomie. More and more every day." He tells me how glad he is that he came and how good it is to be around people who get it. Once he said that I suddenly realized that I was completely surrounded by people and yet felt, for the first time in ten years, completely relaxed.

So many soldiers gathered to remember and reconnect and yet not all that could attend were here. Some were simply not able to handle the emotional load and had opted to stay home. How well I recognized that fear.

I found the one guy I had been missing on the outside of group. The guy who had faked his orders so he could return to Afghanistan after being wounded. The warrior who still patrolled his land every day with a loaded M4 just so he could feel normal. Carl Wild toted a back pack and wore an olive drab jacket—1st CAV patch on the right shoulder—against the cold. His companion was a service dog, still a puppy, which was drawing more attention than Wild seemed comfortable with. He still did not like crowds. I spoke with him a while and rode the bus with him to the luncheon at the new 2/5 CAV headquarters. As everyone unloaded, he asked if the driver would take him back to his car off-post. The excitement was getting the better of him.

"Carl, before you go, would you mind taking a picture with me?" I asked.

He agreed and climbed down so my wife could snap a photo. After he turned quickly to get on the bus. I called to him again and he turned slowly, eager to escape.

"I never had a brother until I fought with you," I said.

He shook my hand and threw the other arm around my neck. "I love you, man," he said.

I watched him get onto the bus with a lump in my throat, not really knowing what to say. As I watched him go, I reflected on everything that I had tried in the last ten years to reclaim who I was. Hours of counseling with therapists and chaplains, drugs to help me feel happy, drugs to numb my anger, drugs to sharpen my concentration, drugs to help me sleep, Emotion Replacement Therapy, Cognitive Behavioral Therapy, biofeedback, and on and on. Normal was out of the question, but I felt that there was at least the prospect of peace. Peace and maybe something more. It was out there. I felt it. It seemed that all of us there were feeling it. You could tell in their smiles, Ben's laughter, Carl's arm around my neck like a lifeline. Maybe if healing was out there for us, we would be the ones to find it, stumbling toward wholeness arm in arm with that man to the right and left. My brothers.

# Lancer Legacy Ranch provides a new life for veterans with PTSD

Plans for a self-sufficient community and therapy center
By Alex Meachum, KTAL News, 10 November 2015

Driving outside of Mt. Pleasant down the long, gravel County Road 4315 in Cookville, Texas is where former members of the military are creating a self-sufficient community for fellow veterans suffering with PTSD to live and recover.

The Lancer Legacy Ranch grew from an idea to a cooperative effort by a group of platoon members who fought alongside one another in Iraq and Afghanistan experiencing the most intense combat situations including sustaining injuries during an ambush attack.

Retired US Sergeant and now Operations Manager for the ranch, Carl Wild, said when he came back from overseas, he didn't feel like the same person, even adjusting to basic parts of life was difficult.

"I had a lot of trouble adapting. I came home and didn't feel the way I used to feel. I was angry a lot, upset a lot and didn't feel comfortable in normal situations. I couldn't deal with crowds. I just wasn't the same person I used to be," Wild said.

Wild, along with Retired US Army Sergeant and Captain Matt Fisk, say PTSD feels unshakeable and hopeless at times. They suffered and dealt with its symptoms for years. The only difference came when they reunited with members from their platoon. As though it gave them a sense of normalcy again. Forming a unit again gave them a calmer, more comfortable sense of attitude.

"We noticed after being apart for so long and being around our friends again we felt like our old self," Wild said.

It made them want to do something. They joked about living out on a commune together but after time passed and the symptoms of PTSD persisted Fisk thought it was actually a good idea. With help from his fellow veterans along with his wife Lisa, they embarked on establishing a livable, sustainable plot of land where veterans could recover together.

"We had each other's backs in combat and we have each other's backs now," said director, Fisk.

Still in the early stages, they've spent the last half of this year working to make their own sources of water and power, constructing temporary homes with plans for permanent ones, and growing crops and raising livestock.

"To be able to feed and care for ourselves and 25 veterans on this ranch at all times," Fisk said.

Feelings of wanting to be isolated is strong once back from combat, Fisk said. They understand it because they lived it he says and hopes his dreams for the development of the Lancer Legacy Ranch will ultimately help other veterans adjust back into life at a quiet pace. Away from busy cities, crowds of people, and the daily pressures of society in general, Wild said it can provide an alternative lifestyle for people seeking something more than what they've been offered so far.

"Instead of sitting in doctors' offices and doing therapy and having prescription medications thrown at you, there's other ways you can find to cope," Wild said.

They will also focus on peer-to-peer therapy where veterans can work, live, and recover together. Several veterans have stayed on the ranch so far and Fisk's wife, Lisa says she has noticed the impact it's had on them.

"Just talking to the ones who have been out here, I've seen a change," Lisa Fisk said.

She said it wasn't easy at first but she acts as the "mom of the ranch" along with already being a mom to their newborn baby.

"I do the cooking and cleaning, you know those things men don't always do themselves," Lisa said.

She said she wanted to support her husband, but sees the kind of change they can have in people's lives.

"Well it hasn't been easy but I just want him to be well and be happy so I'm here for him and anyone else who needs me," Lisa said.

They say PTSD can feel like a losing battle, but there is hope. Wild believes he is an advocate of how the idea will work.

"It's greatly helped me. I'm not the same person I was a year ago. I'm more outgoing, I'm more talkative, I feel comfortable around strangers, I can do groups. I'm just a completely different person altogether. I feel confident that it helped me adjust back to society," Wild said.

They say there will be work catered to physical and mental capacity of each individual and with each new building, plant or cattle it will give them mental relief to be working purposely again.

"Perhaps you've reached a point in your live where you feel it's never going to get better, I will never recover, I'm a completely broken individual. I would just tell you that's false. We've seen it, we've lived it and done it. There's hope for you. There's people who understand your struggle and your journey," Fisk said.

They offer the ranch to any veteran seeking help and will provide them access to programs where they can learn about how to live off the land. They have a partnership with other organizations in the region that teach farming and outdoor living skills. Fisk said he believes they can make an impact into the epidemic of PTSD and appreciates all the support he has received so far from the community and the county.

If you would like to learn about what they can offer you can visit their website: http://www.lancerlegacyranch.com/

# About the author

MATT FISK WAS BORN in DeQueen, Arkansas and entered the Army in 1997. He served 8 years in the infantry as an enlisted soldier before crossing to the dark side for another 8 years as an officer in the logistics corps. He has a degree in criminal justice though he is not currently involved in either the criminal nor justice systems. Matt spends his days in east

Texas developing a self-sufficient homestead with his childhood sweetheart and their lovely baby girl. And 10 goats. And two horses. And 11 bobwhite quail. And about 20 gazillion chickens. And a bad dog. And three disdainful cats, excellent examples of their species.

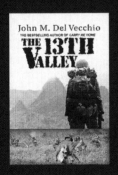

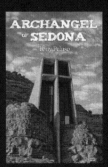

66432060R00178

Made in the USA
Charleston, SC
18 January 2017